Just Cause

Revised & Expanded Edition

A *Just Cause Universe* Novel

IAN THOMAS HEALY

To Susan and Luke!

Local Hero Press

Just Cause: A Just Cause Universe Novel
Published by Local Hero Press, LLC
http://localheropress.ianthealy.com

1st Printing
Local Hero Press: trade paperback, October 1, 2012
2nd Printing
Local Hero Press, LLC: trade paperback, April 15, 2014

ISBN: 0615701086
ISBN-13: 978-0615701080

Cover art by Jeff Hebert
Book design by Ian Thomas Healy

Praise for *Just Cause*

"Ian Healy's *Just Cause* is a slam-bang good superhero story: part *JLA*, part *Young Romance*, with some splashes of *Our Army at War* to keep you on your toes. I thoroughly enjoyed Mustang Sally's adventure and look forward to reading more of Healy's work."

—Rob Rogers, author of *Devil's Cape*

~~~

"Ian Healy's *Just Cause* is solid, serious superhero action in the classic tradition, with tons of interesting characters, extremely well-crafted action scenes, and real depth. Highly recommended."

—Van Allen Plexico, author of *The Sentinels*

~~~

"The best thing about Ian Healy's books is the accessibility of their worlds and characters. He welcomes us in and takes us for a fun and memorable ride, and unlike other superhero universes, we never feel like the understanding of an entire mythology is out of our grasp—or would take thousands of reading hours to accomplish."

—Allison M. Dickson, author of *Strings*

"Ian T. Healy's fun, engrossing, and thoroughly-realized *Just Cause* universe will make you want to break out your own cape and cowl."

—Jeff Hebert, creator of the *HeroMachine*

~~~

"Mr. Healy clearly loves superhero fiction. He has taken tried and true superhero tropes, made them his own, and crafted an excellent world, story, and characters. I highly recommend."

—Corey L. Bishop, *Creative Commoners* podcast

~~~

"Ian Healy's *Just Cause* is a great superhero book because it creates a world that is so close to our own we almost think that maybe these things did/are really happening, it's just that we don't live in the right city, and don't maybe have that special brick touch pattern to get us to Diagon Alley."

—Jenn Zuko, *Nerds in Babeland*

~~~

"It almost feels like you're watching a movie instead of reading a book when the superheroes are battling the villains."

—Megan Bostic, author of *Never Eighteen*

Books by Ian Thomas Healy

The *Just Cause Universe*
Just Cause
The Archmage
Day of the Destroyer
Deep Six
JCU Omnibus, Vol. 1
Jackrabbit
Champion (Fall 2014)

JCU Short Stories
Graceful Blur
The Steel Soldier's Gambit

Short Stories
1001001
Dental Plan
Footprints in the Butter
In His Majesty's Postal Service
Last Year's Hero
The Mighty Peculiar Incident at Muddy Creek
Plague Ship
Pressure
Rookie Sensation
Tuesday Night at Powerman's
Upon A Midnight Clear

The Pariah of Verigo
Pariah's Moon
Pariah's War

Other Novels
Blood on the Ice
Hope and Undead Elvis
Making the Cut
Rooftops
*Starf*cker*
The Guitarist
The Milkman
Troubleshooters

Collections
Tales of the Weird Wild West, Volume 1
The Bulletproof Badge

Nonfiction
Action! Writing Better Action Using Cinematic Techniques

This edition of this book would not have been possible without the assistance of several people. I have the utmost gratitude to Allison M. Dickson for her constant efforts to improve my work; to Jeff Hebert for his wonderful illustration of Mustang Sally; to Kate Jenkins for her help in a difficult situation; to my family for their unwavering support; and to my fans, who keep clamoring for more tales from the *Just Cause Universe*. Thanks and much love to you all.

Foreword

They're all a little messed up, aren't they? Superheroes, I mean. One of the truest lines from the Christopher Nolan *Batman* trilogy, and in this particular case *Batman Begins*, is when Bruce Wayne says to a table of dinner guests, "A guy who dresses like a bat clearly has issues." And of course, anyone who is familiar with Batman's origin story (orphan of murdered parents turned lonely billionaire seeks closure and justice from beneath a cowl and cape) knows that Mr. Wayne, well, he does have issues, and he'd be the first to admit it. Alan Moore seemed to delve deepest into this particular topic with his iconic graphic novel, *Watchmen*. Many of those so-called superheroes weren't particularly heroic. Their deeds seemed to come off more as compulsions to act out in a world that was well beyond saving itself. Look at the canon of Marvel and DC and everything in between, and you will see similar tropes played out time and again. Only the costumes and the names have changed.

I'm not an expert on comic books or super heroes. I leave that stuff up to the experts, like Mr. Healy here. But I can say that his *Just Cause Universe* stories seem, well, different somehow. Maybe it's because the heroes don't have "secret identities." Granted, he's not the first person to do this. Iron Man is the first character to come to mind, and I guess the rest of the Avengers, but doesn't that still seem refreshing in a way? A hero who is completely "out of the closet," as it were. A hero who can live out in the open world without all the loneliness and deception that comes from leading a double life is, well, invigorating. They are who they are, and everyone knows it. The heroes in Just Cause are, like The Avengers, an elite special force, but they're more regulated and organized. People love them. They're like celebrities or Olympic athletes. Of course, this doesn't mean our heroes don't struggle. A story isn't a story without conflict, both internal and external, and just because you can wear your costume and use your real name in public doesn't mean you don't have problems finding a place in the world, as we see Mustang Sally face in this first tale in the *Just Cause Universe*.

No, I think *Just Cause* is different because in an era that struggles to justify even a modicum of money on investments that could move humanity forward or could perhaps save us from the increasingly oppressive climate of our own hubris, these stories portray a society that embraces justice and progress and understands that it's worth the cost. It doesn't force its would-be heroes to live in secrecy and become vigilantes because our government, our law enforcement, our society as a whole either can't or is just too corrupt to care. The cynicism that underlies other comic book stories greatly reduced here, leaving in its place a sense of optimism about people and our potential to still do good things.

Just Cause believes in a world that, while imperfect and filled with danger, still gives a damn about saving itself. I think our world needs that more than ever.

—*Allison M. Dickson*
August, 2012

Introduction to the Revised & Expanded Edition

"HEY DAWG, I HEARD YOU LIKE SUPERHEROES . . ."

I do like superheroes. Reading about them, writing about them, and even at one time drawing them—that is, before I learned that I have no facility with a pencil, unless it's to put words down on the page. This book represents close to a decade of my writing life, and I'm very proud of this final version. I promise not to re-revise it in a few years, like certain directors have done with their movies set in a galaxy far, far away. What you are reading is the definitive *Just Cause*. It has gone through several iterations over the years, from a bloated 106,000-word opus to a post-liposuction 60,000 word novella to the tome you hold today. It's gone through name changes, three agents, two publishers, and several burro-loads of Colombian coffee.

". . . SO I PUT MORE SUPERHEROES IN YOUR SUPERHEROES . . ."

The original draft of *Just Cause* was very different, with chapters alternating between Mustang Sally's story and the backstory of some sixty years of history, spread across her parents' and grandparents' generations. All that backstory was part of the forty-thousand words I cut out in one glorious orgy of excision. I saved it, of course, because one should never waste the words one writes. Some of those stories have since transformed themselves into novels in their own right, and you'll be able to read them someday soon. Others simply languished unattended until this edition, where I have included three of those stories at the end of the book. I call them, collectively, *Those Who Came Before*, and they, like the short stories available all over the internet, add more depth to the illustrious history of Just Cause.

". . . SO YOU CAN HAVE SUPERHEROES WHILE YOU HAVE SUPERHEROES."

I had great fun putting all this together for you, and I hope you enjoy the heck out of it.

—*Ian Thomas Healy*
August, 2012

Chapter One

"We have not passed that subtle line between childhood and adulthood until . . . we have stopped saying 'It got lost,' and say 'I lost it.'"

-Sydney J. Harris

December, 2003
Chicago, Illinois
Lucky Seven Headquarters

"Happy birthday, dear Sally, happy birthday to you!" sang the group assembled in the Lucky Seven's conference room. Salena Thompson hunched her shoulders at the cacophony and squirmed in her seat. She wished something—anything—would happen to cut short the embarrassing spectacle of seven adults fawning over her. Maybe aliens could decide today was the day to invade Chicago, or the Moon could slip out of its orbit, or zombies would choose today to begin crawling from the frozen ground in search of brains. Any opportunity for her to bolt from the room and do what she'd been trained to do instead of suffering the attention and adulation of the others.

"Go on, dear, blow out the candles and make a wish." Tremor's fashion-model looks and height made Sally feel like a clumsy adolescent next to her. Only a shade over five feet tall, Sally had developed a perpetual kink in her neck from always having to look up at the

1

statuesque men and women who populated the parahuman community.

Sally leaned forward and held her long blonde braids back from the eighteen yellow candles on the cake. The frosting was the same scarlet as her superhero costume. It would probably turn her tongue the same color, what with all the food coloring. She knew Bullet had slaved away in the kitchen for hours, wrestling with recipes and mixing ingredients in his giant, ungainly hands. More than once, the entire Lucky Seven headquarters had rung when he punched a counter top in frustration. Juliet had taken Sally aside before the party and made her promise to love the cake no matter what. And to Bullet's credit, it was a very pretty cake, with yellow swirls decorating the frosting that reminded Sally of her braids or the golden trim of her costume.

All things considered, she'd much rather have been on duty in costume, helping to patrol the city or telling school kids not to use drugs or even filling out paperwork. Instead, she took a deep breath and tried not to grimace as Juliet snapped a picture from across the table. A moment later, she extinguished the candles to thunderous applause. She looked around the room at her friends, the privately-funded team of superheroes which had adopted her for the past six months.

"Hey, get the gift." Stratocaster snapped his fingers as if he'd just remembered. His vibrant purple mohawk stood proud and spiked. His guitar, the conduit for his magical power, hung at his back. He'd dressed in his nicest t-shirt for the occasion, one printed with a tuxedo shirt and bow tie, and his Doc Martens had been polished.

"Oh, yeah . . . we almost forgot!" Spark made a show of searching his pockets and rubbing his beard thoughtfully. "Who has it? I don't." Unlike the others on the team, Spark had no innate parahuman abilities of his own. Instead he used his acrobatic skills and electrical gadgetry to hold his own. And it didn't hurt that he ranked pretty high on Forbes 400 list either, thanks to his electrical engineering and business acumen.

Bullet stepped forward. He was as large and imposing in his civvies as in his black-and-red costume. His craggy, scarred face split into a wide grin as he held out an envelope to Sally. "Happy birthday," he said in his cracking, rumbling voice. A piece of rebar had pierced his throat once, and even though he had healed from the injury within minutes, it had left his voice a ruin. "I hope you like the cake."

"I'm sure it's delicious. I can't wait to taste it." Sally took the envelope and glanced around at the others. Statues might as well have surrounded her for all the expressions displayed by the Lucky Seven. Even Carousel, the artificial being who delighted in expressing human emotions, made her face an impassive wall.

"Go on," said Juliet. "Open it." She was the only one of the Lucky Seven who didn't use a superhero name. She had wanted to call herself *Jedi* because of her psionic powers, but Lucasfilm wouldn't permit it, so she just worked without any special name. Her dreadlocks were held back by a tie-dyed scarf with a batik pattern on it and her teeth sparkled like mints in the chocolatey glow of her face.

Sally slid a finger underneath the envelope flap and withdrew two folded pieces of paper.

"Read them out loud." Trix shook his '80s rock-star hair. Like Stratocaster, he would have been far more comfortable in a ripped t-shirt and jeans with a studded belt, but he'd found a dark blue turtleneck and some chinos somewhere in the very bottom of his wardrobe.

"*To Juice, Field Commander and Administrator of Just Cause,*" read Sally. "*We, the undersigned, are pleased to recommend Salena Thompson, also known as Mustang Sally, for an internship with Just—*" She stopped as she felt her throat tighten up. She tried again. *"Internship with Ju—"*

Her vision had grown far too blurry with tears to read more.

"There's more," said Spark. "Since we'd gone to all the trouble of writing this referral for you, we thought we might save you some time and effort and sent in the application on your behalf. The other page is—"

"Shush, let her read it herself." Juliet placed her hand on Spark's shoulder.

Sally flipped over to the other sheet of paper. She saw the official Just Cause stationery and the brief letter written on it. Certain words jumped out at her: *interview . . . Just Cause Headquarters . . . Intern.*

"Th-thank you." Tears streamed down her cheeks. "It's the b-best gift ever."

All her life, Sally had wanted to be a superhero in Just Cause, like her mother and grandmother had been. Now she would have that chance.

Tremor brushed her crimson curls away from her face and smiled at her with the fashion-model looks that had graced a hundred different magazine covers. "Sally . . ." The crimson emergency lights in the corners of the conference room illuminated and a sudden klaxon wailed from the speaker system throughout Lucky Seven Headquarters. Echoes chased up and down the halls of the building.

The heroes looked at each other in disbelief.

"It's five days before Christmas. What the hell could possibly need our attention?" said Stratocaster. "Don't supervillains have last-minute shopping to do?"

"Maybe one of them is working a five-finger discount," said Trix.

Spark touched a button on the intercom that connected him to the team's dedicated monitoring center, modeled after the much larger and more comprehensive one used by Just Cause. "Spark here.

What's going on?"

"I've got the police commissioner holding for you, Boss," reported a voice from the center.

"Patch him through."

"Spark, we've got a giant robot thing breaking up the Science and Technology Expo at McCormick Place. I have officers down and possible civilian casualties!"

"Understood, Commissioner. We're on our way." Spark turned to Sally and the rest of the Lucky Seven. "Let's move, people."

They hurried to the locker rooms to change. Sally, with her super-speed, was in and back out again in costume well before any of the others. She tapped her yellow boots on the floor with a rapid-fire patter, impatient for the rest of the Lucky Seven to finish.

The rest of the team rejoined her within minutes. They'd transformed themselves from civilian attire to their colorful costumes.

"Trix, can you fly today?" Spark checked the clips which held his electro-whip.

"Not sure, man. Let me give it a try." Sally and the rest of the Lucky Seven members tensed as Trix rose into the air. His random powers came and went with alarming frequency. Sometimes he could fly, other times he couldn't. More than once he'd tried to use an ability only to get something unexpected, like an explosive fireball or a tornado from a clear blue sky. He gave them a thumbs-up.

Spark nodded. "Good. Sally, Carousel, you're with me. Bullet, you're on point. Trix, Tremor, flank us. Strat—"

A whine of mystical feedback echoed through the conference room as Stratocaster turned the knobs on his guitar up to the proverbial eleven.

"Bring Juliet along and we'll meet you there."

Juliet rolled her eyes and dug her fingers into her ears. Stratocaster fingered the fretboard and with a long-practiced move, leaped into the air, swung his pick hand around in a windmill circle, and slashed the pick across the strings. He landed with his legs spread apart, pointed the neck of the guitar toward the ceiling, and stuck his other hand in the air in a pose straight out of a rock video. A wallop of solid sound smashed through the conference room. Bright energy sparks flowed from the guitar strings in every color of the spectrum. They coalesced into a violet glow that enveloped him and Juliet and they disappeared to leave only a reverberating echo of the power chord in their wake.

Sally's ears rang like church bells tolled in her head. She winced and hoped the damage wasn't permanent.

"Move out, Lucky Seven," said Spark.

Sally thrilled to those words. In the six months since she'd joined up with the Seven, this was only the second time they'd been called out on an emergency. The first time was to assist with rescue and recovery efforts after Hurricane Isabel smashed into the East Coast.

She'd spent years training for this, her first potential parahuman combat. Three years of her life had been spent under the tutelage of the Academy combat instructor. Before that, her mother and grandmother had coached her on the unique methods a speedster could use against opponents like disarming their weapons before they could be used, wrapping them in yards of tape or rope in mere seconds, and pummeling them with fists like machine gun bullets.

Spark's motorcycle screamed out of the garage, weaving in and out of holiday traffic. Sally and Carousel kept pace with him, one clad in scarlet and the other in naught but nearly-frictionless metallic skin. A younger Sally might have charged ahead—she was fast enough to cover the distance to McCormick in less than a minute—but years of training had tempered some of her natural impetuousness. She would stay with her team and follow the orders of her commander.

Her mother had warned her about going solo in a

combat mission. *It's easy to run ahead of everyone else,* she'd said, *to think that just because you're faster, you're better. Use your speed and accelerated perceptions to think before you act. You have the time. Use it wisely.*

Sally reminded herself of the basic combat tenets taught at the Hero Academy, all of which boiled down to: *protect the innocent, support your teammates, and come home alive.*

Good advice, she thought. She intended to follow it to the letter.

Chapter Two

"When soldiers have been baptized in the fire of a battle-field, they have all one rank in my eyes."

-Napoleon Bonaparte

December, 2003
Chicago, Illinois

Traffic clogged the roads for miles around the Convention Center as people tried to get away and emergency vehicles tried to get through. Sally and Carousel scouted ahead at high speed to find the best route for Spark to steer his motorcycle. Finally, they reached an impasse as the throng of evacuated conventioneers and onlookers became too thick to avoid.

Spark brought his cycle to a halt, dismounted with an acrobatic leap, and uncoiled his whip. He swung it up into the air and snared the flying Bullet, who wrapped one of his huge hands around the tip. Spark's momentum continued unchecked as Bullet lifted him up and over the crowd. Sally and Carousel picked their way through the thick crowd beneath the flyers.

They reached the police line in seconds, where officers struggled to keep curious people back from the buildings and helped others maintain an orderly exit. The members of the Chicago Police Department looked relieved as the Lucky Seven heroes arrived on scene.

"Fill us in, Lieutenant," said Spark to a short, stocky

woman who wore a helmet and armored vest.

"It's a giant robot thing," said the officer. "It entered the main exhibition hall and began firing off tear gas canisters. Cleared the place out pretty fast."

Sally looked around and noticed many people in the crowd were coughing, with red faces and streaming eyes. Her breath mask would give her some protection from gas but it didn't have a self-contained air supply, so she'd get a dose of whatever it was too.

"Do you know what it's after?"

"What it's after? Not at the moment. Security converged on it but it's carrying some pretty heavy weaponry and they couldn't get close to it." The lieutenant pushed her helmet back and wiped sweat from her brow even in the freezing temperature. "We've got four officers unaccounted for, and there may be civilians stranded inside. Goddamn, but I'm glad you're here."

A whine of feedback and a thrum of distortion filled the air as Stratocaster and Juliet materialized out of the sound and appeared right next to Sally.

"Not late, are we?" Stratocaster flashed a tight grin at Spark.

"What, did you stop for a latte and biscotti?" Spark snorted in derision.

Stratocaster patted his vest pocket. "I saved you a couple. You want one with almonds or white chocolate?"

Spark didn't bother to reply and instead turned back to the lieutenant. "Has anyone possibly got a picture of this thing?"

She nodded and pulled out her cell phone. "One of the missing officers was able to send this from his phone before we lost contact." She held it up. The Lucky Seven members all crowded around to get a look. Sally strained to see past Bullet's bulk, and just caught a glimpse.

The blurry image showed an angular humanoid

figure in dark blue and gleaming chrome, with four arms and two legs and a large bulky object on one shoulder. It was caught in the act of firing some kind of weapon from one of its intermediate limbs. A gout of flame jetted out and washed out part of the image from overexposure.

Sally drew in a sharp breath. She knew this figure; he had haunted her dreams since she'd been old enough to understand what had happened to her father and who was responsible for his death.

Destroyer.

Destroyer had taken away half her family before she was even born, and she hated the coward inside his powered armor because of it.

Destroyer.

She whispered the name aloud and felt her perceptions accelerate out of fear. When she ran and moved at super speeds, her perceptions and thought processes accelerated as well, allowing her mind to keep up with her body. It could be a hindrance in a non-combat situation though, as everything seemed to slow down around her. She forced herself to calm down so she could still interact with the others.

Spark confirmed her identification. "That's got to be Destroyer. High-tech battlesuit and weapons, clearing out a science and technology expo. Just his style."

"But why is he still here?" asked Tremor. "I'd think smash-and-grab would be more his style. Why hang around to risk facing us?"

"Because he never has," said Juliet. "He longs to test himself against anyone and everyone. What better opportunity to face us than by attacking this facility?"

"It has to be more than that," said Spark. "He could have drawn us out anywhere, anytime. There must be something here he wants. Let's make sure he doesn't get it."

Sally trembled at high speed. She was terrified of

Destroyer. He killed without compunction, without mercy. He'd killed her father.

Now he was here, ready to kill her and her friends and teammates.

"Let's go," said Spark. "Stay alert, don't bunch up. Bullet, Tremor, Trix, flank him and keep him from escaping. Carousel, Sally, try to disarm him. Juliet, if you can shut him down telepathically, do it. Strat—"

Stratocaster slid his fingers down the strings of his guitar as sparks of energy danced away into dimensions unknown; he knew his role.

"*Lucky Seven, let's roll!*" Many of the onlookers took up the battle cry, made famous after fifteen years.

The long lobby of McCormick Place was eerie and dark, only lit by emergency lighting. Sulfurous tendrils of bitter gas twisted around their feet as they entered. Sally adjusted her breath mask a little better to cut out the worst of the acrid stink.

Spark uncoiled his whip and held it in both hands. At a moment's notice, he could flick it out and send an electrical charge through the bare wire braided into the leather. Sally didn't think it would do much damage against a heavily-armored villain like Destroyer, but Spark carried himself with such confidence that it made her feel a little braver.

Stratocaster's fingers still moved across the strings and fretboard of his guitar, but he'd muted the volume and only a slight purplish glow emanated from it. The others advanced with careful purpose, ready to let their powers fly.

Carousel whispered to Sally, "I'm scared."

"Me too." Sally felt the muscles all through her torso tighten and clench at the approach of combat.

Two of the large doors leading to the exhibition hall had been wrenched off their hinges and the frame twisted into a semblance of some bizarre modern art sculpture. Beyond, Sally could see the flickering firelight of burning displays and carpeting.

The Lucky Seven moved into the main hall. Right away, Sally noticed two security officers slumped against the wall, their uniforms blackened around smoldering holes in the chests. She pointed them out to the others.

Juliet knelt down beside them, opening her mind to seek signs of life. She looked up toward Trix. "They're both alive, but fading fast. Can you get them out?"

He nodded, raised his hands, and willed his power to function. Sally's ears popped as air rushed in around the two victims and gently lifted them as if they were on an air hockey table. He turned and guided them out, leaving eddies of smoke and gas in his wake.

A crumbling sound echoed through the main hall over the crackle of flames. Sally caught a glimpse of motion overhead. Her perceptions shot into high gear and she realized a large chunk of cement was hurtling toward the group. Carousel reached for Spark to shove him out of the way. Sally wrapped her arms around Juliet, strained to overcome stubborn inertia, and yanked her to safety.

Having done her best to protect Juliet, Sally checked on the others. Overhead, Bullet moved with glacial slowness to intercept the tumbling debris, one fist cocked in preparation to smash it into gravel. Tremor dodged upward, and Stratocaster thumbed his volume knob up. Satisfied that there wasn't anything she needed to do, Sally relaxed her perceptions and the world snapped back up to speed.

Bullet plowed his fist into the cement and shattered it into fist-sized chunks. The others dove away and cried out in surprise.

With a whine of high-powered servomotors, Destroyer stepped through a burning display, a metallic demon. Humanoid but with four arms, the fifteen-foot-tall suit contained a small, angry man who gloated over the havoc of his own creation. All blue metal and chrome, the battlesuit looked like the nightmare of a Japanese toy designer, except Sally knew there was no whimsy at all in the sharp angles. In all the years since his debut in 1977, Destroyer had only ever lost to Just Cause once, and that was in his first battlesuit, built from junkyard wreckage.

"*WELL LOOK WHAT I'VE FOUND. SNOW WHITE AND THE SEVEN DWARVES.*" His voice modulated through high-end speakers into earth-shaking tones. "*I WONDERED WHEN I'D RUN ACROSS YOU SO-CALLED HEROES.*"

"Surrender, Destroyer. We've got you outnumbered. Power down your suit and exit it before we peel it off you." Spark stood defiant despite a tear in the side of his suit. Sally could see a stain of blood on his side and wondered how badly he was hurt.

Destroyer laughed, a mirthless chuckle that echoed off the high ceiling of the main hall. "*I'VE FOUGHT JUST CAUSE AND WON TIME AND TIME AGAIN, SPARK. WHAT MAKES YOU THINK YOUR PITIFUL LITTLE CLUB CAN STOP ME?*"

Bullet and Tremor took up positions over Destroyer. Stratocaster played a low, throbbing riff, building power with each strum of the strings. Carousel touched Sally's elbow. Sally turned to look, startled; she'd been almost hypnotized by Destroyer's sheer size. Carousel held out a two-foot-long piece of steel rebar. She must have picked it up from some of the debris. Sally took it, feeling clumsy and awkward with it, and wondered how she'd ever disarm Destroyer with such a simple tool. "What about you?" she whispered to Carousel.

Curved blades like scythes grew from the metal of Carousel's arms to extend past her hands like deadly ribbons. "I'll be fine with these."

"Last chance, Destroyer. Surrender," called Spark.

"*YOU'RE BORING ME,*" said Destroyer, a hint of glee in his voice. "*LET'S FIGHT!*"

Destroyer didn't wait for the Lucky Seven to make

the first move. The unit on his shoulder swiveled and a missile the size of Sally's arm burst out of it to impact point blank on Bullet. Instead of exploding in flames, the missile burst into a sticky, ropy substance that wrapped around Bullet's arms and legs to cocoon him in less than a second. Destroyer pummeled him with a heavy metal fist the size of a mailbox and sent the enshrouded hero crashing into the ceiling in an explosion of ceramics, glass, and masonry.

Tremor hit Destroyer with a blast of concentrated vibratory energy from one side while Stratocaster launched dissonant power chords at him from the other. The shoulder unit ripped away in the combined blast. Unfazed by the double-sided attack, Destroyer crowed "Suck on this, heroes," and dropped a small spheroid onto the floor which flashed into smoke when it hit.

Spark yelped as his batteries shorted out. Sparks shot from Stratocaster's guitar as the internal circuitry melted into so much slag. It must have been an electromagnetic pulse bomb, thought Sally, to have shut down all the electronics.

The guns mounted on Destroyer's intermediate arms chattered as he fired large-caliber bullets toward them all. Sally and Carousel ran faster than the arm could track after them. Sally glanced up and saw the air around Tremor shimmer as she transmitted vibratory power through it at the battlesuit. Destroyer swung a gun at her and she barely had time to form a wall of vibration waves in front of her to deflect the bullets. Destroyer stepped toward her, firing nonstop, and drove her backward toward the wall.

Sally saw an opening and ducked around Carousel to move in close to Destroyer. Although his intermediate arms were higher than she could reach, he'd stepped close enough to the wall that she could try a maneuver she'd practiced many times at the

Academy. She accelerated in the blink of an eye and rushed at the wall on an oblique angle. She stepped up onto the wall and pushed off it to drive herself higher, the rebar raised and ready. Her perceptions fluttered into overdrive as she drifted toward Destroyer. A bullet left the mouth of the gun on a plume of smoke and flame, moving with the gentle pace of a curling stone on the ice. Sally ignored it and stuck the rebar underneath the gun barrel, put her feet against the intermediate arm, and heaved.

Her mass was slight but her momentum was terrific, and she felt the barrel move as she levered it up and away from the firing mechanism. The gun discharged again, but this time a fountain of sparks erupted from it as the bullet lodged inside the barrel and twisted it into uselessness.

Carousel attacked from the opposite side and sliced through the other gun's firing mechanism with her wicked sharp blades. Destroyer reacted with the cold precision of an automatic, computerized response. His primary arm swung down and caught Carousel across her legs as she retreated. Sally heard a snap that made her feel ill. Carousel screamed in android pain and crumpled to the ground. Sally avoided the opposite descending arm only because she was faster than her friend.

Given a momentary reprieve from Destroyer's onslaught, Tremor blasted her powerful vibratory energy at the battlesuit's head. Sparks flew from it in all directions, making a noise like a rotary grinder. Sally tumbled to the ground near Carousel, whose legs canted off in unnatural angles. She grabbed underneath her friend's armpits and pulled her to safety while Destroyer was busy with Tremor.

"It's all right, you'll be okay," Sally gasped, trying to catch her breath.

Carousel weighed next to nothing. Or maybe the adrenaline gave Sally unusual reserves of strength as she dragged the moaning speedster to safety behind a pile of debris. Sally had basic first aid training from the Hero Academy, but everything she had learned flew away in her panic. All she could think of was to keep her friend warm. Even androids felt shock, didn't they? She zipped over to a display that hadn't yet caught fire and snagged the cheap curtains.

"Here," she said. "I've got to wrap you up."

"Do . . . do what you need to," whimpered Carousel. "It hurts. It hurts so bad."

"I'm sorry." Sally couldn't imagine how bad her friend's injuries might be. She'd never been seriously hurt herself. Carousel's broken legs terrified her. "Can you turn off your pain sensors?"

Carousel nodded and her face grew serene and calm. "That's better."

Sally nodded and wiped away tears she didn't have time for. "I'll get you some help as soon as it's safe."

"Go get him," said Carousel. "I wish I could be more help to you."

"Just don't die."

"Androids don't die. They just go into p-permanent hibernation." Carousel managed a wink.

"Well, don't do that either." Sally glanced toward Destroyer. Tremor blasted bursts of vibratory power at him while dodging shots from his secondary cannon. Spark tried to cut Bullet free from the goop that enshrouded him. Stratocaster, powerless without his guitar, stayed under cover as much as possible. Juliet likewise could do very little to help in a straightforward combat situation; she couldn't get close enough to Destroyer to try to shut his mind down with her telepathic powers. Trix was still missing in action.

The Lucky Seven were about to lose the fight.

Sally had to do something, but didn't know what. "Hey, Destroyer, over here!" She leaped out from cover and brandished her piece of rebar to distract him enough to let Tremor get a telling shot in on his armor suit. He cut loose with a hip-mounted chain gun that swiveled to track her almost as fast as she could run away. Bullets chipped into the floor just behind her with every step. She skidded around a corner and gasped for breath.

Angry tears blurred her vision. She felt helpless and afraid. What good was *running*? After more than ten years of training to be a superhero, she didn't know what to do. Destroyer had made a mockery of the Lucky Seven and they would be very fortunate if all of them survived.

Sally banged her clenched fist against her forehead. "Think. Think!"

She stepped around the corner just in time to see a device detach from the back of Destroyer's leg, hit the floor and bounce up into the air, spinning like a top. She dove behind the corner once more as the device exploded with a bang so loud it took her breath away.

Underneath the ringing in her ears, a floor-shaking thrum echoed amid the destruction. Sally staggered to the edge and peeked around the corner. Destroyer had picked up a large case and fired his boot rockets. She wondered what was in the case but had no time for curiosity; somehow, she had to prevent his escape. The others lay sprawled amid the wreckage. She hoped they were only unconscious.

She charged at him, but he sprayed something onto the floor behind him as he flew toward the exit. Sally couldn't avoid the puddle and lost all her traction. She flipped into the air as her arms and legs pin wheeled. The stuff coated her like oil and she bounced and slid all the way to the front doors. She skittered over shards of glass and steel and her costume shredded against them.

Destroyer burst out of the building. Trix tried to engage him but was slapped aside for his efforts, crashing through one of the few undamaged windows on that side of the building. Sally watched, unable to do anything as Destroyer's main engines glowed white hot and launched him into the overcast skies like a missile.

Sally watched the bright spark of engine exhaust recede into the distance, and then bowed her head and felt every bit a failure.

Chapter Three

- Parahumans exhibit a common genetic marker.
- The presence of the genetic marker doesn't guarantee active parahuman abilities.
- Parahuman abilities violate known physical laws.

To summarize: There's far more that we don't know than we do know about parahumans.

-"The Origin of Parapowers", Dr. Matasuko Musashi, 1995

January, 2004
Denver, Colorado
Just Cause Headquarters

Sally sat in the oversized chair and tried not to squirm. She had only been in Juice's office for a few minutes, but it felt like hours while he glanced through the pertinent parts of her file. She fumed with each slow and deliberate turn of a page.

Patience was a challenge for a speedster.

She'd debated whether to wear her costume, and even went so far as to discuss it with her mother, who suggested that business attire would be more professional. She wanted to make a good impression on the man whom she'd known as long as she could remember, but the mere idea of a blazer and skirt made her itch and chafe. Her mother even offered to go shopping with her and played the ultimate card of offering to pay for it, but Sally wouldn't hear of it. She dug through the recesses of her closet and found a pair of slacks she could stand to wear and a silky white button-down shirt. She added a muted navy cardigan and figured she looked good enough for anything Juice could throw at her.

Juice had always looked big from afar when she'd seen him at various events attended by Just Cause. As a Just Cause alumnus, her mother often went and brought Sally along to introduce her to heroes past and present as my future Just Cause member. Now that she sat in front of him, he seemed gigantic. He was the kind of black man who looked stylish with his head shaved, and he dressed in Italian silk and leather. He'd gone to law school and been a part-time member of Just Cause in his early twenties. Her mom swore he was the smartest man she'd ever met.

He leaned his considerable frame back in an expensive chair as he turned the pages in Sally's file. His build and demeanor gave no indication of his unique ability to absorb electricity and convert it into pure strength and resistance to physical damage. "Hmmm . . ." He looked over the edge of his reading glasses at her. "So you'd like to join the team?"

Sally swallowed and licked her lips, her mouth dry as the air in her hometown of Phoenix. She stammered "Y-yes sir," and hated herself for it. In the Hero Academy, oral exams had always made her queasy. So did interviews, she was learning.

"Why?"

Sally had a thousand reasons to want to be a part of Just Cause: because her mother had been a member; because her father had been killed by Destroyer; because her grandmother was one of the first American superheroes; because she'd watched while members of Just Cause had lost their lives in the destruction of the World Trade Center and the Pentagon in 2001; because she wanted to be part of the greatest superhero team in the world. She opened her mouth to reply and all her pat answers flew away like dandelion seeds on a puff of prairie wind.

Juice smiled. "Tell you what, Sally. This office feels pretty formal. Let's head down to the cafeteria. The coffee's fair and the sandwiches are pretty good." His chair creaked as he drew himself up to his full six foot ten. He held open his office door for her. Sally felt like a toddler next to him. "How is Arizona?"

She shrugged. "I don't know. I didn't get home much this fall."

"Beautiful country down that way. If it wasn't so hot, I'd enjoy it more. I've still got enough East Coast in me to prefer a more urbane setting. How do you like it here in Denver?"

"It's nice," she said. "Running's easier up here."

"Even though there's less air to breathe?"

She shrugged. "You get used to it after awhile."

They took the corridor from Juice's office to the main lobby. A Native American woman with magnificent feathered wings had just checked in through Security and stepped away from the retinal scanner. She smiled at them with dazzling white teeth, which contrasted her flawless brown skin. The woman's eyes had bright yellow irises and large pupils like those of a bird. Sally recognized her as Desert Eagle, although they'd never met before.

"Hi, James. Who's your friend?" Sally felt very small; the winged woman was over six feet tall as well.

"Sondra, this is Salena Thompson, also known as Mustang Sally. Sally, Sondra Eagle, also known as Desert Eagle."

"Pleased to meet you, Salena. Are you attending the Hero Academy?"

"I just graduated. And you can call me Sally. Nobody calls me *Salena* except my mom when I'm in trouble."

"Are you going to do your internship with us?"

"I hope so," Sally said with a sidelong glance at Juice, who beamed back at her.

"What's your gig?" Sondra flexed her wings. Her broad and powerful shoulders filled out the custom overcoat she wore against the freezing wind outside.

"I'm a speedster."

Sondra smiled. "I thought so. I'm sure you'll do just fine. We need a speedster to fill out the ranks." Sondra said farewell and headed off into the depths of the headquarters building.

The cafeteria was larger than Sally expected, but then she remembered it catered not only to the team, but also to Just Cause's hundred-and-some civilian employees.

"Would you like some coffee?" Juice asked her as he poured a large cup of his own.

"Uh, not really. It makes me jittery at super-speed." Sally had been prepared for a typical job interview, not Juice's casual friendliness. She didn't know how to play along with his game.

"Grab whatever you want, then come and sit down and we'll finish." He strolled over to a table and sat down.

She didn't know what else to do so she took the first thing she saw—a bag of chips—and went over to him.

Juice had appropriated a large blueberry muffin and was spreading butter on it as Sally sat down. He smiled at her. "Did you always want to be a superhero?"

"Well, sure. I mean, my mom and grandma were, and I'm faster than both of them. What else could I do?"

"You could have a normal life. Go to college, get a job, meet the right guy. Ever think of doing that instead?"

"No, not really. I guess I always wanted to do this."

"You got very high marks in combat training at the Academy. How was training alongside the Lucky Seven?"

"It was cool. I learned a lot from them."

"Before the incident with Destroyer, had you ever been in a real combat situation before?"

Sally shook her head. She still had bad dreams

about the giant blue battlesuit and her hatred of the man it contained.

"I've read the reports, of course, but I'd like to hear it in your own words. Tell me about what happened in Chicago." Juice swallowed the last of his muffin and took a sip of his coffee.

"Destroyer took out Bullet with some kind of goopy stuff that wrapped him up. Then he used a portable electromagnetic pulse to ruin Spark's equipment and Stratocaster's guitar. He broke Carousel's legs when we tried to take out his guns. He knocked out the others with a stun grenade." She bowed her head. "I guess we didn't give a very good accounting of ourselves."

"What about you?" Juice finished his coffee and set the cup back on the table.

"He sprayed some kind of lubricant on the floor." Sally felt her face grow hotter. "I hit it and slid across some broken glass. Tore up my costume some."

"Were you hurt?"

"Not really. Just my pride." Sally sighed. "I didn't really accomplish much either. It's hard discovering that you're ineffective in a real battle after spending so many years in practice."

Juice smiled. "Listen, Sally, Destroyer has taken down heroes far more experienced than you. You've got nothing to be embarrassed about. Quite the contrary, you should be proud you even faced him at all."

Sally couldn't look at him. "Even though I didn't do anything right?" She couldn't believe herself. Worst. Interview. Ever.

"You survived your first real parahuman combat with nothing worse than a wounded pride. That is a lot better than how most heroes fare. They can teach you all the great theories and situational tactics they want at the Academy, but when you get right down to it, real life has very little to do with the classroom. Believe me, any fight you can run, walk, limp, or crawl away from is one in which you did well."

Sally felt her admiration grow for him. As a lawyer, he'd learned to use language to great effect, and his words soothed her discomfort like aloe on a sunburn.

"How are the others in the Lucky Seven?"

"They're okay. Mostly they were just stunned— minor bumps and bruises, that sort of thing. Carousel's back on light duty. Her systems self-repair so long as she has access to power and raw materials."

"Good. Now then . . ." He leaned back. "Sondra was absolutely right. We do need a speedster. Think you're up to the task?"

Words jammed up Sally's mouth so she could only nod in stunned silence. She'd known for years Just Cause was her destiny, but it surprised her to have the opportunity in front of her all the same.

Juice grinned back at her and pulled a phone from his pocket. He thumbed a switch on it. "Harris?" A voice responded in acknowledgement. "We've got a new intern. Can you please prepare her quarters and arrange for her paperwork and badge?"

"*Yes, sir.*"

Juice switched channels and spoke again. "Jason?"

"Yeah?" said a different voice from the phone.

"I've got a young lady here who is in need of a tour. I think you're just the man to handle that job."

"*I'll be right there, boss.*"

"Give her about an hour to settle into her quarters."

"*Yes, sir. One hour, sir.*"

Juice chuckled to himself, closed the phone and tucked it back into his jacket pocket. "Do you remember Jason Tibbets? He graduated from the Academy two years ago."

"I'm not sure, uh, sir." Despite throwing herself into her studies at the Academy, she couldn't have forgotten the tall blonde boy who had been two years ahead of her even if she'd wanted to. All the girls in her dorm had spoken at length about his dreamy eyes and gentlemanly manners. She'd been enamored of him at first, although she found her studies to take far more of her time than she could spare for crushing on boys.

"Perhaps you'd know him as Mastiff," said Juice. "And you can knock off the *sir*. Jason just does that to needle me. I'm not one for military formality and all that. Just make sure you follow orders when we're out in the field and you'll be fine calling me Juice, or James, or even *Hey You!* Just so long as I know it's me."

"I will, sir. I mean, Juice."

The big man leaned his head back and laughed. "You'll fit in just fine here, Mustang Sally. Welcome to Just Cause."

Chapter Four

"The most common occurrence when two parahumans meet is a fight, ostensibly blamed on 'mistaken identities.' It's a form of establishing dominance like one might find in any other type of social situation. The second most common occurrence is mutual attraction. If parahumans are truly genetic mutants they could conceivably be a separate race from mankind. And like any other race, they must propagate or risk extinction."

- Dr. Lane Devereaux, *Larry King Live*, March 4, 1993

January, 2004
Denver, Colorado
Just Cause Headquarters

"Just breathe into the tube," said the balding man named Harris.

Sally blew into the glass tube that emerged from his device. The machine emitted clicks as it processed information and spat out a credit card a minute later. "What is it?"

"Genetic key," said Harris. "It's the best security we have. Your genetic code is imprinted upon the badge. It'll only work if it has contact with your living skin. If someone else tries to use your card, it raises an alarm in the Command Center. Can't be too careful these days."

Sally picked up her new badge and looked it over. It identified her as a Just Cause intern. "What if I lose it?"

"Come back here and we'll retest your code. If it matches, we'll just issue you a new card. If it doesn't, well, it's probably not really you so it becomes our problem, not yours. You don't have an evil twin, do you?"

"No. I'm an only child."

"Good." He handed her a box from inside a cabinet. "Here's your duty gear."

She examined the items in the box as Harris inventoried them for her. "Walkie-talkie satellite PC phone . . . these are state-of-the-art, but we replace them every six months whether they need it or not, the way they keep improving the technology. These babies work anywhere in the world as long as you're not deep underground or underwater."

"Cool."

He pointed out the uniform and clothing requisition form. "Just fill in your sizes now. The tailor will get your costume specs later. Our in-house shop will handle all your costume needs from here on out." Next, he held up a Just Cause Visa card. "This is for emergencies only. No shopping sprees. You swipe it anywhere, you gotta fill out an expense report." Finally, he showed her the gear and equipment requisition form and said, "I'll approve damn near anything. How the hell do I know what you really need?"

"I need a Top Fuel dragster. You know, for training." The whirlwind of being accepted onto Just Cause, even as an intern, had made Sally feel cocky and special. Every hero who had ever interned with the team wound up on the roster. Many of them filled out the ranks of the Just Cause Second Team, which had its headquarters in Virginia, but a few, like Mastiff and Forcestar, had been selected onto the main team. Sally hoped for that to be her eventual assignment.

"Yeah, right." He escorted her from his office down a hallway and up a flight of stairs to the dormitory. "The whole team's on this floor. Promotes unity or something. All I know is that it's a lot like my college dorm, only louder and with more muscle tone." He chuckled. "Everybody gets a suite. Bedroom, closet, living area, full bath, and kitchenette. Most of 'em eat in the cafeteria, probably because they're too busy being superheroes to cook a decent meal." Listening to Harris was like being assaulted by a verbal machine gun, thought Sally. "You get regular laundry service and cleaning, just like in a hotel. Here we are, then."

He stopped at a door that had *Mustang Sally* stenciled on it. He motioned to her to use her badge. She pulled it out and slid it through the reader. The door unlocked and she swung it open. The suite seemed cavernous to her after her shared dorm room at the Academy. It was like an entire apartment. Her luggage sat in the middle of the living area, waiting to be unpacked. The room had decent carpet, a soft couch, a stocked entertainment center, and a computer desk. Off to one side she could see the kitchenette with a small refrigerator, microwave, coffee pot, and hot plate. A small table with two chairs was tucked against the wall. On the other side, she discovered the bedroom with a queen-size bed, a walk-in closet, and a nice bathroom. The entire suite had a faint mulberry scent, as if the housekeepers had sprayed the carpeting with it.

"Whaddya think?" Harris asked her after she'd had a few moments to check out the place.

"It's nice," she said. "It's huge. All this just for me?"

"Yeah. Just you. You need anything, hit star-eleven on the phone. I'm out. I got a thing to do." He headed down the hall, punching keys on his phone.

Sally left her luggage for the moment and kicked her shoes off. She scrunched her toes through the deep pile of the carpet, which felt comfortable and soft enough to sleep upon. She moved into the bedroom and lifted the shade so she could look out across the grounds.

The Just Cause compound consisted of four main buildings. Besides the dormitory, there was the training center, the Command Center, and the hangar/motor pool. The countryside around the facility was mostly dry grassland with an occasional stunted tree. Although she couldn't see it from this side of the building, she knew the Hero Academy was less than a mile away.

It all seemed very alien to her. Even though she'd spent the past three years at the Academy, and become very familiar with the surrounding area, she felt like it might as well have been in a different state; or on a different planet. She sat on the edge of the couch, and wondered what to do next. What was an intern even supposed to do?

A knock sounded at the door.

Sally went to the door, opened it, and looked up . . . up . . . *up* into his face and all of a sudden she was fifteen again and crushing on Jason Tibbets. He was as tall as Juice with a muscular, athletic build. His straight, straw-colored hair fell from the top of his head to float around his jaw line and cover his ears. Blond stubble dotted his chin and his blue eyes sparkled with amusement. His t-shirt read *Property of Just Cause—XXXL* and his sweatpants were so cavernous that Sally could have fit her entire body into one leg.

"Hi, you must be Salena. I'm Jason. Juice asked me to give you the tour since I'm off-duty today." He had a mild Southern drawl that Sally could tell would put just about anybody at ease. No wonder Juice had detailed him to the task of orienting her. Surely it wasn't just because he was gorgeous.

She realized she was still staring open-mouthed up at him. "Ulp." Sally's tongue had stuck to the roof of her mouth.

"Do you, uh, want to, uh, put on some shoes or anything?" His demeanor changed to uncertainty as he tried to interpret Sally's lack of vocal coherency.

"Shoes? Oh, uh, yeah. Let me change my clothes real quick. It'll be real quick because I'm a speedster and I do everything quick. Well, not everything. I mean, uh, I'll be just a minute." She slammed the door in his face before she babbled any more and spun around to fixate on her bags, still unopened in the middle of the floor. In a blur of motion she grabbed the one with most of her clothes and yanked the zipper open. A minor hurricane of fabric ensued as she dug through her wardrobe to find the perfect outfit. Even at super-speed, she had a difficult time deciding on a blouse.

She popped a button off her dress shirt in her hurry; she'd find it later. She didn't want to appear too formal for Jason, but didn't want him to think she was trying to impress him too much either. She settled on a sleeveless pink hoodie, low-rise jeans and high-tops without socks, and then dashed into the bathroom to check herself. Her hair was in disarray after her frantic clothes change. She fussed with it, but then realized it would take more time to fix it than she felt she had, so she plaited it into a single French braid and coiled the braid up into a ballet bun.

Clothes were scattered all over her suite as if a tornado had tossed them. She couldn't let Jason see it, so she cracked open the door, slipped out as fast as she could, and slammed it shut. "Okay, I'm ready."

She made extra effort not to act like a moonstruck teen while Jason showed her around the dormitory. The recreation room had multiple entertainment centers and game systems. The big-screen TV was state-of--the-art high definition, and the stereo looked big and expensive. Besides the electronic entertainment, there was a pool table, air hockey, foosball, and a couple of old-fashioned pinball machines. Off in one corner sat a terminal with a large flatscreen monitor.

"Juice said you spent some time hanging around with the Lucky Seven." Jason slouched against the back of a couch. Sally envied his ability to seem so comfortable in his own skin. "Why'd you do that instead of coming here first?"

"I was only seventeen when I graduated from the

Academy. We tried to pull strings with Homeland Security—me, my mom . . . even Vice Principal Stone wrote a letter to the Director on my behalf—but they wouldn't budge on the age requirement."

"I see."

"So there I was, six months away from turning eighteen with nothing to do and nowhere to go. I was going crazy staying at home with my mom, because we don't get along so well. I was actually looking through the Want Ads, thinking maybe I could just get a regular job or something."

"A regular job?" Jason sounded stunned. "But you're a parahuman, and an Academy graduate. You'd be wasting yourself punching a clock somewhere."

"I was thinking about being a pizza delivery girl," said Sally. "Except without the car. *Your pizza guaranteed anywhere in Phoenix in eight minutes or it's free.*"

Jason burst out laughing. "That's awesome. I'd have called you every day. I mean, uh . . ." His face reddened a bit around the edges. "Because I love pizza."

"Anyway," said Sally, "that's when Spark called me and invited me to come hang out with the 'Seven until I turned eighteen. So I did."

"No pizza?"

"No, no pizza."

"Man, I'd love a pizza about now." Jason rubbed his belly like a hungry toddler and made Sally giggle. "But then I couldn't show you around the rest of HQ. You want to see the rest?"

"Yes, please."

The Command Center fascinated Sally. It was the central hub of many Homeland Security operations, with one section dedicated to monitoring parahuman activities around the nation. Huge banks of monitoring stations and supercomputers fed data to a giant multicolored map of the United States with various marks and lights detailed. The background color of the map was yellow to signify the nationwide threat level of *Elevated*.

"There are forty duty stations," Jason said. "Some people think monitor duty is you hanging out here by yourself trying to keep tabs on the entire world and stuff. Actually, you hardly make any decisions at all when you're on duty. That's up to Homeland Security. The only reason you're even in here at all is to provide a parahuman perspective on anything that the brass wants to know about, whatever that means. Nothing's ever happened when I was on duty. I'm not really sure what I'd do if it did. I'm better at hitting stuff."

"So what so you do when you're here?" Sally asked.

"Surf the Net, mostly." He gave her that grin which made her insides turn to water. "Eric's in the hot seat right now. You want to meet him?"

Sally nodded. They ascended a short stairwell to the dais, where a few screens summarized all the data from various monitoring stations. Four people sat at their stations on the central platform. Jason introduced her to Forcestar, part of the Just Cause team. He was Asian-American, in his mid-twenties, and spoke in quiet, pleasant tones. "I'm Eric Lu. Pleased to meet you, Mustang Sally," he said.

"Please, just Sally's fine," she said.

He smiled. "Of course. Welcome to Just Cause."

"Thanks. You guys are all really nice."

"I'm guessing that you haven't met Doublecharge yet."

"No. Isn't she nice too?"

Eric glanced around to see if anyone else was listening in, then spoke in a hushed voice. "She's kind of a cast-iron bitch."

Sally's eyes widened in surprise. "Oh!"

Jason laughed. "Catch you later, dude. We've got a tour to finish."

"Is she really that bad?" Sally asked Eric.

He shifted his body and Sally realized that instead of

sitting in the chair, he was actually floating a few inches above it. "I'd say for you to keep off her bad side, except I'm not sure she's got a good one."

"Wow. So you're not one big happy family?"

"Sure we are. Only a bit dysfunctional at times." Eric looked past Sally's shoulder. "Whoops. Looks like I'm getting the stink-eye. Time to get back to work." He clicked on his mouse and Sally saw a game of solitaire displayed on his screen.

She glanced behind her to see a military officer regarding them from his own duty station with a disapproving glare. "Sorry to have interrupted your duty."

Eric waved them off. "It's fine. Nice to get a break in the nonstop action, you know? Nice to meet you, Sally."

"Nice to meet you too." Sally followed Jason toward the exit. "He's nice. And I don't care if Doublecharge isn't. I'm glad to be here."

"I'm glad you're here too. Everybody else here is all, you know, old and stuff."

"How often do you get monitor duty?" Sally asked Jason as they left the Command Center.

"Twice a week for twelve hours at a time," he said. "Same as everyone else on the team."

"How often does something happen?"

"Oh, things happen all the time, but mostly it's stuff that doesn't require Just Cause intervention. They don't call us out for normal street crimes or run-of-the-mill emergencies. It's got to be something major." He showed her the main conference room, which was all shiny black plastic and chrome. "You want to see the hangar and motor pool?"

Sally shrugged. "I guess."

"We could skip it. We've got a supersonic jet and a bunch of vans and that's Dully McDullsville." He grinned at her. "I'll bet you want to see the Bunker, though."

"The Bunker?"

"It's what we call the Combat Training Facility.

Nobody else has anything even remotely like it."

"I can't wait!" Sally clapped her hands together. She'd been excited to see it ever since she'd first heard about it. She'd hoped there might be a tour during her time in the Hero Academy, but the CTF was off-limits to everyone except Just Cause personnel because of the dangerous and experimental technology contained within its walls.

The CTF was the largest part of the Just Cause complex, but it didn't seem that way at first because it was mostly underground. The main level consisted of the locker rooms, gymnasium, sauna, and the pool. They rode the elevator down to the main training floor. Sally had seen the hour-long special on the Discovery Channel, but had never actually been on the training floor in spite of her mother's connections to the team.

Jason recounted the salient points of the Bunker's development. Fifteen years ago, a pair of techno-logically minded heroes had put their heads together and developed the basis for a fully flexible training facility for parahumans. The key points were that it had to be configurable into different settings, sturdy enough so heroes could use their powers at normal levels, and self-contained so harmful powers couldn't exit the facility. The Architect, a minor-league parahuman with the ability to reshape earth, stone, and metal, collaborated with Particle, an engineer who could shrink to molecular size. By studying the Architect's powers on a subatomic level, Particle developed a molecule-sized robot to duplicate them.

They built a machine to churn out billions of the nanobots. After fifteen years, there were enough nanobots to function effectively on a macroscopic scale. Construction began on the training chamber itself, using the nanobots as the primary workers.

The army of miniscule devices built a meter-thick

lattice of structurally-perfect walls from the surrounding bedrock. The finished material was hard as diamond with an energy-absorption index of close to one hundred percent. By loading a programmed scenario into the nanobot control computer, the nanobots could now transform a pool of raw materials in the training room into any configuration. Urban settings were common for training purposes, but Just Cause taught its members to work effectively in every imaginable setting from underwater caverns to rocky cliffs to open plains.

"What keeps them from flying out through the entrances or down the drains or anything?" Sally asked.

"I don't know for sure. Something technical."

"Probably a force field of some kind or a signal barrier. Something cool like that."

"You know about this stuff?" Jason goggled at her.

"No, but I'm kind of a sci-fi nerd. Books, movies, you name it."

"That's cool."

Sally wondered if Jason's comment was just his way of brushing off her admission of nerd-dom or if he actually thought it was cool. Being superheroes was like living inside of a great science fiction or fantasy story.

The elevator doors opened to the observation bay and Jason led Sally over to the large bank of windows. "They're actually diamond, not glass," he said with pride, "the most expensive windows in the world." The observation deck overlooked a space big as a domed football stadium. Bright arc lights illuminated a floor covered with the partially-finished renderings of buildings, cars, and pedestrians. It looked like a child's clay modeling project. Sally watched as one building's walls flattened and took on the aspect of brick. It was like watching an ice sculpture melt, but in reverse.

"Looks like we're having an urban session next," said Jason. "I like those the best."

"Why?" asked Sally.

He blushed. "I like having so many cars and stuff to throw around, even though we're not supposed to because of our insurance and all that."

"Insurance?"

"Sure. There's a lot of collateral damage in real parahuman combat. The government has to pay out damages. That's why we're supposed to try to limit combat to open areas away from structures and civilians. It just doesn't always work out that way."

Sally remembered all the damage from the fight between Destroyer and the Lucky Seven in the Convention Center in Chicago. She'd never given any thought about the aftermath until now. She wondered how many millions of dollars in damage their battle had cost. "What about private teams?"

"I don't know. They probably have to have some kind of liability insurance, but I'm no expert on it. You should ask Juice if you're really curious."

Sally shrugged. "I'm not, really. I was just wondering."

Jason introduced her to the technicians who monitored the training room's transformation and asked how long it would take to complete. They told him it should be ready to go within seventy-two hours.

"I like to try and find out," said Jason. "If Juice doesn't schedule a training session, it means we're going to have an emergency drill coming up and I don't want to go in completely blind."

"Doesn't that kind of defeat the purpose of the drill?"

He paused as he considered her statement. "Well, yeah, I guess so. But I promise you, we all do it. There's no such thing as too much information when you're going to have your butt on the line."

He showed her the other areas on the training floor: the emergency medical room, the weight room, which had machines for both normal and enhanced-strength team members. "How much can you lift?" Sally asked.

Jason shrugged. "About four tons on a good day."

They returned to the surface. The pale winter sun hung low over the mountains to the west. A cold wind blew across the quadrangle. Sally shivered and her teeth started to chatter when Jason opened the door.

"Yuck," he said. "We'll take the tunnel. I don't really feel it or anything, but I hate cold weather."

"Me too," said Sally. "I'm from Arizona. I'm at my best when it's really hot."

"I know what you mean," said Jason. "I'm a Georgia boy myself. Nice place if you don't mind a little humidity. Do you want to go get a hot chocolate or something from the cafeteria?"

Sally's heart fluttered. Now that the tour was over, he seemed much less confident and more human, more approachable. "That sounds great."

As they strolled down the underground tunnel toward the cafeteria, their phones beeped to announce incoming text messages. They each pulled them out to look.

Dinner tonight in Main Conference Room. Full Dress. 1900 hrs. Juice.

"What's that mean?" Sally asked as Jason held open the cafeteria door for her.

"He's probably going to introduce you to everyone. *Full Dress* means in costume. We don't normally dress out here in headquarters unless there's a tour coming through or something." Sally caught Jason's eyes wandering up and down her slight figure.

His attention made her feel odd, like she understood at last what people meant by *butterflies in one's stomach*. She wished he wouldn't stare, but she also wished she had more of a figure to show off to him. If anyone in the past had ever looked at her that way, she'd never noticed. She was too busy studying and training at the Academy to pay much attention to the socializing that went on between the students. She knew she wasn't any good at it, which felt every bit as humiliating in its own way as it had been to lose Destroyer. She felt her ears burn. "How about that hot chocolate?"

Chapter Five

"A costume is more than just eye candy. It's a statement, an image, a brand. A costume can inspire self-confidence or fear in an opponent. Why wear them at all when they make you into a target? You might as well ask a Hollywood starlet why she wears expensive fashions and designer jewelry. It's because parahumans crave the attention. It's because we are actors as much as anyone you see in a movie. The only difference is that our roles are in real life and we don't have stunt doubles."

-Gloria Echevarria aka Sundancer, *Playboy,* February, 1976

January, 2004
Denver, Colorado
Just Cause Headquarters

The conference room was a masterpiece of contemporary architecture and interior design. Expansive black reflective surfaces redirected the cool lighting. The table was rich polished hardwood with varnish so dark it nearly appeared black as well, but contained unimaginable depths. Recessed computer terminals sat before every overstuffed, leather--upholstered chair. Juice had kicked off the meal by formally introducing Sally to the rest of the team, speaking in his best courtroom voice while she stood beside him and tried hard not to blush or fidget or do anything that made her look amateurish. At last, relieved, she got to return to her seat to enjoy her dinner. They'd been offered choices that sounded like something from a fancy restaurant, and Sally had

43

picked pork loin stuffed with apricots, parsley potatoes, and cranberry-walnut salad. "God, this is amazing," she said between bites.

"Our house chef . . . Everyone says he's a low-grade precognitive," Jason said to Sally. He was in his brown and gray Mastiff outfit. It was skintight, and showed off every muscle contour, which Sally found distracting. He had his mask pulled down around his neck so as not to hinder his food intake and his gloves lay folded neatly next to his plate.

"What does that mean?"

"He knows exactly what you want to eat even before you do." Jason smiled. "All I know, though, is that I've never been disappointed."

Sally grinned. "I can't imagine you turning down food." During the meal, he'd put away enough food for three normal people, and ate with incredible enthusiasm and gusto.

"Yeah, watch out for Jason," said Jack Raymond from across the table. "Get too close and you're liable to lose an arm." Known as Crackerjack, he was the public face of Just Cause and acted as the team's press agent and publicist. Sally remembered his Saturday Night Live hosting gig back in 1999, and people still aped his tagline from the skit spoofing Just Cause—"*Whoa . . . I didn't expect* that *to happen!*" His unique power was total invulnerability. No known weapon or force could injure him. He specialized in espionage and dirty tricks. He eschewed a traditional superhero costume for a SWAT outfit instead. Jack was dangerously handsome, with his curly hair, just starting to go gray around the temples, and devilish good looks. A couple of days' stubble only added to his roguish appearance. His eyes sparkled with amusement.

"My mom can't cook to save her life," said Sally. "And before that was dorm food at the Academy. I'd be happy with anything edible."

"The food here is more than just edible," said Sondra—Desert Eagle. She sat near Jack but far enough apart from the others so as not to inconvenience anyone with her wings. Normally, she wore thigh holsters loaded with custom-manufactured large-caliber automatic pistols and bandoleers of clips, but she had come to dinner unarmed. "You'll have to step up your workout routine just to keep from filling out your costume in the wrong places."

"Yes, indeed," said Eric, resplendent in his bright blue Forcestar costume. He created and controlled force fields that were virtually unbreakable. He could wrap one around himself to fly, or he could use them as great clubs, wedges, and walls. "The trials and tribulations of the Spandex set."

"I'm glad I don't have to worry about that," said Jay Road, known as Glimmer, the psionicist. He had no set costume and generally wore jeans and a denim jacket in public. Authorities had found him wandering along a country road in Oklahoma after a series of tremendous thunderstorms and tornadoes several years ago. He couldn't remember anything about his past—not even his name—but had strong psionic abilities from telepathy to levitation to psionic healing. He could even see occasional glimpses of the future, although the power was uncontrolled and visions came to him without warning or planning. Doctors, psychologists, and other psis had examined him, but ultimately all they determined was a portion of his mind was simply *gone*. He had taken the name Jay Road, after the place he had been found.

Juice sat at the head of the table in his utilitarian gray costume with the triangular yellow high voltage warning graphic centered on his chest. He leaned back from the table and wiped his mouth with a napkin. "Well . . ." He cleared his throat. "Since we're all in the same place at the same time, I think we'll have a short staff meeting."

Muted groans sounded around the table, the loudest from Crackerjack.

"Hush, you," said Doublecharge, second-in--command of the team. Stacey Martin carried an aura of quiet competence. She remained content to let Juice lead conversation during the meal, except when she offered up a thoughtful and well-constructed opinion or comment. Her black and white costume was trimmed with stylized yellow lightning bolts, a graphical representation of her ability to project electricity.

Juice glared at them. "Listen, we've got a new intern and I'd like to show her how we ought to operate. I promise to keep things short. After this latest masterpiece from Juan, I'm sure we'd all like to take some time to sleep it off. We'll go around the table. When it gets back to me, we're done, unless something comes up."

"Nobody bring anything up," Crackerjack stage-whispered.

"As far as old business goes," said Juice, "a date has been set for Anchor's trial." Sally didn't recognize the name, but knew as an attorney specializing in parahuman case law, Juice was often involved in courtroom proceedings.

"How does it look for her?" Sondra asked.

"I'd be lying if I said I was sure she'd walk free on a self-defense plea. It's going to be a tough fight, given her background, which I'm sure the prosecution will make sure is brought forth in all its vivid glory." Juice took a sip of coffee. "For new business, I'm altering the duty schedules to include Sally. Expect the changes posted by the end of this week. We'll also have team training next Saturday from eight to five." Crackerjack raised his hand as if to ask a question. "No." Juice cut him off. "Everyone needs to be there, no exceptions. Whatever it is, you can reschedule it."

Jack sighed with exasperation, then grinned and winked at Sally.

"Stacey, anything to add?"

Doublecharge toyed with a fork and made sparks dance between the tines. "There was a confirmed sighting of Harlan Washington this morning in Guatemala."

Sally gasped. Harlan Washington was the man inside the Destroyer battlesuit.

"Guatemala?" Forcestar looked baffled. "Strange place for a high-tech guy like him. Especially since he was in Chicago just a month ago. We sure it was him?"

"The report came from the CIA, so it's probably credible. We're moving a recon satellite into position to try and learn more. I'm working to obtain permission from Homeland Security for us to go in if needed."

"Just Cause has a satellite?" Sally asked, but then wished she hadn't; she sounded like such a rube.

"Actually we have four, but it's not public knowledge," Doublecharge said. "I'll update you all as I get more information. I don't have any other business."

Juice nodded. "Jason?"

Jason shook his head. "Nothing." He smiled at Sally.

"Oh, uh, I don't have anything. Except I'd like to know what else you all know about Destroyer," said Sally.

"Destroyer's been a thorn in the side of Just Cause and other hero organizations for years. We've got an extensive file on him, in fact," said Stacey.

Sally nodded. She knew she had to get into that file to see what information Just Cause possessed about the man who had killed her father.

"Glimmer?" asked Juice.

"I'd actually like to know a little more about our newest member," said the psi with a nod toward her. "I don't know anything about you or your background except that you come here highly recommended by the Academy staff and the Lucky Seven."

Sally squirmed in her seat. "There's not much to tell. I'm a third-generation speedster. Actually, I'm the first known third-generation parahuman. Both my parents and at least my mother's parents were parahumans as well. My grandpa and grandma were Dr. Danger and Colt in American Justice back in the '40s and '50s, and then my grandfather helped found Just Cause after Congress blacklisted American Justice. My mom was in Just Cause from '70 to '85 as Pony Girl. My dad was too, although he wasn't a speedster. He had enhanced hearing abilities. He was the team administrator up until . . . until Destroyer killed him at Tornado's funeral."

Sally paused in her tale. She needed a moment to catch up with herself. Talking about her father was always difficult when she'd never had the chance to know the man. Sondra reached out and patted her hand, and it comforted her more than she would have expected. It gave her strength to continue. "Anyway, my mom raised me and trained me until I was old enough to go to the Academy. I graduated last June and then spent half a year training with the Lucky Seven and now I'm here."

"And you all faced Destroyer just last month?" asked Doublecharge, intense and focused.

"Yeah. He broke into a science convention and stole some kind of high-tech energy monitoring system thing," said Sally. "And then he disappeared. Until now, that is."

"Interesting." Doublecharge looked troubled.

"Sondra, what have you got?" Juice nodded toward the winged woman.

"There were three new applicants to the Hero Academy this week; a brick and two blasters. All are underage but were accepted provisionally when they hit sixteen. No surprises—we knew about all three already." Sondra ticked off each point on her long brown fingers. "Other than that it was the usual batch of cranks, including that one Exhibitionist guy for the, what, fifth time?"

Laughter blossomed around the table. "You mean the Visible Man?" Jack asked, his eyes sparkling.

"I thought he was calling himself The Streak." Forcestar snickered.

"Before that it was Naked Guy," said Doublecharge with a rare smile.

Glimmer turned to Sally. "This guy gets his jollies by applying for Just Cause membership, saying he's bulletproof, but only when he's naked."

"Is he?"

Fresh peals of laughter exploded. "No idea. Nobody's let him get any further than his skivvies. He shows up like clockwork every six months with a new nickname and—"

Glimmer's coffee cup slipped from his fingers to shatter against the edge of the table. He flung himself backward. Sally scooted around the table in a blur of motion before anyone else could react and caught him just before his head slammed into the floor.

"Holy shit!" Jack flung himself across the table as Glimmer convulsed. "Get him onto his side!"

Sally ducked Glimmer's thrashing arms and rolled him over. "Shouldn't I hold him or something?" She chewed on her lip in fear. Glimmer's eyes had rolled back into his head and foamy spittle leaked from his mouth as he quivered and shook.

"No, no. He's precogging. Never seen him this bad before," said Jack. "We have to let it run its course. He'll come out of it in a minute or two."

In a few hot and sweaty minutes, Glimmer's spasms subsided and his eyes cleared. He relaxed his tightly clenched muscles and started shaking, but from exhaustion instead of a seizure. Jack soaked a napkin with ice water and brushed it tenderly across the smaller man's face. The change in Jack's personality from sardonic and wry to solicitous and worried was amazing. Sally realized the gentle compassion was closer to his true personality than the sharp, witty attitude he affected most of the time.

Glimmer struggled to sit up. Jack and Sally helped to prop him up against the wall of the conference room. Forcestar pressed a cup of sweetened hot tea into Glimmer's hands. He took a grateful sip.

"That one looked really bad, Jay," said Juice. "Want to talk about it?"

Glimmer took a shaky breath. "Millions died . . . by fire. Never saw anything like it."

"You mean like a nuclear explosion? A terrorist device or an accident?" asked Doublecharge.

"Yes. No. I don't know. This was worse, somehow. Bigger. Like cracking a hole in the planet."

"Is he . . ." Sally felt her nerves sing like an over-tightened cable. "Is he accurate in his predictions?"

"Sometimes," said Juice. "He sees the most likely outcome of a future event, but the most likely is not always what occurs. Often the very knowledge of something allows us to circumvent or prevent it outright. Sondra?"

The others made room for the winged woman as she knelt down and checked Glimmer's vital signs with the practiced ease of a paramedic. She dug in a pouch strapped to one of her legs and withdrew an inhaler, which she metered and administered to him.

"Does he have asthma?" Sally asked.

"No," said Jack. "Most of our emergency medication is delivered orally or via inhaler. Some of us—like me, for example—can't be injected with anything. And in the field, it makes more sense to have a universal delivery system instead of one customized for each of us."

"Can you tell us when and where this event might happen, Jay?" Doublecharge knelt down next to him.

He nodded, his face white as a sheet of paper. "Here. Denver. Soon. Maybe by tomorrow." He swallowed the rest of his tea. His shakes started to subside as the drug from the inhaler worked into his bloodstream. "There's something else. Right before it hit me, I sensed a powerful psionic usage. Someone used a heavy-duty power. Like, with global reach."

"Can you tell what kind of power?"

"Not sure. It was targeted at a region instead of an individual. Maybe telekinesis or teleportation."

The lights in the conference room flickered. Several beeps emanated from the walls and a recorded voice announced emergency power had been activated.

Juice yanked his phone from his belt. "Command Center, Juice. What's going on?"

The reply came over the speaker, loud enough for everyone to overhear, drenched in static and distortion. "Just about to call you, sir. We have a catastrophic failure of the local power grid. It's dark from Idaho to New Mexico, west to Utah and east into Nebraska."

"Complete power failure?" Juice's face fell in dismay and amazement. "That should be impossible. The grids are all connected for redundancy."

"We're working on it now, sir. No answer yet. Only the fiber optics communications lines are working. Something's interfering with regional telephone and cellular networks, including our own."

"Get the *Bettie* on hot standby. We may need to move in a hurry."

"Right away, sir."

"There are going to be a lot of very cold, frightened people if we don't get the lights back on," said Sondra.

The Command Center beeped the team's phones. "New information coming in. Surrounding power grids report an abnormally-heavy draw from our region. It's not that the power's gone, sir, but something is siphoning it off. They've severed connections to us until we resolve the problem or else they might risk going down as well."

"Well, at least it isn't serious." Jack's joke fell flat.

"Is there any information about a possible cause?" asked Doublecharge.

"Not yet. Wait a moment . . . stand by . . ."

They waited, impatient. Sally's foot tapped like a drum roll.

"All right, people," said Juice at last. "Sondra, Jason, and Jay are on standby. The rest of you are with me. I want everyone geared up and at the hangar in five."

The hangar doors rolled back as the team assembled. A jet with the sleek angular lines of a stealth bomber sat under the lights. Its turbines spun with a whistling roar. A painting of a posed pinup girl gleamed beneath the canopy window. Sally shivered as a blast of icy wind and displaced snowflakes circled through the hangar. The storm had worsened, and Sally didn't relish the prospect of having to be a hero in the dismal weather.

"We have a report from a Wyoming State Trooper. He says there's some kind of bright, glowing figure in the vicinity of the Medicine Bow Power Plant."

"Relay that information to Ace," said Juice.

"Yes, sir."

"Well, Mustang Sally, it looks like you're going to get to see some action on your very first day." Juice smiled, his teeth as white as the falling snow outside. The bomb bay doors underneath the jet swung open and a heavy ladder lowered. "Everyone on board."

The heroes climbed the ladder. Sally found it led to a spacious, executive-style cabin with plush seats and plenty of legroom.

A diminutive pilot stepped through the door from the cockpit. She wore a fully insulated pilot suit. Her dark olive skin gave her an exotic look, offset somewhat by her boyish hairstyle. She stepped forward and extended her hand to Sally.

"Hello," she said in a rich, accented contralto voice. "I'm Fairuza, your pilot."

"Pleased to meet you, Fairuza," said Sally.

"Call me Ace. I just wanted to take a second to meet

you, since I'll most likely have to save your life someday." The woman spun around and hustled back into the cockpit.

Sally looked around at the others, who grinned back at her.

"Don't worry about Ace," said Forcestar. "She's always like that. There's nobody better behind the stick than her, though. She's a veteran from the Israeli Air Force."

The engine noise increased from a whine to a scream as the jet taxied out of the hangar. Sally expected the plane to turn and head for a runway, but instead the engines powered up even more and the jet lurched straight up into the air like a helicopter. Clunks sounded underneath the plane as the landing gear retracted. The plane continued to rise almost vertically and Sally could see only darkness and blowing snow out the window.

"Nice, huh?" Jack called to her.

"What?" she yelled back.

"The *Bettie*," he said. "Company in Vermont built her custom for Just Cause."

"Is it always this loud?"

"Only at take-off and landing."

The plane accelerated and replaced vertical thrust with horizontal. True to Jack's word, the engine noise diminished to a more tolerable howl. Ace swung the plane around onto a northern heading and poured on the power.

Chapter Six

"These men and women in their colorful costumes; they charge toward danger when a sane man would flee. They hold the line that cannot be held. Why else do we call them heroes?"

-Dr. Georges Devereaux, 1953

January, 2004
Medicine Bow, Wyoming

"Ace, what's our ETA to Medicine Bow?" asked Juice.

"That depends upon whether or not I have permission to exceed the sound barrier, sir," said the pilot over the cabin intercom.

"Permission granted."

The plane shuddered as it blew through the sound barrier. Noise levels in the cabin diminished as an electronic sound-dampening system came online. "Twelve minutes to point of last contact."

"Notify me when we're T minus two minutes."

"Roger."

Juice turned to face Sally and took on the tone of an instructor. "We don't have much information to go on, so our first priority is to gain intelligence. We'll do a flyby first to see if there's any sign of our mysterious glowing figure. The *Bettie* has some advanced sensing devices that will also help out beyond simple visual identification. If we find our target, we'll deploy after the initial flyby. Deployment is hot, so get out fast. I want you to stay by Jack at all times unless I give you other orders. Put these on." He handed her a featherweight earpiece and throat microphone with a small magnetic plate backing.

"Yes, sir." She fit the earpiece as comfortably as possible beneath her tight-fitting cowl. Doublecharge showed her how to slip the magnetic plate inside her costume so the throat mic would sit outside it.

"Once we get your costume up to Just Cause standards, the plate will be incorporated behind the fabric so you won't have to feel it," she said. "It'll probably seem a little strange at first. We're all tied into the same frequency so you can hear everyone and we can all hear you, including Ace."

"Assuming the network interference doesn't knock these out too," said Forcestar.

"I'm an optimist," said Doublecharge.

"In that case, we're all doomed," muttered Jack.

Juice continued, "Forcestar and Doublecharge, stay aerial and provide containment and ranged attacks if required. I will handle any brute physical needs. Jack and Sally, stay on the periphery and provide additional intelligence and support as needed."

Sally nodded as she tried to take it all in. She felt like her body was stuck in thick, hot glue while her mind raced in circles.

"First priority is to contain any damage and protect any civilians threatened. Second priority is to remove the individual to a safe and secure location by whatever means necessary and to determine if the individual is in fact responsible for the power failure. Third priority is to secure the area and to ensure no additional threats remain. Finally, we provide whatever assistance we can to bring power back online." Juice ticked off each point on his fingers.

"Two minutes to Medicine Bow," said Ace over the cabin speaker. "No sign of the contact yet."

"Stand by," said Juice. "Stacey, charge me up."

Doublecharge placed a hand crackling with

electricity on Juice's arm. He absorbed the power to fuel his strength and toughness. When he nodded at last, she stopped. The air inside the cabin smelled of ozone. Juice didn't seem any different except for frequent pops of static electricity as the charge he'd absorbed slowly bled off. He would be powered up for about fifteen minutes before he would need to be topped off once more.

"Stacey, Eric, get to the lock."

Doublecharge and Forcestar moved to the rear of the cabin and through a double-hinged door into a small chamber beyond.

Jack swung the door shut and dogged it tight. "It's an airlock," he said to Sally. "It lets the fliers deploy without landing the plane."

"One minute," said Ace. "I have visual confirmation of the target. Humanoid, estimated height ten meters, radiating energy of some sort."

"Bring us around to port. Give me one complete circle so I can see it. Stand by on the lock."

"Trust me, sir, you can't miss it." Ace banked the *Bettie* hard on her right wing. Juice, Jack and Sally all pressed their faces against the windows to see. The figure was pudgy and devoid of details, like an unfinished clay model of a person. It glowed a bright yellow-green. Purple-white energy bands arced across its surface. A shapeless dark mass lurked at the center of the torso. The figure lurched through a stand of snow-covered trees, which exploded in clouds of steam from vaporized snow.

"What is it?" Sally asked. "Is it a person?"

Juice said, "It's humanoid, at least. We'll figure out details as we go. Right now it's a threat and we have to treat it as such. Ace, open the lock, then bring us down."

Sally heard a thump from the rear of the plane. A moment later, Doublecharge and Forcestar cruised past the windows, she with electricity crackling around her and he surrounded by a blue energy nimbus.

The *Bettie*'s engines howled as Ace brought her down to hover at zero altitude. The bomb bay doors folded open, aligned to protect the heroes from the blast of the angled jet nozzles. "Go," said Juice, and the heroes jumped to the steaming ground. Juice led Jack and Sally past the front of the plane. "Ace, get clear." The pilot powered up the engines and lifted the *Bettie* back into the air once more.

They had landed in free-range territory, with no dwellings or roads nearby. Six inches of snow covered the fields, and it fell steadily from the thick clouds. The glowing figure trudged slowly about fifty meters away and did not seem to take any notice of Doublecharge and Forcestar overhead.

"Sally, give me a sweep in a quarter mile radius around the thing. I want to be sure we are in open country and there isn't a town or anything just over the next rise. Also, report on its trail and heading. And be careful. We don't know what we're dealing with yet."

Sally peeled out across the snow, leaving a pair of frosty rooster tails in her wake. Everything was happening very fast, even for a speedster like her. She told herself to stick to what she knew—*running*. Sprinting through the snow with no path or road was hard work when she was used to pavement. She stepped lightly to keep her feet off the ground as much as possible. If she turned an ankle on something hidden beneath the snow, she would be useless.

She made her circuit around the thing in less than a minute. Its trail led in a straight line to the north, and it continued to plod in the opposite direction. The surrounding area was just open range with a few scattered stands of evergreens and rocky ridges. She skidded to a stop by Juice and Jack, who had taken cover behind a large rock to formulate a plan.

"Nothing around for miles," Sally said. "It looks like

the creature is heading straight south from Medicine Bow. On foot. No vehicle tracks of any kind. The footprints just start in the middle of nowhere."

"Teleportation," said Doublecharge over the radio. "Glimmer was right."

Juice frowned. "Jack, where does that take it if it stays on course?"

Crackerjack consulted the GPS strapped to the back of his left arm. "Cheyenne, then towards Denver."

"Stacey, any change in the creature's behavior?"

"Negative." Doublecharge's voice on the radio was overlaid with static, which Sally figured was caused by the creature. "It's moving slowly but steadily."

"Give it a warning shot. Get its attention."

Juice, Jack, and Sally moved around the rock to get a better view. Doublecharge hummed with electricity, and lightning arced from her to strike directly upon the creature.

"I said a warning shot!" Juice shouted.

"I did," Doublecharge said. "The thing drew in my shot like a magnet."

"Eric, try to confine it."

Forcestar created a glowing blue dome of energy around the creature. The being ignored his barrier and stepped through it as if it didn't exist. He tried again, but his field seemed to have no effect whatsoever.

"Regroup," said Juice. "All right," he said when Doublecharge and Forcestar dropped to the ground by the others. "Analysis. Stacey?"

"It absorbs electricity, like you do," she said. "And it's destroying things it encounters explosively, although not the ground beneath its feet for some reason."

"Eric."

"I can't contain it. It's the first thing I've ever encountered that I can't hold inside a field."

"Jack, your thoughts?"

"Putting some wildly disconnected ideas together, I'd

say that it teleported or was teleported by an external agency to the vicinity of Medicine Bow. It must require electricity because it drained the power plant and absorbed Doublecharge's blast. The military base in Cheyenne has its own power plant that is not connected to the local grid. If the creature needs electricity, that's the next closest major source. Given its course, it either can sense the source or has been programmed. I'm not yet convinced it's alive and not some kind of machine."

"Hmm. And we'll need to stop it before it gets there. After that, it's the generators at Just Cause HQ. Sally?"

Sally watched the creature with curiosity. An idea had formed in her mind, borne from her love of science fiction. She hesitated for almost a second, an eternity for her. "What if . . . it's made of antimatter? Maybe the glowing part is just a containment field."

"That would explain why it's not reacting to my own force fields," said Forcestar. "Polarity's all wrong."

"Which is why it attracts my lightning. A containment field would need a tremendous amount of energy, and electricity is easy to come by. The thing could require electricity to maintain its field." Doublecharge circled around them and kept an eye on the creature as it continued its slow trek southward.

"What happens if the containment field fails?" Juice asked, staring at the creature like he was sizing it up.

"There could be a couple hundred pounds inside the field, if that's what that dark mass is at the center," said Jack. "That kind of potential explosive power could blow a crater the size of Wyoming in North America. It matches Glimmer's hole-in-the-planet vision."

"All right," said Juice. "Let's presume for the moment Sally's theory is correct. We can't let it take any more power, obviously, but we have to stop it in such a way that it doesn't lose its field integrity. Eric, you said something about polarity being wrong?"

"Yeah," said Forcestar. "My fields are energy, of

course, but they are charged to affect positive matter. If I could reverse the polarity, I should be able to hold the thing."

"What would that take?"

"A big jolt from a capacitor might do it, but I don't exactly have a power station handy. Oh, wait . . ." Forcestar grinned as Doublecharge made electricity crackle between her fingertips.

"All right, that's a plan. Let's try to resolve this peacefully first. Forcestar, you and Doublecharge take high point. Jack, Sally, with me. We'll get in front of the thing and try to communicate. Ace?"

"Yes sir," said the pilot.

"Contact Deep Six and see if they can rig up something to contain antimatter."

"Roger that."

"Move out," Juice said. He and Jack jogged after the creature while Sally flanked them.

In a few minutes, they had caught up to and then passed the creature and took up positions in front of it. It seemed to take no notice of them. Juice stepped up and held up his hands.

"That's far enough," he called. "We can't permit you to continue. Come quietly and we'll try to help you with whatever you require."

The creature lowered its featureless head and halted in its stride. A sound emerged from it, a low thrum of a growl that seemed subsonic rather than audible.

"I've got a bad feeling about this, Boss," said Jack as he raised his submachine gun.

Juice took a step closer toward the being. "We don't want to fight you, and we don't want to hurt you, but we can't allow you to continue harming others through your actions."

"*You are hereby ordered to return to your place of origin or the nearest convenient parallel dimension,*" murmured Jack. Sally looked at him. "*Ghostbusters.* I quote movie lines when I get nervous."

The creature's ominous growl rose in volume. It lifted an arm to point down toward Juice; it didn't have a hand, just a thickening at the end of a wrist. Time shifted into slow motion as Sally's perceptions accelerated to their maximum.

A glowing particle emerged from the end of the creature's arm, like a bubble in molasses. The instant the particle broke contact with the creature's arm, the field around it contracted. Sally knew she only had a moment to react. She couldn't pick up Juice and move him out of harm's way; he must have weighed more than three times what she did. Instead she accelerated and body-slammed him at three hundred miles-per--hour. She had absolute control over her speed and the ability to stop and start instantaneously, but she still gave herself a terrific wallop and knew she would be hurting for weeks. Her check knocked Juice backward with the slow grace of an astronaut but quickly enough to avoid the onrushing particle. Once he came off the ground, Sally shoved him a second time, this time with enough force to push him several yards. She hoped it was enough.

A quick glance at the particle showed the glow around it was almost gone and its trajectory headed toward where Juice had stood a second ago. Sally turned and covered several hundred feet in an instant as the containment field collapsed. A powerful explosion tore through the air. Juice tumbled to the ground clear of the blast radius.

Sally dashed up to him, and made herself slow down enough that she could speak to him. "Are you all right, sir?"

"Yes. Ow." He shook his head to clear it. "Do you think that was antimatter?"

"Maybe. We shouldn't break the containment field."

"Jack, no shooting at it," Juice called.

"Don't worry." Jack sounded disgusted. He tossed away his rifle, the barrel twisted and smoldering. His clothing was singed but he seemed otherwise unharmed.

"Juice?" Doublecharge's voice came from overhead.

"I'm all right," he said. "Thanks to Sally. Negotiations are over. Wrap it up, Eric."

Forcestar gathered his reserves of power and Doublecharge did the same. He cast another cylindrical field around the creature. Doublecharge sent crackling bolt after bolt of lightning into the cylinder. "More power," said Forcestar.

"How will you know when it's enough?" Doublecharge called as more and more electricity coursed from her.

"It won't be able to get out," said Forcestar. The creature raised its arms to the field. "It's working," he said. "Pour it on, Stacey. I can feel it changing."

The creature swung an arm at the field, which crackled, sparked, and rebounded like gelatin. Another subsonic roar emerged from the creature. It released another particle, which bounced off the inside of the field wall and detonated within the enclosed space of Forcestar's field.

"I got it!" Forcestar lifted the creature off the ground. It struggled within the blue field, but couldn't push its way out.

"How long can you hold it like that?" Juice signaled Ace to bring the *Bettie* back around.

"I have no idea. It's not very heavy, but the energy is making it tricky."

Doublecharge slumped to the ground and yanked off her mask. Blood ran from her nose and she looked pale against the snow. Sally rushed over to help support her. A sharp smell of ozone permeated her skin and costume. She had released a tremendous amount of electrical energy, like hundreds of lightning bolts all going off at once, and Doublecharge seemed to have come close to overloading herself.

The *Bettie* roared in to stand on her jets. Sally and Jack helped get Doublecharge on board. Juice secured Forcestar in the airlock, since his powers wouldn't function through the walls or windows of the aircraft; he would have to ride exposed to the cold and altitude. He strapped an oxygen mask over Forcestar's face and wrapped him up in a thermal blanket, plugged into the side of the airlock.

"You need anything? Ace says it's about thirty minutes to Deep Six."

"How about a half dozen chicken tacos and a mocha espresso with extra whip?"

"Oh, sure, I'll have Ace hit a couple drive-throughs in Butte," said Juice as he closed the airlock door behind him. "Ace, we're clear."

The Bettie's engines responded with a new whine as Ace tapped emergency reserves of power to coax just a little more speed from the craft. Sally wrapped a blanket around Doublecharge while Jack administered a sedative through an inhaler.

Juice came up from the airlock and knelt down in front of his second-in-command. "You did good, partner."

In spite of her exhaustion, shock, and the onrushing effects of the drugs Jack had administered, Doublecharge managed a slight smile before her head lolled back.

The Bettie left sound behind her as she tore up the miles on course for Deep Six. Sally knew the parahuman prison facility in Montana would have the best chance of holding a creature made of antimatter until they could figure out what to do with it. She was disappointed that there wouldn't be time for a tour, but there was going to be a lot of work to do even after they relinquished their captive. She yawned.

A hero's work was never done.

Chapter Seven

The "activation" of parahuman abilities is a myth perpetuated by the media. There is no way to tell whether someone who has the so-called "power gene" will develop abilities, and if so, what those abilities might entail.

I've been asked if it is possible to create parahuman abilities in someone who has the power gene. I do not know, but I believe they may be triggered through evolutionary pressures. I've also been asked if parahuman abilities can be bestowed upon someone without the power gene.

I do not believe that is possible.

-From "The Origin of Parapowers", Dr. Matasuko Musashi, 1995

January, 2004
Denver, Colorado
Just Cause Headquarters

Sally flopped onto her bed, too tired to do more than kick off her cracked and friction-burned boots. Her last coherent thought was that she really ought at least to pull off her bodysuit before she passed out for good. Blissful sleep overtook her as she fumbled for her uniform zipper.

It seemed like she had slept for only minutes when somebody knocked at her door and jolted her awake.

She grimaced as she staggered over to the door on tender bare feet. "Yeah?" Her voice croaked like a frog's.

"It's Jason," said a voice behind the door. "I came by to see how you were feeling today. Juice said you had a rough time of it last night."

Sally rubbed her eyes, still feeling like her head was full of cotton. "Give me a minute, Jason . . . I just woke up." She squinted at her bedside clock. *3:06.* For a crazy moment she thought Jason had come to talk to her at three in the morning, but then she realized it was the middle of the afternoon and she'd slept all day.

"Oh, sure. I can come back later if you want."

She almost said, yes, please do, but her heart was already racing and if he left she would only lie awake on the bed and wonder if it had been the right thing to say. "No, it's okay. Can I meet you in the rec room in a few minutes?"

"Sure. See you." She heard his footsteps recede as he tromped down the hall.

The bed called to her with a mighty voice, but she gave it a wide berth, lest it reach out and snag her. She grimaced because she still stank of copper cable. After they had delivered the antimatter creature to Deep Six, Juice had Sally running all over the area, helping to get the power grid back online so the citizens of the Mountain West wouldn't freeze overnight. She'd run cable and installed fuses; she might have qualified as an apprentice electrician after all the work she did the night before. It had been sometime past way too late and before way too early when they'd gotten the grid back up. Forcestar had stayed behind at the prison facility, Deep Six, to help contain the creature until the staff had a chance to devise a suitable containment system. Doublecharge had been treated by the Deep Six medical techs and was recuperating in Just Cause's medical wing. The rest of the team had worked like over-caffeinated speed freaks to get the power back on, and Sally ached all the way down to the marrow in her bones.

A hot shower helped to improve her disposition. She luxuriated in the steamy spray for a quarter of an hour, much longer than her normal three-minute shower. She spent the next few minutes fighting with her hair under the comfort of the heat lamp. "Honey, there's a reason speedsters have short hair," she said to herself in the mirror as she worked out a tangle.

After a couple more minutes that felt like an eternity, she dressed in a pair of jeans and an oversize flannel shirt, because she still felt the chill of the previous night in her bones. When she finally checked the clock, she saw that almost half an hour had passed, and she hoped Jason had waited for her.

Her worries turned out to be unfounded. Jason was lounging in one of the overstuffed chairs, his feet up on a coffee table, and watching classic rock videos on one of the big screen TVs. "Hey." She sat in the chair next to his.

"Hey," he said. "I brought you coffee."

"Oh, uh, thanks," Sally said. "I don't really drink coffee, though."

Jason looked surprised. "You don't? Why not?"

"I don't know. I just never started." She picked up the cup and sniffed it, wrinkling her nose.

Jason shrugged and took a deep sip from his own cup. "You will," he said, sounding confident. "I didn't used to drink it, but a month on night shift monitor duty cured me of it."

"I actually stay away from caffeine as much as I can," said Sally. "Imagine having jitters at super-speed."

"I never thought of that. Must be uncomfortable."

"Yeah." Sally smiled. "It was a nice thought, though. Thanks anyway."

"No problem. So, how was it last night?"

"Scary. We could have all died if Stacey and Eric hadn't been able to contain the thing."

"Juice said it was you who identified it as antimatter. How'd you know?"

"Just lucky, I guess."

"Don't worry about being scared. I was terrified the first time I got deployed. At least you guys got the power back on."

Sally laughed. "Yeah. You want to know anything about power lines, transformers, or fuses, just ask me. I'm like an expert or something now."

Jason smiled and brushed his hair out of his eyes. "Listen, I did want to ask you something. Do you like rock music?"

"Sure, I guess so. Why?"

"Well, my band is playing Friday at a club downtown and I was wondering if you'd like to come hear us?" Jason blushed.

"You're in a band? What do you play?"

"Guitar."

"What's it called?"

"Velma's Glasses." He blushed even more. Sally thought it very, very cute.

"Like in *Scooby Doo*. That's cool. How do you find time to be in a band?"

"Well, we're not on duty all the time. I try to have a life outside of being a superhero."

It was Sally's turn to blush. Very little went on in her life not somehow tied to her powers. Having been raised by a mother and grandmother who both had the same powers had meant much of her life had already been planned for her. She'd trained to be a superhero from early childhood and had gone from home--schooling straight to the Hero Academy. Summer "vacations" had consisted of visits to different heroes or coaches around the country with her mother. She didn't even have a drivers' license, never having needed a car to get from point A to point B.

"I'd love to come hear you play," she said.

Their radios beeped. "Anyone who's not busy, come to the conference room or log into the primary feed," said Juice.

Jason and Sally looked at each other and shrugged. He clicked off the TV and picked up his coffee. "We're playing at eight o'clock. Do you want to ride over with me? Then you could meet the other guys before we do our sound checks."

"Sounds fun." She wondered if that counted as a date. She'd never dated during her time at the Academy. When she wasn't in class, she studied or trained. It occurred to her that she didn't even know how to date.

Jason led her to the workstation in the corner. She sat in front of the keyboard. He spun his chair around behind her to look over her shoulder. It felt almost intimate to Sally the way she could sense his presence behind her. He showed her which icon enabled the feed. The light on the workstation's webcam brightened. Multiple camera images on the flatscreen showed Juice, Forcestar, and Sondra in the conference room, while Jack was logged in remotely from the firing range. Neither Glimmer nor Doublecharge had signed in. "We're here, Boss, me and Sally."

"Good," said Juice. "We've got a call from Deep Six and I wanted anyone available to listen in." The word *CONNECTED* flashed on an otherwise blank window. Juice tapped a control to reveal the warden of Deep Six.

William Silbersack had once been a hero known as The Neutralizer, for his ability to prevent other parahumans from using their powers. Upon his retirement, he'd gone into corrections and had been instrumental in the development of the ultra-secure underground prison for parapowered felons. He had long since foregone the trappings of costumes and now wore a dark blue jumpsuit with the Deep Six insignia over the breast pocket. He had gray-streaked black hair and sharp blue eyes. "Hello, James and company."

"Bill," said Juice. "How's your newest inmate?"

"Well, that's why I'm calling. Your creature is not a creature, she's a human, and I think she's a victim of some sort of cruel experiment." All traces of humor left the Warden's demeanor. "We've got her de-magnetizing slowly in a containment sphere that we rigged up.

We've worked out a method to keep her body sufficiently charged without her innate fields degrading and allowing her antimatter particles to come into contact with any matter. It's not been easy." He ran a hand through his thinning hair. "Frankly, I'm surprised we didn't blow ourselves right out of the ground."

"What makes you think she's a victim of an experiment?" Sondra asked.

"She doesn't have any memory of the events of last night. The last thing she said she remembered was walking home from her job. As near as we can tell, that was something like a month ago. She doesn't understand what's happened to her."

"Does she remember her name? We should at least notify her family what's happened to her and that she's going to be okay," Juice said.

"Well, that's another problem altogether. She's from San José, Guatemala. It's a coastal town. She doesn't speak any English and her Spanish is pretty bad. She's mostly using some kind of local ladino tongue that nobody here can understand."

"Guatemala," said Sondra. "That's where Destroyer is."

"Could be a coincidence," said Forcestar.

"Yeah, right." Jason snorted in derision.

"Agreed," said Juice. "Bill, keep talking to the woman. Get whatever you can from her. In your opinion, is she no longer a threat?"

"That's my assessment."

"I'll make a call to Dr. Devereaux in Paris. She'll make sure that your captive gets proper care and treatment," Juice said.

"Fair enough. I'll notify you if there's any change in her condition. Deep Six out," said the Warden, and broke the connection.

Juice leaned back and pinched the bridge of his nose. Sally squinted into the screen. The bags under his eyes had bags of their own. She suspected he hadn't slept since they'd deployed the night before. "What time is it in Paris? Anyone know?"

"Quarter to midnight," Sondra answered.

"Grace is probably gone for the day. Everyone's got to sleep sometime." Juice yawned. "I'll shoot off a quick email."

"Then you'd better hit the sack yourself, boss," Jason said. "You look like shit."

Juice gave him a weary smile. "Thanks, Jason. I wasn't sure until you mentioned it. Sondra, since Stacey's still out of commission, request permission from Homeland Security for us to leave the country on an investigation. We should follow up on this sighting of Destroyer. I don't believe this is a coincidence for a second."

"I'm on it."

Juice yawned again. "Okay. For the next six hours I don't want to be disturbed for anything less than imminent global destruction. Meeting adjourned."

Jason reached past Sally and closed the feed program. She caught the scent of his skin as he did so—clean, with a hint of some kind of sweet soap and under that the tang of sweat. It made her shiver in a delicious way. The response of her body to his nearness frightened her a little, and she almost leaped out of the chair.

"You okay?" he asked her.

"Yeah," she said. "I just remembered something I was going to do. I'll . . . I'll talk to you later, Jason."

He smiled at her. "Count on it."

She forced herself not to run at super-speed down the hall as she retreated into her quarters. She closed the door behind her and put her back against it, as if to make sure it would stay shut. Her heart threatened to hammer its way out through her ribs. Her cheeks burned and she felt dizzy. "Stop it," she whispered. "You're being silly." However, when she closed her eyes, she saw the blue of Jason's sparkling eyes and the curve of his chin dotted with blonde stubble.

Sally stalked into the bathroom to splash some water on her face. She glared at her reflection with a droplet of water perched precariously on the end of her nose. "Get a hold of yourself, you." She pointed at herself. "You're here to become a superhero, not to get a . . . a *boyfriend.*" She spat the last word with as much venom as she could muster.

Nevertheless, Jason had asked her out, and she'd accepted the invitation without so much as a moment's hesitation. Backing out would be awkward. Very well, she'd go to hear his band play. It wouldn't be a date, it would be two friends going out together. That was an idea she could accept without wincing at the thought of dating a coworker.

Pleased with herself, Sally turned her attention to other matters. The recent mentions of Destroyer had her desperate to learn more about what Just Cause knew about him. She knew the team kept terabytes of information in the supercomputers beneath the complex, but there was also a sizable repository of non-electronic media. It was a trophy room of sorts, filled with sixty years' worth of items and objects that had helped to shape the team's history.

She'd begin her research there. She examined the map of the compound until she felt sure she could find her way down to the Archives, and then left her room.

"Oh, hi Sally," said Sondra as she passed down the hall, her wings held back out of the way. "What are you up to?"

"Hey Sondra, I was just going down to the Archives."

Sondra smiled. "I love the Archives . . . so much history. I majored in History. In fact, I'm still working toward a Ph.D in it."

"Cool. What's your specialty?"

"Indigenous tribes of the American Southwest. Doesn't that sound impressive?"

Sally nodded.

"People always expect me to say *parahuman history*, but that's already been done to death by so many others. Besides, a girl likes to know a bit about her ancestry." Sondra flipped her wings for emphasis.

Sally started to reach out to touch one, but stopped for fear she might offend the winged woman.

"It's all right. I don't mind. Just don't yank on a feather that's still attached. It hurts like tweezing out nose hairs. If you want a souvenir, just stop by my room." Her voice dropped to a conspiratorial whisper. "I'm always molting."

Sondra folded one wing around to where Sally could stroke the long brown and black feathers. Soft and smooth, they exuded a comforting, familiar scent. "Is that . . . baby powder?"

"Yes," replied Sondra. "My natural oils have kind of a funky odor, so I powder the feathers. It keeps the smell from getting overpowering, since bathing with them is a major operation."

"I never thought about that. It must be pretty difficult. Same as for dressing, I bet."

"Oh, it's not so bad." Sondra chuckled. "Especially if I have help. I can't shower unless I'm not going to fly for a full day, but I love to take baths. All my clothes are specially tailored. It's not really any tougher to put them on than to put on a bra. I hate wearing them, though. I can't fly with one on." She sighed. "If only I were smaller."

Sally laughed. "I've wished I was bigger for years. Maybe we should switch."

Both women giggled at the thought.

"You know," said Sondra. "I'm not doing anything at the moment. Want company in the Archives? I know my way around down there pretty well. When we moved everything out here, I oversaw the setup."

When the terrorists destroyed the Twin Towers in 2001, Just Cause lost several members and its New York headquarters. Some items in the Archives were destroyed as well, although the majority of them had been stored off-site in the Second Team's facility in Virginia. Some remained there, while others had been brought to the new Denver headquarters.

"Sure, I'd love the help," admitted Sally. "I don't really know my way around here yet . . . or around Just Cause systems, for that matter."

Sondra led her down the hall to the elevators. "What are you looking for?"

"I want to know more about Destroyer."

"Well, we've got a lot about him. He's been a thorn in our side for a quarter century." They boarded an elevator and headed down.

The Archives were stored in a long, wide room. File cabinets lined one wall, which contained documents dating back to Georges Devereaux's original pre-World War II research into parahumans. Adjacent to the paper files were microfiche copies of the same things, all of which had since been converted into electronic files. Nothing had ever been intentionally discarded, in case a crucial piece of information didn't get transferred between formats. The wall opposite the files was lined with racks, shelves, display cases and free-standing objects which were somehow relevant to Just Cause history. Each object was tagged with a bar code linked to the total of all related information about it in the computer system. The labels had fantastic-sounding names for often-mundane objects. A twisted steel shaft caught Sally's eye. *Arrow belonging to Dr. Danger, Irradiated by Unknown Parahuman, 1949.* She reached out to touch it.

"What is it?" asked Sondra.

"This was my grandfather's," Sally caressed the arrow as if she could feel the history in the blackened metal.

They moved on, past *Tyrant I's Mind Control Device (deactivated), 1957* and *Voltage's Mask, 1972.* Sally stopped in front of a large display case, which contained an unrecognizable piece of burned machinery and read the placard. *Remains of Destroyer's Left Medial Arm, v. 1.0, 1977.*

"That's it," she whispered.

Sondra moved next to her, her wings rustling. "1977," she read. "That would have been his first appearance. New York Blackout. He was thirteen years old."

"How does someone so young have so much hate?" asked Sally. "I read about this. He killed like fourteen or fifteen people in his neighborhood."

"And his mother too. They should have executed the little shit," said Sondra, "but he was a juvenile. They wouldn't try him as an adult, even when the Feds tried to intervene."

"Let's go look at his file."

"You get started," said Sondra. "I'm going to go get some coffee. From the look on your face, we might be down here awhile. You want some?"

"Coffee? No thank you, but I'd take some hot chocolate if there's any."

"You got it." Sondra paused by the elevator. "Sally?"

"What?"

"We'll catch him. He'll be brought to justice."

Sally smiled. "I know we will. Someday." She opened his file, and her mother's name jumped out at her. It was the original report on Destroyer's first appearance in 1977, written by her mother. Sally calculated the dates and figured her mother would have been twenty-three years old at the time. She read the page-long report, then set it down, taken aback by her mother's careless typing and lack of detailed information.

"Come on, Mom," she grumbled. "This is the best you could do?" She turned the page in the hope there would be more, but the next sheet was blank except for a stamp: *MULTIPLE PAGES MISSING 10/28/2001.* Sally shuddered at the innocuous words. This file had survived the destruction of Just Cause headquarters in the World Trade Center. She wondered how much of the original file on Destroyer was simply gone. She went to the computer records and discovered the same missing information. Obviously, the file hadn't been scanned before its recovery.

"Well, crap." She pulled up a list of Just Cause members from '77. Her mother was still alive, but Sally hadn't ever been able to extract much information from her. The woman didn't want to talk about the events that had taken away her husband. What Sally knew, she'd had to glean from other sources. Most of the other heroes from what people referred to as the Second Generation era were deceased. Tornado had succumbed to AIDS in '85. Six more of them were killed when Destroyer hit Tornado's funeral in a devastating sneak attack. The rest had died in the World Trade Center, except for one. The last name on the list jumped out at her: John Stone.

John Stone was not only still alive; he was the vice principal for the Hero Academy. He'd been part of Just Cause when they first encountered Destroyer, and he had survived the attack at Tornado's funeral. If anyone could shed some light about Destroyer's past, he could. And with his open, cheerful demeanor, he might answer the questions that Sally's mother wouldn't.

Sally pulled up the number for his office and dialed.

Chapter Eight

"With the growing numbers of parahumans and the increasing diversity of powers, it was only a matter of time before someone successfully duplicated some of the abilities technologically. We just didn't expect it would be a thirteen-year-old boy."

-Rick Lyons aka Lionheart, Press conference, 1977

January, 2004
Denver, Colorado
Hero Academy

The Hero Academy campus was less than a mile from Just Cause headquarters. Sally had lived and studied there for three years. She and her classmates would often sit up on the dorm roof, stare across the distance toward Just Cause headquarters, and discuss which of them might have the chance to join the big team. Most of them had agreed Sally was the candidate Most Likely to Join Just Cause, given her lineage and her exceptional parapower. Sally's class was the largest ever for the Academy at the time, graduating a total of seven. The current crop of seniors counted eight, and the two younger grades both stretched into double digits.

True to her classmates' predictions, only Sally had made it to the Big Time—the main Just Cause team. Just Cause's Second Team in Virginia had picked one of the boys, a technical genius who called himself Orb. Sally's roommate, Vapor, had chosen not to join any team, instead opting to head straight off to college. She would just be starting her second semester of her Political Science major by now, thought Sally. The other four graduates had banded together to form their own team, and were doing their best to police New York as the Young Guns.

Sally felt pangs of guilt as she thought of them; she had promised to stay in touch with all her classmates after graduation, but she'd failed in that regard. She told herself as soon as she got her feet underneath her with Just Cause, she'd organize a reunion or something. They'd watch movies, eat popcorn, and share tales about what they'd done since graduation.

First, she had a reunion of a different sort to arrange.

She had taken special care to check her costume for stains and dirt, so she'd make the best impression possible on John Stone, the Academy's Vice Principal. She slipped into her overcoat and walked briskly through the cold wintry air down the path to the Academy.

She'd never been much of a troublemaker during her time at the Academy, so she didn't have the same awkward feeling of waiting outside the office that someone like, say, Surfboy or Johnny Go might have. Instead, she felt a profound sense of nostalgia in the familiar halls, even though it had only been half a year since she'd last been in them as a student.

"Goodness, is that Salena Thompson?" asked the elderly receptionist as Sally stepped into the administrative offices.

"Hi, Mrs. Adams," said Sally. "Yes, it's me."

"Congratulations on your internship with Just Cause. I understand you've made quite a stir over there so far."

Sally shrugged. "I guess so. I'm still finding my way at this point."

"You must be Mr. Stone's two o'clock. He's waiting for you. Please, go on in."

Sally thanked her and knocked on Stone's door.

A gravelly voice bade her to come in. She turned the knob and stepped into the office, a cheerful place painted in a pastel yellow with heavy hardwood furnishings. John Stone sat behind his desk like a granite statue. He smiled at her. His face didn't look like it was capable of movement at all. Despite the appearance of rock, Stone's body was actually flesh, but compressed to a molecular density approaching that of his namesake. He'd joined Just Cause back in the Sixties and spent nearly twenty years fighting the good fight on their behalf. After retiring, he'd devoted his life to teaching what he'd learned to the next generation of heroes, and eventually became instrumental in the creation of the Hero Academy.

"Welcome back, Sally," he said, "or do you prefer Mustang Sally now?"

"Just Sally's fine, Mr. Stone."

"Then by all means, please call me John. Can I get you a soda or water or anything?"

"No thank you." Sally sat down and clasped her hands over one knee.

"Well don't keep an old man in suspense. Why are you here?" He clasped his fingers on top of the marble surface of his desk.

"Mr. Stone—John—I was wondering if you could tell me about Destroyer."

Stone stiffened in his reinforced chair, which still made dangerous creaking sounds under his seven hundred pound body. "Perhaps this might be a better discussion for you to have with your mother." His voice was a soft rumble.

Sally shook her head. "Mom can't talk about Destroyer objectively. She won't even talk about the day my father was . . . about Tornado's funeral." She shifted positions in the chair. "But Destroyer's actions shaped my entire life, made me who I am. I think I deserve to know as much as I can about him."

"Is this some sort of revenge trip?" asked Stone. "I'd hope we taught you better than that in your time here."

"No, of course not." Sally felt a desperate need to do something with her hands, and settled for toying with the end of one of her braids. "But I had to face him in Chicago last month with the Lucky Seven, and now we've got information that he might be working out of the country, and nobody alive knows more about him than you do."

Stone laughed. "Flattery will get you everywhere, Sally. Certainly there are detailed reports in the Just Cause archives you could look at."

She shook her head. "The file is incomplete. It didn't all survive 9/11."

"I see." Stone scraped his hand across his chin; it sounded like cinderblocks rubbing together. "I suppose I should tell you what I know. Especially in light of this being an official Just Cause investigation." He fixed a firm gaze upon her. "This is an official Just Cause investigation, is it not?"

"It is." Sally berated herself for not thinking of that phrase sooner. She promised herself to remember it; a phrase like that could open doors in the parahuman world.

"Where would you like me to begin?"

"At the beginning, I guess. His first appearance back in '77." Sally pulled a small notebook from the pocket of her coat.

"So . . . 1977," began Stone as Sally wrote the date on the top of her page. "It was July. New York City. We'd been in the World Trade Center for three years then. It was a crazy, decadent time for superheroes. The parahuman villain community was laying very low back then, so we didn't have much to do except throw parties, go out on the town, and Wednesday Night Poker. Your mother was quite a player, Sally. She could bluff anyone except Lionheart, but that's only because he said he could smell dishonesty." He chuckled. "I even remember one night she cleaned out the Steel Soldier in one hand. He said she must have cheated because he'd calculated probability to nine places and she still beat his hand."

"I didn't know Mom played poker," said Sally. "She always told me that Just Cause was all training and patrolling and stuff."

"Oh dear me, no. No, we did that—patrolling and such—but we were young, powerful, and it was the height of the Seventies. I'm ashamed to say that we didn't cut a very professional image back then." He coughed, embarrassed. "Alcohol, drugs, promiscuity. We had as many vice problems of our own as we were fighting on the streets. Not your mother and father," said Stone quickly, seeing how Sally had stopped writing. "But the rest of us had our problems. Far be it from me to speak ill of the dead, though. In our defense, it was the culture of the time."

"What about Destroyer?" Sally tried to steer the conversation back on track.

"Of course. Forgive me, I do enjoy reminiscing about the past." Stone poured water from a heavy stoneware pitcher into a similarly heavy tumbler and took a sip. "It was a Wednesday night. Normally that meant poker, but Tornado, Sundancer, and I had decided we'd take in the night game at Shea Stadium, so the others decided to throw a party back at headquarters."

"A party?"

"Are you familiar with Studio 54?"

Sally shrugged. "I saw the movie with Mike Meyers. It was pretty good. Was that how your parties were?"

"At a certain level, yes. Lots of young, famous people. Up-and-coming actors, musicians, celebrities. One of those parties was going on that night when the lights went out."

"That was the Blackout?"

"Yes. The infamous Blackout of '77. Many people still think Destroyer was responsible for the lights going out, even though it has since been proved that lightning strikes were the culprits. Anyhow, it was about 9:30 that night when Shea Stadium went dark, along with the rest of New York City. After a few minutes of darkness, people began to get a little upset. Somebody must have gotten a backup generator running, because the stadium organist started playing *Jingle Bells*, of all things." Stone laughed. "It truly was Christmas in July. People started singing along and pretty soon we had an entire stadium full of people singing Christmas songs in the darkness. I don't know what might have happened if the lady on the organ hadn't started playing."

"So what did you do?" asked Sally.

"Sundancer, bless her heart, flew out over the pitcher's mound and lit herself up. She looked like a star out there hovering over the infield. She made enough light for people to find their way toward the exits. It was about this time your mother came to meet us. She'd run all the way from headquarters to come find us."

"Why didn't they just call you?"

Stone took a sip of his water. "We didn't have slick little phones back then. State of the art meant a military-spec walkie-talkie. They were big and heavy to carry around and when we weren't on duty we didn't often bring them along."

"Was this when Destroyer showed up?"

"Oh, dear me, no. Not yet. Faith came from headquarters, as I said, and told us the entire city had lost power and people were beginning to panic. Your father Bobby was standing on the roof of the Trade Center, using his hearing powers to locate the worst trouble spots. He was coordinating for us, sending each of us to where he thought we could do the most good. Your mother went to Harlem along with Imp, whose family lived there. I went to help folks stuck in subways."

"Wasn't Imp Destroyer's sister?"

"Yes." Stone pushed his chair back and gathered up the titanium cane, which rested at the side of his desk. Sixty years of fighting against gravity in his seven-hundred-pound frame hadn't been kind to his body. He leaned on the cane and limped casually over to look out the window at the overcast sky. "We didn't know that right away, of course."

"Mr. Stone, please . . . tell me what you do know about Destroyer." Sally kept her pen poised over the notebook. "It's important to me."

"Of course. Harlan Washington was thirteen years old at the time of the Blackout. He'd apparently been spending time in a junkyard at one end of Harlem and turned it into his own personal engineering lab." Stone shook his head in amazement. "The boy was some kind of sick genius. He had booby traps all over this junkyard, where he'd hidden his younger sister. We found automatic sentry guns that fired engine block bolts. Javelin was almost killed by one. He was lucky."

Sally shuddered. "That's horrible."

"An excellent word to describe Washington," said Stone. "He lived with his mother and two sisters in a tenement. He was a poor student, forced to go to summer school, and apparently not well liked by the other kids in his neighborhood. They teased him about his tinkering and loitering in the junkyard. When his older sister Irlene discovered her parapowers, she came and talked to us and we immediately brought her into Just Cause as Imp. Harlan was quite jealous of her success. I suspect that may have been the event which sent him over the edge into the chasm of his psychopathic madness."

"And he built his first suit?"

"Yes. It was a terrible thing to behold. I didn't get to

see it because I was underground, helping to clear people from stalled trains, but your mother and the others described it for me. Two semi-truck cabs stacked on top of each other, with heavy armor welded all around. Hydraulic arms and legs, driven by twin Diesel engines and heavy-duty transmissions. The way he'd managed to put it all together by himself, with no help, was simply amazing. He had bolt guns, a giant sawblade, and a flamethrower. A flamethrower, for God's sake, in Harlem!" Stone shook his head. "So many of those tenements were already rat-infested firetraps, ready to go up at a moment's notice. When the Blackout hit, he must have decided the time for his revenge was at hand, and he took his suit on a killing spree."

Stone paused, as if he waited for a question or interjection, but Sally didn't interrupt him. This was the part she'd wanted to hear about.

"He took his infernal creation through his neighborhood, destroying vehicles, buildings, and terrorizing the residents. Fifteen deaths were directly attributed to his actions, either directly at his hands or indirectly from fires he set." Stone turned away from the window. "Including his mother."

"God!" Sally wondered what would cause someone that age to go suddenly berserk.

"Your father heard the sound of Destroyer stomping through the streets. He radioed us to say it sounded like Godzilla was in Harlem. Imp and your mother encountered Destroyer first. They could do little against his devastating weaponry and heavy armor. I believe your mother managed to knock out a couple of his cameras, but the suit was far too large for Imp to affect it with her shrinking powers."

"At least they got a couple licks in, right?"

"Indeed. They were able to draw Destroyer's attention away from civilian targets and keep him occupied until the heavy hitters arrived. Tornado,

Sundancer, and Javelin—the fliers—got there quickest. Lionheart was too far away to get there in time, especially with the gridlock from traffic signals being out. Destroyer held his own against Tornado's winds, Sundancer's energy beams, and Javelin's lasers. He wasn't able to hurt them, but neither could they punch through his armor."

"So what happened?"

"The Steel Soldier finally arrived."

Sally recalled the Steel Soldier had been a highly advanced android. The robotic being had successfully won a legal battle in the Supreme Court to be recognized as a sentient being. "The Soldier succeeded where the others failed?"

"In a manner of speaking. He used his cannon to punch through Destroyer's fuselage, holing the fuel tank and leaving the suit unable to move. But before the Soldier could tear open the armor, Destroyer caught him in a burst from his bolt guns and chewed the Soldier's torso to shreds."

"That must have been scary."

"It was, without question. Destroyer's spilled fuel caught fire from the brief fight with the Soldier. Only Imp was small enough to get inside the armor quickly enough. That was when she discovered her brother, nearly overcome by the heat and smoke, was driving the suit. She shrank him down and pulled him to safety."

"And then you all had him arrested?"

Stone bowed his head. "No, not immediately. He claimed he could repair the damage he'd done to the Soldier if we could get his sentence reduced. May God have mercy on our souls . . . we accepted his deal."

"You *what?*" Sally couldn't believe what she'd just heard. "You made a deal with him? With Destroyer?"

Stone sat back down at his desk, heavy and despondent. "The Soldier was dead, or at least nonfunctional. He was our companion, our teammate.

Harlan had already proven he was a genius of engineering. Javelin watched him closely while he repaired the damage to the Soldier and reactivated him."

"You let him work on one of the most highly advanced machines ever built." Sally's tone grew accusatory. "Did any of you even think for a second that he might learn something?"

Stone shook his head. "Not until it was far too late. I believe our actions gave him the tools and knowledge to build his next battlesuit . . . the one he used when he attacked us at Tornado's funeral."

"God," Sally struggled to find the right words to say. "It must have felt like . . . I don't know what it must be like," she finished, unable to complete the thought.

"It's a terrible feeling," said Stone. "I try not to feel guilty about it. His actions are not due to mine. I didn't kill all my friends and teammates in '85. He did. But some days I feel like I might as well have been the one hurling that plane down upon them." A tear rolled down his angular nose to drip from the end.

Sally reached across the desk and touched Stone's rocky hand with her own. "Don't blame yourself, Mr. Stone. He's devious and scary smart. He would have figured out the tech sooner or later anyway."

Stone wiped his eyes with his thick, granite fingers. "It was because of him that I chose this career after my retirement. I swore on the graves of those he killed I would take it upon myself to teach other heroes, to train them to fight evil more effectively than we ever did in our day."

"Well, you've certainly done that. Look at what you have done here with the Academy. I'd never be where I am today without you."

A ghost of Stone's prior jovial demeanor danced across his face. "I can't tell you how proud I am of you, Sally. You were one of the best students ever to pass through this school. You're a real credit to your mother, who was always a very good friend during and after our time together in Just Cause."

"Oh stop." Sally felt herself blush. "So what happened after Harlan Washington was arrested?"

Stone glanced over Sally's head at the clock on the wall. "I'm afraid we'll have to take this conversation back up later, Sally. I have a class to teach."

Sally's face fell. "Really? Okay. What class?"

"Parahuman History," said Stone. "I'd be honored if you'd sit in. After all, you're very much a part of that history with your lineage."

"I guess I could do that," said Sally. "How come you're teaching it instead of Griego?"

Stone smiled. "I'm just subbing. Mr. Griego is sick."

Sally glanced around, just in case anybody else might be listening in, and then said in a conspiratorial whisper, "Good. I think he's a lousy teacher."

Stone dropped his own voice low. "So do I."

Chapter Nine

I declare to you, brothers, that flesh and blood cannot inherit the kingdom of God, nor does the perishable inherit the imperishable. Listen, I tell you a mystery: We will not all sleep, but we will all be changed—in a flash, in the twinkling of an eye, at the last trumpet. For the trumpet will sound, the dead will be raised imperishable, and we will be changed. For the perishable must clothe itself with the imperishable, and the mortal with immortality. When the perishable has been clothed with the imperishable, and the mortal with immortality, then the saying that is written will come true: 'Death has been swallowed up in victory.' 'Where, O death, is your victory? Where, O death, is your sting?'

-1 Corinthians 15: 50-55

January, 2004
Denver, Colorado
Hero Academy

Sally spent an enjoyable hour in a class of seniors at the Hero Academy with kids who were only a year behind her, but seemed frighteningly young and inexperienced. John Stone set aside the syllabus for the afternoon and instead led the students through a question-and-answer session with Sally, who answered everything she could. As the kids asked their questions, they seemed respectful and subdued, as if they had a real live hero in their midst instead of someone who graduated only six months ago.

"I'm nothing special, really," Sally said as kids fawned

over her. "I got the same education you all are now. I just happened to get an internship with Just Cause."

"But you already got to deploy. You stopped the Antimatter Woman from blowing up the planet!" said a sharp-faced boy.

"They've already named her? I don't think it was quite as exciting as that," said Sally. She wondered who of the current class would make it onto Just Cause next. Certainly the organization would have to start taking more interns as the pool of available talent grew. Maybe more than one of these kids would be on the team with her next year.

Mr. Stone ended the class and reminded the students they had assignments due at the end of the week and that Mr. Griego would be back tomorrow. Collective groans issued from the kids as they filed out of the room to head back to the dorm.

"Thank you so much, Sally," said Stone. "The class really enjoyed having you stop in. I hope you will again."

"Of course, Mr. Stone. I mean John."

"Now then, you wish to continue our discussion about Destroyer?"

"Yes, please." Sally fumbled for her notebook and pen.

"Perhaps you wouldn't mind if someone else joined us? I normally have dinner with Mrs. Echevarria on Wednesdays."

Estella Echevarria was the Principal of the Academy. Like Stone, she had also been a long-time member of Just Cause. She'd certainly had experience with Destroyer, but Sally wasn't sure how much she'd want to talk about him. Destroyer had killed her sister in his sneak attack in '85. "If you think it's okay," Sally hedged. She didn't want to definitively say yes or no.

"It's fine. She'll be happy to have you join us. If you don't have dinner plans already, that is."

"No, I don't have anything."

Stone retrieved his briefcase and hat—a fedora he'd

worn for forty years—and led Sally across the campus to his bungalow. "They said I didn't have to live on campus," he said, "but I'd rather be closer to the students in case something comes up. Besides, there aren't many places elsewhere I can safely go with my weight. I'll crack a normal sidewalk just walking down it, and leave footprints in asphalt."

"I never thought about that."

"Quite all right. After forty years, I'm used to it. Now then . . ." Stone opened the door to his house and turned on the lights to ward off the early winter darkness. "Make yourself at home. I have plenty of furniture available for my softer guests."

The bungalow wasn't much larger than a studio apartment, but Stone had made it comfortable despite the overbuilt furnishings. Sally looked around at the pictures on the walls from his days as an active Just Cause member. One picture in particular caught her eye. It was undated, but there inside the frame stood her parents and Lionheart. They must have been in their early twenties, thought Sally. They all looked so young and vibrant. Her mother was laughing between the two men while her father mugged at the camera from one side and Lionheart snarled like he was about to roar in mock fury from the other.

Stone clattered around in the kitchen. "I hope you don't mind spaghetti and meatballs," he called. "It's what I planned to make anyway. Estella should be here in a few minutes. Can I get you something to drink?"

"No thank you." Sally moved on to examine other pictures of the past. "I have to say, this is a little weird, Mr. Stone. I mean John. Nobody ever thinks about principals or vice-principals having any kind of life outside of school."

Stone broke into guffaws that shook his little house to the rooftop. He came out of the kitchen with a large stoneware tumbler. "Now then, where were we in the story of Destroyer?"

"He'd just been arrested after his rampage." Sally checked her notes.

The doorbell rang. "That'll be Estella. Come in!"

The principal of the Hero Academy strode into the bungalow. Formerly known as Sunstorm, she had led Just Cause for more than a decade. Her auburn hair, now shot with gray, was pulled back into a severe bun rather than the wildly flowing mass of her youth. The best skin care regimen could not hide all the wrinkles, but age hadn't dulled her fiery temperament in the least, something misbehaving students were quick to learn. Her mind still burned as quick as dry kindling, much to the chagrin of those who would try to outsmart her.

"Hello, John," she said in her soft contralto. She paused as she recognized Sally. "Miss Thompson. This is a surprise."

"Hi, Ms. Echevarria." Sally offered up her best winning smile.

"Sally is here on official Just Cause business," said Stone. "We've been discussing Destroyer. Perhaps you'd share some of your own insights with her."

Color rose in Echevarria's cheeks. "Insights? I'll give you insights. The bastard murdered my friends and my sister, and he deserves to die for his crimes."

Sally gasped at the woman's sudden vitriol. The pain of her loss was evident in her voice, even eighteen years after the event.

"Easy, Estella," said Stone. "It's hard to discuss, I know. I lost friends as well that day."

"I'm sorry, Salena," said Echevarria. "It's still like a fresh wound to me."

Stone clattered some pans in the kitchen as he began to prepare the dinner. "We had just covered Washington's first appearance in '77. Despite all the evidence against him, the Judge wouldn't permit him to be tried as an adult for his crimes. He was remanded to the custody of the state and sent to a juvenile detention facility, where he stayed for six months."

"Only six months?" Sally gaped in astonishment. "For everything he did?"

Stone smiled sadly. "He cut his own sentence short. He escaped on his fourteenth birthday."

Echevarria had brought a bottle of wine to share with Stone, and poured herself a glass. "We don't have any specific information about Washington's activities over the next seven years. He had no money, no home, and no surviving family. He was a zero, completely off the grid." She sipped at the wine. "But I think I can fill in some of the blanks."

"Well, he had to build the battlesuit he used in '85," said Sally.

"Requiring materials well as the tools to build it, a facility in which to work, and financing," said Echevarria. "And he was just fourteen years old. I suspect he used his intellect to work his way into organized crime. One thing about those groups is they respect intelligence, and Washington always was a pretty large cut above most people in sheer brainpower. It wouldn't have taken much for him to impress someone powerful, and then it would just be a matter of playing the system."

"You think it was really that simple?" The smell of Stone's dinner preparations made Sally's stomach rumble in anticipation.

Echevarria shrugged. "This is all conjecture on my part. I couldn't have done it, but you have to remember Washington is dangerously brilliant. He sees people as tools, nothing more. A means to an end. The crime families in the late '70s would have been the best resources he could find."

"It makes sense to me," said Stone from the kitchen. "Sally, do you want salad?"

"Yes, please," she said. "Dinner smells really good."

"Thank you."

"What's your interest in Destroyer?" Echevarria asked Sally. "Does this have something to do with you running across him in Chicago? Yes, I follow the news." She held up a hand to forestall the inevitable question of how she knew about it.

Sally shrugged. "Kind of, but it also really is part of an official Just Cause investigation. As I was researching, I discovered most of his file was lost on 9/11, so I'm trying to recreate what I can of it."

Echevarria raised an eyebrow. Sally was certain the woman didn't buy her answer. "Very noble and professional of you."

"Look, Ms. Echevarria, you lost your sister to him. I lost a father who I've only ever known through other people's stories. I just want to know more about the man who took him away from me, that's all."

Echevarria sighed and drained her wine glass. "'85 was a very difficult year for us as a team," she began. "Tornado, who was calling himself Stormcloud by then, had contracted full-blown AIDS and it ravaged him until there was almost nothing left of him by the end. He was always such a kind man, and a great hero. We never expected to lose one of our own that way. We're supposed to be privileged to die with our boots on in combat, not wasting away to some incurable disease." She made a small sphere of flame jump between her fingers. "How do we fight something like that?"

"We can't." Stone brought salads in from the kitchen. "He was a good friend. He loved baseball and rock music."

"Tornado passed away in October, and his parents wanted him buried in Kansas City. That was his hometown. John—" she nodded at Stone "—and Lionheart had just retired. Only Imp, Javelin, and my sister were still on the team from '77. Your mother had retired when she became pregnant with you, and your father decided he was better suited to administrating the team than being an active member."

"And you were leading the team then?" Sally speared a cucumber and ate it.

"Yes. We were the largest we'd ever been then. We had Fast Break, the Timekeeper, Foxfire, Danger, the Steel Soldier, and even Juice and Crackerjack—both still in college and only on the team part-time." Echevarria shook her head in amazement as she counted them off on her fingers. "Ten—no—*eleven* of us on the team, plus your parents who were still actively involved. A real supergroup. We were the most powerful parahuman organization on the planet. We'd put away the Tyrant, the Malice Group. Parahuman violence was at an all-time low then. Nobody wanted or dared to challenge the might of Just Cause." Echevarria paused to take a bite of her own food.

Stone took up the reins. "So there we were, all of us in Kansas City at Tornado's funeral. Even your grandparents and their surviving American Justice teammates were attending. It was the perfect opportunity for Washington to commit his revenge against us." He shook his head bitterly. "He threw a plane down on the funeral. He'd killed the pilot in mid-air, shut down the engines, and used his battlesuit's strength to fling it at us from on high. We had almost no warning. If it hadn't been for your father hearing its approach, things might have gone much worse."

"My dad heard it?" Sally finished her salad.

Echevarria nodded. "His hearing always was exceptional. I grabbed your mother and flew her to safety. Both Fast Break and my sister tried to get your father clear." She bowed her head. "Neither was fast enough. The plane came down on top of them."

Sally shivered at the thought.

Stone went back to the kitchen and returned bowls

filled with generous portions of spaghetti and meatballs. "At least they didn't suffer," he said quietly. "They most likely died instantly with the impact. A piece of debris decapitated Danger and another impaled Lionheart. Neither of them survived more than a few moments."

"Your mother started to go into premature labor," said Echevarria. "Fortunately Dr. Devereaux was there for the funeral. She was able to get your mother stabilized or else you might have been born three months too soon, Salena. But things had gone crazy. Everyone was running, shouting, trying to clear the wreckage away to find those who were underneath it. That's when Destroyer arrived."

"My mom hasn't ever told me any of these details," said Sally. She felt like she'd been cheated of this her whole life.

"Certainly you can understand her perspective," said Stone with a gentle rumble. "She lost her husband, her friends, and nearly lost you. It is a very painful memory for her. I don't blame her for not wanting to dredge up the details. It's hard enough for me."

"And for me," added Echevarria. "I still miss Gloria even today. Although it's more like the pain of an old injury when the weather changes. I'll see something and think how I wish she could have seen it too."

Sally wound noodles around her fork, careful not to splatter any sauce on her costume, afraid of stains. "So then what happened?"

"Destroyer dropped out of the sky like a blue missile," said Stone. "We didn't know it was him yet, of course. We'd never seen a battlesuit like his before. Nobody had. The Steel Soldier warned him to surrender. Washington just transmitted a signal of some kind and the Soldier exploded. Then he said *stupid machine, I never should have fixed it in the first place*. That's when we knew it was him."

"We think when Washington rebuilt the Soldier back

in '77, even then he was planning on his revenge. None of us understood the technology that had gone into that robot, so we wouldn't have been able to identify a bomb. We're certain that after the Soldier took him down once before, Washington wanted to ensure the robot couldn't do it a second time. Devious little bastard." Echevarria bitterly speared a meatball. "Javelin and I cut loose on him. We were the only ones able to do so. But Destroyer was ready. He had shields to deflect my flames and Javelin's lasers. He shot a brace of missiles at Javelin, who dodged most of them but broke his arm when he caromed off a tombstone."

"The rest of us did what we could to help," said Stone. "Juice tore away one of Destroyer's guns. Estella melted another away with her plasma stream."

Sally turned to look at Ms. Echevarria, who smiled at the memory.

"She was angry, furious at Destroyer for his temerity. She rained so much fire onto him in that suit. It's a wonder she didn't cook him inside it. It was as if she'd opened up the very gates of Hell. She burned the ground all around him into glass and smelted metal out of the surrounding tombstones. I was afraid for my own skin." Stone laughed. "Something that's almost never happened in sixty years."

Sally set down her empty bowl and regarded Echevarria with newfound respect. She'd known the woman was one of the more powerful parahumans ever to be in Just Cause, but the way Stone described it, Echevarria might be one of the most powerful in the world. And with all that power at her disposal, she'd still elected to devote herself to teach the future generations of heroes, like Sally and her classmates. For the first time, Sally really understood the phrase *with great power comes great responsibility*. It occurred to her that her own speed abilities placed her in the top echelon of parahuman performers, and she ought to think about how else she could use those powers to benefit the greater good besides being in Just Cause.

Maybe she'd look into a position at the Hero Academy herself once she retired from Just Cause, although she figured she'd have to be old before she ever considered something like that seriously. At least thirty, she figured.

"Whatever else I did, I scared him," said Echevarria. "He had an escape pod built into the torso of the suit. I must have done enough damage that he used it. It was like a coffin-sized missile shot out of it, driven by an intense rocket that accelerated faster than any of us could follow. The rest of the suit self-destructed and nearly caught the rest of us in the explosion."

"Area radars hadn't tracked him either on his incoming vector or the escape pod's course." Stone collected the empty bowls and headed to the kitchen with them. "We don't know where he went after that, except certainly it was to build the next model of the Destroyer battlesuit. Does anybody want more spaghetti?"

"No thank you," said Sally.

"We only encountered Destroyer once more before we lost Headquarters on 9/11," said Echevarria. "We were fortunate that time—nobody was killed and only a couple of us were hurt. He'd come back to New York and was gunning for us."

"He was gunning for you," corrected Stone. "You were the one to take the suit down in '85. He's always had a strong vindictiveness about him. The Soldier took him down in '77 and Destroyer blew him up. You took him down in '85 and he came looking for you in—what was it, '94?"

"Yes," replied Echevarria. "The same year I retired and handed Just Cause over to Juice. Destroyer tried to attack us in our Headquarters. Fortunately, we were able to repel him without too much collateral damage to the World Trade Center. Not that it ultimately did that much good." A tiny curl of smoke issued from one of Echevarria's nostrils like the fire inside her threatened to spill out.

"Easy, Estella," said Stone.

"He hated us, hated Just Cause so much," she said, still very much angered. "I'm sure he was jumping for joy on 9/11 when the plane hit and took out most of the team in one shot. The only downside for him would have been he wasn't the one to take them down."

"That's awful," whispered Sally.

"He's an awful person," said Echevarria. "In fact, I wouldn't be surprised if he'd somehow had something to do with the 9/11 attacks."

"I think you're reaching, Estella," said Stone in the tone of someone who'd had the same argument many times over.

"Am I? You know how long he's carried his vendetta against Just Cause. You know the depth of his hatred. Do you really think it's so far-fetched that he'd be involved in terrorism? He may not have been at the controls of the plane, but that doesn't mean he couldn't have been involved."

Stone sighed. "No one has ever been able to find any connection to him. And the Feds did look into it."

"Even so, I can't help but wonder what his next move will be." Echevarria sat back in her chair and drank some more wine. "You don't have any idea about that, do you, Salena?"

"No, ma'am," said Sally. "At least, nothing I think I'm at liberty to talk about."

Sparks danced in Echevarria's eyes, but for only a moment. "I understand, Salena. I know I'm out of the loop now that I'm at the Academy, but perhaps you'll let me know what happened when it's all over? If you can take him down for good, I'd like to hear about it. It would help me to finally know my sister can rest in peace."

Sally swallowed a nervous lump in her throat. "I'll

do my best," she said at last. "I should probably get going. Thank you so much for talking with me today, Mr. Stone, Ms. Echevarria."

"It was my pleasure, Sally," said Stone. "I hope we were able to shed some light on Destroyer for you."

"Yes, I'm glad you joined us tonight," said Echevarria. "Please do so again."

"I will," said Sally. "And I'll let you know what happens with Destroyer, so long as I'm still . . . I mean, if I can."

"We understand." Stone smiled at her.

Echevarria's expression wasn't quite so pleasant. "Be careful, Salena. Harlan Washington is a killer, and he won't hesitate to kill again. I haven't had any of my graduates die at his hands and I don't want you to be the first."

Sally shivered. "I won't."

Chapter Ten

"It is a man's own mind, not his enemy or foe, that lures him to evil ways."

-Gautama Siddharta Buddha

January, 2004
Denver, Colorado
Just Cause Headquarters

"I never realized just how much he hated everyone." Sally sounded as glum as she felt. She'd just recounted to Sondra the tales told to her by Stone and Echevarria.

"Yeah, he's really full of anger," said Sondra.

Sally set down a report and picked up one of the recent pictures taken in Guatemala. "I wonder who the other guy in this picture is?" Sally took a sip from her lukewarm hot chocolate. She and Sondra had been perusing the Archives all morning, looking into the life and times of Harlan Washington, a.k.a. Destroyer.

They'd begun with the CIA report which placed Destroyer in Guatemala and worked backwards, tracing his appearances for the past five years. The slow progress tested even Sally's stamina and she felt the beginnings of a headache. Finally, Sondra had leaned back from her terminal, squeezed her eyes shut and massaged her temples. "I need a break, kiddo." She sucked down the last dregs of the black tar she called coffee. "I'm going to go stretch my wings. You keep plugging away if you want to and I'll be back in awhile to help."

Sally gave an absent nod as she paged through the hard copy of the CIA file. It contained four pictures of Harlan Washington. He was engaged in conversation with a tall, muscular man of indeterminate age by a shipping container in Port San José, Guatemala. The stranger was Caucasian, with hair so light in the bright sun Sally couldn't tell if it was merely blonde or white. Inwardly she cursed the CIA stringer who'd shot the pictures for not getting better quality. She could see, for example, the corner of a vehicle in two of the pictures but nothing detailed. The writing on the shipping container was legible and therefore traceable, but not likely related to either of the men. Sally planned to research it only if she had no other leads to follow.

She set aside the picture, the face of the mysterious blond man almost mocking her with his anonymity. Instead, she selected an evaluation of Harlan Washington performed by the psychologist at the juvenile hall where he'd been consigned after his short reign of destruction upon Harlem in '77. She began to read, careful not to skip over anything, and was so engrossed in the details she jumped when Sondra appeared next to her with foot-long sandwiches from the cafeteria.

"I'm sorry, I didn't mean to startle you," said her winged friend. "It's been hours. I thought you might be getting hungry."

Sally's stomach rumbled as she caught a whiff of the toasted bread and tangy mustard. "Oh my, yes." She took one of the sandwiches and took a huge bite. "Ooo are an an-hel," she said around the mass of turkey, bacon, and provolone.

"I know. I've even got the wings to match." Sondra fluttered hers for emphasis. "How's it going?"

Sally chewed a moment, swallowed, and wiped her mouth with the paper napkin. Her stomach clenched around the food with glee. "Pretty good. Did you know my mom wrote the first report on Destroyer?" She turned the monitor so Sondra could get a closer look.

"Wow, no kidding. I was only five when this happened. You should call her up, get her personal take on the whole thing."

"What, you mean talk to her? About this?"

"Yes, Sally. It's all right to talk to your mother. I call mine a couple of times a week."

"Oh." Sally felt guilty about her reticence. She didn't always see eye-to-eye with her mother. She supposed it was normal teenage angst and had always figured she'd get over it sooner or later. If only the woman wasn't so unreasonable about the smallest things! "She's never really wanted to talk about Destroyer."

"Maybe that will change now that we're investigating him. Surely she doesn't want a repeat of any of his past escapades."

"You think there's more than what's just in the file?"

"Look, nobody ever puts everything into a report. You'd go crazy trying to put in every little detail. Trust me, when you have to write your first, you'll gloss over all kinds of things and forget others. But a lot of times, just rereading your words will help you remember important things that you didn't include before."

"I suppose," said Sally. The notion of calling her mother appealed to her far less than the sandwich she was inhaling. She decided to change the subject and picked up one of the pictures with the mysterious blond man in it. "I'm curious who this guy is that Washington is meeting with, but I don't have the slightest idea where to begin."

Sondra studied the picture, and then examined all four side by side. She selected one and discarded the others. "I think this is the best of the bunch," she decided. "We'll put Research on it and see what they can turn up."

"Research?"

"Sure." Sondra took a bite of her own sandwich. "You're in the big leagues now, Sally. Big government. We've got an entire agency at our disposal if we need it."

"Okay." Sally felt her ears redden. She felt like she could trust Sondra with anything, and had a burning need to ask a question. "Sondra, did you ever . . . date someone you worked with?"

Sondra leaned back from the table, flexed and refolded her wings. "Yes. You?"

"Uh, not yet. But . . ."

"Jason?" Sondra's eyes sparkled.

Sally nodded. "How'd you know?"

Sondra ticked off each point on her fingers. "You can't look him in the eye. Every time he speaks to you, you blush. When you don't think he's looking, you watch him all the time. Should I go on?"

Sally hunched down miserably into her chair. "Is it that obvious?"

"Painfully so," confirmed Sondra. "But don't be upset. I've yet to meet a speedster who understood the art of subtlety. Did he ask you out?"

"Yes."

"When?"

"Just today."

Sondra hit a few keys on her terminal and smiled. "Hm. Jack wins."

"Wins what?"

"We had a pool going. He picked today."

Sally stood up, embarrassed.

"Relax, Sally. We're not making fun of you. Jason's a good kid, and so are you. If I wasn't almost old enough to be his mother, I'd have my eye on him myself. For what it's worth, I think it's perfectly all right for you to go out with him. For being such a huge guy, he's really more of a puppy dog than anything else. Go for it." Sondra winked at her and made Sally feel much better.

"I will," said Sally.

Friday afternoon arrived. Stacey returned from her stay in the medical center and was placed on light duty for one week. The team's request for permission to work outside of the U.S. bogged down in bureaucratic red tape at Homeland Security. Juice reminded everyone about full-team training in the Bunker the next day.

Sally tried on everything in her wardrobe twice and decided she didn't have a thing to wear. In spite doing everything else at top speed, she still didn't find enough time to go shopping. As the seconds ticked away, she dressed frantically in a pair of tight jeans and a sleeveless button-down blouse that she hoped was suitable wear for a club.

Jason picked her up at her door at six o'clock and escorted her down to the parking lot. Sally was a little surprised to discover he had a car, or rather, a beat-up old Bronco. She had hung around with so many people in her life that could fly, levitate, or otherwise transport themselves that she forgot some folks still depended on internal combustion to get around.

The previous night's snowstorm was over but for the occasional lonely flake. A slushy mixture of slush, sand, and magnesium chloride covered the roads. Sally buckled her seatbelt, uncertain as Jason headed downtown. "Is this really safe?"

He laughed. "If you take corners slowly and don't jam on the brakes, you'll be fine. It's the other cars you have to watch out for. Chances are the person driving it will be from California."

"Huh?"

"Local joke. The natives say that most people who move here come from California." Jason negotiated the big truck through an icy intersection with exaggerated care. "Besides, I've got precious cargo tonight."

"Your guitar?"

"Well, that too." He grinned sidelong at her, half-joking but half-serious in a way that made Sally's knees watery. She determined a lightning-quick change of subject was needed.

"Do a lot of people come out to hear you play in this weather? It's a blizzard!"

"This?" Jason waved at the snow outside with a dismissive gesture. "This is nothing. People around here don't even notice snow until there's more than a few inches. Half the time it melts the next day anyway. But I'm forgetting that you were at the Academy—you've seen the freaky weather here for the past couple years."

They stopped in front of the club. A neon sign spelled out *Bart's Basement* in sharp red and yellow lights. A burgundy minivan sat in the loading zone. A skinny young man in an oversized parka unloaded large black drum cases from it. "Hey, Chris," called Jason. "Need help?"

"'Sup, Jase. Nah, I got it."

"Chris is the drummer. He's thirty." Jason opened the back of the Bronco and lifted out an amplifier so big Sally could have crouched inside it. He handed her a microphone stand. "Do you mind?"

"Oh, sure, no problem," she said.

"Chris, this is Sally. She's on the team with me."

"Pleasameechoo," mumbled Chris. He shook her hand then grabbed another handful of gear from the van.

Sally followed Jason into the dark club. She'd never been in a place like it before. Tall, narrow tables, each with ashtrays and a decades' worth of beverage stains, dotted a wooden floor with stools around them in a haphazard arrangement. The stage was a large, raised platform, bathed in light with a ratty black curtain for a backdrop. A long bar ran down one side of the room, replete with cracked leather, tarnished brass, and two white-shirted bartenders.

"Am I allowed to be in here?" Sally asked. "I'm not twenty-one yet."

"I'm twenty," said Jason. "But this is an all-ages show. You have to show an ID to buy booze but they'll let anyone in the door—even him." He pointed to the stage.

Another young man was setting up his gear there. He had striking black hair that stood up in random spots and the slanted eyes of Asian ancestry. "Hey, Jason." He opened a black case and removed a large blue guitar.

"Hiya, Matt," Jason replied. "Sally, this is Matt. He plays the bass. Matt, Sally." Matt appraised her body with appreciative eyes. After Chris had just about ignored her, Matt's interest made her shiver a little.

"Nice to meet you." Matt slung the bass strap over his shoulder and adjusted it to hang low.

Jason bent down and whispered in Sally's ear. "Watch yourself around him. He'll try to pick you up, and you don't want to be part of his bedroom parade."

Chris stumbled in, wrestling with an armful of cymbals. "I need a roadie," he grumbled. "Jason, quit fooling with your date and help move my gear."

Jason smiled and shrugged at Sally. "I'll be back. If you want a cola or something, just tell the bartender you're with me. We get a drink allowance, but all I ever have is water." He followed Chris back out to the street.

Matt walked to the edge of the stage, looked down at her, and smiled. "Haven't seen you around before."

"I'm new to the team," she said.

"So you're a para, huh? What can you do?"

"Run, mostly." Sally glanced around to see if Jason had noticed the uncomfortable attention from Matt, but he was nowhere in sight.

"Cool," he said, and ran his fingers over the strings of his instrument. A wallop of solid sound blasted out of the speakers that hung from the club's roof.

Sally stepped out of the way as Jason and Chris brought in the rest of the drum kit. In a few minutes, the three-piece band completed their set-up and began their sound checks. Sally picked a small table at one side of the stage where she'd be able to see, but wouldn't garner much attention. The club filled up with people during the sound check and before long, there wasn't an empty seat in the house. Sally squirmed with a bit of nervous anticipation. She hadn't realized Jason's band was so popular; they must be pretty good.

A thin man with a trucker hat and horn-rim glasses sidled up to a microphone and mumbled into it to introduce Velma's Glasses to the crowd. A cheer went up as they launched into their first number, a tune with a powerful, driving beat.

For the next ninety minutes, Velma's Glasses churned out a sonic explosion of hard-rocking tunes. Jason and Matt cavorted about the stage, chased each other between verses, and mugged at the crowd. Behind them, Chris thrashed away at the drums, doing his best Keith Moon impression. They alternated crooning ballads with screaming anthems. By the end of their set, they had worked the crowd into a frenzy, and the audience formed an impromptu mosh pit at the front of the stage. Sally pressed her back to a support beam so she wouldn't be sucked into the mass of flailing bodies. Her adrenaline flowed as if attached to a fire hose, and it took all her will to keep from snapping into slow-time perceptions.

They finished their last tune. All three musicians stood triumphant with guitars and sticks raised over their heads, their heads back, and their eyes shut as they drank in the adulation of the fans. Almost as one, the crowd raised a hundred arms with lighters extended to light up the entire bar like a star field.

"Well, I guess we could do one more," said Jason into the microphone. He winked sidelong at Sally. The crowd renewed its enthusiasm and the band launched into an encore—a suitably loud rendition of The Who's *Baba O'Riley*.

They finished and took their bows. The crowd cheered and whistled. The stage lights dimmed and the three men broke down their gear and carried it offstage. Just as quick, another band began to set up. Sally watched as many appreciative fans mobbed Jason with handshakes and hearty slaps on the back. He laughed and joked with them. Matt and Chris likewise basked in the attention. At one point, the dark-haired bass player looked casually in her direction and locked eyes with her.

Sally felt a presence at her side and looked up to see Jason's gigantic frame next to her, his face split in a wide grin like a kid at Christmas. "So what'd you think?"

"You guys are really good." She tried not to wince at how trite her words sounded.

"Do you want to stick around for the next band or do you want to get out of here? It's some group called Neville and His Toad Trevor. I don't know anything about them."

Sally caught Matt's eyes on her again. It gave her a funny feeling in the pit of her stomach. "I don't know," she hedged. "Can we take a break, get away from the people here, and then decide?"

"Sure," replied Jason. "I'm burning up right now as it is. A little snow and freezing wind would just hit the spot." He swept her coat off the chair beside her and held it for her in the best southern gentleman tradition. He took her hand and guided her through the crowd. Sally thrilled at the simple, casual contact of his skin on hers. They went up the iron stairs to the street. Clouds hung low over the city, pink and orange reflected from the lights below, with a promise of more snow before morning.

Sally shivered inside her parka. Her mom had bought her the heaviest coat she could find and for once Sally didn't mind it one bit. "Aren't you cold?" Her teeth chattered.

"Not too much," Jason said. "Cold doesn't bother me unless it's arctic. Besides, it feels pretty good after being under the lights. It's not too late yet. You want to go get a piece of pie?"

Sally glanced down the staircase at the club entrance. She wasn't ready to go back in, especially if it meant she'd have to talk to the bass player with the rotating door in his bedroom. "Sure," she said with a smile. "I like pie."

"Everybody likes pie," confided Jason. "Mind a walk? There's a place a few blocks from here, called Lazzarino's. Best peach pie I've had since my grandma's back home."

"Sounds nice." Sally relished the feel of his large hand wrapped around her own small one. For a few moments, they walked in silence as plumes of breath rose in their wakes. "So how long have you been playing in the band?"

"Year and a half," said Jason. "Chris and Matt have been together longer, but they lost their last guitarist to a tragic accident."

"Oh. What happened?"

"He got married. To a woman who didn't think playing music was a very honorable profession. I think they moved to Duluth and he's selling insurance now."

Sally giggled.

"Are the other guys nice?"

"Oh yeah. Chris is married, with a pair of rug rats. His wife's really cool. She's from Mexico and she can cook like you wouldn't believe. She's very supportive of us. Matt is like the total swinging bachelor. I can't believe how he can juggle all his women, but he's still pretty cool. Watch yourself around him." Jason winked. "He thinks you're hot."

She flushed. "Don't worry. I have no intention of becoming another notch on his bedpost."

Jason squeezed her hand. "Good."

"Hey bro, got a light?" A gravelly voice said from the mouth of an alleyway. Sally looked to see a man wrapped in many layers of sweaters topped off by a Raiders hat.

"Sorry, no," said Jason. Sally sensed they were not alone and glanced behind them. Another man emerged from a shadowy doorway. In front of them, a third man stepped out from behind a parked car.

"Gimme your wallet," he said. "And nobody gets hurt."

"You're kidding, right?" Jason said as he released Sally's hand. "You have any idea who we are?"

"He's pretty damn big, dawg," said the second man.

"Jus' a big target, bro." The man in front lifted a small snub-nosed pistol from where he'd held it behind a leg. "Your wallet, asshole."

The world slowed to a crawl as Sally went into high gear. Fighting bad guys was familiar territory to her, something she could get her mind around without letting her emotions get involved. The man with the pistol stood fifteen feet away from them. He might as well have been right next to them and encased in thick clay for all the good the distance did him.

Sally knew several ways to disarm a man with a gun. She stepped forward and reached for the pistol. She flipped the catch, released the cylinder, opened it, poked out all six bullets into her free hand, then snapped the cylinder closed again before he could react.

The man's finger tightened on the trigger. The click echoed across the street as Sally dropped the bullets in her pocket for safekeeping. The man in the alley lifted a piece of rebar; he hadn't yet realized what had happened. In a flash, Sally pulled it out of his hand and pressed it into Jason's. As Sally came to a stop, time sped back up to its normal speed.

The man swung his empty hand.

Jason chuckled and bent the rebar into a loop. "You're outclassed here, fellas. Why don't you call it a night?"

The three men looked at each other in a panic, and ran. Jason tossed the rebar after them, not to hit any of them but to let them know he could have. It clattered in the street behind their heels. The men disappeared with impressive speed.

"Would you mind getting that before somebody blows a tire driving over it?"

Sally nodded and zipped out to the street and back, the rebar hoop in her hand. She was impressed with the casual demeanor he'd used and how he'd defused the situation without hurting anyone. Of course, she'd helped too. "Should we call the police?" she asked.

"To report an attempted mugging of two Just Cause members?" Jason snorted. "Juice'd love that. Those guys won't stop running until they get home. Maybe they won't be back for awhile. Let's just call it our good deed for the day."

"Definitely."

"Now how about that pie?"

"Definitely," she repeated, and took his hand firmly to let him know she didn't mind him holding it.

Chapter Eleven

There are three things to remember when parahumans engage in combat. I refer to them as AKA, which is a familiar acronym for anyone with a secret identity. Over the rest of this book, we will address these three areas.

One: Analyze your opponents. Be aware of powers catalogued, implied, and possible.

Two: Know your own powers. What are your limits? What are your capabilities?

Three: No battle plan ever survives contact with the enemy. Adapt to changing circumstances, because nothing is ever 'by the book'.

-Estella Echevarria aka Sunstorm, *On Parahuman Combat,* 2000

January, 2004
Denver, Colorado
Just Cause Headquarters

Sally squinted at her alarm clock as it chirped at her. It couldn't be seven o'clock already, could it? She and Jason stayed out late the night before; way too late for Saturday morning training. The date had been a lot of fun, though. After their minor skirmish with the would-be muggers, they had some delicious pie at Lazzarino's. Then, they'd both been so wired they decided to go see a late movie. The previews had started at midnight and the credits rolled after two. It was three by the time they got back onto base.

Jason had been a perfect gentleman the entire night. It was really the first time she'd ever gone on a date, and it felt like something out of a storybook. She'd had such a grand time that she let him kiss her goodnight. Still drowsy, she rolled over and kicked off the blankets—even though headquarters was climate-controlled, it was cold outside and she couldn't sleep without being buried in her covers. She smiled as she remembered Jason's kiss, the tickle of his stubble on her nose, the musky scent of his shampoo and sweat.

He had tasted like peach pie.

By seven-fifteen, she was in the cafeteria and couldn't decide whether she wanted the strawberry--banana smoothie or the cherry-lime. Since it would be a full day of combat simulation, Sally wasn't about to eat anything substantial. She learned long ago that light, frequent meals were best for her in situations where she made extensive use of her powers. She selected the cherry-lime and added a small bowl of granola and a slice of cantaloupe with a yawn.

It seemed like she had been nothing but exhausted since beginning her internship. She wondered if it was part of the training. On the other hand, the night before had been her own fault. Well, mostly hers. She smiled to herself because the rest of it had been Jason's.

Jack sauntered into the cafeteria and made a beeline for the coffee bar. In a minute, Sondra joined him. They strolled over to sit with Sally.

"Morning, sugar," said Jack.

"God, Sally, you look like you have two black eyes," Sondra said. "What time did you get in?"

Sally tried not to think of how little sleep she'd really gotten. She yawned. "It was like three."

"Ah, the folly of youth." Jack sipped a drink that wafted a pleasant cinnamon-vanilla scent across the table. "I remember staying out all night once or twice."

"Jack, you're away more than you're here anymore." Sondra laughed. "Honestly, you've never grown up. So . . . Did Jason kiss you?"

"Yeah."

Jack grumbled something under his breath and dug a ten-dollar bill from a pocket. He held it up between two fingers like a cigarette. Sondra snapped it away from him and tucked it into her vest.

"I'd be angry if I wasn't so tired," said Sally. "Is that all you guys do? Make bets about me and my love life?"

"Before you, it was Jay," said Jack. "After you, it'll be someone else. It's just our thing."

"Why don't you get a cup of coffee?" Sondra pointed out. "It's free and chock full of caffeine."

"Why does everybody keep pushing coffee on me here? Is it part of the super-secret Just Cause clubhouse rules that you have to drink the stuff?" Sally glared at them over her granola.

"Well . . ." said Jack. "Most times we don't get enough sleep. It kind of comes with the territory."

Sondra set down her cup. "You're exhausted, dear, and in no shape to train today. If it wasn't your first time, I'd say you should try to take a sick day instead. Let me get you a small cup—it'll get you through the morning, at any rate."

"Please, Sondra, you'll kill her with that mud you drink. Come on, kiddo—I'll introduce you to the joy of cinnamon hazelnut." Jack stood up and escorted Sally to the coffee bar.

"I stay away from caffeine, Jack. It messes up my metabolism." Sally felt her protests grow flimsy and weak against his charm and male-model good looks.

"Don't worry, I'm not going to start you out with a triple espresso or anything. Sondra was absolutely right —you're in no shape to train today. Jason won't be either, but you're going to be the one on the hot seat today because it's your first time. We just want you to survive it . . . metaphorically speaking." He handed her a cup he'd mixed up. He'd topped it with a dollop of whipped cream and a dusting of cinnamon and nutmeg.

She took it from him and wrapped her fingers around the warm ceramic mug. "Thanks, Jack. It does smell good."

He winked. "Trust me."

She took a sip. It tasted like impossibly warm ice cream. "Yum."

He laughed, and then looked past her. "Oh, oh, oh . . . better clear the way. Here comes someone else who needs his extra-large ration of go-juice."

Jason staggered up to the coffee bar. His hair was in disarray and longer-than-usual stubble dotted his chin and cheeks. "Morn'n." He selected a decanter that was half full and dumped sugar and cream directly into it.

"Watch out, that's Sondra's blend," said Jack.

"Doan care." Jason stirred the sludge with a long-handled spoon. He raised the pot to his lips and drained it.

"Urgh. Tar," he said after lowering the pot. Sally thought it was cute.

They kidded around for a few more minutes before all headed for the Bunker. Sondra guided Sally to the women's locker room and showed her how to put on the training suit. Training suits resembled the costumes that the team-members wore, but were loaded with kinetic and energy sensors and made out of high-tech nylon armor composite.

"A helmet?" Sally looked askance at the headgear that looked more suitable for a grade-Z science fiction movie shown on an grade-Z cable network.

Sondra shrugged as she strapped on her own helmet. "Head shots are efficient, whether you're going for a knockout or . . . something else. Jason or Juice takes a swipe at you, you'll be glad for the helmet. It'll still ring your bell like you wouldn't believe."

"Jason better not," Sally said. "I kissed him." Nevertheless, she put it on. They walked out onto the training floor as she adjusted the straps so it wouldn't slip down over her face. The rest of the team assembled in the middle of the facsimile city street. All wore training suits and helmets.

"Good morning," said Juice as the two women walked up to the group. "I trust everyone is well-rested?" There were good-natured grumblings from the rest of the team and face-splitting yawns from Jason and Sally. "Hey, Jase, you look like shit." Juice winked at him.

"Thanks, boss. I wasn't sure until you said," said Jason with another yawn.

"We're going to break in Sally today and start getting her up to speed. We'll start with a Round Robin drill, followed by a Three-Minute. Analysis will follow both drills, and then we'll break for lunch. We'll run a couple of Tacticals this afternoon and wrap up with more Analysis. Any questions?" Juice winced as he realized he'd handed Jack a straight line.

Jack raised his hand. "*Yeah, I got a question. How do I get out of this chickenshit outfit?*"

"Shut up, Jack," said Juice.

"Aliens," said Sally. "Bill Paxton, wasn't it?"

"Good catch." Jack grinned.

"Does anyone have any *legitimate* questions?" Juice asked, enunciating a little more clearly.

Sally raised her hand. "Can you define a Round Robin and a Three-Minute drill?"

"Of course. My apologies, Sally. We've been without anyone new for so long that I forgot you aren't familiar with the terminology." Juice smiled. "A Round Robin is where you try to take down everyone on the team in turn, and everyone has a turn as the Robin. A Three-Minute drill is blatantly unfair. You just have to survive three minutes of everyone on the team trying to take you down together in a coordinated manner. The Tacticals are specific goal-oriented scenarios. Analysis is when we look at what we all did, what we did right, and what needs improvement. You want to go first?"

Sally nodded. "Okay, I'm ready."

"Good," said Juice. "Everyone fan out. Take us on however you want in whatever order. The rules are no killing shots. The suits will extrapolate damage and the computer will report on specific injuries, but try not to actually hurt anyone. Take as long as you need. Ready?" The others split up and headed down the street and into the air.

Sally flexed her fingers and sped up her perceptions to maximum. Sounds dropped into the bass register and Juice seemed to move in slow motion as he pointed at her. "Bbbbb-eeeee-ggggg-iiiii-nnnnn."

Sally sped to the edge of the Bunker. She'd already worked out her strategy: go simplest to hardest. She'd aced all her combat courses at the Hero Academy, but then she had sixty years of speedster experience to draw upon between her mother and grandmother.

Jack would be the easiest. A quick circuit of the Bunker found him crouched in an alley, his paint-pellet rifle held at the ready. She disarmed him in a blur and had a pair of handcuffs on him immediately thereafter. Since his wide range of skills likely included lockpicking, she knocked him down and hog-tied him. Jack barely had time to swear before he was stuck on his belly with his wrists tied to his ankles. She took a moment to giggle at his helplessness before she checked her watch: eight seconds since the beginning of the exercise. That would serve Jack right for making bets on her, she thought as she ran on.

She moved on to find Glimmer. He should also be fairly easy to deal with, in spite of his psionic abilities. His brain didn't work any faster than a normal human's, so once again her speed would give her an advantage. She knew she had to be quick and careful. His precog could have warned of her approach and let him avoid her despite her speed. With his telepathy, he could take control of her mind and force her to stop or induce her to sleep. With his psychokinesis, he could create a wall of tangible mental force off which she would bounce like a bug hitting a windshield. Both her mother and grandmother had warned her about the dangers of psionic opponents. *A low-power psi is potentially much more dangerous than any top-tier brick or blaster*, her mom had said. *Never assume otherwise.*

Glimmer was already spinning around to face her as she rounded a corner and approached him. She knew many of his psionic abilities required both eye contact and concentration, and those were easy to disrupt. She grabbed an aluminum trashcan facsimile, upended it over his head, and pulled it down over his shoulders and upper torso. She then proceeded to beat upon it for several seconds with a piece of broom handle. He reeled from the sudden noise and loss of vision.

"Unconscious," said a voice in her ear as the combat control computer registered a potential knockout blow on Glimmer. The same voice echoed hollowly inside the can and Glimmer stopped struggling.

"Geez," she heard him mumble. Seventeen seconds.

Her instinct was to lift the can and ask if he was all right, but she knew that she needed to finish the exercise first. The two easy marks were down, which left her with the bricks—Jason and Juice—and the fliers: Doublecharge, Sondra, and Forcestar. None of them would be easy opponents, but she would nevertheless try to give a good account of herself. She decided to save the bricks for last, as they were traditionally the toughest opponents.

Fliers were difficult to fight when one couldn't enter their element. Most parahumans who flew could think in three dimensions when most people only thought in two. This gave them a strong tactical advantage in combat situations. Sally had spent a lot of time working on using her speed powers effectively against opponents who could stay out of her reach. She saw a sporting goods store and ducked inside it. One of the beneficial parts of training in the Bunker was that the technicians prided themselves on making the settings as real as possible, all the way down to the merchandise on the shelves of stores. Sally grabbed a pair of tennis ball canisters, and noted that she could have as easily taken golf balls, baseballs, or darts. Armed with fuzzy green missiles, she found her way to the top of a building.

Doublecharge circled overhead and cut loose with a crackling burst of electricity as soon as she saw Sally step onto the roof. Sally dodged to one side. Another blast of lightning scored the roof where she'd been a moment before. Some blasters' powers took time to travel intervening distances, but Doublecharge's moved at the speed of light, and were only limited by her aim. If Sally kept moving, she'd be a tougher target to hit.

She popped open a tube of tennis balls and stood still for a dangerous fraction of a second, hurling them as fast as she could. In her perceptions, they traveled straight and fast as any thrown object might. To Doublecharge, however, the fuzzy green missiles might as well have been bullets. Two impacted on her side while the third glanced off her helmet. She grunted in surprise from the hits.

"Unconscious," said the monitoring system.

"Nice," Sally complimented herself as Doublecharge dropped gently toward the street below.

A series of sharp reports reached her ears. Each one sounded like a bass drum being struck with a mallet. She glanced in the direction of the sound to see Sondra overhead, paint-pellet guns lowered.

A cloud of paint pellets sped toward Sally. She had to bend and twist her body in midair to avoid them. A pellet brushed by her hair but didn't break. She grabbed another tennis ball tube and sprinted to the edge of the building. Although she couldn't jump any further than a normal person from a standstill, she could cover lengthy distances with a running start. She leaped across the street to another rooftop to buy herself some time.

As Sondra swung around and brought her guns to bear, Sally had already thrown another set of tennis balls. She didn't time her throws right, and missed with two of them. The third smacked into Sondra's left wing, and she winced in pain.

"Sorry, Sondra," called Sally.

"Wing damaged, flight must cease," announced the monitor. Sondra spiraled down to the street. Sally unwound the cord from a flagpole on the roof of the building and dashed down the fire escape. Sondra couldn't fly anymore, but she was still armed and able to fight.

Sally hit the street at full speed and as she sped past Sondra, she flipped the disconnect switches from the paint-pellet guns, causing the compressed-air tanks to drop away. Sally immediately reversed direction, looped one end of her cord around a wingtip, and spun it around the winged woman in tight circles. Sondra's wings wrapped around herself in a feathery cocoon.

"Incapacitated," confirmed the monitor.

Sondra wavered and tipped over. Sally slipped her hands under the woman's head to keep it from bouncing off the pavement. "How am I doing?" she whispered.

Sondra winked at her. "Great."

Taking down Sondra had eaten up almost twenty seconds; Sally had nearly completed her first minute of the training exercise and had only three opponents left. Not bad for a rookie, she thought. The last three were going to take some real time, though. Forcestar's force-field powers were going to be difficult to overcome and she had no idea how she'd take down Juice and Jason. In her Parahuman Combat classes at the Academy, the instructors said that the best way to defeat a brick was to let him beat himself. Obviously, only another brick could stand toe-to-toe and trade punches. Other parahumans needed to either put the brick in a position where his strength would be no help or use his own strength against him. At the time, Sally had thought it sounded very trite and esoteric; something right out of reruns of *Kung Fu*.

Now she was desperate for a plan.

Suddenly her time to come up with one ran out as Juice came around a corner and stopped dead in his tracks. He glanced around quickly to locate a likely source of electrical power. Sally knew she couldn't let him draw a full charge if he wasn't already carrying one.

She sought inspiration in her surroundings, hoping to find something that would help, and spotted a hardware store. An idea struck her like a thunderbolt and she ran in and out of the store in a second. In one arm she had as many bungee cords as she'd been able to hold; in the other she carried a can of red spray paint.

As Juice reached toward a street lamp, she ducked inside his guard and let him have a face full of spray paint. He coughed, choked, and reached for his wraparound glasses to yank them off his face. As he raised his hand, Sally moved faster than she ever had before. She wrapped the bungee cords around his arm and looped them once around his arm to draw them behind his head. In a blur of motion, his arm was tightly strapped to his head. The bulge of his bicep strained across his nose and the back of his hand pressed against the back of his neck.

He glared at her from behind his paint-spattered glasses. When he reflexively raised his other hand to try and free himself, she wrapped another batch of cords around it. Soon Juice's head was completely covered by his arms and a mass of bungee cords.

"Can you still breathe?" asked Sally, concerned. This was something she'd never done before and had no idea if she might have hurt him somehow.

"Grmph," Juice said in a muffled voice. He sounded surprised but not particularly upset or panicky. For good measure, Sally wrapped a few dozen more bungee cords around his legs. Then, since she still had most of a can of spray paint left, she took a couple seconds to write MUSTANG SALLY WAS HERE with a flourish on the ground around Juice. She accented it with a smiley face inside of a heart.

"Incapacitated," said the monitor system.

She'd completely depleted the store's stock of bungee cords, and would have to figure out something else for Jason.

Just her luck, he was running up the street towards them in a plodding, slow-motion gait. She hesitated and slipped out of her accelerated perceptions to watch him approach. His muscles moved enticingly under his training suit and she shook her head so as not to become distracted. She sped up her perceptions again so she could take in every detail of him while telling herself it was strictly for the exercise and nothing more. As he passed a small bistro, an idea came to her and she charged up to one of the outdoor tables.

Jason skidded to a halt as she caught back up to him. She waited until she saw his chest begin to expand with a heaving breath and then tossed a handful of ground black pepper into his mouth and nose. His eyes bulged out and filled with tears. He coughed, spluttered, and issued a braying sneeze forceful enough to knock himself over.

"Incapacitated," said the monitor.

Sally's own eyes blurred for a moment as she realized what she'd done, miserable at the thought of the discomfort she'd caused him. "Oh, Jason, I'm so sorry," she cried.

A glowing blue cylinder appeared around her. She yelped in surprise as it formed a floor underneath her as well as a ceiling. In a moment, she found herself lifted off the ground and suspended in mid-air.

Several yards away, Forcestar grinned at her, his arm extended as he controlled the field in which she was enclosed. "I think that we can consider this exercise complete. Sixty-eight seconds and you took out most of the team."

"Is . . . is that good?"

"Are you kidding? I'm the only one right now who can take down everyone and it takes me a good ten to fifteen minutes of hard work. I bet if I hadn't sneaked up on you, you'd have figured out a way to stop me as well. You can color me impressed." He lowered her back to the ground. He looked at Jason, who sneezed so hard that he cracked the side of the building against which he had fallen. "Medical," he said aloud. "I think we'll need your assistance with Mastiff."

Released from the force field, Sally ran up to Jason's side and seized one of his hands. "Jason . . . I'm sorry. It was the first thing I thought of. Please don't hate me!" Although he couldn't speak, Jason managed to give her a weak thumbs-up in spite of his streaming eyes and nose.

Two technicians in white lab coats ran up; one toted a device, which resembled an unholy mating of a vacuum cleaner and a metal detector. One of them adjusted some controls on the machine while the other swept it back and forth across each member of the team. Jack said to Sally that it was a nanobot cleaner, designed to remove material and residue from the team without requiring cleaning, chemical solutions, or hacksaws and cutting torches. The tank on the back of the device filled with sludgy liquid as the nanobots removed the paint from Juice's face and the pepper from Jason's sinuses, particle by particle. The flagpole cord around Sondra dissolved into nothing.

Juice dry-scrubbed his face, as if he still had paint caked on it. "Well . . ." He looked across the rest of the team. "I suppose we all needed that. It's been far too long since we had any real challenges as a team. Thank you, Sally, for reminding us that we're not totally infallible."

"Uh, you're welcome," she said. "Did I do all right?"

"Are you kidding? I can't remember the last time anyone took us all down as quickly as you did," Jack said. "You're tops in my book."

"All right, Jack, don't go and give her a complex or anything." Sondra rubbed her wing where the tennis ball had hit it.

"Very impressive debut, Sally," said Doublecharge. "Does anyone besides Jason require medical attention?"

Jason shook his head, a grin spread across his blotchy face. "I'm good to go, boss. Just feel like I stepped into a *Tom and Jerry* cartoon. Nice move with the pepper, Sally. Don't let that one get around or everyone will be trying it on me."

Sally shrugged. "It's not easy to take on a brick when you're as fragile as everyone else."

"Much less two of them," said Juice. "If everyone's all right, we'll move on to the next Round Robin. Jack, you're up."

Jack was fearless in his turn as the Robin. Of course, mused Sally, it helped that he was completely invulnerable. He took on the fliers first with surprise, grappling hook, and rope. Like Sally, he was halted by Forcestar, but not before he'd laid out Glimmer, Sondra, and Doublecharge.

Glimmer took his turn as the Robin and brought down both bricks with his telekinetics. He put Sally to sleep with a sneaky telepathic attack. When the drill was over, she discovered he'd managed to also nab Forcestar before exhausting himself. The curse of his psionic abilities was too much use fatigued him.

Forcestar rounded up virtually the entire team in short order, clearly determined to improve on his time after Sally did it so quickly. His tactics were simple—he surrounded his victims in bubbles of force and kept them held aloft in the glowing blue spheres of energy. He saved Doublecharge for last, as her electrical powers could disrupt his force fields, and closed with her to fight hand-to-hand over the street. She fought him off and caught him inside his guard with a point-blank electrical blast. He spun away and cursed aloud as the monitor declared him incapacitated. He grumbled as he released the others from his force bubbles, left with a zero for a score.

Jason seemed to delight in going toe to toe with Juice and Jack. The former was physically stronger but not as quick. Juice's strength drained rapidly when he fought and the younger, faster man eventually overpowered him. Jack cheerfully taunted Jason and soaked up everything the young man had. Eventually Jason picked him up bodily and wrapped a light pole around the man. He didn't get any further than that as Glimmer zapped him to sleep. He grumbled when they woke him and asked if maybe Glimmer could do that little trick again so he could catch up on the missed sleep from the night before.

Sondra used straightforward tactics—telescopic vision in conjunction with her highly polished pistol skills took out Doublecharge, Glimmer, and Forcestar. She incapacitated Juice and Mastiff by well-placed shots that struck eyes; even bricks could be temporarily blinded by impacts to the face. She fired a few experimental shots in Sally's direction but to no avail. Her talents were likewise wasted against Jack, but she used another, sneakier tactic against him that had him crying foul for hours afterward. As she glided toward him, she holstered her pistols and yanked the front of her vest down to spill out a breast with a star-shaped pastie over the nipple. Jack dropped his rifle in surprise just before Sondra landed in front of him and wrapped him up in a feathery kiss. When she pulled away, she left one of his own tangler grenades stuffed down his pants. It went off and wrapped him in sticky tendrils that required multiple passes of the nanobot cleaner to remove.

"She cheated!" Jack said, pouting.

"Wardrobe malfunction," said Sondra.

Juice laughed so hard he had to call a ten-minute break to compose himself.

Doublecharge took down most of the team in a cool, professional manner. She started with Forcestar and worked her way through the others until only Juice and Sally remained. Eventually they called a stalemate because she couldn't hit Sally, and all her blasts did was feed Juice's strength. In the field, that was actually a planned tactic.

Finally, Juice took his turn. He used the environment to great advantage. Well-flung awnings caught Doublecharge and Sondra in mid-flight. He hung Jack from a flagpole by his belt. The monitor system declared Glimmer unconscious after a stop sign clipped him in the head. To her own surprise, Sally bit on a skillful feint on Juice's part and she dodged at high speed right into a fist the size of an Easter ham. Unlike when Glimmer knocked her out, there was nothing gentle about it.

She awoke on a bed in the medical wing with her ears ringing and persistent blurriness of vision. The rest of the team waited in the room with her while the medical techs checked her over. They diagnosed her with a mild concussion.

"I'm very sorry, Sally," said Juice. "Honestly, I didn't expect that feint to work so well. You're excused for the rest of the day."

"No," she said through lips that didn't seem to work quite right. "Wanna c'ntinue."

"Sweetheart . . ." Jack sat down at the foot of her bed. "I've seen people take hits like that and never get back up again. We'd rather you not die in your first week on the team. Or at all, of course." He raised a remote control toward a monitor screen overhead. "You've got to see this, though. This is better than any highlight reel on ESPN."

"Right now?" Jason asked, and Sally realized her hand was in his, which felt kind of nice.

Doublecharge nodded. "She'll never fall for that trick again if she sees how it happened."

Jack pushed the button and Sally saw a slow-motion replay of her contact with Juice. He had just hurled a stop sign at her, which she had dodged easily. She then ducked under his spinning kick and rammed her forehead right into his left hand, which clearly had been his intention. She winced as she watched the replay. Her feet continued forward and her entire body flipped up into the air to pivot around her head. She smashed into the ground like a rag doll but bounced up a heartbeat later.

"Pause it," said Doublecharge. Jack complied. "Look at her. Look at her eyes. She's not conscious at all, but she's still preparing to run. If Juice hadn't caught her right after, who knows how far she'd have run in reflex, and how hard it would have been to catch her."

"I've never seen that happen in anyone," said Juice. "It's like your super-speed is controlled at a fundamental level of your brain, like respiration and heartbeat."

"Like sleepwalking," said Glimmer. "You ever do that?"

Unpleasant memories surfaced in Sally's mind. "Uh, once or twice, I guess."

"How far did you get out of the house?" Jack asked.

"Tucson," Sally said.

"All right," said the medical technician. "Enough. She needs some peace and quiet. You can question her tonight if we've cleared her to leave by then."

Juice motioned to the others. "All right, guys, you heard the doc. Out. Jason, you can stick around until afternoon training if you want to and Sally says it's okay."

Sally smiled, causing her whole face to hurt, and closed her eyes. "It's okay." She felt Jason's hand around hers and hoped it would still be there when she awoke.

Chapter Twelve

"You are not here merely to make a living. You are here in order to enable the world to live more amply, with greater vision, with a finer spirit of hope and achievement. You are here to enrich the world, and you impoverish yourself if you forget the errand."

-Woodrow T. Wilson, 28th President of the United States

January, 2004
Denver, Colorado
Just Cause Headquarters

"Do you feel any pain?" The doctor worked Sally's head to one side and the other with gentle motions.

"No." The truth was that her whole body felt like a truck had hit her. At least a more generalized body ache had replaced the acute head pain, but she didn't want the doctor to know that. She tended to heal from injuries at a rapid rate thanks to her parahuman abilities, so if she was still exhibiting symptoms, she must have really gotten her bell rung.

"Hmmm," said the doctor the way doctors do when they know someone is lying to them. He took a penlight and shined it into her eyes.

Two days spent anywhere with little to no activity for a speedster ought to count as cruel and unusual punishment in most jurisdictions. At least Jason had spent most of the first day with her. They played Uno and he brought in his iPod so she could hear some tracks from his band's CD. The next day he had monitor duty and couldn't come see her. Juice and Sondra had stopped in to check on her. The wait for medical clearance was stretching out into hours of interminable boredom. Channel-surfing was bad enough when she had the attention span of a goldfish, but when it was all she was permitted to do, it nearly drove her crazy.

"Well," said the doctor at last, "I'm going to release you. But . . ." He held up a warning finger and glared at her over his bifocals. "Light duty for a week. No training sessions or deployment before I check you over again next week. And keep the super-sprinting to a minimum. Concussions are funny and we still don't know how they'll affect parahuman abilities."

"Thanks, Doc!" Sally grinned and gathered up her things, eager to be released from medical jail.

"One week," he said. "Light duty until then."

"Yes, sir."

Sally skipped out of Medical. She felt like she could fly as she scampered up to her room. She was so lost in her happy feelings she nearly bowled over Harris as he came out of the elevator.

"Oh, hey, there you are." He picked up the boxes he had dropped in their near-collision. "I just heard from the Doc that he cut you loose and I figured you'd wanna see this."

"What is it?"

"Your new costume—redesigned to official Just Cause specs." He opened the first box with a flourish and showed off a pair of shiny yellow boots.

"Ooooh!" Sally reached out to touch the smooth polymer with such low friction coefficient that it felt greasy. She started to peek into the other box, but then paused and glanced at Harris. "This is really for me? You're just giving it to me?"

"Yep, that's right," he said. "Tell you what . . . you go and try it on real quick and then I'll come in and you can give me any notes about problems you need to have resolved. I'll take them back to the Costumes department and let them wrangle 'em for you. We can't have you running around in a substandard outfit when you're out and about town at your charity functions."

"Charity functions?" Even with her advanced perceptions, Sally found it tough to keep up with Harris' sudden subject changes.

He raised an eyebrow. "Didn't anybody tell you? Well, part of your job with Just Cause is to keep up a good relationship with the public. And the way we do that is by associating ourselves with various charitable foundations. You'll need to pick a couple and spend some time volunteering with them. Keeps us looking good in the public eye, and these days that's critical, since many government stooges don't like parahumans too much. Wouldn't take too much negative publicity for 'em to re-enact the PRA all over again."

"The Parahuman Registration Act," said Sally, nodding. After his retirement, her grandfather had devoted much of his time to his fight against the laws enacted in the paranoid Fifties that had kept parahumans from enjoying the same rights as other citizens.

"So anyway, get yourself dressed up and let me know if there are any problems. I'll wait here for you. I figure you probably don't take more than a minute to get dressed. Unlike my wife. I tell ya, that woman can spend an entire day just futzing with her hair." Harris laughed.

Sally took the packages and went into her room. She opened the boxes, spread out the costume on her bed and looked at it in wonder. The costumiers had duplicated the look of her old costume but had still managed to make this new model look fresher and more contemporary. It was shinier and smoother. Like the boots, the body suit had a slick feel to it. It was thicker than her old suit, but not noticeably heavier. The extra thickness came from two new layers: an interior liner to provide insulation from heat and wick away moisture from her skin, and an unusual material that Sally figured could only be some sort of flexible body armor. The new suit was easier to get into and out of, which would make the inevitable bathroom break much less of a major operation.

The boots had soft cushiony interiors that were so comfortable she considered violating the doctor's orders and go sprint for a while. Unlike her old boots, these were adjustable along both the shin and calf. The soles were thicker too, which added an inch to her height and made her feel like she would tower over everyone. Well, she'd tower over anyone under five feet tall, she thought.

The new goggles and breather mask fit her face without feeling as if the edges were biting into her skin. More importantly, they were less clunky than her originals, making her head much more streamlined than before. She could only barely feel the throat microphone and knew she'd quickly forget it was even there.

She examined herself in the bathroom mirror for a few minutes before she remembered Harris waited outside for her. She went to her door and opened it.

"Oh, hey." He looked up from his tablet PC. "Any problems with the new threads?"

"No," Sally said. "They're really great. Is it armored?"

"Yep. Artificial spider silk. It has better tensile strength than steel. Our techs developed it using nanotech from the Bunker. Pretty cool, huh?"

"I've never even heard of such a thing."

"Well, it's kind of our own little secret," said Harris. "Lawmakers get all funny about nanotechnology. They think it's a stepping stone to super-soldier programs and tailored viruses and stuff. Of course, that wouldn't stop 'em from co-opting the technology for strict military use."

"Wouldn't soldiers like to have armor like this? It feels like I'm wearing hardly anything."

"I dunno. I'm just a glorified quartermaster here. I figure the fewer people who know about the armor, the better. Look at it like this . . . as soon as somebody knows you've got better armor, they figure out a way to shoot through it. You're in Just Cause, you already got a target on you. Better if they're shootin' at you with popguns and peashooters, know what I mean?"

"Oh, I guess I never thought about it like that."

"Anyway, you got any issues you need me to take back to the Costume shop?"

"No, I guess not. Can I let you know after I've taken it out for a test drive?"

"Sure thing." Harris beamed. "But I know you're on light duty, so I'll check with you after the doc clears you."

"Sounds good."

Sally went to visit Jason in the Command Center. She strutted through the halls like a preening supermodel. She couldn't help it; she felt sexy and powerful, like a superhero ought to. She strolled into the Command Center and watched from behind her goggles as every head turned to look at her. Some women glared with open hatred at her slender body. Some men turned away but watched her nevertheless out of the corners of their eyes. It almost made her giggle.

Jason's mouth hung open as she walked up to him. "I got my new costume," she said, and twirled around once in front of him with an audacity that surprised her. "What do you think?"

"Wow," he said. "It's . . . wow. You look great." Jason's cheeks turned red.

"That's sweet." She pushed her goggles up onto her forehead and pulled the breather mask down to dangle at her throat. "I don't get to break it in for a week though. Doctor's orders."

"Oh. That sucks."

She stepped around behind him to peek over his massive shoulder at the monitor before him. "What are you doing?"

"Nothing much," he said. "Working on my band's website. It's slow going. I'm no code monkey."

"Can I see?"

"Sure." He opened a new window, clicked on the link, and showed off the Velma's Glasses site to her. He pointed out the features, demo tracks, and some pictures of the three members as they goofed off with each other or rocked out onstage.

"What time are you off?" she asked.

"Six. Then I'm spending a couple of hours down at the Foundation. I'm free after that."

"Foundation?"

"The Devereaux Foundation. It's a center for underprivileged children that Just Cause sponsors. I go down there a couple times a week and hang around with the kids."

Sally raised her eyebrows in surprise. "You do?"

He shrugged. "I've got two brothers and about twenty cousins, all younger than me,. They grow families big down south where I'm from. I don't ever remember a time when I wasn't surrounded by kids."

"I bet the kids just love you," said Sally. "You're like a great big huggy bear."

"Sometimes," he said. "But I just like going down there. I think I'd want to keep working with kids after I retire." Jason grinned.

"Retire?"

"Sure. We can't do this forever, you know. Everybody leaves the life one way or another. Look at all the staffers at the Academy. They're mostly retired heroes."

"I guess I never really thought about it."

"So did you want to do something after I get back?"

"Sure," said Sally. "Only . . ."

"What?"

"Harris said I need to get involved with some charities and stuff. Could I come to the Foundation with you and check it out?"

Jason's face split in a wide grin. "I'd like that."

"Do I need to bring anything?"

"Only your smile. Oh, and a coat. It's going to be pretty cold by tonight."

"I can do that. Should I wear my costume?"

"Definitely. The kids'll love it."

"Then I'll see you at six, Jason."

"That's a date."

"Yes," Sally said. "It is." She tried to force her heart to stop pounding with incipient terror.

The Control Center techs grinned at one another as she walked out of the room. She could feel Jason's eyes following her all the way to the door.

Her sense of invulnerability lasted long enough for her to stop by the cafeteria and get a bowl of chicken tortilla soup. She didn't feel like being around people, so she carried it back to her room and ate it in silence in front of her terminal reading news reports. Suddenly she set down her spoon, leaned back, and stared up at the ceiling.

"What the heck are you doing?" she asked herself aloud. "You don't know anything about kids."

For the next forty-five minutes she tried to think of a way she could gracefully bow out from going to the Foundation. She'd survived three years of the toughest tests the Hero Academy could throw at her; she'd faced Destroyer and not flinched; but to volunteer to surround herself with hundreds or thousands of screaming kids, with their runny noses and grabby hands and grubby faces, made her shake in real terror.

She was about to go ask Sondra to break one of her legs when she heard Jason's knuckles rap on her door. Her knees turned to water and she wondered if she could maybe give herself a convenient heart attack. Or

137

develop a sudden virulent case of bronchitis. She tried to cough. Nothing.

Then, from outside, Jason's soft tenor with its Southern twang: "Sally, are you in there?"

All her resistance melted away at the thought of getting to spend a little more time with him. He'd protect her from the hordes of screaming toddlers. She found her voice. "Just a minute . . . finding my overcoat." She swept it off the back of her chair and slipped into it. Her low-friction bodysuit slid easily into the lining like a second skin. She took a deep breath and opened the door.

Jason smelled good. He must have just showered and shaved; his normal chin stubble was missing. He wore a long dark trenchcoat, which must have been the size of a tent to provide enough space for his massive shoulders. His gray and brown costume gleamed underneath it in the warm hall lighting. "Ready to go?"

Sally slipped her arm around his. "As much as I'll ever be. Those kids . . . do they bite?"

"Only if they don't like you. Be brave, for they can sense fear and ticklishness."

Sally poked him. "I'm not ticklish."

"Everyone says that."

"I'm not!"

"Of course you aren't."

Jason led her out to where he'd parked the Bronco. The air was cold and had a damp chill that froze Sally to her bones. She squealed as she shivered in the passenger seat. "People shouldn't live where it gets this cold!"

"Heater's on. We ought to warm up pretty soon." Jason backed out of the spot and headed for the headquarters exit to the city streets, unmindful of the occasional patch of snow or ice on the road. Sally's teeth chattered and she tried not to flinch as the truck rolled down the road; she expected it to skid out of control and flip at any moment.

Jason drove through town for about twenty minutes before he pulled into a parking lot next to a well-lit building painted in cheerful colors with tasteful neon lighting that spelled out *Devereaux Foundation.* A small cluster of people stood under a streetlight near the door and smoked while they conversed. One of them noticed Jason and Sally and called to them with a loud *yoo-hoooo!*

"Crap," muttered Jason.

"Who is it?" Sally whispered as the woman in the raspberry-colored overcoat and white hat and scarf hurried toward them.

"Theresa Lupe. Society reporter. Leech."

"She's the press? What does she want with you?"

"Not just me. Us. Just Cause. She's always trying to dig up something on us."

"Mastiff darling! So wonderful that you came out here tonight." The woman clutched a small handheld recorder like it was a rosary.

"Hello, Ms. Lupe," said Jason.

"And this must be Mustang Sally, Just Cause's newest member. Are you two an item? Have you already made your move on the parahuman community's most eligible young bachelor?"

Sally blushed and wished she'd had the foresight to have her breather mask and goggles on. She had never considered the implication that being in Just Cause would make her a *celebrity*, with all the public interest that went along with such a moniker.

"We're just here to play with the kids, Ms. Lupe." Jason steered Sally away from the reporter with the buzzard's gaze. "Perhaps you'd urge your readers to make a donation to the Foundation."

"Give me an exclusive interview with the two of you and I'll consider it."

"No thanks. Have a nice evening, Ms. Lupe." Jason opened the door and gave Sally a gentle but firm shove inside ahead of him.

"You two make a lovely couple," called the cackling reporter after them.

"I can't stand that woman, but Juice made it clear we have to be polite to her. A lot of people read her column. She could do a lot of damage to our reputation if she tried."

"Why would she want to do that?"

Jason blushed. "Because she's a vindictive bitch."

Sally burst out in laughter as they walked through the foyer and stripped off their coats. Jason pushed open the door into what he called the *romper room* and he and Sally went inside.

Sally saw fifteen to twenty kids as they played games in the room, roughhoused, chased each other, and climbed all over an indoor playground. Cries of "Jason!" and "Mastiff!" echoed around the room and the kids charged over like little bundles of boundless energy. Sally locked a smile on her face and hoped it didn't look like a rictus of death.

"Everyone, this is Mustang Sally. She's new on the team and came out to hang with you all tonight," said Jason to the excited children.

"Hi, Mustang Sally!" several of them chorused. Sally thought they sounded like a juvenile Alcoholics Anonymous meeting.

"Da-a-a-amn," called two young boys who couldn't have been more than eight or nine years old and looked so much alike they had to be twins. One had an afro so large it made his head twice as large as normal while the other sported short dreadlocks. Their clothes looked worn, like hand-me-downs, but clean.

"Sally, these are the Kingston brothers. The one who looks like he stuck his finger in a socket is D'Angelo. And his brother is Jamal."

"You better hang with us," said D'Angelo. "A lot of these older kids'll be mackin' on you because you're lookin' so fine."

"Yeah," said Jamal.

"Jason? Help?" Sally hoped the tone of her voice would convey to him her discomfort.

"You'll be fine." Jason's voice was muffled by the ten children who climbed all over him. "Just don't let them sell you anything."

"Hey, you can't blame a li'l brother for tryin' to make a buck," called D'Angelo.

"Yeah," said Jamal right on cue.

"You're a superhero, so show us somethin'," said D'Angelo. "What's your power?"

"I'm a speedster. That means I can run really fast."

"That ain't a real power. Anyone can run."

"Yeah."

Sally cracked a wry grin at the two young skeptics. "Not like me." And before he could yelp in surprise, she swept up D'Angelo in her arms and made a couple quick circuits of the room—not so fast that her doctor would have a reason to complain but certainly fast enough to make D'Angelo's hair blow around like a thistle puff. She skidded to a stop and set him down. He staggered a couple steps and sat down.

"Whoa!" He gasped for air.

"Word," Jamal said, moved to great expressiveness by Sally's display.

Suddenly she was surrounded by all the children who'd been dog-piling on Jason a moment before, all clamoring for a ride.

Sally felt like she had a spotlight on her. "What do I do?" she asked Jason, who seemed a little taken aback at suddenly being relegated to second banana.

"You started it," he said. "How about making a run around the room the prize for a game?"

"We could do that. What game?"

"*Red Light, Green Light!*" shouted several of the kids.

Soon Sally found herself in the middle of a game of Red Light, Green Light as serious and intense as any training session she'd had at the Hero Academy. After a few minutes, she realized she really enjoyed playing with the kids.

She'd never gotten to just be one herself.

They all played several rounds of the game with different winners each time. Sally carried each victorious child piggyback around the room a couple times at speed. Parents began to come by to collect their children, who zoomed around pretending they were Mustang Sally, much to her amusement.

D'Angelo and Jamal were the last ones to leave, picked up by their mother who smiled warmly at Sally and Jason and threatened to beat the boys with a skillet if they didn't stop runnin' around like damn wild monkeys.

"She don't really beat us," D'Angelo confided in Sally as he left. "We're too pimpin' for that."

"Yeah," said Jamal. "Ow!" He yelped as his mother grabbed him and his brother by their ears and led them out of the playroom.

"Think that'll do it, Cerise?" Jason asked the Foundation employee who had kept track of the kids and signed them out to their parents.

"Yes, we're going to go ahead and close up for the night. Thank you so much for coming out tonight. The kids always love it when you drop in. And it was a real pleasure to meet you too, Sally."

"I had fun," said Sally. "I'll be back again. I promise."

She and Jason walked outside into the chill night air hand in hand. "So what'd you think?" he asked.

"It was fun," she said. "A lot more than I was expecting. Thanks for bringing me here."

"My pleasure." Jason grinned. "So it's still pretty early. Do you want to go get something to eat? I could go for a few burgers. Playing is hungry work."

Sally's stomach rumbled. "Yes, please," she said. "On one condition."

"Name it."

"Can we go somewhere quiet? My ears are still ringing." She stuck a finger in one of them.

Jason's laugh made her feel warm enough that the cold air wasn't quite as bad as before.

Chapter Thirteen

"Know thy self, know thy enemy.
A thousand battles, a thousand victories."

-Sun Tzu

January, 2004
Denver, Colorado
Just Cause Headquarters

Jason squeezed the Blazer through a narrow drive-through and bought a half-dozen burgers for himself and one with a side of fries for Sally. She noticed he asked them to hold the onions so she did the same, just in case. "What do you want to do?" he asked her.

"I don't know," she said. "We could just drive around for awhile. Listen to music. Talk."

"Sounds good to me. Unwrap this for me, will you?" He held out a burger to her.

They wandered along the streets, as Jason stuffed his face. He did take smaller than normal bites and attempted to chew quietly in a real effort to be polite. Sally thought it was very dear of him to do so.

Sporadic fog began to appear in the darkness. Jason flipped a switch on his dash and powerful lights mounted underneath the Blazer's bumper illuminated the road despite the growing mist. Sally saw something that pegged her interest off to the right. "Hey, slow down. What is that?"

Jason braked and stared into the darkness. "Looks

like a park. There's a lake. See all the fog rolling off it?"

"Can we park there?"

He steered into the gravel lot and swung the Blazer around to face the water. "Ask and you shall receive."

"Turn off the engine," said Sally.

"It'll get cold pretty quickly," said Jason. "Not much insulation in these old trucks. But I've got a blanket back there somewhere. I use it to protect my amps."

"Good enough." Sally scrambled over the back of the seat and began to rummage around through the stuff in the back. "Look at this mess! Don't you ever clean out your truck?" She held up for emphasis what had once been a soda can, crushed into a golf-ball-sized spheroid.

Jason laughed and blushed. "I don't ever have anybody else in here with me. Seriously, the other guys in the band don't even ride with me. Hey, can I have a fry?" He reached over, took one of Sally's fries, and popped it into his mouth.

"Oh, it's on now," yelled Sally, and jumped back into the front seat. "Nobody takes my fries, mister!"

Jason took another one.

Sally giggled and grabbed the small carton with her super-speed. She kept it away from Jason's big mitts with ease.

He reached out and poked her in her ribs as he laughed like a hyena. She shrieked, doubled over, and kicked at him.

"You said you weren't ticklish." He laughed as he tried to get her again.

"You cheater!" she gasped.

He grinned and ate another fry. She realized while tickling her he'd taken the carton away. "Mmm, good," he said around a mouthful of processed deep fried potato.

She reached for them, but he held them up out of her reach. Not to be deterred, she scrambled right into his lap, straddled him, and fished the remaining fries out of the carton to leave him holding the empty container. She sat there for a heartbeat and her whole body tingled in a pleasant way as she looked down at him. He returned her gaze, locking eyes with her. Their battle for the fries forgotten, Sally took his head in her free hand and kissed him slow and tender, like in a movie. He tasted a little like french fries and faintly of burger, but mostly he tasted like himself.

His arms encircled her and pressed her to him. She felt a thrill course through her as he nuzzled the spot where her neck met her shoulder. "Mmm," she breathed. "That's nice."

"Glad you like it." He brushed his fingers across her cheek, making her skin feel warm and prickly.

"Have you been with lots of girls?" she asked. "You know, big celebrity, rock star, you must have quite a stable." She stroked his hair.

He raised an eyebrow. "You brought me all the way out here to talk about that?"

Sally kissed him on the tip of his nose. "It doesn't bother me. I was just curious."

"No, I haven't. I don't have that kind of free time. Just one. Back in the Academy."

"Really?"

"Really. It's been a long dry spell."

"You certainly seem to know what you're doing." Sally nibbled on his ear and made him jump beneath her.

"I'm making it up as I go along." He kissed her again. The fries tumbled from her hand to lodge between the seat and the door. She didn't care. She wanted her hands free to caress him.

Jason's interest in her, the desire she could feel in his lips, his hands, and his lap, made her feel invincible. He wanted her, she was the object of his affection, and it felt so good she could barely stand it. The steering wheel jabbed into her back as she shifted her position a bit. She could do something about that, though. She pulled away from Jason's mouth, although loathe to do so, and fumbled around the side of his seat.

"What'sa matter?" he asked, his voice hoarse.

She found the release handle and yanked on it, which caused Jason to fall backward. She slid from sitting on his legs to his hips, a position she found much more comfortable and intimate. She leaned over and kissed him again. She enjoyed the feel of him beneath her. His arms slid up inside her coat to caress her back. The cold outside forgotten, she flung away the coat. She wanted to feel him, his hands on her skin.

A tiny voice in the back of her mind asked her what she thought she was doing. It sounded like her mother, but she didn't listen. The sound of her heart beating drowned it out. She sat up and looked down at Jason, who gazed back up at her with wonder in his eyes as she undid the Velcro tabs and hidden latches along her costume's front.

Jason's eyes widened and she felt him grow harder beneath her as he took in the sight of her small but firm breasts. Her tiny nipples stood out hard like pebbles. He reached out to touch them, but stopped; his hands hovering in uncertainty. Sally took his massive wrists in her slender fingers. "No, I want you to," she breathed, and guided his hands to her skin. The sensation made her head spin and sent little electric shocks running up and down her as if Doublecharge had fired tiny lightning bolts at her from afar.

"You're beautiful," whispered Jason.

"So are you." And in that moment, Sally knew he would be her first. The thought warmed her in the cold air inside the truck and she reached up to let her hair down.

A light shined into the driver's side window, diffused by the frost all over it, and somebody knocked on the door.

Sally yipped in surprise. In a flash, she closed her

top, slithered back into her coat, and sat primly in the passenger seat as Jason sat his side of the seat back up and tried to get himself back onto an even keel. As casually as possible, he rolled the window down to reveal an earnest young police officer, dressed in her heavy coat to ward off the night's chill.

"All right, you two lovebirds, hit the road. This park closes at eight." She squinted into the truck's interior. "Do I know you?" she asked Jason.

"I'm Mastiff, uh, ma'am. From Just Cause. And this is Mustang Sally," stammered Jason.

"Hi!" Sally winced at the saccharine brightness in her own voice.

"We're, uh, we're working on a case?" Jason asked as if trying it out.

"Yeah, sure. I wasn't born yesterday. I used to come out here and make out too. But it's late, and it's cold, and you're supposed to be setting some kind of example, so what say you call it a night and head back to the clubhouse, huh?"

"Yes, ma'am. Right away." Jason fumbled with the keys in the starter.

"Behave, you two, and have a good evening," said the officer.

Jason backed the Blazer out of the parking spot and pulled onto the road rather faster than might have been advisable, given the police officer was still watching.

"Oh my God, I'm so embarrassed." Sally buried her face in her hands.

"Yeah, me too."

They drove in silence for a few minutes. Then Jason snorted. "I wasn't born yesterday."

Sally snorted; she'd thought the same thing. "Let's hurry back to the clubhouse."

That got them both laughing. Soon both had to wipe their eyes from tears of amusement. By the time they parked in the Just Cause garage, their laughter had subsided somewhat.

"Do you want to come over?" Jason asked. Sally could hear the longing in his voice. It matched a similar longing she felt deep within her, but somehow the magic of the earlier moment had passed. She wasn't worried; she knew there would be another moment, and it would be soon.

"No, not tonight," she said. "But you can walk me home, okay, cowboy?"

He smiled and tipped back an imaginary cowboy hat. "It'd shore be mah pleasure, ma'am." He held out his arm and she took it with glee. Arm in arm they walked through the halls of Just Cause until they stood outside Sally's door.

"Overly curious cops notwithstanding, I had a really good time tonight, Jason." Sally gazed up into his eyes, so far above her own.

"Me too. I only wish . . ." He didn't finish the thought, but Sally knew what he would have said.

"So do I," she whispered. "We'll have another chance." She winked at him. "Soon, if I have anything to say about it."

He bent down and kissed her. The touch made her tingle all over once more. "I'll see you tomorrow, Sally."

"Thanks, Jason. I had a lot of fun tonight. Good night." Sally went into her room and shut the door. Her heart raced as if she'd been doing four-hundred mile-per-hour wind sprints. She almost talked herself into going to his room anyway, but headquarters didn't feel private enough. It was like somebody having sex in his or her office at work. She'd have to see about working around that feeling, though, because she was desperate to feel Jason's hands on her, his bare skin against hers. Maybe she should check around for skeevy motels, she thought in amusement. Or nice ones, she added after a moment's consideration. He drew a decent salary as a federal employee. She was still unpaid as an intern, but she had some money saved up from birthdays and such. No reason to shortchange herself.

She was falling for him, this giant of a boy with the gentle demeanor of his namesake. She could sense his loyalty to her, and felt he would stay with her for a long while. It felt comfortable to be wanted, to be desired. She wondered if he felt the same way. She knew she could ask him and he'd tell her. He'd been so forthright and upfront with her she almost didn't know how to deal with it. She'd been brought up to expect men to be creatures of difficulty, impossible to please or understand, and that she'd have to use her feminine wiles to get what she wanted. The idea of just getting to be herself with him and him being okay with it made her feel like the luckiest girl in the world.

She stripped out of her costume and cranked up the heat in her room to luxuriate in the warm air as it blew gently across her skin. She didn't want to dress yet. She felt sexy in her nakedness. Instead, she sat down at her workstation with a half-formed idea about perhaps composing a naughty email to Jason. When she opened the *JCMail* program, though, she found a message waited for her with such an intriguing subject line and sender's address that she decided Jason would have to wait.

The message was from an Intelligence Analyst of the CIA, with a subject of *Your intelligence request #20040112-1825-003*, with an attached archive file. She'd asked the CIA—something she still couldn't believe she had the ability to do—to try to identify the mysterious blond man with Harlan Washington in the pictures from Guatemala.

She slid her card through the workstation reader to unlock the file and began to scroll through it.

The analyst gave a high probability the man's name was Heinrich Kaiser. He was a naturalized Guatemalan citizen who had lived in the country for an indeterminate amount of time. Records were available that showed someone with his name lived in the town of San José that dated back to the 1940s. The analyst theorized that the man might actually be the son of the original Heinrich Kaiser, and included a grainy photo of the senior Kaiser as evidence. Sally looked at them side by side and she could see a definite resemblance.

Kaiser Junior was a wealthy businessman involved in construction and imports. He was heavily involved with the Guatemalan power infrastructure. His company built new substations and generating plants and laid transmission lines across the great mountain ranges that divided the country. He was a mover and shaker in the local economy, a real powerhouse, Sally thought, and smiled at the joke. No wonder Harlan Washington was meeting with this Kaiser; the man owned half of the docks, a couple of freighters, and numerous buildings throughout the small town of Puerto San José. With his ability to import nearly anything into the country undetected, and his sizable power base, Kaiser was the perfect accomplice for Destroyer.

The question that stumped Sally was why Washington would choose Guatemala at all. There was so little there to appeal to the engineering wizard. As resourceful as he was, Washington could have disappeared just as effectively within the United States, where he would have easier access to the high technology, tools, and materials he needed to build his battlesuits.

Well, that was a problem for analysts, she decided. She'd solved the mystery she of the blond man in the picture. She picked up her phone and paged Sondra.

"What's up, Sally?"

"Not much, I'm just hanging out tonight. I got an email back from the CIA on our mystery guest."

"The blond guy?"

"Yeah. They sent me a whole file on this guy. Want to see?"

"Sure. Want me to come to your room or do you want to come here or what? Ow, stop it!" Sondra sounded like she had to bite back giggles.

Sally blinked. "Stop what?"

"Oh, sorry, Sally. I wasn't talking to you."

"I see." Sally looked around her room. As usual, it was a minor disaster area. "Tell you what, give me about fifteen minutes and then I'll come by if we can use your terminal."

"Deal."

Sally took a shower and washed her hair, then wrapped herself up in her fleecy pajamas. She stepped into her fuzzy bunny slippers and robe. At last, she felt warm and cozy and dried her hair lackadaisically. She decided to leave it down instead of coiling it back up into her customary braids.

She slipped her ID card into her bathrobe pocket and left her room. As she walked up the hall toward Sondra's room, Jason came out of his door. He had changed into sweats, a tank top, and cross-trainers. Sally almost turned around and sprinted back to her room to hide from him, but instead took a deep breath and made herself smile. It was one thing for him to see her all dressed up in her costume, or even partway out of it, but she was in her robe and pajamas! Her hair hung halfway down her back, a little wavy from the constant braiding, but frizzy from constant windburn. She figured she must look pretty awful.

"Hey, Sally. I was just going to the gym."

"Oh. I'm, uh, going to go over some Destroyer stuff with Sondra."

"Cool. See you tomorrow." He started down the hall.

"Jason?"

He turned. Sally jumped up into his arms—she had to leap to reach his face as it was a good eighteen inches over hers—and kissed him full on the mouth. "Thank you for tonight," she whispered in his ear.

"You're welcome." He set her down as if she were made of glass.

She wanted to say something more, something which would make him think only of her until the next time they got together somewhere private, but words failed her.

"Enjoy the rest of your evening, Mustang Sally," said Jason with that smile which made Sally want to knock him on the head like a cavewoman and drag him back to her room. He whistled a Velma's Glasses tune as he headed on down the hallway. Sally watched him go. When he reached the end of the hallway, he glanced back over his shoulder and saw her looking at him. He winked and then continued on his way.

She turned and knocked on Sondra's door.

"Come in," called Sondra from inside.

Sally opened the door and nearly bumped into Jack. "Hey, darlin'," he said. "Don't mind me, I was just leaving. Girl talk makes me all oogie."

Sondra threw a pillow from her couch at him.

He laughed and handed it to Sally. "You girls behave yourselves." He shut the door as he left.

"Goodness," exclaimed Sondra. "Sally, are you ill?"

"N-no. Why?"

Sondra stepped over to her and laid a hand across Sally's forehead. "No fever," she said. "Do you know you're blushing so much you look sunburned?"

Sally could feel her face prickling. "Yeah." She let her hair fall forward.

"Oh, don't be silly. Do you want some ice cream and then we'll look at that file?"

Sally nodded. "I'm sorry. I just wasn't expecting to run across Jack here. I mean, I'm not even dressed."

Sondra laughed. "You don't have to be ashamed. We're all friends here. I'm the team's field medic. I've seen most everybody naked at some point."

"Even Jason?"

"No, so far he's managed to keep his clothes on around me. Poor boy embarrasses easily. You kids and your hangups." Sondra came back from her kitchenette with two pints. "I look at the two of you and all I can say is I'm glad I'm not a modern teenager. Chunky Monkey or Cherry Garcia?"

"Chunky Monkey, please. I never really thought of myself as a teenager. I mean, I'm out of school now. I'm here, right?"

"Sally, dear, you're young." Sondra chuckled.

"You don't look very—"

"Watch it." Sondra raised a finger in warning. "I'm not that old. Although . . ." She sighed. "I do find the occasional gray hair amid all this luscious black." She shook out her head for emphasis.

"You've got beautiful hair," said Sally.

"So do you, but you need a different conditioner. And you've got terrible split ends. You really need to trim them off. I could do it if you want. If you don't mind losing a couple inches, that is."

Sally shrugged. "It comes from all the running. Wind damage." She pulled a plait around to look at it and clucked her tongue at the ends. Sondra was right. "Yeah, I guess you can trim it. *Trim,*" she said with heavy emphasis. "Not *cut.*"

Sondra set down her pint and picked up a hairbrush from the end table. "Here," she said. "You sit at the terminal and get that file open and I'll take care of your hair."

Sally found it hard to even get started on the file because having Sondra brush her hair felt so good. Her mother used to brush her hair when she was younger, before she'd left for the Hero Academy. It was something they'd done to bond. Sally would have returned the favor, but her mother always kept her hair practical and short. As she sat and Sondra's strong fingers worked patiently through the tangles, she realized she really did miss her mom a lot. Maybe she'd see if she could head home for a visit.

"Okay, I'm going to *trim* it now. I promise, no more than two inches."

"You're sure?"

"Honey, I can plug a quarter at a hundred yards and give you twenty cents change. When I say two inches, I mean *two* inches."

Sally gritted her teeth. She hated haircuts and had since she was a toddler. She remembered screaming tantrums from those days until her mom had given up ever approaching Sally with a pair of scissors. "Do it."

Sondra snipped. "Done." She showed Sally what she'd cut. If it wasn't two inches, it was awfully close. "I'll finish brushing it out in just a minute." She paused in her brushing to eat a couple spoonfuls of ice cream

Sally opened the file and zoomed in on the first picture. "Sondra, meet Junior. Junior, Sondra."

Sondra raised her spoon in greeting. "It's a pleasure."

Sally continued skimming down the first page of the report. "Junior's real name is Heinrich Kaiser. He's the son of a German national and possible Nazi war criminal who immigrated to Guatemala sometime after World War II."

"That's him all right." Sondra looked at the picture with her odd, bird-like eyes. "And why's he involved with Washington?"

"His specialties include construction, power infrastructure, imports, and buying off local government."

"I imagine that's not so tough in Guatemala," said Sondra. "Okay, so he's a local celebrity with his fingers in the kind of pies Destroyer likes. That's a good starting point. He can bring stuff into the country without nosy customs inspectors and provide Washington with a suitable power base for his work. The question is, what is Washington doing for him?"

"Paying him?" asked Sally.

Sondra shook her head. "Look at the money this guy is making through his legitimate business." She pointed to some figures on the screen. "He's not lacking in funds. Shoot, he might be the wealthiest man in the country, maybe all of Central America. You don't just pay someone like that. You give him something he wants."

"He's rich and powerful. What does he want that he can't get himself?"

"More power. His own battlesuit. I don't know. Harlan Washington is a very intelligent and resourceful man. Who knows what he's put on the table?"

"I'd like to know."

"So would I." Sondra fluttered her wings and a few pinfeathers dropped onto the table. "Hey, is that supposed to be Kaiser Senior?" Sally looked up. They were on the page that showed Kaiser's father. Sondra didn't seem to have trouble reading the small print on the screen even though she stood well back.

"Yes."

"Sally, that's the same man. I'm sure of it."

Sally looked. They had similar facial features but the hair was all different. Oh, thought Sally as she looked down at her own hair trimmings on Sondra's coffee table. Haircuts change. But still, she couldn't tell from the quality of the old photo of the father, and she asked Sondra about it.

"I'm looking at ratios," said Sondra. "The size and placement of the eyes in relation to the rest of the face. The angle and width of the nose. The way the lips press together. I'm telling you, this is the same guy."

"But this picture is from . . ." Sally consulted the file. "1950. And he doesn't look a day older. That's more than fifty years. That means . . ."

"He's got to be a parahuman," said Sondra. "This just got a whole lot more interesting."

Sally smacked her forehead. "My grandma and granddad dealt with a German parahuman after the

IAN THOMAS HEALY

war. Grandpa wrote about it in his book. I remember."
She turned to look at Sondra. "I wonder if this is the
same guy."

Sondra raised an eyebrow. "How are your
grandparents these days?"

"My grandpa died when I was just a baby, but
Grandma Judy is just fine."

"Overdue for a visit from her favorite grand-
-daughter?"

"Yeah, I haven't been to see her since I went to the
Lucky Seven last summer."

"Then we should go talk to her." Sondra ate another
spoonful of ice cream.

"We can do that? I was hoping to maybe go home to
visit my mom sometime soon."

"Yes, we can. That's the great thing about being part
of a government law enforcement agency. We can go
anywhere as long as it's for an active investigation. We
just have to clear it with Juice."

"It'd be nice to go home," said Sally, full of wistful
thoughts of the warm winter temperatures in Phoenix.

"Then it's settled. We're going. Pack your bag."
Sondra grinned. "It's been too long since I felt warm
sunshine on my wings."

Chapter Fourteen

"I have the greatest respect for my grandfather and the American parahumans he recruited, for without their tireless efforts against the Axis powers, the world might have been a very different place for me to raise my own children."

-Dr. Grace Devereaux, *The Oprah Winfrey Show*, Feb. 21, 2002

January, 2004
Denver, Colorado
Just Cause Headquarters

"I'll only be gone a couple of days." Sally punctuated her promise with a kiss. She perched in Jason's lap in the lounge as they pretended to watch a bad science fiction movie on the big screen. "You know, visit my mom and my grandma, do a little shopping, warm up my toes." She wiggled them for emphasis, wrapped up in two pairs of thick socks. "It's not supposed to be this cold where people live."

Jason curled a hand around one of her feet. "Like five little ice cubes," he said. His hand was pleasant and warm, like the rest of him, so Sally jammed her other foot in between his thigh and the chair.

"You know what they say about cold feet?"

"That you need electric socks?" asked Jason.

"No, silly. Cold feet, warm heart."

"I thought that was hands."

"Cold feet, warm hands?"

"No . . . You're making fun of me."

"And they said you were only good at picking up heavy things."

"Who said that?"

"They."

"Ah. Them."

"Them too."

Jason covered her mouth with his. She opened up to him, reveled in his attentions. Gradually, she became aware of someone else in the room with them and she turned to see Sondra staring at the wall with feigned interest.

"I've got to go," said Sally.

"I know," said Jason. "I'll miss you."

"I know." She winked him. "Call me after your gig tonight."

"It'll be late. Probably after one."

"I don't mind." She kissed him on his nose and climbed out of his lap.

"Ready to go?" asked Sondra.

Sally nodded. "Let me just grab my bag. I won't be a moment." She'd packed upon waking that morning so that chore would be out of the way.

Juice waited in the hangar to see them off. Just Cause had a small civilian jet at its disposal, and Ace's backup pilot would fly them to Phoenix aboard it. "Have a good trip," said Juice. "Give my regards to your mother, Sally, and invite her to come visit us up here. It's been far too long since we've gotten together."

"I will, Juice. Thanks for letting me go."

He smiled. "I'm pleased that you've taken such an interest in this case. I hope you find out some useful information. Make sure you share anything you learn with us."

"Will do."

Sally and Sondra boarded the jet. It was well-appointed and comfortable inside, with plenty of room for Sondra to stretch out her wings instead of having to fold and sit on them like she had to do most times. Sally had a hard time sitting still in her seat and buckling up for takeoff. She was excited to return home. She wanted to show her mom the new costume, tell her about the Antimatter Woman in Wyoming, and . . . Well, she wasn't quite sure she was ready to discuss Jason with her mother.

"You and Jason make a cute couple," said Sondra as the jet taxied onto the runway and picked up speed. "It makes me remember what it was like when Jack and I first got together."

Sally chuckled. "I guess I've fallen pretty hard."

"He's a lovely boy. He's head over heels for you too."

Sally's heart fluttered. "Really?"

"Oh my, yes," said Sondra. "I can see it in his face when he talks to you."

They chatted throughout the ninety-minute flight. Sondra recounted some of her stories about growing up on a Reservation in New Mexico, and Sally told her best tales about the shenanigans her class perpetrated upon the Hero Academy.

As the jet traveled south and left the snow and cold behind, Sally peeled off successive layers of clothing until she was down to shorts, a t-shirt, and her tennis shoes. Sondra watched the striptease and laughed. "Ready for warm weather, are you?"

"Oh my God, Sondra, I checked the weather and it's supposed to be eighty degrees today. Eighty! I might never go back to Just Cause again."

"Except for a certain blond-haired boy."

Sally nodded. "Yeah, he's worth going back into the stupid arctic conditions for."

The pilot notified them they were on the final approach to Phoenix Sky Harbor. Sondra folded her wings, buckled in, and waited for the jet to land.

A few minutes later, the jet rolled to a stop on the tarmac and Sally skipped down the steps to let the warm sun caress her. Sondra unfurled her wings, leaped from the doorway, and circled for a few seconds before she touched down next to Sally.

"That feels good. Is your mom meeting us?"

Sally's phone beeped to announce an incoming text message. She flipped it open to look. "She's stuck in traffic. Do you want to go meet her?"

"Sure." Sondra slipped her arms through the straps of her backpack. She had to wear it unconventionally across her chest so it wouldn't interfere with her wings.

Sally keyed her mom's cell number into her phone. "Hi, Mom," she said when Faith answered. "We're here. Don't bother with the traffic, we'll come to you. Where are you?" She waited while her mom said. "Okay, just pull into that parking lot. We'll be there in a few minutes." She shut her phone and looked at Sondra. "I'm not supposed to run really fast yet. Doctor's orders."

"Don't worry about me. I can keep up." Sondra grinned and spread her wings.

Sally shouldered her own bag, glad she'd packed light, and ran off toward the airport exit. Sondra followed after her and flew low and fast so as not to be a hazard or distraction to civilian air traffic.

They were off airport grounds in about a minute, and only took a few more minutes of weaving through lunchtime rush hour traffic to find the parking lot where Sally's mom awaited them.

Faith Thompson was still fit even at nearly fifty. Her skin was a bit more weathered than her daughter's was, but they both sported the same shade of blonde hair. She drove a Cadillac convertible, and the weather was nice enough she had the top down. She'd pulled her hair back in a short ponytail with a bandana over it to keep the wind from blowing it loose. She removed her sunglasses as Sally and Sondra approached and waved, smiling.

A moment later, Sally hugged her mom as Sondra beamed at them both. "Look at you," said Faith.

"Carrying on the family tradition." She paused, sniffing. "Are you wearing sunscreen?"

Sally rolled her eyes. "Mom, it's winter. There's no sun back in Denver. It's above the Arctic Circle or something."

"Bull. I know what the weather's like out there. Now I won't have you ruining that gorgeous complexion of yours. There's a tube in the glove compartment."

"Do we have to do this right now?" asked Sally through gritted teeth.

"I'm sorry," said Faith. "You must be Desert Eagle."

"Sondra, please, and it's an honor to finally meet you, ma'am."

"Please call me Faith." Faith put her sunglasses back on. "Your wings are lovely."

"Thanks."

"Sally, why don't you hop in back and let Sondra sit up front here?"

"Oh, that's all right," said Sondra as she saw the look of disgust on Sally's face. "There's more room for me to spread out my wings in the back anyway."

Soon their bags were stowed in the Caddy's trunk and Faith pulled the car back into traffic. She snarled at other drivers and wove from lane to lane the way she always had. Sally had long ago learned to ignore her mother's driving habits for fear they might make her give up riding in cars for good.

"How's Grandma?" Sally asked in an effort to distract her mom before she triggered fatal road rage in somebody.

"She went to the doctor last week," said Faith. "You know she's been having some trouble walking?"

Sally recalled her grandmother's careful, deliberate footsteps. "Yes?"

"She's going to have to have both hips replaced."

"What?" Sally couldn't believe she'd heard right.

"Sally, her joints are coming apart. She's been in pain for years."

"Why didn't she ever say something?"

Faith shrugged. "She's a proud woman. She always was. I already had this out with her last week. She never said a word of complaint."

Sally shrank back in her seat. "I can't believe she'd do that."

"There's more," said Faith. "The doctor thinks it's a likely side effect of super-speed running. He wants to check me as well."

"Are you going to go?"

Faith's mouth tightened to a fine line. "I have to. I've been hurting too. I always thought it was just arthritis, just getting old."

"Mom . . ." Sally couldn't think of anything to say. Was this going to be her legacy as well?

Sondra leaned forward. "As I understand it, hip replacement is a pretty common procedure these days. Almost routine."

Faith nodded. "The doctor said he doesn't foresee any complications. She'll be in a wheelchair for awhile afterward and in physical therapy, but she's feisty and fit. She's a veteran. She'll be fine."

Sondra placed a solicitous hand on Sally's shoulder. "Nothing to worry about, Sally."

"You're staying the night?" asked Faith. "Or are you rushing back up to Denver when you're done *Mom*-ing me?"

"We could stay, I guess," said Sally. "Unless we're called back or something."

"You're both welcome to stay with me. Goodness knows I have the room. The house has felt a lot bigger to me recently." Faith looked over at Sally. "I've missed you, Sally."

Sally blushed. It was weird being nice and pleasant to her mom after so many years of butting heads with the woman. But in the end, honesty won out. "I've missed you too."

The rest of the drive passed without incident. Sally noticed people raising their camera phones to snap pictures of them as they passed by. Even with her wings folded, Sondra was still recognizable as a fifteen-year veteran of Just Cause. Phoenix wasn't a hotbed of celebrity sightings, so even Faith and Sally rated interest.

Eventually, Faith cut across two lanes of traffic to pull into the lot of the assisted-living complex where Grandma Judy lived. It had galled the eighty-one-year-old lady to move into the place where, as she so often said, *old people waited to die*. However, the staff had been very polite to the veteran of World War II and the American Justice superhero team, and when Judy saw that she could still be as independent as she desired, she accepted residency without too much of a grudge. Since then, she'd become active in the bridge club, painted watercolors, and played a lot of *Call of Duty* on her computer.

Sally heard through the apartment door the faint sounds of electronic destruction being perpetrated against virtual opponents. It ceased when they knocked. "Hold your horses," called Grandma Judy from inside. "I'm not as fast as I used to be." She still chuckled at her joke when she opened the door. Her lined face brightened as she saw her daughter and granddaughter stood in the doorway. "My goodness, what a wonderful surprise to see you!"

"Stop that, mother," said Faith. "You knew very well we were coming over to see you."

Grandma Judy hobbled across the room and eased herself onto a chair. "One must keep up appearances," she said, "if one is to live among the old and decrepit. When in Rome . . ."

Faith snorted. "Please, mother."

Judy smiled. "Don't argue with me, young lady. I'm old enough to accept that I'm old, and decrepit enough to accept that I'm going to have both my hips replaced next week. It's high time you accepted that as well."

"Grandma," interrupted Sally before her mother could argue. "How are you?"

"Old and decrepit." Judy cackled with glee. "I'm thrilled you came to see me." Her voice dropped to a conspiratorial whisper. "I understand you're involved with a boy."

Sally's mouth dropped open, an expression matched by Faith's.

"You are?" cried her mother. "When did this happen? And how does mother know and I don't?"

"It was on *Good Morning America.*" Judy turned to look at Sally. "He needs a haircut, your boyfriend."

Sondra laughed. "He's not so bad, really. His hair is charming when it's all messy like that."

"Could we maybe not talk about my social life and look at the real reason why I'm here?" said Sally.

Sondra settled down, an indulgent smile pasted across her face. Faith looked scandalized. Grandma Judy snickered. "Oh, to be eighteen and in love again."

"I'm not—look, I'm not here for that, Grandma," said Sally. "Mom, stop shooting me that look."

"I'm not giving you a look. I'm just concerned—"

"Mom, please?"

Sondra wrapped an arm around Faith's shoulders and steered her toward the door. "Let's give Sally a little space. I'm sure you'll have plenty of opportunity to grill her about Mastiff. In the meantime, let's go get something to drink."

"But I—oh, all right," said Faith. "But we will discuss this, young lady."

Sally fumed in silence as Sondra and her mother left the apartment.

"I wish you two wouldn't fight so much," said Grandma Judy. "And I wish you'd be a dear and get me a ginger ale from the fridge."

"Sure, Grandma."

"You remind me so much of her when she was your age. No wonder you two butt heads so much. There were days when I could have cheerfully strangled your mother. She was quite the little hellion in her day. If she wasn't so much faster than me, you might never have been born."

Sally handed Grandma Judy a glass of ice and poured the soda into it. "I'm not really a troublemaker. I've tried really hard to be good."

"I know, dear. You've never had the chance to stretch your wings. Between home schooling, training, and that Academy, you missed out on your childhood." Grandma Judy clinked the ice in her glass for emphasis. "Now, while your mother is off fuming about your boyfriend, what did you want to ask me?"

Sally slipped the file folder from her bag. "I know you and Grandpa fought a German parahuman the night you met. He wrote a little about that in his book. Do you remember much about it?"

"Oh my, yes. I may joke about being old and decrepit, but I promise you my mind is as sharp as ever, Sally." Grandma Judy smiled. "How well I recall that night. Your grandfather looked so handsome in that ridiculous pirate shirt he wore, so young and vital. And he was such a good shot with his bow. We never even considered that he might be a parahuman until long after he'd retired and the test confirmed it."

Sally thumbed through the file until she found the best picture of Heinrich Kaiser and showed it to her grandmother. "Do you recognize this guy? Is he who you fought that night?"

Judy took the picture and stared at it with intensity. Sally chewed on her knuckles while she waited.

"I'm not sure," said her grandmother at last. "It's been more than fifty years. I wish your grandfather was still alive, God bless him. He always had a better memory for details. It was the writer in him." Judy gazed at the picture once more. "This could be him. It's so hard to tell. Oh!"

"What is it?"

"I've just thought of something else. Will you go to my closet? On the top shelf is an old file box filled with his papers."

Sally was in and out of her grandmother's bedroom in a blur.

"So fast," smiled Grandma Judy. "The speed runs in our blood, Sally, and you're the fastest of all. Your daughter will be faster yet."

Sally burst out laughing. "I've only barely even got a boyfriend. I'm in no hurry."

"Of course, dearie." Judy opened the box and riffled through the papers within. "These are your grandfather's notes for *Dangerous*. He was meticulous about keeping them so he would have all his details in order. I wonder if he has anything here about your mystery man."

Sally moved to stand at her grandmother's shoulder and looked with interest at the notes, sketches, and faded newspaper clippings.

"Aha!" crowed Judy in triumph. "Look at this." She held up a rough pencil sketch of a glowing figure that floated over water. In the corner was a more detailed study of the face. It had an uncanny resemblance to the photo of Heinrich Kaiser, enough so that Sally whistled in surprise. She held the two pictures side by side.

"That might really be the same guy," she decided. "You only dealt with him the one time, right?"

"Yes. He disappeared that night and we never did find him again. We always suspected he'd left the country.

"Do you remember anything else about that night? Anything Grandpa didn't write in his book?"

Judy shook her head. "I don't, but your grandfather undoubtedly does."

"That doesn't really help me."

"Ah," said her grandmother. "This will." She held up a sheaf of papers.

Sally perked up. "What's that?"

"The original draft of that night's events. The first chapter of his autobiography. What appeared in the book was much shorter. His editor thought the detail would bore the readers."

"Really? Grandma, could I maybe borrow it?"

"Of course, dear. It would all come to you eventually anyway. Take the whole box."

"Wow," said Sally. "This is awesome, Grandma. Thank you!"

Judy beamed. "I hope it brings you the answers you're seeking."

Sally smiled back. She knew what she'd be reading later that evening before bedtime.

Chapter FiFteen

"People say they fear us because they don't understand us, and people always fear what they don't understand. They should fear us because of what we are."

-Isaiah Mohammed aka Flashpoint, 1965

January, 2004
Phoenix, Arizona

Sally looked up as Sondra set down the manuscript, a thoughtful expression on her face. She lay on her stomach on the bed in the guest room, her wings spread out like a feathery cloak. Sally sat on the floor and worked her way through her grandfather's papers.

"I can see why his editor suggested the change," said Sondra. "This reads more like a chapter from an adventure novel than an autobiography."

Sally shrugged. "He was a superhero. Our lives by definition are adventurous."

"Good point," said Sondra.

"Okay, I have a theory," said Sally.

Faith bustled into the room. "Sondra, can I get you anything in here? More pillows? A blanket?"

"I'm fine, Faith. This bed is lovely and comfortable."

"Well, I came up to tell you the pizza's here."

"That's fine, Mom. We'll be down in a minute." Sally gave her mother a tight smile.

Faith left and headed back downstairs.

"You ought to be nicer to her," said Sondra. "You only ever get to have one mother."

Sally stretched her arms up to work out a kink in her neck. "She's just so hard to deal with sometimes."

"Think of her as part of your adventurous life."

Sally snickered at that. "Her cooking is adventurous, that's for sure. Trust me, you'll be glad we ordered pizza."

Sondra patted her belly. "I love pizza far too much for my figure, I'm afraid. Extra time in the gym for me this week."

"Do you want to hear my theory?"

"Of course I do, but why don't you tell me downstairs. Your mother might have some insight to share."

Sally sighed in exasperation.

"Sally, she's not your enemy and this shouldn't be a secret," said Sondra as they left the guest room and followed the scent of pepperoni and green peppers that wafted up the stairs.

Faith already had one of the boxes open and got drinking glasses from the freezer with one hand while she balanced a large slice in the other. "God," she said around a mouthful. "I haven't had pizza forever. Sondra, what would you like to drink? A beer?"

"Beer's fine. If I'm going to let myself go to hell tonight, I might as well take the full tour."

"Sally? I've got soda and iced tea."

"Tea is fine, Mom."

Faith handed out plates and beverages. "Don't be shy, ladies."

For a few minutes, the only sound in the room was that of the women scarfing down the pizza. Sondra punctuated the brief binge session with an unladylike belch that made Sally and Faith crack up.

"Now that I've gotten that out," said Sondra. "Sally, please, tell us about this theory of yours."

Sally wiped her mouth with a paper napkin and took a sip of her tea. "Say that this guy Kaiser is the same guy Grandpa wrote about. He's a parahuman, and he seems to not be getting any older. Plus he's a Nazi, or at least he used to be. That means he's got a pretty twisted sense of the proper way of the world."

"I'm with you," said Sondra.

"I'm not, but keep going. I'll catch up," said Faith.

"Okay. According to Grandpa's manuscript, Strongman's parahuman commando unit found a reactor of some sort when they were in Germany during the War. They also found evidence that the Germans had managed to create a parahuman, who might have possibly been Kaiser." Sally took another drink. "So if they made one, why didn't they make more? Where was the army of Nazi supermen?"

"The reactor blew up," said Sondra. "Small-yield thermonuclear explosion. It killed Sounder and Meteor. That's when Flicker lost his arm and both he and Strongman suffered the radiation scarring. The War in Europe ended shortly after that. The only information anybody had about the project was in a notebook Strongman and Flicker managed to retrieve before the reactor went."

"Is there going to be a test on this?" asked Faith. "History was my worst subject."

"Okay," said Sally. "So we've got this guy, a parahuman created through technology and a Nazi to boot, who's built himself a cozy little empire in his corner of the world. But now he's looking to expand and thinks he'd like to recreate the experiment that created him. Only this time, he wants it to work right and to work better. So he enlists the help of a technological genius who's already known to have psychopathic tendencies. Destroyer."

Sondra set her empty beer down on the table. "You think they're trying to make parahumans?"

"I think they already have," said Sally. "That Antimatter Woman in Wyoming. She's from Guatemala and she doesn't have any idea what happened to her. What if she got fed into this . . . this machine, this reactor, whatever it is, and came out changed?"

"That's horrible!" cried Faith. "But how did she end up in Wyoming?"

Sondra rubbed her chin. "Glimmer said he detected a massive expenditure of psionic energy right before everything fell apart. There must be a psi user there with enough strength to teleport someone half a world away."

"Someone like that might be able to reprogram freshly-made parahumans," said Sally. "And there's your army of supermen, led by a Nazi warlord, built by a psychopathic genius, and controlled by a mysterious telepath. All they need is a target."

Silence reigned around the table for a few minutes as the women considered the implications.

"God, I hope you're wrong, Sally," said Faith at last.

"So do I, Mom."

"We'd better head back first thing in the morning," said Sondra. "We ought to at least tell Juice about this. Even if this is mostly conjecture on our part, he'd say this is worth investigating further."

Over the rest of the evening, the three women demolished the pizza and a quart of mint mocha ice cream Faith found in the back corner of the freezer. Afterward, they argued about movies and finally settled on *Beaches*, Sally's preference of *The Matrix* having been outvoted two to one. Sally suffered through the two hours of angst in silence, then was shocked to find herself in tears along with Sondra and her mother at the end despite her avowed cynicism toward chick flicks.

After they'd all had a good cry, they decided to call it a night. Sally made sure Sondra was settled into the guest room before slipping into her own bed for the first time in six months. She'd forgotten how much she missed it. Her bed at Just Cause headquarters wasn't nearly as comfortable. She'd have to check with Harris to see if he could replace her mattress with something a little softer. Superheroes needed their sleep to be restful, she reasoned, since it seemed to be in short supply.

Her phone beeped quietly but insistently and woke her from a dream of running endlessly through the darkness. She looked at her bedside clock as she fumbled for the elusive device. *1:48.*

"H'lo?" she mumbled into the phone.

"Hey, beautiful, did I wake you?" It was Jason.

"Yeah," she said. "But it's okay. How was your gig?"

"Lousy sound. The guy running the board was pretty wasted. But we played well."

"That's good." She yawned. "It's really nice to hear your voice."

"Likewise. Did you get to talk to your grandma?"

"Yeah. We got some good stuff from her. We're coming home tomorrow. I mean, we're coming back. I guess I'm home now."

"Cool. I'm on duty the next two days, but stop by and see me when you get back."

"I will. I think I'm on duty the next two. Stupid work schedule."

Jason laughed. "Well, I've got to get a few hours of sleep. Juice looks down on dozing during monitor duty."

"Imagine that."

"I missed you today, Sally."

Sally smiled. "I missed you too, Jason."

"See you tomorrow."

"Okay."

Sally felt warm all over and content as she hung up. Jason had missed her, and he'd told her so. That thought comforted her and lulled her back to sleep.

Breakfast was low-key in Faith's house. Cereal and tea. Faith admitted to Sondra she didn't often get inspired enough to cook anything early in the morning. She referred to anytime before nine AM as *Grumpy Hour*, which meant you were on your own. She did manage to find enough coffee to make a pot for Sondra, who confided to Sally that it was about as stimulating as colored water.

Sally's phone beeped once to announce an incoming message. She checked it.

Heading off 2 duty. Thinking of u.

She smiled and sent a reply text. *Have a good day. C U l8r.*

Faith raised an eyebrow. "What's all that about?"

"Just work stuff," said Sally.

"I see." Her mother didn't seem like she was fooled in the least.

Sally was astonished to see a few people with cameras loitered outside the house when they left. They snapped pictures as the women got into Faith's Cadillac.

"Who are they?" Sally whispered to Sondra.

The winged woman shrugged. "Fans. Paparazzi. They turn up whenever we're recognized somewhere, especially in civilian garb. I'm not exactly anonymous with these extra appendages."

"Jason and I got cornered by a reporter at the Devereaux Foundation the other night," said Sally. "I'm not sure I'll ever get used to that."

"We'll probably see something about our kinky lesbian tryst in the tabloids next week." Sondra laughed.

"What?" Faith's grip on the steering wheel wavered.

"Most of the time, they just make me laugh, although I wish I had Jack's equanimity when it comes to dealing with the more aggressive paparazzi." Sondra smiled. "Although I can always fly away and then all they get are pictures of my ass. It's gotten more press than I have, I think." She slapped the portion of her anatomy in question. "That's why I have to keep working out."

Faith dropped them off in front of the terminal. Sally hugged her mom and thanked her for the hospitality. Somehow, she felt she'd gotten a little closer to her mother in the past day, and decided she ought to nurture that feeling.

"Don't mention it," said Faith. "But don't let another six months go by before you come back. Seeing you twice a year isn't nearly enough. You too, Sondra, come back anytime."

"We will, Mom. I love you." Sally turned to go, but then stopped. "Mom? I . . . I talked to John Stone and Ms. Echevarria about the day Dad died."

Faith gasped and one of her hands flew to her mouth.

"I'll meet you inside, Sally." Sondra disappeared into the terminal.

"Mom, I'm sorry. I just wanted to know what happened that day. I wanted to know about Destroyer. I wanted to know about you . . . and Dad."

"I was going to tell you myself someday," whispered Faith. "I've always meant to. I just never could find the right time. It still hurts every time I think about it."

"I know, Mom. I'm sorry about Dad. I know you loved him very much."

Faith's eyes grew bright with tears. "I still do, Sally. I miss him every day."

"Are you mad at me for asking someone else?"

"No. I'm glad you found someone to talk to. Someone stronger than me." Faith sniffled.

"Mom, you're the strongest person I know. Everything I'm doing with Just Cause is because I'm trying to honor you."

"Oh, Sally." Sally found herself in her mother's arms and didn't remember ever crossing the distance between them. They embraced one another. "I'm so proud of you, honey. You've gone and grown up into a real hero."

"Only because you taught me to be one."

They finally broke their hug. Faith smiled at her daughter and wiped the tears from her cheeks. "You go on, Sally. Go be a superhero for me. For your father. For yourself."

"I will, Mom." Sally wiped her own eyes.

Sally turned and headed for the terminal.

"Sally!" Faith called. "Come back soon."

"I will."

Sally met Sondra inside the terminal. Once they presented their identification to Security, they were allowed to bypass all the checkpoints and were given a ride out to the hangar on a whisper-quiet electric cart.

Sally dozed most of the flight back to Denver. She didn't even stir when the jet landed. She'd drifted off right after takeoff and the next thing she knew, Sondra was shaking her awake. The jet was already in the Just Cause hangar and the engines powering down.

"Wow." She yawned. "I didn't know I was so tired."

"Same here," said Sondra. "But your mom's coffee was pretty weak."

"Compared to that tar you drink, I suppose so." Sally collected her bag and followed Sondra out of the jet. She shivered in the cold. "It doesn't take long to get used to the warm temperatures again, does it?"

"Definitely. Let's get inside."

They called Juice to let him know they had returned. He asked if they could meet with him in an hour to go over what they'd learned from Sally's grandmother. They agreed, and went to their respective rooms to drop off their bags and freshen up after the flight. Sally took a quick shower and dressed in slacks and a button-down shirt, so she'd look a little more professional for a meeting with her boss. She had enough time to stop in the Command Center for a few minutes, so she went in to see Jason. He smiled at her, but was busy as he kept tabs on a developing situation in San Francisco with the New Guard responding to a high-profile bank robbery with possible parahuman involvement.

"Are we on alert or anything for that?" she asked.

"Probably not," he said. "The Guard should be able to handle it. We couldn't get there very quickly anyway. If they get into trouble, we'll send a squad out. I'm sure they'll be fine though."

Sally squeezed his arm and left to go meet Juice.

Sondra already sat in the office, her wings draped over the back of her chair. Juice smiled as Sally slipped into the room with her grandmother's box clutched in her hands.

"Welcome back, Sally. How is your mother?"

"She's fine. She sends her best."

"And your grandmother?"

"Not so good. She's going to have to have both of her hips replaced."

"I'm sorry to hear that."

Sally shrugged. "It's for the best. She'll be in less pain afterward."

Juice leaned back in his chair. "Now . . . tell me about your investigation."

Sally cleared her throat, nervous all over again. Stick to the facts, she told herself. Let him ask the questions, let him make the decisions on how to proceed.

"So you're saying you believe he's trying to create an army of parahumans?" asked Juice after Sally finished her briefing.

"Yeah, I really think that's what he's trying to do. Destroyer has the technological skills to recreate that original experiment with a higher rate of success. And if he's using the local population, it would explain why the Antimatter Woman came from the same area."

"And he has a pet psi to keep everyone in line and teleport out the ones who are the worst?"

"He's got to, or else the Antimatter Woman would still be down there on a rampage through Central America in search of power."

"Too dangerous to keep around as part of his army, so he teleported her away," said Juice. "It's a good theory, Sally. You've tied it all together very nicely."

"But?"

"No buts, Sally. I might consider the idea of an artificially-created parahuman far-fetched if we hadn't had to deal with the Antimatter Woman. It could be simply a coincidence that she turned up when she did. Coincidence has certainly been part of parahuman history. Have you ever heard of Occam's Razor?"

"Aren't they a band?"

Juice smiled. "Probably. But in this case, it's a method of solving a problem. Essentially it means that given multiple theories behind a specific outcome, the simpler explanations are generally better than more complex ones."

"*Generally* isn't very scientific."

"No, but it's a reasonable assumption. Your theory ties together Destroyer, the Kaiser fellow, Guatemala, and the Antimatter Woman quite reasonably."

"Thanks, sir. I mean, Juice."

He smiled. "Now I'm afraid I have to play devil's advocate here for a moment. I know you have a lot of personal history tied up with Destroyer. I can't help but wonder if you're trying to attribute too much to him."

"I don't understand," said Sally.

"Have you considered that perhaps he's just down in Guatemala to acquire something from this Kaiser fellow, after which he'd simply return to whatever construes his current work?"

"N-no." Sally suddenly felt only about six inches tall. "What could he only get in Guatemala that he couldn't get here?"

"You tell me, Sally."

"I can't think of anything."

"James," said Sondra. "She's not on the witness stand."

"My apologies, Sally. No further questions."

Sally sat back in her chair. Her hands shook as if she had just gone through a Three-Minute Drill in the Bunker. Sondra reached over and squeezed her shoulder in a friendly way.

Juice leaned forward. His chair creaked with the shift of his weight. "Sally, I'm proud of you. This theory is solid, and right or wrong, I'm going to present it to Homeland Security as part of my argument why we should be cleared to go investigate the matter ourselves."

"Really?"

"Really. Good work, kiddo."

Chapter Sixteen

*"The problem with being the world's policemen is that the world
usually doesn't want policing. American parahumans have character-
-istically been unwelcome beyond our own borders. Since parahuman
abilities aren't constrained by political boundaries, other countries are
as likely as not to possess parahumans of their own."*

-Dr. Lane Devereaux, *Larry King Live,* March 4, 1993

February, 2004
Denver, Colorado
Just Cause Headquarters

"We're cleared to go to Guatemala," announced Juice at
the first-of-the-month meeting.

"How'd you swing that, boss?" Jack stopped toying
with his pen and looked up with interest.

"Sally put together a very convincing argument for
further investigation which I relayed to Homeland
Security. They bought it."

Jack grinned. "Good job, Sally. What was your pitch?"

Sally blushed. "I think Destroyer is working with a
guy my grandparents fought to artificially create
parahuman abilities." She took a sip from her caramel
latte. Between Jason and Jack, she'd experimented with
coffee and had discovered a weakness for the frothy
sweet beverages. As long as she mixed decaf and
regular shots, the jitters didn't get too bad.

"And the right people at Homeland Security agree
with her assessment, which is why they're sending us
in," Juice said. "There is a catch, though."

"Always is," Jack muttered.

"With the complications in Iraq and the terror threat high, Homeland Security isn't allowing the whole team to travel to Central America. They're going to let four of us go. The rest stay here on heightened alert status."

Grumbles resounded around the table. Since the early days of Just Cause, whenever the team split up, missions became more complicated. It was always better to have the entire team present to give the field commander maximal options when making spot decisions.

"Stacey will be in command of the mission, and she's selected her team. Stace?"

Doublecharge stood. "This will be a reconnaissance mission in a foreign country, not a combat mission. Jack, Jay, and Sally are with me."

Jack sighed. "Super. I hear the wet season doesn't start for two more months."

Sondra touched Sally's hand. "Don't take this the wrong way, Sally, because this is in no way a reflection of your capabilities." She turned to Doublecharge. "I'm going on record as against Sally's participation in this assignment. She's an intern, not a full member. This could be a very dangerous mission and she's been with us only a month."

"Three reasons." Doublecharge ticked them off on her fingers. "First, she's already proved that she's very capable in the use of her powers. Second, her investigative efforts are directly responsible for us even being allowed to go there at all." Her eyes narrowed at the rest of the team. "I notice none of you took that extra step. And neither did I, for that matter."

"Easy, Stacey," said Juice.

Doublecharge cleared her throat. "Finally, besides Jack and Sondra, she's the only one on the team who speaks Spanish."

Sally sank lower in her seat, somehow embarrassed by the attention.

Jason raised a hand. "Stacey, I speak some Spanish."

Jack snorted. "The menu at Taco Bell doesn't count."

"Sorry, Jason," said Doublecharge. "Sally's had five years of it. She's fluent."

Jason shrugged, miserable. "I'd still come along."

"Not this time. I'm sorry." Doublecharge touched a key on her terminal. "I'm sending what little mission briefing I have to each of you. We leave in two days. If you have questions, you can ask me later."

Jack lifted a hand. "*How do I get—*" A tiny bolt of lightning shot across the table to hit him square in the teeth. It didn't hurt him, of course, but startled him into silence. Doublecharge lowered the finger that she'd pointed at him.

"I meant any legitimate questions."

"And on that note, we'll consider this meeting adjourned," said Juice, intervening before anything else could happen.

Outside the conference room, Sally slipped her small hand into Jason's great palm. She took comfort in the way he gently squeezed it. "Walk me to my room?" She asked.

"It'd be my pleasure."

Neither of them spoke to each other during the short trip back to the dormitory. Sally keyed her door and noticed Jason's shuffling feet. "Do you, uh, want to come in?" she asked, not daring to look into his eyes. Her mind whirled like an out-of-control carousel.

"Sure."

The door slid shut silently. Sally made a couple frantic laps of her suite to pick up stray underwear and rolled-up socks. Jason's hair flapped in the breeze that swirled in her wake.

"Sorry," she said, embarrassed. "I'm a terrible housekeeper." She neglected to turn on the suite lights, which left the room, bathed in the low light from her terminal's screensaver.

"It's okay," Jason smiled, and then they stood very close to each other, the contours of his cheekbones highlighted in the dim lighting and his eyes sparkling pools of obsidian. "I'm . . . going to miss you." His voice was husky.

"It was very sweet of you to offer to come along. I don't even know how long we'll be gone. Maybe just a couple of days."

"You should probably check the briefing," he offered.

"In a minute." Sally surprised herself with her conviction as she reached up, grabbed hold of Jason's sweatshirt hood and pulled herself up to his face level. His arms encircled her legs to support her gently with muscles that could bend girders. She kissed him hard and tasted his lips and tongue with hers. He staggered backward, caught his leg on the couch, and jarred her loose as he sat down hard.

"Sorry," he mumbled. "Clumsy."

"That's okay," she said, her voice shrill. "It was kind of a spur-of-the-moment thing."

He rubbed a hand across his jaw and smiled through a deep blush of his own.

Sally turned away quickly and slid into the chair by her computer desk. "I better check that briefing . . . see how long we're going to be gone."

"Shorter would definitely be better." Jason moved over to her and knelt down so he could read over her shoulder. He used the proximity as an opportunity to nuzzle her neck.

She gently slapped him away. "Stop." She tried to be authoritative. "I'm working."

"Mmm." He blew a gentle breath on the back of her neck, right where her two braids parted. It made her delicious and shivery inside.

Sally sped through the mission briefing. As Doublecharge had implied, there wasn't much: try to locate Destroyer; try to find a positive connection to the Antimatter Woman; try to find a positive connection to Heinrich Kaiser; objective is to gain intelligence, not to engage; projected mission length of two weeks. *Two weeks?*

"That's crazy," she said aloud. "I can't spend two weeks down there."

Jason spun her chair around to face him. "Maybe she'll let you come home on the weekends. How long would it take you to run that far?"

Sally fiddled with her hands because she didn't know what to do with them. "It's south of Mexico. That's a long way." She draped her restless hands around his neck, which immediately felt better. "Furthest I've ever run in one stretch was from Phoenix to Anaheim." She smiled wistfully. "I went to Disneyland."

"Well, look at the bright side," Jason said. "You get to take an extra-long Spring Break in the tropics a month before everyone else does."

Sally kissed him again and rested her forehead against his and drank in the scent of his skin. It was nice. "Do you want to stick around for awhile?" She felt her skin prickle from a ferocious blush.

"Sure."

"Good." She covered his mouth with hers.

They kissed for some time. Sally wasn't quite sure when they wound up on the couch. He leaned back and rested his head on the overstuffed arm, and she half-laid, half-sat on him. He reached a tentative hand under her blouse to caress his fingertips across her back. The heat rose off them in palpable waves and made her feel like she was back in Phoenix. Without stopping herself to think about it, she lifted her blouse off completely. This was better, but she wanted to feel his skin too, and helped him yank off his sweatshirt. Little golden curls of hair dotted his massive chest and washboard abs.

Back at the Hero Academy, she and the other girls in the dorm sat up many late nights and compared notes on who were the hottest boys, who would be the best kissers, and what really happened when you had sex. Only one girl had actually hooked up with a boy in school, or at least admitted to it. At the time, Sally had been convinced that she would never want to have a boy do that to her. Now, though, she felt desire quiver through her that could only be fulfilled by giving all of herself to him.

Sally felt like taking a chance. In one definitive motion, Sally slipped her sports bra over her head and sat up to allow Jason to drink in the sight of her. "I want you."

He nodded, his eyes as wide as saucers. "Should I, uh, run back to my room for a minute? I gotta get, you know, something."

"It's okay. I'm on the pill." Her mother had lost her virginity at Woodstock, when she was only fifteen. She'd put Sally on the pill as soon as she left for the Academy. I know you'll be smart, she had said, but I don't want to take any chances.

Sally lifted his hands up to cup her breasts. He caressed them and brushed his fingertips across her nipples with curious delight. "Are you sure?"

"Mm . . . yes," she said. "You know what to do, right?"

"Um, I think so. I mean, of course."

"Good." She bent forward and kissed him again, hard. "Because it's kind of my first time."

They shed their remaining clothing and scattered it about the room. Sally rolled onto the floor, Jason matched her every move. He supported himself on his arms so he wouldn't crush her.

Sally's perceptions flipped into full acceleration to allow her to experience every nuance of sensation. She immersed herself in the sensuality of touch, from the initial sharp pain to the waves of pleasure that followed. Musky, exciting scents swirled around her and made her gasp. She hadn't known something could feel so good. If she had, she reasoned later, she'd have been having sex a lot earlier in her life. His muscles felt like iron sheathed in velvet, his breath hot in her ear, stubble on her cheek. She felt something building up and wrapped her legs around Jason's back to pull him even closer. His muscles clenched, he closed his eyes, and stopped moving. Sally could feel him, hot like a steel ingot, and then . . . nothing. It was like a door starting to open then shutting in her face. She gasped again, but from an overwhelming sense of disappointment.

"I'm sorry!" Jason panted. "Did I hurt you?"

She squeezed her arms and legs tighter around him as she tried to regain that sensation of going up the roller coaster hill, but to no avail. "No," she managed to whisper at last.

The look of concern on Jason's face was so earnest and honest that she broke into giggles. "Sally?"

She hugged him, and then realized she was crying even while laughing. She felt a sudden panic starting to creep in around the edges. "I'll be right back."

"Sure thing," he said as he pulled on his briefs.

Sally retreated to her bathroom and locked the door. She gulped down a glass of water and then cleaned herself up. She felt a twinge of disgust at the smear of blood on her thigh. She caught a glimpse of herself in the mirror and glared at her reflection. She should have been feeling sexy and glowing. Instead, she felt a little sick to her stomach and shocked that she'd just given up her virginity. "You're a superhero, stupid. You faced Destroyer. You can face this." She scolded her reflection. She wrapped her bathrobe around herself.

Jason lay on the floor, wearing only his shorts, with his hands behind his head. He yawned. "Anything in your fridge? I'm starving."

"No, silly. I only eat in the cafeteria, because I don't cook. I'll burn a pot of water if you give me half a chance." She made herself calm down, to bring back a semblance of normalcy.

"Really? I'll have to cook for you one of these days. You like jambalaya?"

"That's Cajun, right?"

"One of my many specialties. I'm a closet chef, but only for a few select friends. And for my girlfriend."

"Is she prettier than me?" Sally asked. "I'm kidding," she said as she saw an expression of mock hurt cross his face.

Somebody knocked at her door. Jason grabbed his pants and made a discreet exit into the bedroom.

"Salena? It's Harris. Got your luggage for you."

She opened the door and smiled nervously at Harris. The short, balding man held up a nondescript black pull-along suitcase. "Custom bag for your trip. Were you sleepin'? I'm sorry if I woke you up."

Sally's hands flew to her head of their own accord. One of her braids had come undone, and the untamed hair flopped about. She began to plait it again as a way to burn off her tension. "Uh, yeah. I was. Sleeping, that is." She forced a yawn.

"Sure," said Harris. "Everyone else has one of these but you. It's for when you gotta travel incognito. There are two complete costumes in special compartments here . . . and here." He pointed out two nondescript pockets. "One's all black for night work. They're vacuum-packed and compressed into the smallest possible space. I'll personally guarantee that you won't raise any suspicions at any airport security, no matter where you go. You open one up, you better plan to wear it because you'll never crush it back into place once you break the seal."

Sally nodded and hoped he'd wrap up his spiel as quickly as possible so he'd just leave.

He glanced past her into the darkened room beyond. She imagined he'd seen everything, and felt herself flush. She yanked the case from his grasp. "Thanks very much, Harris. I'll get busy packing right away. Goodbye." She backed into her room and shut the door as fast as she dared. She dropped the valise on the floor and stepped into the bedroom.

Jason had stretched out on her bed, his hands behind his head and his eyes shut. She thought he might be asleep but he spoke without opening his eyes. "Harris?"

"Yeah," she said.

"The man's a menace. Hell of a quartermaster, but has the worst timing in the world. He's always showing up at just the wrong time."

Sally climbed onto him and straddled his waist. Just being close to him again was enough to start her tingling all over once more. "You think he knows?"

"Probably. He's pretty sharp. I wouldn't worry too much about it, you know? Secrets don't stay secret long in this place. We all gossip like old ladies." As he yawned, he lifted her knees off the bed from his chest expansion.

"You're tired?" she asked, incredulous.

"A little. It's a guy thing. Aren't you?"

"I guess." She leaned forward to rest her cheek on his chest and listened to the patient thumping of his heart.

"Might as well sleep now. You might go kind of short the next two weeks." He rolled onto his side. She squealed with glee and dove under his arm to wind up holding his hand against her chest with her back pressed against him. With his arm around her she felt safe, warm, and suddenly drowsy as well.

"I guess I could take a nap." A deep vibration rattled behind her and she smiled to herself.

Jason snored.

Chapter Seventeen

'Tis a far, far cry from the "Minute-Men,"
And the times of the buff and blue
To the days of the withering Jorgensen
And the hand that holds it true.
'Tis a far, far cry from Lexington
To the isles of the China Sea,
But ever the same the man and the gun—
Ever the same are we.

-Edwin Legrand Sabin, "The American Soldier", July 1899

February, 2004
Denver, Colorado
Just Cause Headquarters

Sally awoke with a start. Jason was still sprawled on her bed. His snores had subsided to low rumbles like a tiger purring. Her clock read *2:24* and she realized they had slept through dinner. She felt jittery and a bit out-of-sorts with herself, like she'd drunk strong coffee for too long. She carefully disengaged herself from Jason and slipped out of the bed.

She still felt restless. She went into her bathroom and brushed her teeth, then brushed her hair until it snapped with static electricity. She glared at it in the mirror and considered how it would look if she acceded to her mother's wishes and cut it short. Right now she looked like a walking haystack, she thought. She stuck her tongue out as she rolled the mass of hair into a haphazard pile balanced on top of her head and stuck long pins through it more or less to hold it in place.

She still wore her robe. She found a pair of cotton leggings and pulled them on, and then slipped her freezing feet into her moccasins. She still felt odd and decided a walk might help clear her head.

The corridor was quiet, the lights darkened for nighttime. She strolled up to the deserted recreation room. None of the chairs felt comfortable, and she knew because she tried all of them twice to be sure. She ambled back down the passageway and stopped in front of a door—not her own room, but Sondra's.

She agonized for several minutes about whether or not to knock, but finally her need for some company won out and she tapped on the door. In a minute, she heard some movement behind the door and Sondra slid it open a few inches, rubbed her bleary eyes, and held a robe up to her chest.

"Sally?" she whispered. "Are you okay?"

"I don't know," Sally said. "I can't sleep."

"Do you want to come in?"

"Yeah." She stepped into the darkened room. Sondra clicked a lighter and lit a candle, which filled her living room with a warm orange glow. Sally curled up on the end of the couch, drew her feet up under her, and wrapped her arms around her knees.

"I hope you don't mind." Sondra fumbled with the robe. "I'm not usually dressed at this time of morning."

"That's okay." Sally dropped onto the couch beside her friend.

Sondra looked at her with compassion, her dark eyes finally clear of sleepiness. "Are you sure you're all right?"

Sally opened her mouth to say she was, and tears just started to run down her face. As Sondra curled one arm and wing around her, Sally buried her face against Sondra's shoulder and cried. Sondra whispered soothing nonsense into her hair and stroked her arm.

After a few minutes, Sally's tears stopped as quickly as they had started, and she shivered a bit.

"Do you want something to drink? Coffee? Or maybe hot chocolate?"

"Hot chocolate. I've seen what you call coffee." She smiled just a little and sniffled.

"Chocolate it is." Sondra went to the kitchenette. She fluttered her wings slightly to realign the feathers. "Want to talk about it?"

"Yeah." Sally wiped her eyes.

Sondra returned in a minute with two ceramic mugs filled with thick chocolatey goodness. She sat next to Sally and arranged her wings so they'd be out of the way. "So what's going on?"

"Do you promise not to tell anyone else?" Sally asked as she felt her face grow hot.

"I swear on my brother's grave not to repeat anything you say to me tonight." Sondra's voice was so deadly earnest and her face so serious that Sally shrank back a little. Sondra cracked a little smile. "You can trust me. You know that."

Sally took a sip of scalding hot chocolate and burned her lips and tongue. "Me and Jason . . . well, we kind of . . . hooked up."

"Really?" asked Sondra. "I'm not surprised."

"What do you mean by that?" Sally stiffened and set her mug down on the end table.

"It's okay, kiddo. Think of me like your big sister. You can tell me anything."

"I never had a sister. Or a brother," said Sally. "Mom always said she couldn't possibly keep up with two of us. Although she never remarried after Dad died."

"I only had a brother, myself," said Sondra. "He died when I was about your age, but that's another story. About Jason . . . did he treat you okay? He didn't hurt you or anything, did he?"

"No, no," said Sally. "He was very careful . . . very nice about it all. I just, I mean, uh . . ." She trailed off as tears threatened to overflow once again.

Sondra's eyes widened. "Was it your first time?"

Sally nodded and sniffled.

"Oh, honey . . . no wonder your emotions are out of whack." Sondra handed her a box of tissues. "It's an intense emotional experience." She took a sip of her own chocolate. "Did it hurt?"

"Only for a moment. Then it was . . . I don't know how to describe it. Like riding on a roller coaster, I guess." Sally giggled, then started to cry again, then tried to do both at the same time and failed.

"I'm going to talk to you like a big sister for a minute, okay?" Sally nodded her head. "It's okay to have sex. Most everybody does, one way or another. You're going to be confused a lot. You're going to wonder if you love him or if you don't want to see him anymore. One second you're going to think he's wonderful and the next you'll be so steamed you'd rather kick him in the face than have to look at him. He'll charm you, irritate you, put you on a high pedestal and knock you off of it. He won't understand what he does wrong when he does it, and he won't understand why you get mad." Sondra leaned back on the couch and smiled. "This is perfectly normal. We'll never understand men as well as we understand each other, and they'll never understand us. It's why we go to the bathroom in groups and they don't."

"How is that supposed to help me understand what I'm feeling?" asked Sally in irritation.

"It's not. You may never understand it. But you can decide to enjoy it anyway. Sex can be fun or it can be a chore. If it becomes a duty instead of a pleasure, you're with the wrong person. Sometimes you'll come. Sometimes you won't. Sometimes you'll need to help yourself along. Sometimes it won't matter." She gave Sally an encouraging smile.

"How do I know he's the right person?" Sally mumbled as she finished her chocolate.

Sondra shrugged. "You may be asking yourself that for the rest of your life. If you believe he is right now, then he is, and he will be as long as you both feel that way."

"Do you think I did the wrong thing? Was it too early? Should I have waited until after the mission?"

"Who knows?" Sondra smiled. "Do you have regrets? Would you do it again? Will you?"

Sally thought for a minute as she remembered how tenderly Jason had kissed her and how they had snuggled in the bed. "Yeah, I'd do it again."

"Well, there you go," said Sondra, as if that settled the matter. "Because don't you think for a minute I'm letting Jack out of here without getting some from him."

"How long have you and he been together?"

"Eight years or so."

Sally's eyes widened. "Wow. Why don't you guys just get married or something?"

"Oh, we probably will someday. When we get around to it, I suppose. For now, though, it amounts to a lot of flirting and as much sex as we can get around duty schedules, missions, and his public relations work."

"Does Juice know?"

Sondra laughed. "Juice knows damn near everything that goes on in this place. I swear, if I didn't know better I'd say he was a mind reader. He told us both that he didn't want to have to make a policy expressly forbidding it, and that we'd better not let it affect our job performance, and that was that."

"I had a poster of Jack in my dorm room at the Academy. *The Face of Just Cause*," said Sally in amazement. "Is he . . . good?"

"Jack's a very skilled lover. He's worth clearing my schedule for. Believe me," Sondra dropped her voice to her favorite conspiratorial whisper. "It's like he was trained in a brothel or something."

Sally blushed at the thought of Jack and Sondra together, but then a question burned into her mind that wouldn't leave her alone until brought to light. "Can I ask you something?"

"Anything."

"What do you do with your wings when you're . . . you know . . ."

Sondra burst out with infectious laughter, which made Sally giggle too and soon both women roared in amusement and had to wipe tears from their eyes. "Oh, Sally." Sondra gave her a hug. "You're precious. I can lie on them if I'm careful. And there are plenty of other ways to do it besides on your back." She took a deep breath to calm herself. "So . . . I told you, you have to tell me. How was Jason?"

"I, uh, don't have a basis for comparison."

"Empirically, then."

"I don't think I came. I mean, it's different with someone else, right"

"It can be. Some women don't without help."

"Help? You mean I still have to do it myself? I thought that's what he was for!"

Sondra laughed. "You can still have a lot of fun that way. Trust me. Foreplay is a wonderful thing."

"Is it always that . . . messy afterward?" This sent both women off into peals of laughter once again.

"A real gentleman would offer to sleep in the wet spot." Sondra's dark eyes sparkled.

"Didn't have to . . . it was on the floor." Sally giggled.

By the time they finally wound themselves down, the clock had bypassed four in the morning. Sally yawned so hard she thought she might dislocate her jaw.

"Do you want to stay here the rest of the night?" Sondra asked.

"No, I think I'll be okay." She hugged Sondra. "Thank you. I really mean that."

"Anytime, kiddo. It's nice to have another girl to talk to for a change. Stacey's so cool and distant and I've never seen her let down her hair at all. You're in for a real treat going on a mission with her in command. I hope you don't wind up hating her."

"Me too," replied Sally. She left the room and went to her own door. She fought back an urge to knock on her own door, took a deep breath and walked into the room. It was strange and quiet, and she realized she couldn't hear Jason's breathing. She peeked around the corner to look into the bedroom.

Jason was gone, but he'd been busy. He'd made the bed, with one corner turned down. A folded card made a little paper tent atop one of the pillows. Mystified, she unfolded it and read what he'd written.

YOU'VE GOT MAIL.

Even more mystified, she went to her computer. The screen was dark and it took her a few moments of wiggling the mouse and punching keys before she realized her monitor was actually turned off. She switched it on and a picture of a bright bunch of roses filled the screen. A card-shaped icon flickered, which invited her to click on it.

Sally,

My mom says I could wake the dead with my snoring, so I figured I'd give you a few hours of peace in case I woke you up. This pic is the best I could do for flowers this time of night. Hope you like them! I'll see you at breakfast. Thanks for everything!

J.

Sally dropped her hands away from the computer. Of all the things he could have done, all the things she might have expected, he'd surprised her. In a very pleasant way, she thought. She wasn't really that tired, but decided that she could curl up in bed with the lights out and the covers pulled up to her chin anyway.

The pillow Jason had lain upon had just a slight hint of his shampoo, and it made her smile into the darkness. She wondered if he'd be able to come back tomorrow night and her belly tingled a bit at the thought. But then again, she was a bit sore and tender, she discovered.

Two weeks away from him seemed like a really, really long time.

The next two days passed in a whirlwind of activity. Juice, Doublecharge, and an earplug-wearing man in a nondescript suit from Homeland Security each conducted a last-minute briefing. Harris showed his prescient side as he always popped up with whatever the expedition team seemed to need before they even knew it. Sally passed through the hours in a happy daze and stole kisses from Jason whenever she found the opportunity. Definitely a keeper, in Sondra's words. The night before their departure, she visited his room.

He answered her knock right away. He wore his ubiquitous sweats, a tank top, and a Colorado Rockies ball cap, and held an acoustic guitar.

"Hi," she said.

"Hi yourself." He stepped aside. "I'm writing a song. Want to come in?"

"Nice hat." She punched him gently in the arm. "They play baseball, right?"

"They suck," he said. "But I like the colors."

"Oh, I don't know," she said. "Purple and white? I think you look much better in gray and brown. Or buff." A slow blush crept up Jason's neck. Sally couldn't believe herself; she was already becoming as much of a smart-aleck as Sondra.

She jumped onto the couch and looked around. His room was immaculate; everything clean, straight, and organized. "I had no idea you were such a neat freak. I hope my sloppy tendencies don't drive you away."

"It's okay. My dad was in the Navy, and he made us run a tight ship at home."

"Us?"

"Me and my two brothers. Justin and Jordan."

"And Jason. Your folks like the letter J?"

"Yeah. We all have the same middle name too."

"What is it?"

"I'll never tell." He grinned and set his guitar on a stand by his desk. "Okay, it's Aries. My folks have a twisted sense of humor."

"Mine's Judith, after my grandma." Sally walked over to Jason, sat on his lap, and put her arms around his neck. "Our family joke is that speed runs in our blood. How about you? Are your brothers paras too?"

"Yeah. Well, kind of. Justin's two years younger than me. He tested positive on the Musashi test, but hasn't ever shown any kind of powers. Jordan's fifteen and starts at the Academy next year. He's strong like me, but not nearly as tough. I can whip him if I need to."

"Take off this stupid hat." Sally pressed her lips to his. After a few minutes, she smiled down at him. "I thought I'd come and give you a going-away present."

"Are you sure? I mean, you're not . . . like . . . sore, or anything?"

Sally smiled. To tell the truth, she was still a bit tender. On the other hand, she'd spent her free time earlier reading online about certain techniques and hoped she might get him to try a few of them. "I'm a speedster," she whispered and nibbled his ear. "I heal fast."

Jason grinned and threw away his hat.

Duty call was at five the next morning. After an evening spent in some very pleasant close proximity to Jason, Sally almost missed the alarm he had set for her. She'd told him she only needed five minutes to get herself ready, and he'd set the alarm for four fifty-five. She'd gone to sleep, satiated after his ministrations, and didn't move the rest of the night.

At the alarm's first beep, she sat up in surprise, wrapped in his sheets. Her hair was a mass of tangles and much of it hung in her face. Jason rolled over and murmured "'snot timma geddup yet," and shut off the alarm, more asleep than awake.

She rubbed her eyes and then grabbed her clothes and his Rockies hat on impulse. "You're amazing," she whispered in his ear, and kissed it.

Without opening his eyes, he grinned, which tempted her to stay a bit longer.

"I've got to go. I'll see you in two short weeks." She peeked into the hallway to see if it was deserted and found herself looking right at Jack as he headed for his first cup of coffee like it was the Holy Grail.

"Morning, sugar," he said with little enthusiasm.

"Uh, hi," she said. He walked a bit further up the hall, then stopped and turned around to look in confusion at the door in which she stood. She smiled and shrugged. Realization dawned on his face and he smiled back, not so sleepy that he hadn't figured it out.

She dashed into her room, showered, dressed, and tucked her plaited hair through the back of Jason's cap. By the time she was done and back in the Command Center with her luggage, Jack had just sat down.

"Sleep well?" He eyed her latte with interest.

"As well as you, I'm sure." Sally noticed something stuck in his hair and pulled it out with a gleeful squeal. "Look, a feather!"

Doublecharge walked into the room with her wheeled suitcase behind her. She looked out of place wearing jeans and a button-down blouse, like a business executive on a weekend trip. "Good morning." She leaned her bag against the conference room wall. "I trust you're both ready to leave?"

Sally nodded while Jack muttered something incomprehensible into his coffee cup.

"I didn't quite catch that, Jack."

He set his cup down and gave a world-weary sigh. "Yes, I'm ready."

"Morning, everyone," said Glimmer as he walked into the room, pulling his wheeled bag behind him and whistling a cheerful pop tune.

Doublecharge ignored him. "Since we're flying as civilians, we need to be at the airport by six o'clock. That gives us just about half an hour to eat and review the mission." She motioned to someone outside the room, and Juan walked in with a tray piled high with fruit and fresh pastries.

While they dug into the delicious home-baked pastries, Doublecharge went over the salient points of the mission. The primary objective was to locate Destroyer's base of operations. They had the name and contact information of the CIA's operative who had originally tipped off the team to Destroyer's presence. He would be their starting point for the investigation.

The secondary objective was to find out any information about the antimatter woman's origin. To that end, they would visit her hometown of San José to retrace her steps.

"Guatemala is a small country," said Doublecharge. "I don't believe for a moment that her sudden appearance and Destroyer's presence are unrelated. We'll try to establish that connection and find out what he's up to."

At the end of two weeks, the expeditionary team would return to the States to make a report to Homeland Security. At that point, a decision would be made whether to follow up further and if such follow-up would be performed by Just Cause or by more covert operations.

"I don't see why the CIA doesn't just handle the whole investigation on its own," said Jack. "They've got plenty of experts and resources in that part of the world. And they've certainly got their own parahuman assets."

"Any CIA paras are most certainly being used elsewhere in the world at this time, probably in the Middle East," said Doublecharge.

They filed out of the conference room and headed down to the parking lot. Despite the freezing temperatures and the early hour, the rest of the team had turned out to see them off. Juice wore an oilskin duster and wide-brimmed leather hat over his bald pate. Sondra covered herself with a heavy Navajo blanket and wrapped her wings close about her for more warmth. Beside her, Jason yawned in his sweats and a rag hat. Forcestar kept a shimmering force field around him to trap his body heat and keep out the cold. A man Sally didn't recognize stood with them in an overcoat and with curly hair around his shoulders.

It began to snow as the van pulled into the circle. Juice stepped forward and shook everyone's hand. "Good luck," he told Sally. "I know you'll make us proud."

Without much preamble or fanfare, Sondra stepped up and gave Jack a deep, passionate kiss. In a moment, she stepped away and bussed Sally on the cheek, and whispered that she'd had to drag Jason out of bed because the poor kid was all worn out.

Jason stifled his yawns enough to wrap his arms around Sally, who shivered inside her coat. "I'll miss you," he whispered. "Be careful."

"I'll miss you too, and I will." She kissed him to savor the experience for as long as she dared delay their departure.

As she regretfully drew away from Jason, she saw Doublecharge embrace the curly-haired man. "Who's that?" she asked Glimmer.

"That's Mike, her husband."

"She's married?"

"Why not? Lots of people are." He winced as the wind began to pick up, adding a bite to the snow.

"I'm surprised she has time. That's all." Sally climbed into the van. "Don't you have someone to see you off?"

"Oh, I have a girlfriend," he said, "but she lives in Kansas City. I go visit her on my days off."

"Long distance relationship? That's got to be tough."

"It is at times. But she's worth the extra hassle."

"Are you going to marry her?" Sally had never given much thought to marriage before, but she couldn't help it now. Her developing romance with Jason had given her all kinds of new ideas and perspectives.

"Maybe someday," he said. "She's got a career there and I've got one here and neither of us really wants to pull up stakes and relocate."

The others got into the van while the driver secured their luggage in the rear. Sally wiped condensation off the window and waved shyly at Jason. She kissed her fingertips and touched them to the glass. He grinned and blew her a kiss.

"See you soon," she mouthed at him as the van pulled away.

Chapter Eighteen

"Something people tend to forget is that parahumans are not unique to the U.S. Japan had Rising Sun in World War II. Russia had Steel Wolf. Since then parahumans have surfaced all over the world. Who knows how many there are that we still haven't encountered yet?"

-Dr. Grace Devereaux, *60 Minutes,* October 17, 2000

February, 2004
Porto San José, Guatemala

Sally longed for the hot, dry deserts of home. Phoenix was as pleasant as a city could be this time of year. Guatemala was just as hot, a hundred times as humid, and stank like a cesspool.

Stepping off the plane in Guatemala City had been like getting hit in the face with a hot, wet towel. In climes like this, women were supposed to glow. Not Sally; she sweated and hated it. She couldn't decide which was worse, the droplets which ran down her back to soak the top of her underwear or the ones that trickled between her breasts. As soon as they got through Customs, she ducked into a bathroom with her suitcase and changed to the lightest tank top she had.

The others waited while Jack retrieved a large trunk from the cargo terminal, full of his special gear. He'd shipped it down separately to avoid any complications from flying public transport. A few bribes ensured the release of his property without any awkward questions about weapons, intrusion gear, and explosives. Being reunited with his equipment seemed to energize Jack, and he smiled a lot as he negotiated with a man for his car. "No way do we use public transportation down here," said Jack. "Not if we actually want to get where we're going."

The car in question turned out to be an antiquated Volkswagen bug with its roof and fenders cut off and no engine cover. It bore oversized tires that wouldn't have looked out of place on a military truck. A bank of headlights had been bolted to the hood, with exposed wires that ran along the flanks held in place by duct tape.

"Very good car, very dependable," said the owner. "Never had a problem with it." He patted it carefully, as if he expected the car itself to contradict him.

Jack had talked the guy down to two hundred American dollars plus two extra gas cans full of whatever passed locally for fuel. Most of the bags fit in the small trunk between the front wheels. They lashed the extra bags to the doors like saddlebags.

"If it dies while we're still in town, I'm coming back for my money," Jack told the man. He slipped behind the wheel while the others climbed in and got as comfortable as possible on the patched and cracked vinyl seats.

"Never had a problem with it." The man tucked the cash into a pocket.

Jack snorted and turned the key. The Volkswagen coughed and spat out a glob of thick smoke before it caught and exhibited a steady if uncertain purr. "Very reliable car." The man nodded encouragement as Jack ground the gears to find first. The car jerked forward as Jack negotiated his way through the congested streets of Guatemala City. By the map, it was only about fifty miles to Porto San José, where the Antimatter Woman had originally lived.

"How long do you think it'll take to get there?" Doublecharge called over the thrum of the motor.

"No idea." Jack leaned on the horn to encourage a man with a troop of mules to move them aside. "It could be late afternoon before we even get out of the city at this rate."

Glimmer leaned back in the cramped seat. His eyes were closed behind his sunglasses which reflected the swollen clouds that promised heavy rain later. Sally saw his lips twitch. "What is it?" she asked him.

"I can feel something here. Something hidden."

"Something bad?"

"It feels bad," he said. "I foresee we'll have a big problem when we find it."

"Precognition?" she asked, wide-eyed. Psionic powers had always fascinated her.

He took off his glasses and looked at her, his intense gaze unfaltering. "No, pessimism."

Jack burst out in laughter and even Doublecharge cracked a smile. Sally realized she'd been had as Glimmer finally broke his composure and chuckled.

"Jay follows the philosophy of hope for the best but expect the worst," said Jack. "That way he covers all bases and still gets to act all mysterious."

They drove for a couple hours before Jack got them onto the road to San José. They stopped on the edge of town at a roadside market and bought some rolled sandwiches, fruit, and bottled water. "Don't drink anything not in a bottle or can," said Jack. "I'm immune, but I'd rather not truck around a carload of dysentery sufferers."

"Hey, has Jack been here before?" Sally asked Doublecharge while Jack checked on road conditions from some of the other shoppers.

"I don't know. He's been a lot of places." Stacey rolled the remains of her sandwich up in the wrapper and stuck it in a pocket. "I want to talk to you about Jason."

Sally almost choked on a sip of water. "Uh, what about him?"

"I don't have a problem with the two of you having a relationship, but it had better not affect your performance as part of this team."

"Don't worry, it won't," said Sally with a frosty tone.

"Good. Then that's all I'll say on the matter. You're a valuable addition to this team, and based on what I've seen so far, I'll recommend you for full membership at the end of your internship." Doublecharge stood up. "See to it that doesn't change." She walked away and headed for the car.

Sally didn't move, not sure whether to be insulted, angry, pleased, or worried. She settled for worried, since that was the expression on Jack's face as he came back to the table.

"What is it?" Sally asked as he sat down.

"Road's washed out about halfway between here and there."

"And?" She sensed there was more to come.

"There's a group of bandits, preying on travelers."

"Is that all? Um, they should be the ones worried about us, shouldn't they?"

"Under normal circumstances, yes. But right now we're trying to keep an extremely low profile, and it's hard enough just being foreigners. If Destroyer's really here, he's going to have one ear to the ground and he'll find out if any of us use our powers publicly."

"Oh." Sally suddenly felt very small.

"And we're just the sort of stupid tourists bandits will love."

"So what do we do?"

"Plan B." Jack collected the remains of his lunch and stood up.

"What's Plan B?"

"I haven't figured it out yet."

They got back on the road. Within an hour, the clouds broke open. Sally knew rain, but this was more like steady sheets of warm water, reminiscent of a waterfall in an amusement park ride. She was soaked through in moments. They had to open the doors of the Bug to keep the seats from flooding.

As quickly as the rain started, it stopped. Sally felt miserable, hot and wet, and the heady smells wafting from the soaked jungle made her nose itch. After only a few minutes, it started to rain again.

"Lovely country." Jack blew raindrops away from his eyes. "I'm thinking we ought to open a satellite headquarters for the team here."

The Volkswagen bounced across muddy ruts. Jack had to fight the wheel the whole time. This became the pattern over the next two hours: drenching rain showers punctuated by brief bursts of calm. In several places, the road was so bad they had to act as spotters, guiding Jack so the Bug's wheels didn't slip into deep ruts or catch the frame on jutting rocks. By the time they ran into the washout, they were all soaked and covered with mud, and only Jack had any marginal sense of humor remaining.

Sally had never really considered what the term *washout* really meant until she stared at one before her. A wall of mud had poured down the side of the mountain earlier, and several trees below the road level were mutilated. No longer anchored by roots, the road had collapsed into a trench almost four feet deep. A heavily tricked-out four-wheel drive might have made the crossing okay, but their Bug wasn't going to get across without some serious labor.

Glimmer suggested they use logs to make a temporary bridge over the trench and ropes to anchor the Bug so it wouldn't slide. "Great idea if we had any ropes," said Jack. "Maybe you could lift it across telekinetically?"

"I wouldn't want to risk it. I've never moved anything that heavy, and if I dropped it we might lose it completely. Besides . . ." His face darkened in consternation. "There's still something out there. I think it would be best if we all avoided using our powers as much as possible. It could be like striking a match in a dark room."

Jack sighed. "I guess we do it the old-fashioned way." He opened his bag and withdrew an axe and a saw.

"What, no chainsaw?" Glimmer grinned.

Jack shook his head. "Too noisy. Let's see if we can find some deadfall long enough to make a good bridge. I'd rather not have to cut something down."

They spread out and ranged up and down the hillside to look for fallen trees. Several were available, but they were all wet and extremely heavy. It took all four of the heroes to drag the logs over to the road and to place them over the trench.

"I wish Jason was here." Jack wiped sweat from his brow. "He digs on heavy work like this."

"That'd keep Sally happy," said Glimmer.

Sally glared at him as she tried to dig out a splinter embedded deep in her palm. "Does everybody know about us?"

"I don't think anybody's called the Lucky Seven yet," said Jack, chuckling.

"All right, you two." Doublecharge wrapped an entire roll of duct tape around the logs to keep them from slipping once the Bug's weight was upon them.

The sun had already dropped behind the mountains when they finished building their makeshift bridge. *Don't travel after nightfall,* advised the State Department's Consular Information Sheet for Guatemala. *Extremely dangerous.* Sally looked with apprehension into the darkening jungle as they moved all their gear to the other side of the washout. If the Bug slipped and got stuck or fell altogether, at least they'd still have their supplies.

Jack started the Bug after they were all safely clear. "If it starts to slip, I'm jumping out," he informed them. "I'd rather not spend the night hiking back up here.

And the longer we wait it out, the more likely we are to run into the bandits." He flipped on the Bug's lights and began to nudge the car forward. It hung up on the raised edge of the bridge until Jack goosed the throttle and it climbed the bump.

Timbers creaked and duct tape stretched as the logs shifted a couple of inches. "Jay, are you helping?" Doublecharge asked.

"No."

"Do it if the car's going to fall. I don't want to spend the night in this jungle under any circumstances. I'll take the chance that we won't be discovered."

The Bug inched forward as Jack tried to look in every direction at once. One of the logs cracked and splintered, causing the left front wheel to slide to one side. Glimmer raised his arms in preparation to focus his telekinesis, but Jack managed to save it. The falling rain somehow increased in intensity to a roar as the front wheels dropped off the bridge onto the muddy road.

Water coursed down through the washout as Sally watched in concern. "I think this washout is going to get worse fast."

Jack nodded, white-knuckled, as the Bug's rear wheels spun against the edge of the bridge without climbing up onto it.

"Shit!" He turned around in his seat to see where he was stuck.

"You're going to have to get a bit of a running start," said Doublecharge. "It's like jumping a curb."

"Says the woman who can fly," said Jack. "*All things being equal, I'd rather be in Philadelphia.*"

"*Die Hard,*" said Sally. "We watched that last week. Jack, you'd better hurry up. I can see more mud washing away."

Jack carefully backed up the Bug until the front wheels sat just over the bridge's edge. He took his hands off the wheel for a moment and flexed all his fingers. Then he took a deep breath, hit the throttle, and popped the clutch. The Bug's rear tires spun in the mud for a moment then bumped up onto the bridge. Wood cracked and duct tape split. Jack floored it in pure panic. The Bug skittered across the bridge and slid to a stop in the mud beyond. Their makeshift bridge collapsed into the trench and washed down the side of the mountain by the torrent of muddy water.

Jack pushed his soaked hair back from his forehead, leaned back in his seat, and closed his eyes. "That's the longest four feet I've ever driven. I'm done for the day. Can anyone else drive a stick?"

"We're surprised you made it at all, *norte americano,*" said a voice from the trees. Several men stepped out onto the road, both in front of and behind the team. All wore threadbare fatigues and carried automatic rifles. Several also carried plastic coolers. The brightly-colored plastic was incongruous amid the greens and browns of the jungle. "Hands up." The speaker was a heavyset man with a thick mustache and a white scar on his chin.

Sally glanced quickly at Doublecharge to see what she should do. Doublecharge raised her hands cautiously, as did Glimmer. Sally lifted her own as well, but shifted her perceptions into high gear in preparation for fight or flight.

Jack stuck his hands in the air. "Easy, pal. You're getting no trouble from us. We'll pay whatever toll you want if you'll let us go on our way."

"You're a long way from the tourist spots," the scar-faced man said. "No *policía* this far out. We'll take what we want as we please. Paco, Eduardo . . . get their bags."

Two other men slung their rifles and dragged the heroes' bags over to the bandits' leader, who waved the tip of his rifle at Jack. "Out of the car, *señor.* Let's have a look at the four of you." He handed his rifle to another man, drew a pistol, and advanced on him.

Sally quivered like a racehorse before the starting pistol. Running would be treacherous on the slick mud, but it would hamper the bandits' movement just as much as it would hers. The leader examined each of them close enough that they could smell the stink of his breath. "Nice and healthy, yes? No alcohol, no tobacco. Good clean living. I love *americanos*. You take such good care of your bodies."

Several of the men burst out in laughter at this. The others looked confused until one of them translated in rapid-fire Spanish.

"I'll tell you what," said the leader. "I'm in a great mood today. I'll let three of you go, and I'll even let you take the car. The fourth one . . . stays with us."

"Take me," said Jack.

"Shut up, Jack," said Doublecharge. "No deal. We all leave together."

"What? You let your woman speak for you, *señor*? I'm shocked!"

"Not as shocked as you're going to be." A tiny spark snapped in one of Doublecharge's eyes.

The leader smiled at her with a mouthful of rotten teeth. "I'll take this one. She looks like she'll provide a bountiful harvest."

"No!" Jack leaped toward the leader. Several guns thundered and Jack spun about in midair as the bullets impacted all over him. He tumbled to the ground and lay still. Sally and Glimmer threw themselves to the ground, as did Doublecharge and the bandit leader.

"Goddammit, don't shoot while I'm out here, you assholes!" The leader shook his fist at his men. "Somebody check that *pendejo* and see if we can salvage anything."

Sally began to get an icky, cold feeling in the small of her back as she saw two men come forward with large coolers and knives. Salvage? What did that mean? Suddenly it came to her. In the Consular Sheets, she'd read a short little blurb about people being kidnapped for their organs. The State Department had discounted the tales as rumors.

Something colorful flashed past her, fast enough only to be a blur to everyone else. Her brain protested that such a thing had to be a figment of her panicked imagination. It was a feathered, winged snake with a razor-sharp blade for a tail that whipped past the two men who approached Jack. It caught each one across the throat with its tail and left a spray of bright arterial blood in its wake. Everyone froze for a moment as the two men swayed before they toppled, and then all hell broke loose.

Doublecharge hit the leader with such a hard jolt of electricity that he flew backward through the air, knocked right out of his boots, and bounced down the slope until he fetched up against a tree with his fatigues and skin blackened and smoldering. Glimmer grunted with the effort of concentration and three men dropped to the ground, either unconscious or dead from his psionic attack. Jack uncurled from his fetal position to reveal a short, ugly pistol in his hand. He fired the entire clip into the largest grouping of opponents, unconcerned about their return fire.

Sally wavered, uncertain what to do. A man who aimed his gun at Doublecharge galvanized her into action. In a flash, Sally moved next to him, dropped his clip from the weapon and popped out the unfired bullet. He pulled on the trigger, but got only an empty click. Before she could do anything else, the feathered serpent looped around his head and stuck its tail straight through the back of his neck. Blood spattered Sally and she recoiled in shock.

As suddenly as the fight had begun, it was over. Silence reigned across the mountainside except for patter of rain on leaves and a few muffled gurgles from men as they bled to death.

Jack got to his feet, his clothing shredded from the gunfire. "Everyone okay?"

Sally's stomach clenched and she barely remembered to hold her braids back as she vomited up her lunch.

Doublecharge was by her side in a moment, her hands cool on Sally's head. "You all right, Sally?"

Sally wiped her mouth with a hand that shook like a leaf in a gale. Glimmer handed her a water bottle. She spilled half of it.

"You've never been in lethal combat before, have you?" Stacey asked.

Sally shook her head, glad it was still raining so they couldn't see her tears.

"Listen, Sally . . ." Jack slipped a new clip into his pistol, and tucked it back into his belt. "These guys were bad. Real bad. They would have killed us all without a second thought and stolen our body parts to sell on the black market. It was either us or them. Me, I'm glad it was them."

She nodded and risked a tiny sip of water into her queasy stomach. The winged snake had curled around a low tree branch and regarded them with curious, bird-like eyes. "What is that thing?" Glimmer asked.

"I think it's called a *Quetzalcoatl*," said Jack. "It shouldn't be here. They're mythical." The snake stuck a forked tongue out at Jack and flicked it back and forth, tasting the air.

Sally got the distinct idea that it was laughing at them. "Do you think it understands us? *Hola, señor serpiente. ¿Usted me entiende?*"

The snake bobbed its head up and down in an unmistakable *yes*.

"This is all very interesting." Doublecharge looked around. "But it's not getting us to Porto San José any faster. If the snake wants to talk things over, it can do it on the road. I've had about all the surprises I want for one day, and I want to get out of this goddamned rain." She shook her bedraggled locks for emphasis.

The snake dropped from its branch to the ground. With a flash and a smell of ozone, rain flashed into steam and instead of a winged snake, they saw a slight boy, maybe sixteen years old, huddled naked in a fresh crater in the hillside.

Jack's pistol appeared in his hands so fast that even Sally didn't see him draw. "Hold it right there."

The boy raised one hand to comply but left the other to cover himself and stayed hunched over. "Please, *señor*, no be afraid. I no speak when I am *el Quetzalcoatl.*" His accent was thick but decipherable.

"Who are you?" Doublecharge asked. Lightning crackled around her fist.

"Diego. You American superheroes, *sí*?"

"Whatever gave you that idea?" Jack's eyes narrowed.

"You shot lots, not hurt. She shot lightning. She very fast." He pointed to each of them in turn.

"You were watching us?" Glimmer asked

"*Sí.* I follow *los bandidos de riñónes y de ojos.*"

"The what?" Sally didn't recognize the words he'd used, but her Spanish classes had been lacking in criminal vernacular.

"Stealers of kidneys and eyes," said Jack.

"Very bad men. Deserve to die."

"No argument from me there," said Doublecharge.

"You here for compound?"

"A compound, Diego?" Jack asked.

"You destroy it? Bad place." The boy's voice was hopeful, but his face fell as he looked at the four of them. "Only four of you. Not enough"

Doublecharge and Jack exchanged glances. "Diego, where do you live?" asked Stacey.

"Porto San José, with *mi madre.*"

"Want a lift back to town? You can ride on the running board."

"I fly back, but then I no speak to you." He looked down at himself. "*Lo siento*. My clothes lost when I become *Quetzalcoatl*."

"We'll see what we can round up for you," said Doublecharge. "Sally, you're the only one small enough to have anything that might fit him. Think you could find him a pair of pants?"

Sally nodded. Diego was an attractive boy, with smooth brown skin, shoulder-length black hair, and straight teeth. Although he wasn't bulked-up like Jason, she could see the play of every muscle under his skin. He smiled up at her from his crouched position. "*Gracias, señorita*."

"*De nada*." She blushed.

They left the bodies where they had fallen. Jack said the jungle would take care of them with its own quick and unique efficiency.

In a few minutes, they had stowed the luggage back onto the Bug and were on their way. Diego stood on the passenger-side running board and held onto the door for balance. He wore only a pair of Sally's cutoff jeans around his narrow hips. Although he mostly spoke to Doublecharge, he often glanced back at Sally in a way that made her feel embarrassed. This Guatemalan boy had a raw sexuality about him that had her hormones all in a twist. Maybe it was because he was foreign. Maybe it was just her body's reaction to the high stress of the combat.

"Tell me about this compound you mentioned, Diego," Doublecharge said.

"It there long time. Tribes afraid. Many people gone. Whole villages in mountains gone. Maybe people there."

"Who's in charge of it?" Glimmer asked.

"I no know English word. *Un extranjero*."

"A foreigner," said Sally.

"American? A black man? *Un hombre negro*?" Jack asked over his shoulder.

219

"No. White man, yellow hair." Diego reached out and stroked Sally's hair for a second. She was so surprised she didn't recoil from the sudden familiarity from this boy she barely knew. Sally figured the man had to be Heinrich Kaiser.

"Diego, how did you learn what you do know about it?" Doublecharge asked.

"Compound soldiers buy supplies in Porto José. Sometimes they get drunk. I listen. *Mi madre* has a bar."

"How long have you been able to turn into a, uh, *quest* . . . *quelt* . . ." Sally floundered over the unfamiliar word.

"*Quetzalcoatl* is new to me. I get very sick, almost die."

"Have you seen a black American man in town? He'd be about my age and very smart, maybe buying electronic and mechanical parts?" Jack asked.

"*Sí*, I see him. He here very long time. Many crates come to him at port. He no drink. *Mi madre* says never trust man who won't take drink."

"Your mother sounds like a wise woman." Jack chuckled. "Do you know of a place we can stay while we're in the port?"

"Sí. Rooms above the bar. Very clean. Very nice."

"We'll pay cash for them."

"*Muy bueno.*" Diego grinned as his hair flapped in the breeze.

"One last question, Diego," said Jack as the Bug cleared the edge of the trees. The lights of Porto San José twinkled in the near distance. "Do you by any chance know a man named Luís de la Barros?"

Diego's smile vanished. "*El traficante.* He stays at port hotel. Many guns. You buying?"

"*Sí,*" said Jack.

"Who's that?" Sally whispered to Glimmer.

Our CIA contact, said a voice inside her head which made her jump. He turned his head to look at her. *Don't ask too many questions. Diego is telling the truth as far*

*as he knows it, but I sense something deceitful about him,
something hidden deep in his mind.*

"There it is," called Diego as he pointed toward the
ramshackle town crouched on the seaside. "*Hay* Porto
San José!"

"I'm sure we'll find what we're looking for there,"
said Doublecharge.

"I'm sure we'll hate what we find," countered Jack
under his breath.

Chapter Nineteen

The battle between members of Just Cause and the criminal Destroyer dealt a strong wake-up call to the organization. Prior to that event, Just Cause had been primarily a reactionary organization—responding to specific parahuman crimes but not actively attempting to prevent them. The deaths of six past and present members of Just Cause—Lionheart, Sundancer, Danger, Fast Break, Audio, and the destruction of the Steel Soldier—could be linked directly to the failure of Just Cause to follow up on the whereabouts of Harlan Washington, builder and operator of the Destroyer battlesuit after his escape from juvenile detention.

Subsequently, Just Cause became much more proactive: seeking out the criminals before they committed their crimes; building the Deep Six prison facility; performing surveillance and raids.

-Dr. Grace Devereaux, *Just Cause: Sixty Years of Heroism*, 2000

February, 2004
Porto San José, Guatemala

Glimmer hadn't dared to perform deep telepathic scans on Diego or his mother. Since he believed Diego's mind had been tampered with, he didn't want to risk setting off any post-telepathic compulsions. He said it as the telepathic equivalent of a booby trap.

"I don't trust it," he said when they all met in Jack's room after a delicious dinner of spiced pork and rice, courtesy of Diego's mother. "It's all too neat, too perfect. We were expected."

Jack stood by the window, an unlit cigar in his lips that Doublecharge had forbidden him to light or she was going to make him eat it. "You think he's a plant?"

"Absolutely," Glimmer said. "Maybe not for us specifically, but I'm certain his appearance was no accident. Someone intended him to be found."

Doublecharge frowned. "He's a sleeper, then."

"That's my assessment. I've found traces that he's been manipulated, or at least read recently. And by someone talented," he said with a glum sigh.

"Better than you?" asked Jack.

"Maybe. I don't dare scan any deeper."

"We need information about this mysterious compound he mentioned," said Doublecharge.

"He seems anxious enough to please," Sally said as she brushed her hair. "Maybe we could just ask him."

Doublecharge stood up. "You packed a swimsuit, didn't you?"

"Well . . . yes," said Sally, embarrassed.

"Good. Why don't you take our little friend to the beach in the morning and find out what he can tell us about the compound? We need as much information as you can pump out of him."

"You don't mean . . . *that*, do you?" cried Sally.

Doublecharge gave a slight smile, as amused as Sally had ever seen her. "Of course not. This isn't a primetime melodrama."

"Why have me do it? Wouldn't Jay be better?"

"Certainly, but Diego doesn't have a crush on Jay. He does seem infatuated with you. Therefore, you're elected," said Jack.

"There should be a recount, then," said Sally. "What are the rest of you going to do, go shopping?"

"As a matter of fact, yes. Well, sort of," said Doublecharge. "Jay will check with our CIA contact to get any updated information. Jack will search town for signs of Washington, since he's had the most firsthand experience with him. I'll be checking the docks for more information about Washington's incoming freight and his relationship with Kaiser."

"By yourself?" Sally was shocked.

"I don't really think I have to worry about being mugged. Do you?"

"I guess not."

"Good," said Doublecharge. "Then get a good night's rest. Tomorrow we track down Destroyer."

As they broke the meeting, Glimmer asked, "Sally, have you got a minute?"

"Sure."

"Would you mind if I set up a telepathic recorder in your brain?"

Sally stopped in mid-stride. "You want to run that past me again?"

"It's a technique I developed. Basically it optimizes your brain for information retention, keyed to a specific telepathic contact."

"English, Jay. I'm tired."

"I want to turn you into a telepathic camcorder."

"I see."

"Most people have faulty memories. Their brains don't record all information available; just enough to get the general idea. It's not a flaw. It's just how the mind is constructed. We'd all go crazy if we had to store all the information our senses record constantly."

"You're going to make me go crazy?"

"Of course not. You're not going to have direct access to those memories. I'll access them from a telepathic key later. You won't even know they're there. This way we can make sure you don't miss any important details, or even minor details that at the time seem unimportant."

"Oh. Will it hurt?"

"Not at all. You won't feel a thing, I promise."

Sally was about to agree, but stopped. "Don't take this the wrong way or anything, Jay, but you're not going to, like, read my mind or anything like that, are you? I mean, there are things I'd kind of rather you didn't know."

He raised a hand. "I swear. Your thoughts are your own. All I'm going to do is make your memory perfect for the next day or so."

"Well . . . I guess that's okay. What do I do?"

"Don't do anything. I just need a moment." He closed his eyes. Sally concentrated on herself, to see if she felt any sign of him poking around in her mind. Not that she would know what it felt like if he did.

He opened his eyes again. "All finished."

"That's it? No *Vulcan mind-meld* or anything like that?" Sally wondered if she should be disappointed.

Glimmer laughed. "Maybe some other time."

The next morning, Sally put on a bikini top and a pair of shorts and mentioned that she was going to go check out a beach and asked Diego if he knew of any good places.

"*Sí, señorita*," he'd said, and shortly they wound up on a beautiful stretch of white sand. Diego wore only a pair of shorts and a big smile. He'd returned Sally's shorts freshly laundered and folded.

They had walked north through the small town to the beach. The sun shone bright and the sky was an amazing shade of blue without a cloud to mar it, which was quite the contrast to the previous day's hard rains. Sally suffered the walk in silence, which allowed Diego to carry on a happy monologue about the various inhabitants of Porto San José.

"Tell me more about the compound, Diego," she said when he took a break from his bilingual chatter.

"I said all yesterday," he said.

Inwardly cringing, she leaned a little closer toward him to tilt her chest more into his view. His eyes glanced downward before he looked back into hers. She'd never, ever before used what her mother called feminine wiles to get anything she wanted. It felt awkward and uncomfortable. "I know, but there's got to be more. Have you ever been there?"

"Once, as *Quetzalcoatl*," he said. "I fly there to see if stories true."

"What did you see there?"

"Army buildings. Big building too."

"Any people?"

Diego smiled. "Army people." He leaned backward to laze on the sun-warmed sand and folded his hands behind his head. "I show if you want."

Sally was about to say no, but then remembered the thing Glimmer had put in her mind. She debated whether she should risk it without any support from the team. In the end, she decided, she was anxious to prove herself and earn a permanent place on the Just Cause roster. If things got really bad, she could always run away. "Okay, Diego. Show me."

He sat up, brushed sand from his shoulders, and shook it out of his hair. "Come." He held out his hand to her.

She hesitated as she thought of Jason, but she decided holding hands wasn't cheating, and anyway, she was at work. She took the proffered hand and let Diego lead her off the beach. "How do we get there? Is it very far?"

"You fly?"

"No."

"Run then?"

Sally considered it. "Better not. Is there another way?"

"My cousin has motorcycle. We ride there."

Sally's heart pattered a little faster. She'd never been on a motorcycle. "All right, I trust you."

Diego took her to the docks. She kept an eye open for Stacey but saw no sign of the team leader. Diego talked to another man, older and less handsome. They went around the corner of a warehouse. In a moment, Sally heard an engine fire and Diego came back astride a dirt bike. He pulled it up next to her and shouted over the *BRAP BRAP BRAP* of the exhaust. "My cousin say you

227

very beautiful. Please . . ." He motioned to the seat, which looked like it belonged on a touring cycle.

Sally climbed onto the seat behind Diego.

"Exhaust pipe very hot. Don't put leg on it. Put feet there and there . . ." He motioned to two pegs bolted to the body of the bike. "Arms around my waist."

Sally clasped her hands together against his abdomen. In spite of the humidity, his skin was warm and dry and stretched tight like canvas. It was a very intimate position, she thought.

Diego pulled the bike away from the docks, careful to avoid any rapid acceleration or sudden maneuvers. He navigated quickly through the town and took them along a one-lane road that headed northeast. "This road take us up above compound. Maybe you see what you look for."

"Sounds great." Although Sally had been determined not to enjoy herself, she found the feel of the wind whipping her hair very pleasant, like when she ran, but without the effort.

For the next forty-five minutes, Sally had a lot of fun. Diego picked the smoothest path along the rough road. He didn't try to show off with daring maneuvers or riding too fast. Every ten minutes or so, he'd turn his head to shout over the engine and ask if she needed to stop. The road climbed back and forth up the side of an ancient volcano and wound through the trees. They skirted the caldera, which had lush green bushes and a pool at the bottom.

Diego shut off the bike and wheeled it into the foliage at the side of the road. "Guards down below. We walk from here." He pulled a long machete from a sheath strapped to the front shock absorbers. They pulled some broadleaf fronds over the bike to disguise it from anyone passing by.

"How much further is it, Diego?"

He thought for a moment, and said, "Not far. You need rest?"

"No," Sally said with a smile, "but thanks for asking."

He motioned toward a nearby peak that jutted up into the sky. "We climb up there, go around a ways, and then we see the compound." He patted a canteen at his side. "I have water for now. We refill at stream along the way."

"Well, aren't you just the little *Indiana Jones?*"

"*No sé qué es eso, señorita.*"

"It's a movie, about—oh, never mind. Lead on."

Hiking through the mountainside jungle wasn't at all like in the movies. The trees had thick boles, but weren't so far apart to make it hard to pass between them. Vines dangled from overhead branches or clung to the trunks. The ground was damp and little red and yellow flowers grew in clumps, surrounded by clouds of tiny insects. Broadleaf plants grew everywhere, which made a second canopy at knee height. Instead of hacking away at every vine and sapling within reach, Diego barely used the machete at all. He picked a path around the thickest undergrowth. Bugs the size of model airplanes buzzed past her, quick enough that try as she might she couldn't slap one away. After several minutes, she got so tired of slapping at herself that she gave up and knew she'd be one big itchy spot by nightfall.

Diego's canteen was empty by the time they reached the stream; the heat and humidity had taken their toll on the two hikers. "Is it safe to drink?" Visions of dangerous bacteria and viruses danced through Sally's head, courtesy of a thousand hours of late night movies and video games.

"If no," said Diego as he smiled and wiped his mouth. "We get sick. Rest now, *señorita.*"

Sally stripped off her boots and socks and plunged her feet into the stream to let the cool water soothe her feet. Climbing was a lot harder on her than running. She wasn't tired, because she could go for a few hundred miles at a single stretch, but whereas running was nice and rhythmic, hiking through the Guatemalan jungle was a series of starts, stops, and stutters that had her feet aching. Some people might long for a comfortable recliner after a long hike; Sally longed for a long stretch of straight, flat road where she could get up to a comfortable cruising speed and just run.

"Maybe I come with you to America," said Diego. "Be a superhero like you, *señorita*."

"My name's Sally, Diego. It's okay to use it. I don't know if you could join Just Cause or not." She cursed at herself for her accidental slip. She hadn't wanted to mention Just Cause at all. She hoped it hadn't spoiled their plans, but Diego didn't react to it.

"Maybe I just come and visit you, then. You have boyfriend in America?"

"Yes, I do."

He shrugged and smiled. "Is it serious?"

Sally yanked the canteen away from him. "Yes, it's serious. How old are you, anyway?"

He puffed out his chest. "Almost fifteen."

"Well, almost-fifteen-Diego, let me tell you something. When you're twenty-two, you are going to be absolutely stunning. Girls won't be able to keep their hands off you. But for now, you should find a sweet young thing your own age. Now you tell me . . ." Sally took a swig from the canteen. "Do you have a girlfriend?"

He chuckled. "*Sí*."

"Is she pretty?" Sally passed the canteen back to him.

"Not like you, *señori*—er, Sally. She's sixteen and wears glasses."

"I can tell you this, Diego. If she's two years older and still with you, she must think very highly of you. You should be thankful for that."

"Okay," he said as he stood. "Maybe I leave her for someone better someday." He winked at her. "Time to go. We see compound very soon."

The downhill side of the volcano proved much easier hiking. They followed along the stream and only had to worry about slipping in the mud. Even the hot sun relented as puffy white clouds blew in from the ocean.

Soon Diego put his finger to his lips to indicate silence. He motioned for her to get down as he moved with the quiet confidence of a cat. Sally crawled after him until the two of them peeked out into a large clearing from under the shelter of a large fern.

Down below, Sally saw several buildings. Most were made of cinderblocks, but the largest was modern, high-tech construction. She thought it might be a power plant of some sort, since a large smokestack belched forth steam into the already-humid air. It had no windows, but she saw fortifications on and around it, machine gun nests with sandbags and razor wire. One contraption looked like it might be some kind of missile launcher amid a forest of radar dishes. She wished Jack were there, because with his knowledge he'd know immediately what she saw. People guarded the fortifications, inattentive until they heard a distant engine.

In a few moments, an ancient bus wheezed into the center of the compound, flanked by three jeeps full of soldiers. The compound became a flurry of activity as uniformed troops rushed from the buildings to take up positions around the bus. People began to get off the bus. They held their hands atop their heads and trudged at the direction of the soldiers, grim and hopeless prisoners.

Several of the soldiers floated into the air and trained guns or pointed hands at the prisoners. Sally gaped in astonishment. As she looked around, she saw evidence of more parahuman powers: a man whose skin seemed to be metallic, and a woman whose eyes had an unearthly glow.

She whispered, "How many are there?"

"What?"

"Parahumans, Diego. How many?"

"I don't know. Many."

This was bad news. Based upon pure percentages of population, Guatemala shouldn't have more than two or three parahumans altogether, and Sally suspected there were at least ten times as many down in that compound. More, if some of those who held guns had less-obvious abilities.

Two men came out of the large building to inspect the prisoners. One was very old, hunched, and skeletally thin. He leaned on a cane. His skin was very dark. The other was Heinrich Kaiser. He affected a slow pace, either out of choice or out of deference to the older man. He stood, ramrod-straight, while one of the men from the jeeps reported to him. He nodded and gave an order. The soldiers hustled the prisoners into the large building.

The compound went into another brief period of activity as troops opened several round hatches in the ground and climbed into underground facilities of some sort. In a few minutes, the compound seemed entirely deserted and quiet.

"What are they doing?" Sally wondered.

Diego's eyes were wide and sweat ran off his face in rivulets. "Time to go, *señorita*."

"What's going to happen? What are you afraid of?"

Diego didn't have a chance to answer. The ground suddenly vibrated, as if a giant had struck a powerful chord on a subsonic guitar. The vibration made Sally's feet go numb and her eyes water. Something came from the large building, like a shockwave or a ripple that traveled in an expanding concentric circle. She felt a hard prickling in her skin as it passed over them, like her entire body had been asleep and tingled as it awoke. A huge puff of steam emerged from the cooling tower, rivaling a large cloud overhead in sheer volume.

Diego fell down on all fours, cowering like a dog scolded for stealing a baby's snack.

She hauled him to his feet. "What just happened?"

"*El fuego, el fuego*," the boy said repeatedly. *The fire.*

"Snap out of it, Diego!" She slapped him across the face. Hard.

His eyes regained their focus. "*Lo siento*," he said. "Time to go."

"Change into the snake and lead the way. I'll keep up with you."

Diego nodded, and transformed in a flash of light. Sally hoped nobody saw it or attributed it to anything besides lightning. The jewel-toned Quetzalcoatl spun around, hovered like a hummingbird, and lit out up the side of the hill. Sally scrambled after him as fast as she could go.

Unfortunately, Sally stepped in a hole right at the crest of the hill and went sprawling. In a flash, she was back on her feet but her knee already throbbed. Diego swooped around her like a nervous satellite. "I'm okay." She waved at him. "Let's go."

They crossed the ridge they had come up earlier in the afternoon and a few seconds later Sally limped to a halt by the bike.

Diego kept going. "Diego!" She yelled after him. She took a dozen half-hearted steps in pursuit, but her knee felt like it was full of broken glass. She hoped she hadn't torn a ligament or something worse.

Okay, how hard could it be to ride a bike?

She struggled to get it upright and back onto the road. It wasn't a big bike, but she wasn't very big herself. Moving it proved even more difficult when she couldn't put all her weight on her right leg. "Son of a bitch, Diego," she mumbled under her breath. "Shit."

She wondered why she even bothered with the bike at all. She was a superhero, dammit. She thought about running back to town, gimpy leg or no, but she feared her running would be over for a few days, maybe longer if she really damaged herself. She was still supposed to stay incognito, and it would look very suspicious if someone spotted her limping along the road without any obvious transportation. It would have to be the bike, then.

She got herself astride it, held onto the handlebars, and wondered how in the world to start it.

There was no key that she could find, but maybe she didn't need one. She'd always seen guys on the X-Games start their bikes by jumping on one of the pegs. She closed her eyes and tried to access the perfect memory that Glimmer had set up for her the night before, but there didn't seem to be any sign of it. How had Diego started it? Maybe that peg at the end of the arm was it. It didn't have one matching on the left side of the engine.

She tested it with her injured leg, to see if it even moved. It did just a little. That had to be it. She didn't know how she was going to manage to jump on it. Her knee already resembled a balloon, and the idea of landing with even a fraction of her weight on it was enough to make her feel faint.

A small voice behind her said, "I'm sorry, *señorita*."

She turned to see Diego hunched down amid the bushes at the edge of the road. She'd never been so glad to see someone else, and the relief overcame her and her eyes brimmed with tears. "Oh, Diego!"

"I am very scared. Please no be mad." He hung his head in shame.

"I'm just happy that you came back, Diego. I don't know how to drive this stupid bike, and I hurt my leg real bad back there."

"I drive it."

He stood up and stepped out of the bushes. Both he and Sally realized that he was naked. The moment only lasted for a brief second before he hurried to cover himself, but not before she'd gotten a real eyeful.

"I'm sorry!" Diego was mortified.

"Oh, uh, that's okay." Sally turned away from him to save him from further embarrassment.

"I lose all my pants that way. *Mi madre* no understand it."

"Here," said Sally decisively, and slipped her own shorts off. Underneath was the bottom half of the bikini she'd bought on a day when she felt particularly brave. Her mother would have called it scandalous for the lack of coverage it provided.

She tossed him the shorts and turned her back, but not before she caught another glimpse. *His girlfriend is very lucky*, she thought, and almost giggled aloud in spite of her discomfort. In a moment, he hopped onto the bike in front of her.

They rode back to town. Every time the bike jarred Sally's leg, pain shot down to her toes and up to her hip. Diego took her right back to his mother's bar. Glimmer sat outside the building and watched people pass by. He jumped up when he saw the bike pull up and helped Diego get Sally off it, since she couldn't straighten her leg or bend it any further. She'd given up all pretenses of being a tough hero, and tears of pain and frustration streamed down her face.

Glimmer and Diego carried her up to her room above the bar. Diego went downstairs to get some ice. Glimmer inspected her knee. "I'm no doctor, but I don't think it's broken. Maybe a sprain?"

Sally leaned back on the bed and threw an arm across her eyes in frustration. "A sprain. Great. What the hell am I supposed to do now? I could heal a pulled muscle in an hour or two, but a sprain will take at least three or four days."

"There's a technique I can try," he said. "But there's a catch. I'm not very good at it, and it's going to hurt a lot whether or not I succeed. Your call."

"But you said you said you couldn't use your powers here, that the mystery psi would be able to detect you."

235

Glimmer nodded. "That's true, but I've been doing some very light scans around the area, getting a sense of what we're really up against. I think only direct telepathic contact, like mind-reading or psionic attacks will put up a red flag."

Sally tried to make sense of this. She'd never understood psionic abilities or the related terminology. "So you can use some of your powers safely, but not all of them?"

"More or less," said Glimmer. "It's more complicated than that, but you've got it essentially right."

"And you can do . . . whatever-it-is . . . to me safely?"

"I believe so."

"Then do it," Sally said. "Before I change my mind or pass out or something. Can't you just put me to sleep like you did in training?"

"It doesn't work that way. Psionically-induced sleep isn't like anesthetic. It's just sleep. You'd wake up if a dog started chewing on your leg, wouldn't you?"

Sally wiped tears away. "I hope so. Is it going to hurt that much?"

"Worse, I'm afraid. It's why I don't generally use the ability. It's hard to hurt your friends."

Sally glared at him. "I'm no good to you stuck here in bed with a bum leg. I forgive you for whatever I'm going to feel. I forgive you in case it doesn't work. But if you don't try, I'll never forgive you, Jay Road!"

Glimmer placed his hands on either side of her swollen knee and closed his eyes. Searing hot pain exploded in her leg. It made white stars erupt in her vision. She let out a yelp that she muffled in the crook of her elbow. It felt like he was digging around inside her damaged leg with a telekinetic scalpel and pushing every cell back into its correct place by brute force. Nausea roiled her stomach. She could not bear to look, out of fear that he had ripped her leg into fleshy ribbons.

Glimmer leaned back and pulled his hands away from her leg. His hair was damp and sweat poured down his face. "Finished."

"Did it . . . work?" Her leg throbbed, but compared to the pain of psionic healing it was almost tolerable.

"I don't know. We'll have to see how you respond."

"*Señorita?*" Diego stood in the doorway, a plastic shopping bag filled with ice clutched in his hands. "You okay?"

She nodded even though she thought she might faint. "I'll live." It felt good to close her eyes. "Where are Jack and Stacey? I need to talk to you all."

"They're on their way back here. I've already contacted them." Glimmer sounded weary. "I need to rest. And so do you."

"But . . ." Consciousness fled from Sally as if the Quetzalcoatl had flown away with it.

Her eyes flew open and she took a great gasp in surprise. It was dark outside the window. A light burned on the bedside table. She glanced around. Diego sat on the floor next to the bed, asleep against the wall. She looked down at her leg. The swelling was gone. It still hurt, but it felt more like she'd done a heavy workout or run a few hundred miles, instead of the pain of injury.

There was a knock at her. "Yes?"

"Are you decent?" Jack's worried voice came from behind the door.

"Yes, come in."

The door swung open and in walked Jack, Doublecharge, and Glimmer, who still looked exhausted. Stacey sported a fresh suntan, and Jack looked as smug as ever. "Hey, gorgeous, how's the leg?"

Sally slipped off the bed and tested her weight on it. It hurt, but it held. She jogged in place a few steps to check the mobility. "Seems sturdy enough. Thanks, Jay."

"Anytime," he said.

"How about your boyfriend?" Jack asked.

Sally shrugged. "He's asleep. And you know very well he's not my boyfriend."

"He'll stay asleep," said Glimmer. "I still think he's a spy. Induced sleep is the only offensive ability I dare use. We're better off this way. Sally, are you up to a group mindlink?"

"What's that?" Sally rummaged in her bag for a pair of sweat pants and a tank top and pulled them on over her bikini.

"Like a séance without the dead people," Jack said.

"It's how we disseminate the information your brain recorded earlier," said Glimmer. "And no, it doesn't hurt."

Sally yawned. "Oh. Okay. Do we do it for everyone?"

"No," said Doublecharge. "The rest of us weren't set up for it. And I don't have much to share anyway."

"Me neither," said Jack. "This town's full of people who don't know their heads from their asses."

"Or they've been psionically prepared," said Glimmer. "I can sense a lot of low-level psionic usage throughout the area. I think this whole town may be a sham."

"What did you get, Jack?" Doublecharge asked.

"Very little. Nobody seems to remember much about Harlan Washington except that he doesn't talk to anybody when he comes to town and receives deliveries. Everyone thinks of him as a typically rich eccentric American. It's been somewhere between a week and a month since he last came into town. Other than that, no information to speak of. How about you, Jay?"

"De Barros checked out of his room four days ago. Nobody has seen him since then. They think he's left town." Glimmer sat down on the edge of Sally's bed. "I think he's dead."

Doublecharge asked, "What leads you to that conclusion?"

"Nothing that I could get my mind around," said Jay. "But he knew we were coming. He was waiting to meet us. The only reason he'd disappear voluntarily is if he was running for his life."

"Nothing going on at the docks, either. I couldn't find anyone who'd received anything for Destroyer, and no records either. This entire town's a blank book. I agree with Jay. Business as usual around here is to avoid drawing attention to that compound or anything related to it."

"Then you're going to just love what I've got," Sally said. "Do your thing, Jay."

"Everyone get comfortable and close your eyes. I'll set up the link and rapid playback," said Jay.

Sally did so. There was a moment of contact, like a switch being thrown in her mind, and then the day's events replayed like a movie on fast forward. In spite of the speed, she saw and heard everything clearly.

"Holy shit!" said Jack when the events at the compound unfolded. Once Sally's memories got to the part where she and Diego were on their way back to town, Glimmer halted the playback. They all opened their eyes.

"It's a goddamn army," Jack grumbled. "*War's over, man. Wormer dropped the Big One.*"

"So what do we do?" Sally asked.

"Go back home. Forget about Guatemala. Drink margaritas," said Jack.

"We need to get inside that compound," Doublecharge said. "That looked suspiciously like a nuclear reactor from what I could see, and that's way out of league for small-time criminals. Whatever is happening there is huge, and we need to find out what it is."

"Then what?" asked Sally.

"*Nuke it from orbit. It's the only way to be sure,*" Jack said with a grin.

"Enough is enough, Jack." Doublecharge didn't bother to look at him. "We don't have the resources to fight an army of parahumans. We stick with the original assignment. We find out what's going on and report back."

"You think they've worked out a method of creating parahumans artificially?" Jack asked.

"There's too much evidence for it to be all coincidence." Doublecharge stood. "We go in tonight."

Chapter Twenty

"Whoa. I didn't expect that to happen!"

-Crackerjack, *Saturday Night Live,* March 13, 1999

February, 2004
Porto San José, Guatemala

Night settled over the coastal town like a heavy, wet blanket. A storm front had moved across the region, trailing thick moist clouds that trapped the heat of the day. Glimmer kept a psionic eye out for anyone who might observe the group as they hiked out of town, away from anyone who might see. Once they were well clear of town, Stacey ordered them all to change into their nighttime suits.

"No peeking, Sally." Jack whispered at her from behind a tree as he changed.

"Please, you're like old enough to be my father," she said. "Are you taking Viagra yet?"

Muffled snickers came from Glimmer, and she thought she even heard a snort of amusement from the dour Doublecharge.

"Definitely spending too much time with Sondra." Jack tightened his equipment belt as he stepped out from behind the tree. With his face blacked out and a black skullcap over his hair, he looked like a living shadow.

"This is pretty much your element, isn't it?" Sally eyed his matte-finish weapons. She counted at least four guns and three knives before she stopped.

"It's a living." He smiled, teeth white against his darkened face.

Doublecharge and Glimmer added military-issue Kevlar vests over their black suits. Sally had one as well, but she hadn't put it on. Jack offered to help her adjust the fasteners.

"I don't know," she said. "Isn't there already armor built into my suit? How can I run in this thing if I can't move right?"

"Can you actually see bullets coming at you?" Doublecharge asked.

"Most of the time," Sally said.

"*Most* of the time," Doublecharge repeated. "Put it on and keep it on. That's an order." She coiled her blonde hair up and tucked it under her skullcap. It took a little extra work, but they managed to get Sally's braids wrapped around her head and covered as well. "Think you can find your way back to the compound from here, Sally?" Doublecharge asked as she smeared black across her forehead and cheeks.

Sally looked around. The jungle was pitch-black with the stars covered by the thick clouds. The only light at all came from the pale smudge of the obscured moon. "I don't know. I think so. I wish Diego was here to guide us."

"I wish I had a tank with GPS and a cappuccino machine," said Jack.

"Jay, can you help her?"

The telepath nodded and connected with her to trace out a firm map in her mind. When she closed her eyes, she could refer to it and found it like having a *You are here* light in her head. "Okay, yeah, I can find it from here. What now?"

"We move. Jay is slowest, he'll set the pace. We'll rest after thirty minutes or when we get halfway there, whichever comes first." Doublecharge flew a few feet into the air and hovered, waiting. Glimmer closed his eyes and levitated both himself and Jack off the ground. They all looked at Sally.

"This way." She chose the path and led the others along it at—for her—a slow jog.

In a few minutes, Jack stopped her and handed her a pair of night-vision goggles. "They're not much," he said, "but it's better than tripping over every tree root in the dark." The goggles gave everything a bright green tint and made Sally feel like she'd slipped into a video game.

They climbed the route that Sally and Diego had followed earlier in the day. Glimmer couldn't levitate much faster than Diego's dirt bike, so it took almost as long as it had before. She stopped them at the volcanic ridge she remembered and they took a short break. Jack passed out some nutrient bars to everyone, and Sally was surprised by how delicious they tasted.

"Make 'em myself," he said. "Can't tell you what's in them. Trade secret. Besides, if you knew, you wouldn't want them."

"Microphone checks, everyone," said Doublecharge. They all tested their throat mikes and earbud speakers. "Normally under these circumstances we'd operate using Jay as a psionic switchboard," she said to Sally, "but he's uncomfortable with that so close to the target area."

"It's all the evidence of psionic activity in the area," Glimmer said. "With that big-time psi here, I bet there are booby traps in half the minds of San José."

"You're no slouch in the mental powers department yourself, Jay," Jack said. "You really think this mystery psi is that bad?"

"Yes I do."

"Whatever the case," said Doublecharge, "I don't want these radios used except in an emergency. With Destroyer involved in this operation, we can't trust that our signals will be secure, even with encryption. Use hand signals whenever possible."

"I don't really know any hand signals," said Sally.

"Don't worry, neither do we," said Jack. "Except the old standby." He raised his middle finger in salute. "But seriously, they're very straightforward. This means *come here*, this means *get down . . . look . . . go there . . .* and *take him down*." He showed a series of simple gestures to Sally that ended with a finger drawn across his throat.

"Okay, I think I can remember that." She shuddered, wondering if Jack's idea of *take him down* was more permanent than hers.

"All right, it's time to go," said Doublecharge. "The most important thing is we stay safe. If anything goes sour, the standing order is to bug out. This thing is bigger than any of us. It's only a matter of time before we're found out, and we need to get as much information about this facility as we can."

They traveled on through the midnight jungle until they found the clearing that overlooked the compound. A few sentries walked or floated on patrol duty. The compound was well lit by powerful floodlights, which made an unobtrusive approach seem impossible. Jack watched the compound carefully for almost an hour to examine the patrol patterns and habits of those who walked them.

"Okay," he said at last. "On my mark, follow me in. We're going straight across to the near corner of that building." He pointed to the target. "Stealth mode from here on out. Watch yourselves and be ready for anything." He handed pistols to everyone.

"What do I do with this?" Sally whispered. "I never took any firearms classes at the Academy."

"Safety's here." Jack showed her the switch. "It's on. Don't touch it. Parahuman powers aren't always obvious, the locals might not speak English, but everybody understands a gun. If there's going to be any shooting, it'll be by me."

Sally nodded and hefted the unfamiliar weapon. Jack sighed and adjusted her grip on it so it at least looked like she'd held one before.

"Ready? Okay, go."

The quartet crossed the clearing and reached the cinderblock building without incident. Jack peeked over the edge of a window and then ducked back down. He motioned for the others to follow him. They advanced along the side of the building to a metal door. Jack took a device out of a vest pocket and quickly ran it across the edges of the door to check for electrical current. Satisfied with the results, he checked the handle to see if it was locked. The knob turned without a hitch and they slipped inside.

They found themselves in a storeroom filled with cases of personal hygiene supplies. "It's a dorm," whispered Jack, "but it looks empty. All these boxes are sealed."

"That means they're either planning on more people arriving," said Doublecharge. "Or more troops being made."

They all froze as they heard a door open and footsteps outside the storeroom. Jack glanced at Glimmer, who had his eyes shut in concentration. He opened them and held up three fingers.

Shit, mouthed Jack.

Outside, they heard slurred conversation in a language that might have been Spanish with a strong tequila accent. Jack wrapped his hand around the storeroom door's knob and turned it. The only noise it made was a twang of the spring inside the mechanism. He cracked open the door and peeked out. Then he looked at Sally and drew a finger across his throat.

How? she mouthed back at him.

He rolled his eyes, grabbed Glimmer and turned him around. Then Jack reversed a pistol, touched the butt to a spot on the back of Glimmer's head, and looked at Sally to see if she understood. She nodded. He raised his hand, held up three fingers, and gave her a countdown.

When his last finger dropped, he yanked on the door and the world shifted into slow time as Sally ran into the dormitory itself. She saw three soldiers sitting on bare mattresses, smoking cigarettes and passing a bottle back and forth. One of them had skin that looked like blue candle wax.

She swung the pistol into the first man's head. His eyes rolled up and he started to slump forward. Sally grabbed his bottle as it started to fall and set it out of the way so it wouldn't break. The second man just started to turn his head as Sally clocked him. She turned her attention to the waxy-skinned soldier.

When she hit him, the pistol butt sank several inches into his flesh, which started to flow like thick mud. Sally gasped as it enveloped her hand before she could pull away. She couldn't free herself and muffled a shriek as her hand started to burn like it had been dipped in strong acid. In slow motion, the door to the storage room swung open and the others rushed out.

Tears of pain ran unchecked down Sally's blackened face. The guard's entire body shifted and moved like liquid plastic as it crawled up her arm. Jack tried to pull her free, but to no avail.

Electricity crackled between Doublecharge's hands with a sound like paper tearing. Teeth clenched in fury, she placed her hands on either side of the guard's head and let him have a huge jolt. His strange, polymer body insulated Sally from the electricity. A ripple flowed through him and he released Sally. She fell to the ground and held her hand in pain.

"Bastard." Doublecharge growled, upped the voltage and gave him another concentrated blast. The guard toppled into a quivering puddle and remained still.

"Let me see your hand, Sally." Jack pulled a medical kit off his waist. The skin was raw and blistered. He clucked his tongue in sympathy and spread burn cream over the injury.

"I'm sorry, Sally," said Doublecharge as she checked the other guards. "I should know better than to have you taking point with your inexperience."

"I can handle it." Sally winced at the sting.

"How is she?"

"Looks like some kind of acid burn." Jack as he wound a bandage around Sally's hand. "It's good we got to her when we did." He smiled at Sally. "*My advice to you is to start drinking heavily.*"

"*Animal House,*" she said with a sniffle. "I love that movie. What do we do now?"

Doublecharge looked at the guards. "Search them."

Glimmer complied with her request and turned up some basic personal effects and three key cards. "Think these will get us into the main building?"

"We'll find out," said Doublecharge. "Strip their uniforms off. We'll try a more direct approach."

"Good," said Jack as he withdrew some zip-tie binders from a pocket. "*I prefer a straight fight to all this sneaking around.*"

"*Star Wars,*" said Glimmer. "Even I remember that one. You're on a roll."

"You're pissing me off," said Doublecharge. "Stay on task so nobody else gets hurt. These two soldiers we'll lock in the storage room. Jay, see to it they don't wake up anytime soon. Jack, can you find something to pour this other guy into?"

Jack shrugged and vanished into the storage room, to return a moment later with a large footlocker. "He might get out of this eventually," he said of the gelid puddle. "But he'll have to work at it, if he's even alive. How do you check Jell-o for vital signs?"

"Well, scoop him in, Mr. Invulnerability," said Doublecharge, "and you're wearing his uniform when you're done."

In a few minutes, Jack, Doublecharge, and Glimmer had dressed in the three guards' uniforms. Jack passed around a packet of baby wipes to the others so they could clean the black off their faces. "Best cleaning supplies ever," he said with a cheerful grin.

"What about me?" Sally asked.

"Not much we can do. These guys were twice as big as you. Maybe we can find a smaller guard somewhere," Doublecharge said. "In the meantime, we'll take the overt risks and you follow when the coast is clear. Jack, what's the time?"

"Almost midnight," he said. "Think they're going to do a shift change?"

"Let's wait and see."

They watched out the windows of the dormitory, careful to remain in the shadows. Sure enough, outlying guards climbed or flew down from their towers and others came in from the perimeters. Replacements exited the dorms, yawning and flexing stiff muscles.

"Grab something to carry. We're going to go straight across to the power station," said Doublecharge. She picked up a box of supplies.

"Why carry something?" Sally asked.

"Old tricks always work the best," said Jack. "If you act like you're supposed to be somewhere when you're not, and you carry something appropriate in a purposeful way, people tend not to notice you." He picked up a clipboard that he found hanging by the door. "This thing is like a free pass to anywhere."

"We'll signal you when it's clear to come across," said Doublecharge to Sally, and opened the door.

They walked across the hard-packed clay toward the entrance to the power station. Nobody stopped them or even seemed to pay any attention to the three heroes. At the door, Jack swiped the keycard he'd taken from the guards. Sally held her breath and it seemed like eternity before the green light on the security box clicked on. The meter-thick door slid sideways into the frame.

Doublecharge looked back in Sally's direction and nodded. Sally bolted across twenty yards of open space in the blink of an eye and skidded to a stop just inside the corridor as the door slid shut. She glanced around and saw a security camera behind a Lexan bubble.

"Oh, shit!" She ducked.

Jack smiled. "No problem." He held up a small device. "Already took care of it with this little baby."

"Geez, this guy's like Santa Claus," Sally said to Glimmer. "Now what?"

"We go further in," said Doublecharge. "Until we find out what this place is for or we can't get any further with these." She held up a key card for emphasis. "Sally, you make sure our back is clear. You're fast enough to take down anyone who sees us before an alarm can be raised."

They passed through the corridor into a nexus. The interior of the building was much smaller than the exterior, which implied a great thickness of shielding. Glimmer mentioned the discrepancy.

"Yeah, it's making me pretty uncomfortable," said Jack. "Like I might be about to find out the one thing I'm not invulnerable to is an uncontrolled nuclear reaction."

The doors from the nexus were labeled in both English and Spanish. One led to the *Control Room*, one to the *Holding Cells*, one to *Medical* and the last to the *Reaction Chamber*.

"I don't see any sign of more security measures," said Jack after he checked the room. "Maybe they're not expecting anyone to sneak into a camp full of armed parahumans."

"You don't believe that any more than I do," said Doublecharge. "The Control Room is where we're most likely to find an answer. There should be more people in here. I don't like this one bit. Why would there be access into a reaction chamber?"

Nobody could answer her. Weapons drawn, they opened the door that led to the Control Room. A short corridor ended in a rising stairwell. Jack took the point as they advanced. The stairs ended in another door. Jack put his ear to it, eyes closed in concentration.

"I don't hear anything at all. But if this is another foot-thick door, I wouldn't. Jay, anything?"

Glimmer shook his head. "I can't sense anyone."

"Why would a control room for a nuclear reactor be abandoned?" Jack asked. "Is Destroyer so bright that he can build one that runs itself?"

"Maybe," said Doublecharge. "Be on your guard. I think this is a trap."

"Then why are we still here?" whispered Sally.

Jack smiled. "Because we're Just Cause, babe. It's just what we do."

He swiped the card and a motor hummed as the door slid into the wall. Beyond was a semicircular room lined with banks of computers and thick windows. Although they saw several duty stations, the room was empty of people.

Jack stepped forward to look out the windows. "You'd better see this," He had a funny note in his voice.

The others moved up to see what he did. Below them stretched a long, open room lined with metallic cots with manacles at each corner. A thick layer of ash coated the floor. Greasy soot blackened the walls and edges of the observation windows, which were smudged as if they'd been wiped without much regard for perfectionism. At the far end of the room, they saw a heavy industrial door marked with the universal symbol for radioactivity.

"What the hell is this?" Doublecharge asked.

Glimmer motioned to a console that looked like a video monitor. Jack stepped up to it and played with the controls for a few moments. "Ah, here we go," he said as words filled the screen.

24-February 2004
Test #0117
Subjects: 102
Rads: 7,500
Duration: 3.0 seconds

The words were replaced by four video images of different angles from the interior of the room below. They saw people chained down to each of the bed frames. Most struggled; many screamed in fear. Figures wearing radiation suits bustled through the room, checked locks, and set up equipment. A digital readout in the corner showed a countdown of two minutes. As the clock wound down toward zero, the suited figures evacuated the room to leave only the men and women in the beds. When the clock ticked down to five seconds, the large door at the end of the room slid into the roof, which revealed a complex apparatus glowing with unholy radiance. At 0:00 a bright flare emitted from the device that lasted for three seconds and blanked out all video screens.

When the cameras came back online, several seconds later, all the bed frames were empty and fresh ashes swirled through the room. A few seconds later, the recording ended.

"Oh my God!" Sally whispered.

Jack tapped a control and a compact disc ejected from the machine. He handed it to Sally. "Here," he said, his voice rough. "You take this. You have the best chance of getting it out of here if things go badly."

"Let's go," said Doublecharge. "We're pushing our luck as it is."

They returned to the lobby below.

"*I've got a bad feeling about this,*" Jack said.

The large door slid open and they found themselves face-to-face with what looked like the entire camp with scores of weapons leveled at them. Some soldiers' fists glowed with various deadly energies.

Sally spun around and saw more soldiers crouched in the doorways of the lobby, likewise armed and ready for anything.

Heinrich Kaiser stepped into the ring of soldiers, followed by the ancient black man who hobbled with his cane and cackled quietly to himself. Kaiser sized them up with the air of an entomologist who regarded particularly choice insects pinned to a card. "Old tricks always work the best, Mr. Raymond. Wasn't that what you said?"

With a whine of servomotors, Destroyer stepped around from the edge of the power station. "*You just cause losers are so predictable*," he said. "*Drop your guns and don't move.*"

Jack gave a wry half-grin. "Well, which is it, drop our guns or don't move? They're mutually exclusive actions, smart guy."

"You know what I mean, Mr. Raymond," said Kaiser.

Jack and the others dropped their guns. A soldier teleported to the heroes, collected the weapons, and then popped back to the others in a series of rapid reports like gunfire.

"How'd you catch us?" Jack asked.

"Him," said Jay through clenched teeth as he glared at the old man with the cane.

"Bertram has been with me for many years," said Kaiser. "He is very skilled at psionic disciplines. More so, I believe, than you, Mr. Road. He has kept you from seeing our true movements since you came to the camp."

"How'd you even know we were here?" Sally asked. A figure stepped out from behind the blond man.

Diego.

White hot fury filled Sally which blinded her to everything but the smiling boy. She took a step forward. A sudden pain ripped through her entire body and made her gasp in agony. The icy burning was strong enough to double her over.

"Stop it! Leave her alone!" shouted Jack.

"*DON'T MOVE, CRACKERJACK!*" Destroyer said. "*YOU MIGHT BE BULLETPROOF, BUT YOUR FRIENDS AREN'T!*"

"Bertram, please," said Kaiser. "That's not really necessary."

The old man licked his lips with a gray tongue. "A lesson must be taught. She will join us eventually, as will they all, Heinrich. I will see to that."

A voice in Sally's mind cut through the pain, like a spot of pure white on a red wall. In spite of the agony, she locked eyes with Glimmer. *Sally . . . run!*

Time shifted into the syrupy slowness of accelerated perceptions. She tried to scream "No!" at him, but it felt like her vocal cords were frozen.

Glimmer's head turned and his eyes focused upon the old man. His brow furrowed and the pain wracking Sally's body vanished. He grunted with effort and his eyes turned blood red as capillaries burst throughout them. Something powerful passed across the intervening distance to Bertram from Glimmer, with an anticlimactic effect. Bertram's eyes rolled up in his head and he toppled. Blood poured from his ears and nose.

At the speed of thought: *Sally . . . run!*

Sally pushed herself to her feet and ran to the edge of the clearing before she dared glance back. Destroyer's guns roared with a sound like thunder to her accelerated senses. She averted her eyes so she wouldn't have to see the exploding shells tear Glimmer apart.

Flame blossomed under Destroyer's boots as he took to the sky in pursuit of Sally. She saw a familiar flash as Diego transformed into the bullet-fast winged snake and raced toward her like an organic missile.

Half-blinded by her own tears, Sally turned and ran into the dark jungle, frantic to find the road. She dodged past shadowy tree trunks and mercifully avoided stepping in any more holes. In a few seconds she found herself at the road which led back to Porto San José. She glanced back and saw a distant rising star in the darkness that must have been Destroyer. Movement flashed in the corner of her eye and she ducked backward as the Quetzalcoatl's razor-sharp tail lanced through the air her head had occupied a moment before.

Sally dodged the winged serpent as it pursued her, hissing and spitting. The tail flashed so fast that even with her sped-up vision she could hardly see it. She stepped on a loose rock in the road and lost her balance. The tail flashed downward toward her eye and she barely jerked her head aside in time. The razor-sharp tail cut a stinging bloody furrow down her cheek instead.

She rolled and twisted to avoid the tail as it whipped at her with dangerous ferocity. She scrabbled across the road, desperate for a tree branch or anything she could use as a weapon. Her fingers closed around a fist-sized rock and she swung it at the serpent with all her might. She missed its head, but connected solidly with one wing. Diego whirled in midair to try to stay in flight, but he lost all momentum. Sally saw her opportunity. In a blur, she grasped his tail, whipped him around with a strength she didn't know she had, and smacked him into the ground. Her other fist looped down and smashed the stone into the snake's belly with a sickening crunch.

Light flashed and she was straddling a naked Diego in an obscene parody of lovemaking. She recoiled and rolled backward and leaped to her feet, ready to fight again. He didn't move and drew a ragged, forced breath. She stepped closer, stone raised should she need it.

One of his arms twisted at an unnatural angle; a shocking white knob of bone protruded from the place his forearm met his elbow. His broken torso looked as if it had been ripped apart and then sewn back together with crude, uncaring hands. He was dying in the most painful way Sally could imagine.

"Señorita," he whispered through the blood that bubbled on his lips. "Help me . . ."

"I liked you." Sally found her voice. "I even trusted you, you little shit. And you lied to me. You lied to all of us! My friend is dead because of you!"

"Not my fault." He coughed.

A distant sound made her raise her head. The star that was Destroyer had developed several bright trails of flame and smoke that rushed in on her position.

She felt like she should have said something to Diego, but there was no time left. She bolted down the road only a second before the missiles converged on the site. A tremendous explosion tore through the nighttime sky. The heat washed across her back as she fled. She couldn't trust anyone in San José. She didn't know anyone else, and could only think of one place to go.

Chapter Twenty-One

My greatest fear is an all-out parahuman war. The minor fights that take place in the streets and the skies are nothing compared to the devastation that would result from a full-scale battle. It is my greatest hope that by properly training these heroes, they can prevent such a tragedy.

-Lane Devereaux, *Time Magazine*, December 4, 1999

February, 2004
Phoenix, Arizona

Bruised, filthy, Sally crawled onto the dark porch of the house. Her clothing was torn into rags and even her accelerated healing hadn't been able to keep up with all the damage she'd done to herself in her flight. She had faint memories of tree branches slapping at her, falling down steep and rocky slopes, and crossing a river fast enough that her feet didn't sink into the water. Her feet had gone numb inside the remains of her boots and every muscle in her legs threatened to seize up in the most painful cramps imaginable. Her face was covered with dust and road grime. She shivered like someone freezing, despite the warmth of the surrounding darkness.

She lay on the boards of the porch for a few minutes, too exhausted to raise herself up to the door. She felt like she couldn't draw enough air into her cracked and burning lungs or settle her heartbeat down from its rapid patter. Her lips were chapped raw and she had no spit left to wet them. A network of fine scratches covered her cheeks, forehead, and chin. At last, she raised herself onto her knees, which twinged in protest, and pressed the doorbell. Inside the house, the bell buzzed and rang for almost a minute before Sally had no more energy to hold herself up and collapsed back to the porch floor once more.

The overhead porch light turned on and a moment later the door opened.

"What are you doing? It's four in the morning! Get off my porch," said a woman.

Sally raised her head up and saw her mother staring down at her in mute surprise, mouth hanging open in shock.

"M-mom?" she whispered, her voice hoarse with dust and dehydration.

"Sally!" Faith reached down and helped her daughter to her feet. Sally could barely even stand. Her mother half-carried her into the living room and got her onto the couch. "Sweetheart, what happened to you?"

A single tear leaked out of each of Sally's swollen eyes and made a clean track down her filthy cheeks. "I didn't know where else to go," she said, sniffling. "I didn't know what to do. I ran here."

"From Denver?"

"N-no," Sally's voice quavered. "From G-Guatemala."

"Guatemala? Central America?"

Sally nodded. "Something bad happened down there. I . . . I ran away."

"What were you doing in . . . No, wait. First things first. Are you hurt?"

"Just my f-feet." Sally took the CD wrapped in toilet paper from inside her uniform and set it on the coffee table. "That's . . . That's really important," she whispered.

"It can wait. If your face isn't hurting now, it will be, sweetheart. You look like you ran through a sandstorm. Let's get you into the tub. You're probably very dehydrated. I'll get you some Gatorade. Are you hungry?" Faith took the scuffed and split boots off Sally and winced in sympathy at the grape-sized blisters and bruises covering her daughter's feet.

Sally looked at them in horror. "Oh no!"

"Never mind that," said Faith. "They'll heal right up in no time." She lifted Sally off the couch.

Faith was not a large woman, but she hefted her daughter like a rag doll and carried her up the stairs. Sally buried her face against her mother's shoulder and sobbed. Faith set Sally down on top of the toilet and started running water into the tub. "I think we'll give you a good hosing down first so you don't have to soak in this grime," she said. She pulled a pair of scissors from the medicine cabinet and cut away the shredded uniform.

Sally sat numbly for a few minutes as her mother worked. She felt woozy and lightheaded, but she also had a very important mission to complete.

"Mom, I need to call Juice. Can I use your phone?"

"Of course, sweetheart. Let's get you in here and then I'll bring everything you need." Faith adjusted the water temperature. She pulled the shower wand from its clip and handed it to Sally. "Okay, then?"

Sally nodded and let the hot water stream over her.

Faith smiled at her. "I'll be back in a flash." Sally heard the front door bang as her mom ran out into the night. She returned less than a minute later, bearing a quart bottle of Gatorade in one hand and the phone in the other. She pushed the bottle into Sally's free hand. "Drink that, but go easy. If you're too dehydrated, it'll come right back up if you slam it. Sally nodded and sipped at the electrolyte. "Good," said Faith.

"Mom," said Sally, her voice a little stronger than before. "I really need to call headquarters." She turned off the faucet so she could sit in the quiet, steamy water.

"Of course, dear." Faith handed her the phone and picked up a sponge. "Can I do your back?"

Sally nodded. Fresh tears welled in her eyes as she punched buttons on the phone. "H-hello? This is Salena Thompson . . . Mustang Sally. I need to speak to Juice right away."

"Voiceprint confirmed," said the Command Center operator. "I'm transferring you to his line."

Juice answered on the second ring. "Forsythe."

Sally's vocal cords froze. How could she possibly tell him what had happened?

"Who is this?" Juice asked, more awake and with a dangerous tinge to his voice.

"It's Sally," she said.

"Sally? What's going on? Are you all right?" All trace of sleepiness vanished from him and she felt like she was in the glare of a spotlight.

"N-no," she said, afraid she was about to cry again. "Everything's gone wrong. Jay . . . he's dead."

"Dead? Sally, where are you?"

"Home." She hiccupped. "In . . . in Phoenix."

"Is your mother there? May I speak to her?"

Sally pushed the phone at Faith. "He wants to talk to you, Mom."

Faith scrubbed Sally's back as she tucked the phone between her shoulder and ear. "Juice?"

Sally couldn't hear what Juice said, only the baritone timbre of his voice.

"I'd say she's in shock. She apparently ran all the way here from Guatemala. Guatemala!" Faith's voice rose to the borderline of hysteria. "What the hell did you get my daughter into, James?"

Juice asked another question instead of giving Faith the answer she wanted to hear.

"She'll be all right." Faith's tone was frosty. "But you have some explaining to do."

Juice started to speak but her mother cut him off.

"No, you listen to me." Her voice rose in pitch and intensity. "I don't know what you thought you were doing sending my little girl on some mission out of the country, but she's just an intern, for God's sake! You should have known better!"

"Mom," Sally whispered.

"That's not the way we did things when I was on the team. We looked after our youngest members like we were their parents!"

"Mom, they needed me."

Juice spoke for a couple of minutes. Faith listened and then put her head in her hands. "I'm sure you're right, James. You're a smart leader, and I know you wouldn't put her in a position where she'd be in too much danger. I understand." She sighed and turned to look at Sally. "He really does think the world of you. Can you talk to him?"

Sally nodded and took the phone.

"Juice?"

"Hi, Sally. Start at the beginning and tell me what happened."

Taking a deep breath, she relayed the events that had unfolded since the team entered Guatemala. Juice remained silent while she spoke except to make encouraging noises when she paused. Finally, she finished, and he had only one question.

"Do you want us to come and get you before the rescue mission?"

"Why would you want me now? I screwed everything up." Sally felt as low as she ever had.

"That's not you talking, that's your grief. You did everything exactly right, because you got the information out in spite of being captured. I'm proud of you. God knows you've earned the right to sit this one out."

Sally looked at her mother, whose facial lines stood out in sharp relief. "Mom? Stacey and Jack . . . they're still being held hostage."

Faith's mouth was a thin white line. "You want to rescue them."

"Mom, I have to. They're my friends, my teammates."

"I know, sweetheart." Faith lowered her head. "I would do the same if I were you. Hell, if running to the store just now hadn't hurt me so bad, I'd come with you. Finish cleaning yourself up."

"What are you going to do?"

"Well, first I'm going to go and scream long and hard into my pillow. Then I'm going to make you something to eat before you leave. You're thin as a rail. Aren't they feeding you up there?" Faith gave her a sad, brave smile, and stepped out of the bathroom.

"Is there anything you need from your quarters or from Harris?" Juice asked Sally.

Sally glanced at the tattered remains of her black outfit. "A replacement costume, I guess, with boots. About a gallon of foot cream."

"It's hard losing a teammate. I know. We'll take the time to mourn the dead once we've rescued the still-living. Deal?"

"Yeah," said Sally.

"I'm scrambling the *Bettie*. We'll come to you . . . say, about seven-thirty?"

"You can be here that fast?"

"Yes," said Juice. "You rest and we'll see you soon. I'm proud of you, Mustang Sally. Good job."

Sally finished her bath and toweled off. She limped to her bedroom on tender feet and pulled on fleecy sweats and the thickest socks she could find. Delicious smells wafted up the stairs.

Sally found a spread of egg, bacon, and cheese burritos with salsa awaited her. Her mother had gone to the effort to make something palatable for once. Her stomach clenched as she realized how long it had been since she last ate. Faith came over to her and put her arm around Sally's shoulders. "Feel better?"

Sally was surprised to discover that she really did. "Yeah," she said. "I've got about an hour, and then the team is coming to pick me up." She sat down and started to pick at a burrito.

"They're picking you up here?" Faith sat down with a plate of her own. "The neighbors will love that. Is there anything I can do to help?"

"No, I don't think so," said Sally.

At 7:22, a whistling roar shook the house as the *Bettie* made a vertical landing in the middle of the cul-de-sac. Neighbors ran from their houses in surprise. The engines powered down and the rest of Sally's teammates exited the aircraft. She rushed out of the house in a blur, treading as lightly as she could on her sore feet, and threw herself into Jason's arms.

"I'm so glad you're here," she whispered into his ear.

He grinned. "I missed you."

She kissed him then remembered herself. Sheepish, she looked back toward the house where her mother had just disengaged herself from Juice's embrace.

"And who's this?" Faith walked over to them and looked up into Jason's reddening face.

"Oh, uh . . . Mom, this is Mastiff. Jason. My, uh . . ."

"I'm pleased to meet you, Ma'am." Jason turned on his Southern charm as best he could. He took her hand and raised it to his lips.

"I like this one," Faith said. "And my goodness but you're tall. What do they feed you where you're from?"

"All I can eat, Ma'am."

Sally gave Sondra a tight squeeze. "It's good to see you. Jack's okay, as far as I know."

Sondra smiled back even though her eyes couldn't hide her concern. "He's a tough nut to crack, all right."

"Sally," said Juice. "We need to leave. If you still want to go, do you want to change in your house or in the plane? Courtesy of Harris," He held up a bag.

"I'll, uh . . ." She glanced sidelong at Jason. "I'll change inside. I'll just be a minute." She grabbed the bag from him and ran into the house to change.

Inside the package she found a fresh, new costume. She slipped into the body suit and quickly braided her drying hair. It took a bit of work to get the boots on over her extra-thick socks, but when she was done she felt like she'd be able to run pretty well. After all, Mustang Sally at seventy-five percent was still faster than anybody else at full speed. She pulled on her gloves and stared resolutely into the mirror as she replayed Jay's death in her mind once.

Destroyer would pay for it. She'd make sure of that.

She left her room and skipped down the stairs to find her mother waited at the bottom. "You look so beautiful," said Faith. "I'm so proud of you. You're every bit the hero."

"Thanks, Mom, I had the best teacher in the world." She hugged her mother.

"Which reminds me . . ." Faith picked up a flat box from the couch end table. "I have something for you. I meant to give them to you when your internship was over, but I think you should have them now." She handed it to Sally.

Inside sat two gleaming steel horseshoes. "These belonged to your grandmother. She wanted you to have them and passed them along to me." Faith smiled. "Just a little something to give those six-hundred-mile--per-hour punches a little more oomph. And to protect your fingers, too."

Sally discovered a pair of Velcro loops at her waist which hadn't been on her old costume. That sly devil Harris must have already known about the horseshoes. She hung them from the loops and looked back at her mother.

"Now go and save your friends," said Faith. "And you come back and see me when you're done. And bring that charming boy with you so I can get to know him better. I'll make sure he's good enough for my only daughter."

"Mom!"

They laughed at each other, and then embraced. "I have to go," said Sally, and ran out the front door.

Ace already had the *Bettie*'s engines on hot standby. As soon as Sally dropped into her seat, the pilot opened the throttles wide and lifted the jet out of the neighborhood.

"Sally, how are you doing?" Juice asked.

"I'm good. Really," she said. "I'm ready to do whatever we need to do to get Jack and Stacey out of there."

"Good. We need to make one stop first. I've called in some favors and I'm bringing a little extra muscle for this job." Juice's lips parted in a dangerous grin.

"Extra muscle?" asked Sally.

"A few other heroes from around the country. Eric, any change on the imaging?"

Forcestar turned away from the screen he was monitoring. "Negative," he said. "There's no sign of any major movements of troops or materials away from the site. Looks to me like they're digging in. I see lots of firepower—antiaircraft missiles, machine gun emplacements, not to mention whatever parahumans are present. I've tagged at least ten fliers in the group. Since we're only getting stills, it's hard to say."

Juice turned to Sally. "We've had one of our recon satellites monitoring the site, but it's only overhead for ten hours a day. We haven't seen anything to match your description so far, but I have no reason to doubt your report."

Sally nodded. She cuddled up next to Jason.

"Can you give me a clearer understanding of this image, based on your experience?" Juice asked.

Sally pointed to the central building. "This is a power station. They're using some kind of radiation from it to create new parahumans. It doesn't seem to work very well though." She handed Juice the CD she'd carried with her from Guatemala. He put it into a player and they watched the test unfold, expressions of distaste and disgust on their faces.

"The fact that it works at all is very disturbing," said Sondra. "If it's not too complicated a process, we're going to have governments around the world decimating their populations to create their super-soldiers."

"If these people were being taken against their wills, how is it that they're now working to defend the compound?" asked Jason.

"Jay detected a ton of psionic activity in the area. I think it was centered on the guy he killed. He said the other psi was the most powerful he'd ever found. I bet he was reprogramming their minds, just like what happened to Diego."

"Who's Diego?" Jason asked.

"Just some kid they used to trap us. He's dead too."

Juice's brow furrowed. "Psionics are among the least common parahuman abilities. It's likely this man was the only psi on hand, or at least the only one with enough power to accomplish the reprogramming of an entire city." He looked at Sally. "Jay may have put a serious hitch in the operation of this compound before he died. Let's hope he did."

"Maybe some of the people that psi was controlling took off after Jay got him," said Jason. "What do you think, babe?"

Sally snuggled a little closer to him. "I don't know. I didn't stick around to find out."

"Well, there might be a much smaller force waiting for us," said Juice, "but I'm not banking on it."

"Whatever happened," said Forcestar. "They're expecting trouble. This is going to get very ugly."

"Sir, we just received final clearance to land at Tucson Airport," Ace announced over the intercom. "Looks like we're not the first ones to the party, either." The *Bettie*'s forward motion slowed as Ace brought her in to a gentle three-point landing.

Sally looked out the window and saw a plane that could have been the *Bettie*'s twin, except with a different pin-up girl painted under the cockpit windows. "What's that?" she asked Sondra.

"That's the *Marilyn*, as in Monroe. Just Cause Second Team is already here."

"Ace, go ahead and power down," said Juice. "We have to wait for everyone else and have a meeting before we leave."

"Roger."

They disembarked from the *Bettie* and hurried across the tarmac to an open hangar. An informal briefing area had been set up on the hangar floor that consisted of folding chairs and a PowerPoint projector. Several other costumed heroes lounged around, sipped coffee, and munched on donuts.

"I thought you said it was urgent, Juice," said a handsome young black man in close-fitting brushed steel armor and an infectious grin. "We've been here for hours."

Juice clasped the younger man's hand. "Keith, thanks for coming." He poured himself a cup of coffee, appropriated a couple donuts before Jason could get to them, and sat down with the other man to discuss plans.

"You know the Second Team?" Jason asked Sally.

"Only by name," she said.

With a flash of purple light and a howling, dissonant chord filling the air, the Lucky Seven arrived. Sally ran up and distributed hugs among them.

"Any word on the others?" Juice asked Spark as he stepped up and shook hands.

"Haven't heard," said Spark. "Divine Right should be here any moment. I think the New Guard and Young Guns are flying conventional." Divine Right was a team of Christian-themed heroes, who believed their powers had been granted by angels. The New Guard was a young team, formed from some independent heroes and some original Hero Academy graduates that had opted to go into the private sector instead of joining Just Cause. The Young Guns represented the rest of Sally's graduating class at the Hero Academy.

Sally's jaw dropped as she realized Juice had managed to recruit every American superhero team to this mission. "Wow," she said in amazement. "Who's left?"

Spark nodded. "I'm a little curious about that myself, James. Who's minding the store while Just Cause is away?"

Juice rubbed his jaw. "The Homeland Security Director has issued an emergency order authorizing the faculty and students of the Hero Academy to act in an official capacity if needed."

"Wow," said Sally again. She couldn't imagine what it would be like if Ms. Echevarria and Mr. Stone had to lead a group of parapowered kids somewhere to save the world. Juice really had pulled out all the stops to make sure Jack and Stacey would be rescued.

A man in a charcoal gray suit and dark sunglasses entered the hangar. Conversation quieted as he glided toward Juice. He removed his sunglasses and tucked them neatly into his jacket. "Bominger. Homeland Security."

"Juice. Just Cause."

"Great buffalo. Heap-big tree." Sally could see the Spark's grin even behind his full-face mask. Bominger glared at him. "Sorry, I thought we were talking in Tonto-speak."

Bominger took a deep breath. "We've got two supersonic jets bringing in the New Guard from California and the Young Guns from New York. They're expected within the next half hour. Divine Right just arrived."

"Good," said Juice. "Thanks for getting this all together so quickly."

"Wasn't me. These orders came straight from the Director. You've got a lot of pull with someone. I'd like to go on the record as being against Divine Right's involvement in this operation, whatever it is." Bominger frowned.

"Separation of Church and State, I suppose. Your concern is noted," said Juice.

Juice called the meeting to order within minutes after The New Guard and Young Guns arrived. "First off, I want to thank you all for coming on such short notice. I'm pleased that you're backing Just Cause despite our lack of authority to give orders to any of you. You've all read my report and felt it important enough to be here now. This may very well be the most important mission that American heroes have ever undertaken."

Sally shrank against Jason as Juice reviewed what they knew about the Guatemalan compound. His brief elaboration on its methods to artificially create parahumans brought back recent unpleasant memories to Sally, and a tear coursed down her cheek when Juice reported Glimmer's death at Destroyer's hands.

"The long and short of it is that two of my team members are being held prisoner in this compound. We're going to go get them out and then destroy that generator so no more mass murders can take place. And I'm making it a priority for Just Cause to hunt down those responsible for these atrocities and bring them to justice. If anyone wants to back out, now is the time. From here on out, things are going to get ugly." He looked evenly at the gallery of heroes. "Are you all in?"

Everyone stood.

Juice smiled.

Chapter Twenty-Two

"In the paths your lives will take, there inevitably will come a time in which you must fight for that in which you believe. When that time comes, know that you have received the best training from the best instructors we can provide. Know that you can count on each other no matter the stakes, for you are now the newest, the greatest heroes the world has. You have my congratulations on your achievements, both in the present and yet to come, and my blessing for success in your futures."

-Dr. Grace Devereaux, Inaugural Hero Academy
commencement, May 25, 1998

February, 2004
Porto San José, Guatemala

Sally couldn't sleep, despite the white noise of the *Bettie*'s engines and the comfort of Jason's arm around her. Instead, she had a terminal active and reviewed the planned three-pronged attack Juice had designed.

She'd been assigned to the group whose mission was to rescue Stacey and Jack. She had none of her Just Cause team but three of the Lucky Seven with her, so she wasn't stuck with a completely unfamiliar group. Juice placed Spark in command of their unit.

The second group's task was to ensure the reactor could be safely decommissioned. Because it was a nuclear facility, it couldn't just be broken apart. Blueshift of the New Guard was the only nuclear power expert they had, and he was given responsibility for that task. Jason and Juice were on that team.

271

The rest of the group would engage the opposing army and incapacitate as many of them as possible. Juice hoped that their psionic conditioning could be broken and asked that the battle team try to refrain from causing fatalities. *But,* he'd said, *if it comes down to survival, I'd rather bury one of them than one of you.*

Thirty-four heroes.

The *Bettie* flew at top capacity. Besides the five members of Just Cause, all the Young Guns and half the New Guard were on board. The Marilyn was just as full, and held the rest of the New Guard and half the Lucky Seven. The rest of the heroes rode in an Air Force transport jet. Unlike the Just Cause planes, the transport jet couldn't hover, so the occupants would have to make their own way to the ground. Matthew of Divine Right had enough telekinetic ability to lower his team safely as well. The remaining members of the Lucky Seven on board the transport jet could fly on their own.

Sally heard a rumble under the noise of the *Bettie*'s engines and looked up to see Jason was sound asleep. She gave him a gentle shake. "Better get ready," she whispered. "We're almost there."

He yawned and looked around the cabin. All the Young Guns slept except Surfboy, who had produced a Gameboy from somewhere and was deeply engrossed in electronic mayhem. Chrome's eyes were shut, but Sally thought that perhaps he was meditating. The New Guard's Javelin conversed quietly with Juice and planned strategies in her soft contralto.

"Ten minutes to target," Ace reported.

"Ace, coordinate our approach with the other pilots," said Juice. "I want as close to simultaneous deployment from all three planes as possible."

"Yes, sir."

Juice turned around in the cramped cabin to face the others. "Okay, people. We're certainly expected today, but I don't think they're anticipating this many of us. Ace will get us down safely, but she'll come down hard, so expect a real jolt. The *Bettie*'s overbuilt enough to take it. Once she pops the hatch, everybody out of the pool. As soon as we're clear, the *Bettie* will go airborne and provide what support she can. When you're on the ground, rendezvous with your team leader. Above all, watch yourself. We're dealing with an unknown quantity of parahuman adversaries with unknown abilities. I've already lost one teammate to this place and I don't want to lose anymore. Any questions?"

The cabin was silent.

"Jack'd have something smartassed to say if he was here," muttered Jason.

"*You have been recruited by the League to defend the Frontier against Xur and the Ko-Dan Armada,*" Sally quoted. She smiled a little. "I've been saving that one for him." She was met with blank stares from everyone in the plane. "*The Last Starfighter.* Oh for God's sake. It was one of the first movies I ever saw!"

Tension filled Ace's voice as she warned her passengers. "Incoming missile. Stand by for evasive maneuvers."

At that moment, Ace stood the *Bettie* on her port wing and the engines howled. A series of thunks sounded from somewhere near the aft as she released anti-missile flares. Sally glanced out a window and saw a missile streak past only a few yards off the wing. The engine pitch changed as Ace flipped the *Bettie* upside-down and rolled into a screaming power dive.

Sally's stomach pushed upward against her throat as the *Bettie* raced toward the ground. Something banged hard somewhere on the upper fuselage which caused the entire plane to shudder and vibrate.

"Ace?" Juice sounded worried.

"Took a cannon round," said the pilot. "Minor damage. Permission to return fire?"

"Granted."

Minor explosions surfaced on each wing as Ace fired a pair of air-to-ground missiles. "Firing," she announced. A few seconds later she added, "Target neutralized. Stand by for hard landing in fifteen seconds."

The *Bettie* began to level out of her dive. The landing gear hydraulics thumped as they lowered the wheels into position. The jet nozzles angled until the plane plummeted flat; its wings vibrated as they cupped the thick air. The engines screamed as they tried to slow the descent.

"Touchdown in six . . . five . . ."

CLANG!

Another cannon round holed one of the wings and left a fist-sized impact crater in the armor. Ace muttered something venomous in Hebrew before she resumed her countdown. "Three . . . two . . . one . . . impact!"

The *Bettie* smashed down into the clearing. All the windows on one side of the cabin cracked. Sally gasped in surprise; the shock felt like she'd fallen two or three stories. The rear hatch popped open.

"Go, go, go!" Juice exhorted. The heroes poured out of the hatch and got clear as Juice slammed the hatch shut. The *Bettie*'s engines howled in fury and the hardy vessel took to the sky again in a blast of fiery exhaust.

Forcestar wrapped them in a sturdy shield to protect them from the bullets and parahuman energy attacks that started to come their way. A few seconds later, the *Marilyn* slammed down to the ground to discharge her passengers in similar fashion. Like Forcestar had, Stratocaster whipped up a magical force field around them. Above them, Matthew of Divine Right, hands clasped in prayer, lowered himself and the rest of his team to the ground inside a telekinetic shield.

Enemy combatants charged at them on foot and through the air. Juice shouted, "Take them down!"

The battle proper began in earnest.

Later, Sally would only recall the battle as a series of disjointed still images. She was so hyped up that her accelerated senses made the world seem oddly still around her. She had to concentrate even to be able to speak or listen to the others.

"Can you get a fix on them?" Spark asked his teammate Juliet.

"Wait," she said as she concentrated on locating the mental patterns of Jack and Doublecharge.

Enemy soldiers attacked. Bullets and beams of energy lanced toward the heroes. While Juliet focused her psionic powers on the search, the others leaped to her defense.

Sally ran on adrenaline and anger. Every enemy she encountered got a horseshoe in the face. Some of them fell with broken jaws or noses. Against others, the horseshoes merely glanced off impervious skin or flesh made of other, harder materials like stone and metal. Although she knew she moved too fast for her voice to even be heard, much less understood, it felt very satisfying to scream "this is for Jay!" with each blow. She didn't even feel the pain in her feet.

Juliet called out, "Got them!" She pointed at a fortified building across the clearing.

"Couldn't have been a little outhouse or something, right?" Spark shouted as he curled his lash around the neck of a soldier and transmitted fifty thousand volts through the copper wiring braided into the leather. "All right, people . . . The building across the way. Move it!"

They made it to the building where Jack and Stacey were held. Seahawk of the New Guard grabbed the edges of the door, flexed her powerful shoulders and ripped it right out of the wall. A single large room with a dirt floor formed the building's interior. Jack and an unconscious Doublecharge, stripped naked, hung suspended from chains attached to the roof. Doublecharge had suffered a bad beating; lacerations oozed blood and competed for space on her skin with bruises and welts.

Jack remained unhurt but looked exhausted. He managed a smile as the rescue group moved in to secure the building. "Hi guys," he said. "If I'd known you were dropping by, I'd have dressed first."

A strum of his guitar and Stratocaster turned the chains into smoke.

Alloy reshaped her metallic body to support Doublecharge's unconscious form.

Seahawk from the New Guard caught Jack as he fell. "Thanks, gorgeous," he said, displaying only a ghost of his carefree personality.

"What's-your-name, uh, Surfboy . . . you and Luke watch the door." Spark barked out orders. "Esther, can you get them out of here?"

"Of course," said the woman from Divine Right who could teleport people and things away.

"Not yet," said Spark. "Juliet, can you find Ruth? We'd better make sure Doublecharge here is stabilized enough to move."

The Lucky Seven psi nodded and closed her eyes to seek Divine Right's healer telepathically. Sally scooted out of the building in a blur and returned a moment later with the uniforms of two soldiers that were either unconscious or dead and handed one to Jack.

"Thanks, kiddo," he said, "and thanks for bringing out the cavalry. It sounds like World War Three out there."

"What did they do to Stacey?" Sally asked.

Jack swallowed and his voice grew husky. "They were a little . . . upset about losing their psi. We apparently threw quite a little wrench into their plans." He closed his eyes for a moment. "They didn't even ask her any questions."

"Who were they?" asked Spark.

"Harlan Washington, that son of a bitch. Destroyer, out of his battlesuit," said Jack. "He didn't get his own hands dirty, but I could tell he really enjoyed watching the thugs work her over. It was the other guy who scared me, though."

"Kaiser?" Sally asked.

"Yeah. Heinrich Kaiser. He talked to us for a while before turning his dogs loose on Stacey. He wants to take over the world."

"Just another petty third-world dictator." Seahawk waved a hand. "They all have big dreams."

Jack shook his head. "This guy can do it. He's a fanatic, no question, but there's something about him that makes me think he's capable of pulling it off. It's like this was just a setback in his grand plan, like all we did was test his patience. He left hours ago, I think, and now Destroyer's in charge."

Ruth came into the room at a dead run. "Things are bad out there. We're outnumbered three to one. I've got more injured outside." She stopped by Stacey and crossed herself as she stared in horror. "God in Heaven!" She knelt down, took Stacey's hands between her own, and bowed her head in prayer. Stacey's wounds began to close and bruises began to break up.

Juliet suddenly shrieked, "We have to get out of here right now!"

Everyone turned to look at her.

"Esther, get everyone out now!" Juliet cried again.

Esther didn't argue. She raised her hands and the others vanished, except Sally, who ducked out of Esther's line of sight so she could stay and fight some more. They all heard a terrifying roar of heavy weaponry outside the building, louder even than the raging battle.

Destroyer had arrived.

Red anger washed across Sally's eyes and she headed for the door in half a heartbeat with the intent to tear Destroyer apart bolt by bolt if she could. A missile passed over her head into the building. As she turned, it burst apart in slow motion to her accelerated perceptions. Sally looked back at Esther in horror. Their eyes met. In Esther's eyes she saw the reflection of an expanding cloud of burning plasma.

The building exploded in a colossal fireball. Sally turned away so she wouldn't have to see the flames overtake Esther. It happened so quickly that even she couldn't have saved the woman.

She blinked away tears of fury and rounded the corner of the reactor building. There she stopped to catch her breath and figure out what she was going to do. Several of her allies had taken cover near her. Bombshell of the Young Guns winced as she fingered an angry red mark on her side where a laser beam had burned through her denim top. The beam hadn't penetrated her skin but it looked like she'd suffered a third-degree sunburn. Her teammate Toxic cowered in terror as beams passed through the building overhead, her pale skin covered in a fine sheen of sweat. Mark, too, had flung himself to the ground—his so-called angelic strength wouldn't stop him from being holed like a carnival target.

Sally crawled to the corner of the building and risked a glance at Destroyer. The fifteen-foot-tall battlesuit stood in the middle of the compound. It had extended all four arms, which pointed in various directions and swept back and forth. Two of the arms sported the repeating laser cannons that had made everyone scramble for cover. The other two fired a barrage of explosive shells like the ones that killed Glimmer. Missile racks perched on the battlesuit's shoulders, and occasionally it fired one to whiz around after the flying heroes. She didn't see any of the enemy soldiers still fighting; those who could still move tried to crawl away from Destroyer's massive firepower.

"He's gone crazy," she whispered. "He doesn't care who he kills anymore."

Several of the heroes risked their lives to battle the impervious battlesuit. Bullet cracked the speed of sound as he plowed into a spot between two of Destroyer's arms and staggered the behemoth. In reprisal, one of the medial arms bent at an unexpected angle and hurled Bullet into the ground hard enough to leave a small crater.

Superconductor and Mosaic from the Second Team as well as Tremor and Trix from the Lucky Seven laid down a withering crossfire, blasting electricity, vibrational energy, particle beams, and what looked like steam at Destroyer. Somehow, Trix's attack was the most effective as the innocuous-looking vapor stream sliced off a chunk of the dark blue armor. Trix seemed as surprised as anyone that it happened, and he got a shell in the face for his trouble. His body hurtled backward, with nothing left but ragged strips of flesh above his shoulders.

Forcestar wrapped a sphere of blue energy around Destroyer. The battlesuit's head turned slightly, as if it examined its new prison. An arm extended to brush the edge of the field, which caused sparks to streak from the edge of the metal. Forcestar, his costume ripped and his face bloodied, snarled, "Got you, you asshole." The sphere began to contract as Forcestar tried to crush the battlesuit inside it.

"*SO IT WOULD SEEM*," said Washington's modulated voice from external speakers. "*I'M COMPLETELY AT YOUR MERCY. PLEASE SPARE ME.*" Instead of pleading, the tone was mocking.

"Stand down, Destroyer," shouted Juice. "It's over!"

"*IS IT, NOW?*" The underlying venom in the words made chills run down Sally's spine. "*THAT'S THE PROBLEM WITH YOU JUST CAUSE LOSERS. YOU CAN'T SEE BEYOND THE ENDS OF YOUR OWN NOSES. WHEREAS I, ON THE OTHER HAND, HAVE HAD YEARS TO PLAN FOR THIS EVENTUALITY.*"

A screeching tone erupted from Destroyer's

speakers; to Sally's sped-up perceptions it had a distinct pattern that was eerily familiar. He was transmitting an audible data stream, and Forcestar's field couldn't contain sound waves.

Alarm sirens began to hoot around the power station. Liquid sprayed out of several pipes around the reactor building.

"Oh no," cried Toxic in panic, "that's coolant!" She tried to force the fluid back into the reactor with her powers, but to no avail.

"If enough of it all drains away, the reactor will go, and then it's over," said Blueshift.

"*IT'S OVER*," mocked Destroyer. "*WELL, IT'LL BE OVER SOON ENOUGH, ONE WAY OR ANOTHER. REMEMBER CHERNOBYL, KIDS? THAT'LL BE LIKE A PUFF OF SMOKE COMPARED TO THIS BABY. YOU PREPARED TO LET CENTRAL AMERICA BE UNINHABITABLE FOR THE NEXT FEW THOUSAND YEARS, JUICYFRUIT?*" Destroyer burst out in laughter.

"Let him go, Forcestar," said Juice through clenched teeth. "He's right, and we need you more here now."

"Son of a bitch!" Forcestar released his force field. Destroyer instantly opened fire with all four main weapons and ignited his rockets in a blast of flame. Heroes ducked and dodged to avoid the deadly hail of lasers and cannon shells.

A laser pierced Forcestar's chest, and he fell twenty feet to the ground, a look of shock frozen on his face.

"No!" Sally crossed the yards between her and Destroyer in a fraction of a second, and as the battlesuit rose into the air on a column of flame, she grabbed onto one of the arms and held on with desperate strength.

"Hold your fire!" called MetalBlade as heroes raised their arms in attack.

Sally closed her eyes as the ground fell away from her. Destroyer tried to shake her off, but her perceptions let her adjust to his every motion. "*ARGH!*" he shouted. "*GET OFF ME, YOU LITTLE BITCH!*"

Sally struggled to maintain her grip on the giant blue battlesuit. Destroyer's arms weren't designed to scrape over one another. She kept her hold with dogged tenacity. One way or another, she vowed, she would find a way to stop him. "You have to land sometime!" she shouted as wind tore at her.

"*NOT BEFORE YOU DIE OF ASPHYXIATION.*" HE accelerated even faster. They climbed high enough that Sally could see both the Gulf of Mexico and the Pacific Ocean as Destroyer spun to try to shake her loose. Late afternoon sunlight glinted off the armor.

But not in one spot.

The place Trix had cut with his steam jet trailed some wires and tubes. Sally saw her opportunity and knew she had to act now before he took her high enough that it wouldn't matter whether she died from freezing or lack of air first. For one perilous second, she let go with one hand, fumbled at her waist, and finally got hold of one of her grandmother's steel horseshoes.

The entire universe went silent and stopped cold. Her perceptions sang like a high note drawn across a violin string. She crawled up to the exposed section, moving through a thick syrup of atmospheric molecules that grudgingly moved aside so she could pass. Time had virtually stopped for her as she braced herself. With a wordless scream, she plunged the horseshoe deep into the cavity, twisted wiring around it and yanked.

A powerful electric shock made her recoil and she lost her grip on the horseshoe. It stayed buried deep in the components of the battlesuit. Her senses reeled as time sped up to its normal breakneck pace. Sparks shot from the orifice in the armor and something flared deep inside.

"*WHAT DID YOU DO?*" shouted Destroyer, and his voice rose in panic. "*OH SHIT, WHAT DID YOU DO TO MY BATTLESUIT?*" The suit's boot jets flickered and died.

Sally smiled in satisfaction despite the black spots that swirled in her vision. "That's for killing my daddy, you son of a bitch."

With a flash of exploding bolts, a section of Destroyer's torso detached from the main body. No larger than a coffin, rockets flared from it and it accelerated away.

He was getting away again. Like he always did.

Sally's grip failed her as she began to black out. Her hands and feet had gone numb with the cold. She felt only mild disquiet as she thought how easy it would be to just close her eyes and let the darkness overtake her.

Jason was still down there, somewhere below her. Tears leaked from her eyes to freeze on the inside of her goggles. She'd never see him again, never make love with him again. She hoped he wouldn't see her fall. It would tear him apart. He was such a sweet boy.

An image of his face drifted past her eyes with such clarity that she gasped. *Hallucinating already,* she thought. *At least I'll have a lovely view on the way down.* She somehow managed to turn onto her back. That way she didn't have to see the ground as it rushed up toward her. It felt almost like the air buoyed her up, like she floated on seawater. The dark spots in her vision annoyed her, though, and she shook her head a little to clear them. Most of them vanished except for one. At first she thought it was the remains of the Destroyer suit as it tumbled after her, but then she realized it was getting closer. She wondered what could fall faster than her.

As it got closer, she realized it wasn't falling, it was diving. It was the *Bettie*, screaming down in a vertical power dive. *What a beautiful sight,* Sally thought, *but this must be what a bug sees right before it hits the windshield.* As the *Bettie* drew even with her, she could see into the cockpit where Ace had shed her flight helmet, her black hair matted with sweat. The jet drifted further down until Sally couldn't see it anymore. She felt the wash of heat from its engines for a moment. Then silence surrounded her—even the noise of the air rushing past her dulled to almost nothing.

Something blocked the sunlight, seeming to swallow her. She bumped against something firm and unyielding and screamed. Instead of a bone-shattering impact, it wasn't any harder than if she'd fallen off a bed. The whistling in her ears stopped. Suddenly she realized where she'd landed. Ace had somehow managed to fly beneath her and had gotten her to fall right into the rear airlock.

"Hang on," Ace called over the speakers. "No time to wait for you to get into restraints." The engines shrieked in protest as Ace fed them as much fuel as they could take and then some. The *Bettie* began to heave over and pull out of the dive into a spiraling turn that shed momentum.

Sally's vision blurred and everything went fuzzy-red as blood pooled in her head. She felt a jarring impact and the next thing she knew, Ace knelt beside her inside the airlock.

"Holy shit," said the diminutive pilot. "I didn't know if that was going to work or not. I need a raise."

Then Jason was there. He held her in his arms and everything was better. She struggled to pull her goggles and breath mask off with fingers that throbbed from near-frostbite. He tore his own mask off and then he kissed her and held her as if he might never let her go again.

They heard a loud crash outside the plane. Ace jumped and looked out a porthole. "Just the remains of the Destroyer suit."

"He still . . . got away," said Sally in a voice hoarse from the cold.

"Well, he'll have to build a new suit now. That'll take some time at least," said Jason.

"The reactor?" Sally's entire body tingled in an unpleasant way. She suspected she looked like one big bruise from burst capillaries.

"Blueshift is working on it. Stratocaster is helping him. The rest of them are just kind of pushing buttons and pulling levers as he tells them to," said Jason. "They say they're going to get it shut down before . . . before it's too late."

"Of course they say that," said Sally, whose vision started to tunnel and spin. "They're superheroes."

She heard Jason's voice from a long way off as she drifted into unconsciousness. His lips brushed her forehead. "So are you, babe. So are you."

Epilogue

I, (insert name), having been appointed a member of Just Cause under the conditions indicated in this document, do accept such appointment and do solemnly swear that I will use every power at my disposal to protect those who need protection, to aid those who need assistance, and to bring to justice those who require it; that I take this obligation freely, without any mental reservation or purpose of evasion; and that I will well and faithfully discharge the duties of the position on which I am about to enter, so help me God.

-The Just Cause Appointment Acceptance and Oath of Office

March, 2004
Denver, Colorado
Just Cause Headquarters

Four memorial services took place for the heroes who fell in the battle.

In spite of his lost past, Jay Road had touched many lives in the few years he had been part of the Just Cause organization. His girlfriend came out from Kansas City and sat in the front row, her head bowed in sadness over the man she'd only barely begun to know.

Eric Lu, Forcestar, was mourned by his parents and two younger brothers. His father cried more than the rest of them combined.

Trix and Esther were awarded honorary member--ships in Just Cause for their valiant efforts in service to their country. The Lucky Seven would be six for many months before they found someone who could fill the void Trix left behind. The members of Divine Right sequestered themselves, and prayed for guidance in their time of loss.

None of Stacey's injuries were life-threatening, and all healed fully under Grace Devereaux's watchful eyes.

Only Jack returned to the site of the compound before Guatemalan authorities—a phrase that he delighted in ridiculing—took over. He spent a week sifting through the entire compound, searching for any evidence of Heinrich Kaiser or his grand scheme of conquest. He returned empty-handed, his normally cheerful demeanor subdued.

"He's out there somewhere," he said. "I'll bet anything you like we haven't seen the last of that man or his evil plans."

Nobody took his bet.

Juice took considerable time in conference with the Director of Homeland Security. Part of the time was spent in debriefing and explanations of what went wrong. Any time people died during involvement in government operations, someone took the heat, and the obvious culpability lay with Juice, who had planned the entire operation. The Director relented because by some miracle the events had avoided attention from the mainstream press and only made a small blip on the internet news community.

The rest of Juice's discussions certainly involved the future of Just Cause. The team of seven had been whittled down to five in just over thirty hours. The Director talked about the possibility of recombining the Second Team with Just Cause, but Juice argued against it. A larger team was unwieldy and made a bigger target. *Well then,* the Director said, *why not transfer someone from the Second Team to fill out your ranks? Name your selection and it's done.* Juice was against that idea as well. The Second Team held a good balance of powers and personalities. To break it up would only serve to weaken it.

Juice did want a new member as part of his team; someone who had been instrumental in dealing with both the Antimatter Woman crisis and the Guatemalan incident. The Director approved and signed a waiver.

* * *

In the three weeks since Guatemala, Sally's bruising faded and she felt more or less back to her normal self. She and Jason spent a lot of time together since the incident. In fact, she spent more time in his room than she did in hers, which provided Jack and Sondra no end of amusement.

Sondra broke the news to her. "You're on the team full-time, as of tomorrow morning if you want it," she said over a cup of the tar she called coffee. It was unseasonably warm and she and Sally sat outside and enjoyed the spring-like temperatures and sunshine.

"You mean, officially?" Sally asked.

"The Director gave approval to waive your internship, based on your exemplary record to date."

Sally gave a bitter laugh. "Exemplary record. I let Destroyer get away. Again."

"Lots of people have 'let' Destroyer get away. He's not an easy catch. However, in twenty-odd years, nobody's peeled him out of his armor the way you did. He probably has a replacement suit, of course—he's smart enough to do that—but if he doesn't, it could be years before we see him again. And like the rest of us," Sondra smiled, "he's not getting any younger either."

"I never thought of it like that." Sally sipped on a mocha latte Jack had made especially for her.

"That's what makes you such a great addition, Sally. You do what you must, every time without fail, and afterward you question whether you could have done it better. Constant self-improvement is the mark of a true hero."

Sally turned away so Sondra wouldn't see her blush.

"So do you want to go through with it?" Sondra swallowed down the last dregs of her drink and shook out her wings.

"Yeah. I really do," said Sally. "All my life, I wanted to be in Just Cause."

"Can't say I blame you, especially with your heritage. Which brings up another point," Sondra leaned back to turn her face toward the sun. "You do have a lot of history in your family. Your induction to the team is going to be a media event."

"A media event?" The phrase made her feel queasy.

"Don't worry," Sondra patted her arm. "Jack's handling it."

Pure terror washed through Sally's mind. "*Jack*'s handling it?" She put her head in her hands. "I'm so not ready for this."

She was appointed in the auditorium where Just Cause had press conferences. When she peeked out from backstage at the packed audience, she almost bolted. She had thought there might be some of the heroes from other teams, plus her mother and grandmother. Instead, she stared out into a packed gallery, replete with journalists, heroes both current and retired, and what looked like the entire Hero Academy student population.

"I can't do this," she whispered to Sondra, who waited backstage with her.

"Why . . . got a little stage fright?" Sondra stepped around behind her and squeezed her shoulder muscles with strong hands.

"I just can't. I get nervous . . . sick to my stomach."

"Hey, if you gotta hurl," said Harris, who managed the sound and lighting from a console nearby, "try and avoid the costume, you know? That stuff is a bitch to clean."

Sally broke into helpless giggles. She clamped both hands over her mouth to keep from braying laughter.

Onstage, Juice finished his speech of introduction and the audience began applauding.

"That's your cue, sweetheart," said Harris.

Sondra kissed her cheek. "You'll be fine, now get moving, girlfriend." She gave Sally an encouraging slap on the behind.

Sally took a hesitant step onto the stage proper, and the cheering rose to a feverish pitch. Despite the glare of the lights, she could see many familiar faces in the crowd. She drew strength from one in particular, a face with a sincere grin and a stubbly chin. Next to him sat Jack, who gave her a proud smile. She caught his eye and he winked and made kissy-lips at her. It almost made her break out in giggles again and she looked away from him lest she lose control of herself.

Sally blinked under the spotlights as a hundred television cameras stared at her with glassy eyes.

Juice gave her a lot of glowing praise about her abilities and how capable she'd proven herself in such a short time. He said there was no question in his mind that someone of her exemplary caliber belonged as a member of the greatest superhero team in the world. She raised her right hand and repeated the Just Cause Oath of Service, during which a thousand flashbulbs popped from the audience. She managed to survive it without making any mistakes or cracking up, keeping her eyes locked on a spot on Juice's chest.

When he finished leading her through the pledge, he shook her hand, followed by MetalBlade and the Homeland Security Director. Thunderous applause filled the room. The roaring in her ears almost prevented her from hearing Juice announce her officially as Just Cause's newest member and ask her to say a few words to the audience.

Her perceptions shifted into high gear from her fear. She took several deep breaths to try to will herself back into normal time with everyone else. The podium seemed miles away, and the stage exit invitingly close. With a supreme force of effort, she turned and stepped up to the microphone.

"Uh," she began, and hated herself for the weak beginning. "It's a real honor to have been selected to be a part of Just Cause. I'm glad to have the opportunity to do my part . . ."

Suddenly she ran out of things to say and made the mistake of glancing at Jack. He crossed his eyes and stuck out his tongue at her.

"And I want to . . . I want to . . ." *Think, dammit!* she yelled in her mind. Inspiration struck like a bolt of lightning. *Academy Awards*, she thought. *Just thank some people and get the hell off the stage.* "I want to thank my teammates for believing in me. I want to thank my mom and grandma for inspiring and teaching me to become who I am today. I want to thank the Hero Academy for training me, and the Lucky Seven for letting me train with them too." *Running too long now.* "This is . . . what I wanted to do my whole life. I promise not to let you down. Thank you all." More applause and cheers erupted as she walked off the stage.

The rest of the day seemed like a whirlwind even to a speedster like her. She met more people than she could possibly hope to remember. She answered hundreds or maybe thousands of questions from journalists representing everything from local newspapers to national tabloids and all media in between.

After what seemed like hours, she got a few precious minutes alone with Jason. "Welcome to the family, officially." He kissed her.

"Mmm . . ." she said. "I think I'm going to like it here."

"I've got something for you."

"Oh?"

From his pocket, he removed a package wrapped in scarlet paper and tied with a bright yellow bow.

"What's this?"

He grinned. "Open it."

She tore open the paper. Inside she found her missing horseshoe. She held it up in wonder. "Where did you find it?"

"It was in the wreckage of the Destroyer suit. I found it before the military confiscated the remains. I figured you'd want it back. I hear they're good luck, horseshoes."

Sally smiled. "I've heard that too. Thanks, Jason." She kissed him again.

"Do you want to get out of here?"

"I've been waiting for you to ask me that for hours."

"Good. Change to your civvies and meet me at my truck and we'll see about sneaking away."

"Where are we going?" She got delicious shivers at the idea of going anywhere with him.

"Where else?" He laughed. "For pie at Lazzarino's."

She laughed and kissed him again. "Pie sounds lovely," and she ran off to change.

<u>Appendices</u>

-Those Who Came Before
Stories From the History of *Just Cause*

-Roll Call
Teams past and present of the *Just Cause Universe*

Those Who Came Before: The Freakshow

I remember clearly looking down the great hall and thinking to myself what a waste of Aryan blood; one hundred men—one hundred of the best soldiers in the Reich who had volunteered to die for the Fatherland. Each was strapped to a gurney, elevated forty-five degrees. At the end of the hall was Messer's Device. It crouched like some great, hulking beast, barely containing the energies within its carefully-crafted skin.

Messer gave his usual speech—that the men had been selected for their bravery and their loyalty to Germany for a special treatment that would make them into the supermen they were destined to become. His speech was always the same. I had heard it so many times I could have repeated it word for word; so many times he had sent a group of good soldiers like these to their death.

God in Heaven, how could we have known this time he would have been right?

-Dr. Felix Dietrich, 1942

February, 1942
Aufstein, Germany

The way the castle lights dimmed and flickered worried Jim Scott. The American soldier watched the two-hundred-year-old castle through his field glasses, as he sprawled across a high rock ledge that overlooked the castle. Scott could have been a poster child for the Aryan ideal, had he not been a loyal son of America— six foot four, built like a farmhand, with a strong jaw and a shock of dirty blond hair that had grown out considerably since the arrival of his team in Germany.

Officially, their team's code name was *Project Circus*, but everybody from General Eisenhower on down just called them *The Freakshow*.

"Goddamn Krauts don't know a goddamn thing about wiring," grumbled Johnny Stills next to him. He fumbled for his canteen, which Scott knew was full of cheap Swiss vodka. Stills was small, almost rat-like in his appearance and intensity. He was dark-eyed and furtive in his movements.

A few battery-powered lights flickered to life below. "Now's our chance," said Scott. "While they're restoring power."

Stills nodded, wiping his mouth with the back of a grimy hand. "Move out," he whisper-shouted behind him. Two more dogfaces emerged from the low evergreens. William Hester and Ray Downs. Hester was twenty-four, making him the oldest of the group, and wore glasses, earning him the nickname *Professor*. Downs was the youngest, barely eighteen. His overlarge ears made him seem even younger. If it hadn't been for his parahuman ability, Scott would have refused to take him on a mission. It was like having your younger brother along on a date. The four men had infiltrated Germany nearly three weeks earlier with help from the French Resistance and had been making their careful way to Aufstein, where Allied Command said the Nazis were working on some secret weapon.

"Did you guys hear that?" Downs tapped his ear as he attached a rope around a sturdy rock outcropping.

"What do *you* think, moron?" Stills sneered at him, making no effort to connect his own rope.

"Stow that noise, Corporal," said Scott. "We're going to have a hard enough time of this without you announcing our presence to the entire Third Reich. What'd you hear, Sounder?"

Downs shrugged. "Dunno, Sergeant. Sounded like they turned on a big dynamo."

"Couldn't have been," said Hester. "A dynamo makes power, not drains it. Why'd they lose their lights?"

Stills muttered something under his breath that sounded something like "whyncha go ask 'em, shithead?"

Scott ignored his headstrong second-in-command. In spite of Stills' abrasive personality, he was a brilliant tactician and made excellent use of his particular skills. "You guys ready for descent?"

Hester and Downs answered in the affirmative. Downs even sounded eager. They hadn't seen any real action since France, and that seemed like an eternity ago, and more than once, Downs had complained about all the damn sneaking around. "It ain't fair. I want to kill me some krauts," he'd say, fingering his knife.

Scott turned to Stills. "Corporal, secure our landing site. And do it *quietly.*"

Stills drew his bowie knife and saluted. "Yes sir," he said, and vanished off the rock with a soft puff of inrushing air.

Stills was what Allied Command called an *exceptional talent.* They all were. Scott had been the first, found by a displaced French researcher named Georges Devereaux. Scott was strong enough to toss a jeep across a parking lot and tough enough to take a fifty-caliber bullet in the chest without even blinking, much less bleeding. He could also fly for almost a mile at a time, something that was more than a leap but less than actual flight. Devereaux had found Scott, thanks to his odd ability to see parahuman abilities in others, and brought him to see some men in the Army. They liked what they saw and immediately enrolled him in Basic. Then they went back to Devereaux and asked if he could find a few more like Scott, whom they code-named *Strongman.*

John Henry Stills was next. He was a teleport, able to move anywhere he could see without traversing the space between points. He simply vanished from one spot and instantly reappeared in his destination. He was a master knife-wielder, having been working in his father's slaughterhouse. Scott had seen him slice a kraut to bloody ribbons in seconds, flashing all around him faster than could be seen. The army code-named him *Flicker*, which he hated. But they let him get away with his antics because he was a parahuman, and there were only four in all the American forces, plus the wild card of Georges Devereaux.

William Hester could imbue objects he could hold in his hand with kinetic energy and then release them with enough force to rupture tank armor. In spite of his tremendous combat ability, Hester was mostly an intellectual. The soft-spoken, bespectacled man was more likely to be found with his nose buried in a book during down time, instead of chasing women or gambling like normal soldiers. On paper, he was called *Meteor*, but to everyone else he was just *Professor*.

Raymond Downs had lied about his age to get into the army. He wanted desperately to be a soldier and to fight the Axis, joining when he was only fifteen. Four months later his mother had come to pick him up from Fort Bening just before he was scheduled to ship out. Downs had nearly died from the sheer embarrassment of it. Two months later he was back when his family doctor couldn't explain why Downs could hear things that were too quiet, too far, and too high-pitched for anyone else. The Army doctors determined his abilities far surpassed normal, and he received a special dispensation to join and a codename, *Sounder*.

When the Army brass had showed their abilities to Albert Einstein, he said, "that's exceptional." The Army being what it was, the four men were referred to as "exceptional talents" from then on. They had been trained for every possible situation the G-men could devise. Eventually Roosevelt had ordered them deployed and they parachuted into France with a few thousand other dogfaces.

They'd had some success aiding the French Resistance by using their special abilities to complete missions that would have otherwise required ten times as many men. Their standard mode of operation was for Sounder to provide the intelligence via sound cues, then Flicker would secure the site, and finally Strongman and Meteor would go to work. Emplaced machinegun nests were no challenge to the four of them, and they could take out a convoy in a matter of seconds. This particular mission was going to require some different tactics. Their objective was gathering information about the project the Nazis had set up in Aufstein Castle.

Scott hadn't been told, officially, what Army Intelligence thought was going on in the castle. Unofficially, he'd been told that the krauts were trying to make their own *exceptional talents*. Allied Command was very interested in their experiments. Project Circus was to gather as much information about the process as they could, and then permanently disrupt operations. Scott was all in favor of the mission. The idea of an army filled with soldiers like himself marching across the face of Europe gave him nightmares.

He checked his watch. Two minutes had passed since Stills had vanished and he hadn't reappeared. If the area hadn't been secured, he would have popped back to report. He nodded at Hester and Downs, who began quietly rappelling down the rock face. Scott watched their progress, checking the castle for any sign they'd been seen. The castle was still mostly dark. Whatever the krauts had set off was drawing plenty of power. Hester and Downs got down to the ground and took up covering positions with their rifles. There was no sign of Stills, but Scott knew he'd be around somewhere. He took one last glance at the castle, then stepped off the side of the rock, letting himself fall.

Flying took a certain amount of suspension of disbelief. Scott always visualized himself parachuting when he fell. He'd actually been tested from heights of over two hundred feet and always landed safely. Well, not *always*. He could still twist an ankle or something else painful and inconveniencing. At least he didn't have to worry about being shot on the way down, as had happened to so many of the other soldiers. He always tried imagining he was an airplane when he launched himself into the air. After about a mile, his brain couldn't seem to handle the impossibility of his motion, and he fell, which was just as unnerving as flying. The doctors thought that they could hypnotize him so he'd be able to fly for longer periods of time, but Scott wasn't about to let them do that.

He reached the ground and unlimbered his own rifle. He heard a soft popping sound and a sudden breeze on his cheek announced Stills had teleported back to them. The smaller man's knife was bloodstained and his grin was shocking and bright in the dark.

"Two sentries in this section," he said. "Both accounted for." He wiped his knife on an evergreen and tucked it back in his sheath.

By now, Scott was familiar with Stills' bloodthirsty tendencies, and tried not to let it bother him. "How many other sentries on patrol?"

"I counted six. Three pairs of two."

"Sounder?"

The youngest soldier closed his eyes, concentrating on the sounds nobody else could hear. "Confirmed," he said in a moment. He chuckled quietly. "Two of 'em are drunk."

"Okay, here's the plan . . ." Scott began, but before he could continue a loud explosion ripped upward from the middle of the castle, sending cobbles and tiles flying.

"Shit," whispered Stills. "Think that's good for us or bad for us?"

An alarm began to wail, sounding very much like the air raid sirens in London. The four men instinctively looked to the skies, half afraid they would see a flight of B-17s on approach.

"Hey, look!" Hester pointed toward the castle. People were fleeing from the main entrance. Some of them were clearly soldiers, but others were in civilian garb or wearing white lab coats. They fought with each other as they grabbed motorcycles, trucks, or whatever vehicles were available. Engines sputtered to life and headlights illuminated the large cloud of dust that was raised from the explosion.

Within moments, the surge of people leaving the castle subsided. "Krauts might have done our job for us." Scott motioned to the others. "Let's move in. Stay sharp."

A ruddy glow in the smoke over the castle roof was a mute testament to a fire still burning inside. The Americans approached cautiously, rifles at the ready. The darkness seemed thick and oppressive as they reached the road, a muddy mess from the quick evacuation of the German vehicles.

The main gate into the castle hung open.

Advancing in pairs, they leapfrogged each other all the way to the castle wall. The stone was conducting a slight amount of heat. Scott figured that the interior must be like a blast furnace if the walls were already warm.

"Sounder, you hear anything inside?"

The young man removed his helmet, clapped a hand over one ear, and pressed the other against the wall, eyes shut, listening intently. "Big fire, glass breaking from the heat, something making a shrieking sound, maybe a steam valve? Shit, *footsteps!*" He pushed himself back from the wall and fumbled for his helmet.

Stills drew his knife. Scott pulled his pistol from his holster; it would be more useful in close quarters than his M-1. They waited on either side of the doorway. A figure staggered out. Stills' knife descended sharply and stopped short when Scott blocked his strike with the barrel of his pistol.

"What the hell, Sergeant?" Stills looked shocked.

"Look at him, Stills. He's no threat."

It was true. The man was badly burned. His clothes were mostly burned away except for the metal parts, which had cooked into the ruin of his skin. He tripped and fell, landing face down in the mud.

Scott had seen men burned by flamethrowers before, but this was worse than anything he'd ever witnessed. Bile rose in the back of his throat. Behind him, Downs vomited against the side of the castle. The man's limbs trembled as if he was cold, but it was surely from the massive nerve damage he'd sustained. Choking back the bad taste in his mouth, Scott reached out a boot and flipped the man over. Carbonized flesh flaked off him in layers. The man's face was gone, charred bone peeking through the cooked muscle. Incredibly, he was still breathing and *whispering* something through his burned lips and tongue.

"Hester," ordered Scott through clenched teeth. Hester was the only one who spoke German. The Professor spat to one side and kneeled down next to the man, disgust leaching from his pores.

"He keeps saying *übermensch*, over and over," said Hester after a moment, getting back to his feet.

"What's that mean?" Downs wiped his mouth. His face had gone as pale as the moon.

"Super man," Hester answered. Mercifully, the man stopped moving as his injuries overcame him.

Scott felt all the strength drain out of his legs. "Holy Christ. What if they did it?"

Stills' lip curled in disdain. He was undoubtedly still upset about Scott stopping him, since he believed the only good kraut was a dead kraut, no matter the circumstances. "Did what?"

"Made someone like us," said Hester.

"Bullshit! How could you make a parahuman?" Stills shoved his knife back into its sheath.

"Nobody knows how we got our powers," said Scott. "I didn't really know about mine until I hit eighteen. You found out about yours by accident, Stills, and Downs didn't get his until after Basic Training. The Nazis have scientists; maybe they figured something out."

The four men were silent for a moment as each considered the possibility of a Nazi parahuman.

"Okay, let's move in," said Scott finally.

"What, in there?" Stills was adamant. "No way."

"That's an order, Corporal. Salvage any documents you can find."

Rifles drawn, they moved into the castle.

The entryway was filled with smoke. A smoldering Nazi flag hung in the middle of the hall. Somewhere ahead, they could all hear the sounds of a fire.

"How come it ain't burning out here?" Downs asked.

"Stone don't burn, kid," said Stills.

They passed through another doorway into a courtyard. There was the remains of a building in the middle of the courtyard where the explosion must have occurred. Some of the cobblestones around the ruin glowed white hot. The force of the explosion seemed to have blown out most of the fire, leaving behind only the charred inflammables in its wake.

"It does if it gets hot enough." Hester coughed through the acrid fumes in the air. "I never heard of anything making this kind of heat except a volcano."

Shattered Klieg lights and warped scaffolding surrounded the courtyard. Scott looked around intently. Up on the castle wall was a steel and glass booth that was in just the spot he would have picked for an observation gallery. The glass was melted and blackened.

"Stills, can you get up there to check that out?"

"Affirmative." Stills winked out of the courtyard and appeared up on the wall. Rifle out, he kicked open the door and peered inside. In a moment, he called out from the doorway. "Sergeant, you better get up here!"

Scott took as deep a breath as he could in the smoky air and concentrated. His feet left the ground and he flew up to the top of the wall. A reek of charred flesh emerged from the booth. Scott swallowed hard, then stepped into the enclosure.

Everything in the room from window height and up had been charred black. Ash eddied in the air currents. Two people had been seated in chairs, presumably to watch the events unfolding in the courtyard below. Their legs and lower bodies were relatively unharmed, but from the waist up, they were essentially unrecognizable lumps of charcoal.

"What is this?" Scott asked, disturbed at the strangeness the scene entailed.

"Some kinda observation tower. I figure there might be some notes or something here, but I didn't want to touch nothin' without your approval first." Stills glanced at the two smoking corpses. "Shitty way to go. Must have been one hell of a burst to cook 'em like that!"

Scott clicked on his electric torch and began searching for anything he could take with him back to Allied Command. A shelf of notebooks might have been promising, but they had been turned into lattices of ash that disintegrated when he touched them. He began rooting through drawers in a low file cabinet. Nothing. No notes, no binders, nothing to show but death.

"Sergeant!" Downs' voice was urgent from down in the courtyard.

Scott leaned out of the observation booth door. "What, Sounder?"

"Heartbeat, sir, and it isn't one of ours."

A sudden rush of air and ash behind Scott informed him that Stills had just teleported out. Sure enough, he appeared an instant later next to Downs, already drawing his knife.

Scott vaulted the edge of the wall and dropped the twenty feet to the courtyard. For a trained paratrooper, even one who could fly, it was like any other landing. Hester had his pistol out and was slowly circling, like a hawk preparing to strike. His left hand clutched a fist-sized chunk of rock that vibrated with barely--contained kinetic energy.

"Where is it, Ray?" Scott grasped his own pistol at the ready.

Downs turned around slowly, using his ears like a radar set. "Through there." He pointed to the stone building in the center of the courtyard. It was long, stretching nearly two-thirds of the length of the courtyard itself. A large portion of the roof had been immolated in the explosion. "Sounds like he's inside a metal box by the echo of it."

"Maybe he can tell us what happened," said Hester in a hoarse, choking voice.

"Move in," said Scott. "And watch yourselves. It's still damn hot in here."

The four men advanced to the building. The entry doors had been blown off their hinges and lay smoldering on the courtyard cobbles. Two by two, they entered the building.

Inside was a long, low-ceilinged hall. Strange metal implements lined each wall at regular intervals, twisted into unrecognizable shapes by the heat. Small metal boxes were bolted down by each sculpture. Scott approached one cautiously and flipped open the catch with the tip of his rifle. Inside it was a smoke-stained German army uniform. He looked back down the hall, trying to picture it before the accident.

"Beds. These were beds." Hester stepped up next to him. "That's why the footlockers are here."

"That doesn't make sense. Was it a hospital?"

Hester looked grim. "Not a chance. This looks like a lab of some sort. These poor guys were subjects." They glanced down and saw charred bone fragments amid the ash remains of flesh and bedding.

"Sarge, in there." Downs motioned to a bank of heavy clothing lockers against one wall. He and Stills stepped up to them. The young man closed his eyes, listening intently next to each door. He stopped at the third locker, opened his eyes, and nodded. Stills took up a position on one side of the door, Downs the other. Scott and Hester raised their weapons, preparing for the worst. Stills nodded and raised his fingers in a silent count. *One . . . two . . . three!*

Downs yanked open the door and a man pitched forward onto the charred floor. He coughed and choked, rolling onto his side. A rope of mucus and blood trailed from his mouth. His skin had an odd, waxy sheen to it. With horror, Scott realized his eyes had been burned out; their remains leaked down his cheeks.

In his hands, he was clutching a notebook.

"This him?" Scott asked. Downs nodded, eyes wide. "Professor, check him out and confiscate that book. Downs, Stills, check the rest of the lockers, including the footlockers."

Hester dropped to his knees and started to pull the notebook away from the man. The man started and closed a desperate hand around Hester's wrist, babbling something in German. Hester kept his cool and asked the man a question. The man stuttered as if he was drugged.

"Give him some morphine," said Scott. "Maybe it'll help us get some answers from him."

As the drug kicked in, the man became somewhat more lucid. He spoke rapid-fire German, as if he was trying to get all of his thoughts out before he perished from whatever it was that was eating him up inside. Hester took frantic notes in the man's notebook. Most of the man's speech was so jumbled and incoherent that he couldn't make heads or tails of it.

Stills and Downs returned from their search to report. "One hundred footlockers. One was empty, and there was no sign of a body beside it." Stills glanced around the room.

The man on the floor began to laugh. Not just *laughing*, thought Scott with horror, but *cackling* like an insane witch in a motion picture. His whooping laugh degenerated into a thick, bubbly cough that spurted bloody mucus from his mouth and nostrils. Hester recoiled from the grotesque droplets.

"Yah . . . yah . . . one lived!" The man spoke in heavily-accented English.

"You speak English?" Scott stepped forward.

"Ya . . . a little." The man's laughter fell into a hacking cough.

"What do you mean, *one lived*?" Stills eyes narrowed.

"The experiment . . . it was . . . success! Thousands die so that one may live. *Heil Hitler!* We have created . . . your superman!"

"What the hell does he mean by that?" Downs shouted.

"I think that's obvious, kid," said Hester.

"*No!* He's . . . he's sick or something. Look at him. He doesn't know what he's saying." Downs' face grew dark beneath the soot stains.

"At ease, *Private*," growled Scott.

"We're supposed to be the only ones. They told us we were the only ones!" Downs raised his rifle as if it were a club.

"Stills," said Scott. The teleport popped from his spot to reappear directly behind Downs. He yanked the rifle from the boy's hands. When Downs spun around in fury, Stills cuffed him hard across the face, sending him sprawling. "Stills, stand down," Scott bawled in his best drill-sergeant's voice.

Downs didn't rise from where he had landed in a heap. His voice was racked by sobs. "We're supposed to be the only ones," he repeated as he gasped for air.

Scott stalked over to the boy. "We don't have time for this. *On your feet, soldier! Atten-SHUN!*"

Months of conditioned reflexes kicked in and Downs jumped up, ramrod straight, tears tracking clean streaks down his sooty face. "Sorry, sir." He gulped and wiped his nose, and then paused, listening. "Does anyone else hear that?"

The other three soldiers looked around warily, weapons raised. "Hear what?" Scott snapped at him.

"That sort of humming, whistling sound. Kind of like before a steam valve busts."

Another cackling laugh emerged from the forgotten man on the floor. His flesh seemed to be moving from waxy to almost liquid, like it wasn't sticking to his bones anymore. "Ya . . . Messer's Device . . . it will pulse again . . . all will perish."

Hester started as if he'd been goosed. "Device?"

"What's *pulse*?" Downs looked frightened.

"It's bad, whatever it is." said Scott. "Stills, take that journal. If anything happens, you get clear with it."

"But Sergeant—"

"That's an order, Corporal. Move out, boys, asses and elbows!"

The four men ran for it, back down the hall and through the entryway. They cleared the castle wall and were pelting across the mud for the evergreen forest across the road when a light as bright as day erupted from the castle behind them.

Scott had a sensation of being as transparent as glass, followed by a twisting, wrenching pain. His mind whirled madly as it tried to reconcile the fact that he had just been teleported. Acute vertigo hit him like a right hook and he fell hard onto a rocky surface, retching from the dizziness and the awful sensation.

That's when he heard the screaming. He tried to focus his spinning eyes. A fiery orange and red blur resolved itself into the largest explosion he had ever seen. The castle had been flung apart by the force of it, and the evergreens had been knocked flat, burning so fast they exploded as the water within their trunks flashed into steam. He realized he was up on the high mountain that overlooked the castle, or what was left of it. He shivered violently, although from the cold or the altitude or the sudden shift in location he couldn't tell.

The screaming continued and Scott saw Stills writhing on the ground in agony. His left arm was missing halfway through his bicep, as neat as if someone had lopped it off with a band saw. Blood poured out of the stump.

Scott forced himself up to his knees, fumbling for his pack and for the morphine. The world spun around him as he found the emergency kit. He flopped down next to Stills, whose screams had softened to animalistic moans. He ripped off the sleeve of his fatigues and fashioned a tourniquet around Stills' arm. Even in the darkness, with the angry glow of the fire below, the man had gone deathly pale.

Stills had lost so much blood; Scott was afraid that the morphine would kill him, but he wasn't a medic and wouldn't trust himself to alter a dose. In a few minutes the narcotic took hold of Stills and his whimpering subsided.

Scott hunkered down next to him to wait until morning. Neither of them was in any shape to travel, and if Stills was going to die, it would happen in the next few hours. There was no sign of Hester or Downs. Scott was certain they had died down below in front of the castle. The heat from the explosion had been so strong that where there had been mud was now cracked earth with a glossy sheen over it. The forest had been leveled, and what hadn't been blown to splinters was burning away.

He had a fair idea of what happened. When the device pulsed, it had blown up, like an overheated boiler. In the fraction of a second after the burst, Stills had reached out to Scott, who happened to be right next to him, and teleported them both up the mountainside.

Stills was able to move more mass than himself, since he could teleport with a full pack, but he'd never attempted to move another whole person. His body must have rebelled at the attempt and left part of itself behind. Scott felt fortunate to be all in one piece and to not have any parts of the local landscape impaled through him. Teleporting to an unseen location was one of Stills' great fears; he was afraid of materializing in the same space occupied by another object. Army doctors had no idea what would happen if he did.

Scott knew that no matter what else happened, he had to get that notebook back to the Allies. He had to tell them what they'd learned at Aufstein, that the Nazis were trying to create their own parahumans.

And he had to tell them that they'd succeeded.

Those Who Came Before: Arrowheads

There were so many doors open for me then. I was young, rich, smart, good-looking, and I lived in New York City—the greatest place anyone who was anyone should live. I could have done anything I wanted to.

What I chose to do was put on a mask and fight crime with American Justice.

-Adrian Crowley aka Dr. Danger,
Dangerous: The Autobiography of Dr. Danger, 1964

August, 1949
New York City, New York

Adrian Crowley crouched in the shadows of the rooftop overlooking the warehouse. He was a tall man, cresting six feet, with an athlete's build honed from thousands of hours on his private archery range. The tool of his trade rested across his back, a curved piece of yew that hung from custom clips on the back of his quiver.

His costume was piratical in nature; flowing white cotton shirt, dark blue pants tucked into folded-down boots, a dark red sash and a matching kerchief tied around his head, incorporating into it a mask that hid his eyes.

He called himself Dr. Danger; he just liked the sound of it.

He fiddled with a small Geiger counter that he'd removed from a pouch on the side of his quiver. Tiny clicks emerged from it at an elevated rate. He frowned behind his mask and adjusted the dials, but it continued to report that radiation levels were significantly higher than they should have been around the warehouse. It looked like the information from his source was correct. He'd checked the warehouse from three different angles and each time the Geiger counter clicked like a tap-dancing flea circus.

The sound of an engine made him shrink back into the shadows. He replaced the counter into his pouch and watched over the edge of the adjacent building. A long, low Hudson slid around the corner, lights off, engine rumbling just above an idle. Two guys got out of the back seat, wearing trench coats and fedoras. Moonlight glinted off the Thompson submachine guns each man held. They looked around, furtive and suspicious, daring anyone to challenge their superior firepower. Then, apparently satisfied, one of them raised an electric torch and flashed it down the alleyway in three quick bursts.

Headlights appeared around the corner and a step-van rolled into the alley, its badly-tuned engine raising a cloud of black smoke. The other man walked past the front of the Hudson to the delivery door of the warehouse and rapped on it with the butt of the gun in a short, syncopated pattern.

In a moment, light streamed into the alley as the door raised against the squeaky protest of poorly--lubricated bearings. The Hudson glided into the well-lit interior of the warehouse, followed by the belching van. Adrian watched as the door was lowered, leaving the alley once again bathed in darkness. He hadn't realized until the door opened that the windows of the warehouse had been either covered or painted. *Stupid and careless*, he thought to himself. *Never assume anything*. He'd been playing at superhero for almost a year and still felt like a wet-behind- -the-ears novice. It had been a lark, the diversion of a bored rich boy who'd inherited his wealth from war profiteering, who'd been slowly dying of terminal boredom until discovering his uncanny knack for archery.

Who'd decided to become a superhero, like those of American Justice. Unlike them, he didn't have amazing parahuman abilities to bring foes to justice. But they didn't have his archery skills, or his arsenal of special arrows.

With a seasoned eye for gauging distances, he estimated how far away the warehouse was from his vantage point. Alleys in the industrial part of town were deceptively wide; much more so than they looked. To misjudge distance here was to invite a tumble to the pavement or worse. With enough room for the Hudson to have opened both doors and the men to walk past them, he figured it was ten feet across.

Unfortunately the two sentries remained below, slouching in the alley and smoking unfiltered cigarettes. They would have to be dealt with before he could safely leap across the gap, or else they would raise the alarm. He drew one of the ball-tipped arrows, finding it by the shape of the fletching. He machined the special tips on a lathe in his workshop. Instead of a sharp point, this particular type of trick arrow was tipped with a blunt steel bearing the size of a golf ball. They were heavy and ungainly projectiles, and not very accurate over distance. On the other hand, they were useful for knocking opponents down and out, instead of killing them outright.

Adrian had never killed a man, and didn't intend to start. The political climate following World War II had been mostly permissive toward vigilantes, especially with the formation of American Justice by parahuman veterans of the War. South of the old Mason-Dixon line, though, vigilantes were lynching colored folks and burning down churches. Because of that, someone was going to make it illegal sooner or later. Adrian hoped to stave off that time as long as possible, and leaving the bad guys alive and hurt but contrite looked pretty good to the general public.

And a good public image was imperative to a guy who dressed up like a pirate with a bow and lurked around the rooftops of New York City.

He lifted the bow off its clips, its familiar weight comforting in its presence. He measured the distance to the men below at about a two-thirds pull. A ball-tip could knock a man out with a nasty bump on the head, or it could crack his skull. It was a fine line, but he'd spent many hours perfecting his techniques. He took careful aim at the first man's head, using the glowing tip of his cigarette as a reference point.

He released the first arrow. In a blurred economy of motion, he drew a second ball-tip just as the first one struck. As the man dropped like a rag doll, Adrian pulled back on the string a second time. The other sentry was just starting to react to the sudden fall of his partner when he was likewise struck, the impact knocking his hat off into a puddle.

The only sounds from the entire encounter had been the thuds of the ball-tips striking scalps, the crumpling sounds of the men falling, and the clink as the deflected ball-tips bounced to the pavement. Adrian listened intently for a few minutes, making sure that no suspicions had been raised. Eventually, satisfied that he could safely cross the intervening distance to his target warehouse, he took a few running steps and leaped across the alley. Bow in hand, he advanced across the warehouse roof, looking for a way into the building itself. There was a sudden puff of breeze that ruffled the sleeves of his shirt. He stopped, sensing danger.

A long blade slid across his throat.

"Don't move, archer, and lose the bow." Breath redolent with garlic washed past Adrian's face.

"Easy there, chief. You'll get no trouble from me." Adrian relaxed himself, preparing to unleash a flurry of kicks upon his attacker. He dropped the bow carefully, glancing down at the blade across his neck. There was something odd about its shape and position. The arm holding the blade was far too short, and even in the shadows, it was plain that the blade was the length of a sword. With a start, he realized that the man was not holding the blade, but that it replaced his arm altogether.

There was only one man Adrian knew about that had a sword for an arm. "Flicker, I'm one of the *good guys*. We're on the same side."

"Let him go, John," came a voice from somewhere above them. Adrian looked up and saw a man hovering casually in the air, ten feet above them. He knew it was Strongman, of course, but it was still quite a shock to see him flying unsupported. Strongman wore a tight-fitting bronze-colored reflective body suit with red accents, cape, and hood. He'd once explained in an interview that the bright colors made him a better target, and since he was bulletproof, he'd rather that the bad guys shot at him than at his teammates.

The blade was removed from Adrian's throat—not by it being pulled away, but by suddenly vanishing in a puff of air. Flicker reappeared several feet away. He wore a dark body suit, made out of a material that trapped the light. Where Strongman was bright, Flicker was darkness incarnate. Even the blade that extended from the stump of his upper arm was made out of non-reflecting Damascus steel. His face was also masked.

Adrian stooped down to pick up his bow, checking it for damage. He'd built it to be as hardy as possible, because one never knew when a bow would need to be used as a club in close quarters, but it was always good to check.

"You're gonna believe him just like that?" Flicker grumbled behind his mask.

"Perhaps," said Strongman as he dropped to the ground as gently as if he'd been lowered on a crane. "But before you kill him, I'd like to find out more about him." He turned his attention to Adrian. "We've read about you in the papers. It's a pleasure to finally meet you."

"You always make your introductions like this?"

"Please forgive John," said Strongman. "He's never been especially trusting."

Flicker swung his sword blade back and forth. "Yeah, well, he's wearing a mask, isn't he? He's obviously got somethin' to hide!"

"So do we," said Strongman.

"Nobody wants to look at radiation scars, Jim. The pirate over there looks like he hasn't even ever cut himself shaving."

"The mask is to protect my identity." Adrian felt sheepish. He'd thought that his first meeting with American Justice would be more . . . *heroic*. "Unlike the two of you, I have a private life that I'd rather not complicate with my nighttime activities."

"He's got a point there, John," came a new, feminine voice. Adrian looked and saw the other three members of American Justice standing by the edge of the warehouse roof. The three newcomers were veterans of the war, like Flicker and Strongman, but they had fought against the Japanese in the Pacific.

Colt, the woman who had spoken, was pretty behind her short haircut and pilot's goggles. She wore a dark red leather jacket over a stylized ballet leotard and tights. Her heavy black jump boots had thick, knobby soles, and a pair of horseshoes were incongruously slung at her waist. Adrian knew that she could run as fast as a speeding car and her other reactions were similarly accelerated.

Beside Colt was Flashpoint, the colored man. He could generate powerfully bright bursts of light to blind and confuse opponents. He wore goggles like Colt, but his were smoked. His costume was a set of light gray coveralls with numerous pouches affixed to it. A pair of automatic pistols was strapped to his waist in well-oiled leather holsters.

At their feet sat a wolf, tongue lolling out past razor-sharp teeth. The wolf was called Gray, and was a real-life werewolf. Adrian couldn't remember for sure, but he thought that the alter ego of Gray was an Indian from one of the southern reservations.

"All right, we'll concede your identity . . . for now," said Strongman. "What are you doing here tonight, Dr. Danger?"

"Working on a tip," said Adrian. "Someone's buying uranium, and there's a group selling it downstairs in this building."

Colt gasped and glanced toward Strongman. Adrian was sure that either he had shocked her with his revelation, or confirmed a suspicion.

"And you were going to just bust in and start shooting arrows at them?" Flicker sounded disgusted.

"Something like that," said Adrian. "Last I checked, smuggling was still illegal. I don't like the idea of somebody else building an atomic bomb. It's bad enough that the Russians have one now."

"So you've been working the seller's angle?" Strongman asked him.

Adrian nodded. "It's a branch of the Mob. I don't know where they got the uranium . . ."

"Nevada," said Colt.

"We've been working on this case for a few months now," said Strongman. "But from the buyer's angle. We know who's been trying to obtain the ore, and we think we know why. We just found out the transaction is going to happen here, tonight."

"Hell, Jim, why don't you tell him everything?" Flicker scraped the point of the sword across the warehouse roof.

"You know what your problem is, Stills? You don't trust anybody." Flashpoint spoke for the first time, his voice deep and mellow like a French horn.

"That's right, I don't. And it's kept me alive this long!" Flicker teleported suddenly right in front of Flashpoint, who started but refrained from further provocation.

"That's enough, John. If we're going to fight amongst ourselves, we might as well let the Nazis win." Strongman glided in between the two of them, gently pushing Flicker away from the black man.

"Nazis?" Adrian asked. "I thought that show was over a few years ago."

"The buyers are a group of Nazi officers that escaped prosecution and relocated to South America. Specifically, Brazil," said Strongman. "I don't think I have to tell you why they're purchasing uranium."

"To build an atomic bomb," said Adrian, his voice grim. "So they can use it on us."

"Or a reactor," said Flashpoint.

"What's a *reactor?*" The term was unfamiliar to Adrian.

"It's a device that creates power through a controlled atomic reaction. We encountered a prototype in Germany. It's why we wear masks." Strongman's voice took on a note of sadness.

"All right. So we've got the Mob selling uranium to the Nazis. Sounds tailor-made for people like us." Adrian twanged his bowstring for emphasis.

"Us, maybe." Flicker's voice took on a nastier quality than it had before, something Adrian wouldn't have believed possible. "Nobody said nothin' about you."

Strongman sighed. "Well I'm saying it now, or do I have to make it an order, Corporal?"

"Yeah, yeah, I know," grunted the black-garbed man.

"They brought a truck in a few minutes ago," said Adrian. "The whole building's already reading hot on my counter. If they're going to do the deal tonight, it's probably going down soon, if not now. Any idea how the Nazis are going to move out the ore?"

"I'm sure they'll use a boat. They just need time to load it and make their getaway." Colt was quivering like her namesake, anticipating battle.

"All right then, what's the plan and how can I help?" Adrian asked.

"He's the tactician," Strongman pointed to Flashpoint.

"Three-pronged attack," said the colored man. "Strongman goes in through the roof. His objective is to draw fire and cause mayhem. Flicker 'ports in and handles outlying sentries. Colt and Gray work the guys on the floor, herding them away from the ore towards me, where I can incapacitate them. You . . ." He pointed to Adrian. "Hang around in the rafters and take opportunity shots. Make sure nobody gets away with any ore. Our primary objective is to keep the ore from leaving the warehouse, not to pursue the bad guys. Questions?"

Adrian glanced around at the others. They seemed confident in the plan, apparently trusting Flashpoint's ability to formulate strategies.

"Move out," said Strongman. "John, you and Dr. Danger are with me. The rest of you have two minutes to get to your positions, then we enter the building." Colt, Flashpoint, and the wolf slipped away, heading down the fire escape toward the alley below.

"How are you going to go through the roof?" Adrian asked Strongman.

"Just smash through it, I suppose. It can't be that sturdy. It's just a big box. Why?"

Adrian pulled an explosive arrow from his quiver, putting it to the string. "This is loaded with gelignite. The impact on the head will detonate it. It ought to weaken the roof considerably."

"A grenade, huh? Maybe you ain't so bad after all." Flicker's eyes glinted behind his mask. "Where do you buy 'em?"

"Make them myself," said Adrian. "Where do you want it, Strongman?"

The bronze-costumed man flew into the air, drifting toward the center of the warehouse roof. "Think you can hit right here?"

Adrian smiled. "Give me a ten second countdown."

Strongman pulled back his sleeve and checked a slim wristwatch. "Okay. Ten . . . nine . . . eight . . ." Strongman rose higher into the air, inverting himself in preparation for smashing through the warehouse roof.

At four seconds, Adrian released the arrow. It arced up into the night sky. Four seconds later, it dropped and struck the precise spot that Strongman had marked. The explosive charge shook the roof of the building and a burst of flame and smoke rent the sky.

Strongman lunged downward, heedless of the fiery cloud of the explosion, hitting the roof like a missile. The rooftop, overstressed and weakened by the gelignite arrow, split open like an overripe fruit, sending a cloud of dust and debris high into the sky. Flicker chuckled behind his mask. "Nicely done, Doc. That'll get their attention for sure." He teleported to the edge of the gaping hole, looking inside for his first target, then gave a whoop of pure joy and vanished.

Adrian was already running for the edge of the hole as he heard gunfire erupt inside the building. Inside the base of his quiver was a coiled silk rope and a grappling hook. Spying a metal pole protruding from the roof, he looped the hook around it and lowered himself into the hole.

Below him, he saw Colt and Gray running amid a large group of men, all armed, who were trying unsuccessfully to hit any of the heroes. There was no sign of Flicker or Flashpoint, but Strongman had just picked up a shipping crate and was preparing to hurl it at a group of men peppering him with their Tommy guns. Glancing around, Adrian saw a wide horizontal beam that should fit his needs. He kicked his legs, swinging on the rope, hoping that it wouldn't tear on the jagged edges of the ripped roof.

As Strongman threw the heavy shipping crate, sending the men flying, Adrian released the rope and flew across the intervening space to catch himself on the beam. In a moment he had clambered up to straddle it. He unlimbered his bow again, seeing a bright flash like a magnesium flare out of the corner of his vision. Blinking away the spots, he began looking for opportune targets.

The first arrow he fired was a ball-tip at a man carrying one of the ugly-but-efficient German submachine guns. The man was stitching bullets across the floor toward Gray, who was mauling another gunman's hand. The ball-tip smashed into the man's wrist, shattering it and causing him to drop the gun. He let out a yell audible even over the sounds of guns and combat. A second ball-tip silenced him, catching him across the temple.

Colt dashed underneath him, holding her horseshoes like they were boxing gloves. A 60-MPH punch sent a gunman flying in an explosion of tooth fragments. Adrian sent a shower of arrows in her wake, now using pointed arrows to pierce the arms and legs of the gunmen. A new, heavy chatter filled the air as two men raised an air-cooled belt-fed machine gun from the trunk of the Hudson and fired at Strongman. The heavy caliber bullets didn't penetrate his flesh, but their kinetic impacts knocked him into a support beam for the warehouse. Already overstressed by the weakened roof, the beam buckled and Adrian's perch bent almost ninety degrees, dropping him toward the floor.

He knew he was going to land badly. The floor below was covered with splintered shipping crates and debris from Strongman's actions. He tried to twist himself in midair, the way he'd been taught by a French acrobat. A dark red blur smashed into him as he fell, the impact knocking him flying laterally to smash into a stack of cardboard boxes. The empty boxes absorbed much of the force of his landing. He shook his head to clear it as he realized that Colt was lying on top of him. She had deflected his fall into the boxes. She was breathing heavily, her face flushed. Their eyes locked and in that moment, Adrian was hooked.

Her hand, trembling slightly, brushed against his cheek and the edge of his mask, as if she would gently lift it away from his face. Thoughts of preserving his identity were far away in Adrian's mind, and it felt like time itself had ground to a halt.

The feeling only lasted for a fraction of a second, though, because a stream of fifty-caliber bullets tore through the boxes. Adrian jumped one way and Colt the other to get clear. He spotted his bow where it had fallen and dove for it, yanking one of the Japanese frog-crotch arrows from his quiver. The man firing the machine gun by the Hudson had a terrible grin on his face as he swept the barrel this way and that, driving Strongman back into the warehouse walls. In one smooth, sweeping motion, Adrian grasped his bow, drew the arrow back, and let fly.

The forked arrow sliced neatly through the belt feed of the machine gun and in a moment the thunderous fire halted. That gave Gray and Flashpoint an opening. The wolf leaped across the Hudson, his claws scrabbling on the shiny black paint, and came down hard on the man who'd been feeding the chain to the machine gun. The man's scream turned into a gurgle as Gray clamped his jaws down on the man's throat, tearing it out as neatly as a sculptor removing a lump of clay. The man who'd been firing the gun staggered as a dark third eye appeared in the center of his forehead. He crumpled to the floor. Beyond him, Flashpoint lowered one of his smoking pistols and winked at Adrian.

For a brief moment, all gunfire in the warehouse stopped and Adrian thought that perhaps they'd won. Suddenly four figures in gray overcoats and helmets rushed in from the dockside entrance. Almost in unison, they each tossed a handled grenade in a carefully-planned dispersal pattern. Two of them impacted right where Strongman was digging his way out from under a collapsed wall. The resulting explosion demolished the remains of that corner of the warehouse, burying him under several tons of debris.

The four newcomers raised their rifles, advancing into the warehouse, which was starting to burn from the various detonations. A black blur appeared among them, swinging a bloodstained sword. A surprised head parted from its shoulders in a spray of blood. The other three reacted with impressive speed, firing toward the teleport. Adrian thought he saw Flicker stagger even as he teleported away.

Flashpoint popped off three flashes in rapid succession, bringing his pistols to bear on the three remaining overcoats. Gray yelped as a burning crate exploded, scattering fiery splinters across his coat. Even though he had to be seeing nothing but spots from Flashpoint's powers, one of the men snapped his rifle around and fired at the sound of the wolf.

Adrian, realizing at last that this engagement would require him to cross the line he'd set for himself, drew a broad-tipped hunting arrow and put it through the throat of one of the three men. The remaining two fired back, taking cover behind a forklift.

Colt was frantically trying to pull flaming debris away from the pile that had trapped Strongman. Even though he couldn't be hurt by the crushing weight, he could still be burned or suffocated. She was moving faster than she ever had before.

"Danger, help Gray!" Flashpoint called as he crouched behind a packing case and reloaded his pistols.

Adrian looked around and saw the wolf was pulling Flicker across the floor by his good arm, a trail of blood streaks in his wake. He lunged for the wounded man, helping to get him behind some cover just as the two overcoats opened up again.

"Who the hell are those guys?" Adrian shouted over the din.

"SS," coughed Flicker, pulling his mask off. Adrian started with revulsion, realizing why the man wore a mask. His face was terribly scarred, as if he'd been burned. Blood trickled from a corner of his mouth. "Got a . . . real good look . . . at the guy I cut."

"SS?"

"Yeah . . . *Schutzstaffel* . . . I really hate . . . those assholes." Flicker grimaced from the pain of his wounds. He'd been shot in the torso and abdomen. "Can't feel . . . my legs."

Colt appeared beside them, her costume blackened and smoke still rising from it in places. "I can't get him out! I can't even tell if he's alive under there!"

More gunfire came from the SS troopers, providing cover for four other men to grab a pair of heavy strongboxes and head for the dockside entrance. The entire front wall of the warehouse was burning.

"That's the uranium!" Flashpoint shouted.

A voice outside the warehouse urged the men to hurry in German.

"They've got to have a boat," said Adrian. "If they get to it, we'll never stop them. We need a diversion so we can get past those troopers!"

Flicker coughed, spattering blood flecks. "I can . . . still do that . . ."

"No!" cried Colt as the teleport vanished.

He reappeared in midair, several feet over the *Schutzstaffel* who were firing from behind the forklift. He tumbled down on top of them like a giant rag doll, swinging his sword at them as he fell.

Adrian was already up and running, reaching for another hunting tip. Gray was even faster, closing on the men carrying the strongboxes. Behind them, Flashpoint used his powers again to try and blind anyone trying to draw a bead on them.

The two SS troopers made short work of Flicker. They raised their rifles again, preparing to fire at Adrian and Gray. Suddenly Colt whipped past from behind them. As she dashed past Adrian she hung something on the arrow he was about to release.

Arming pins.

The troopers blew up.

A furry gray body staggered away from the explosion to collapse on the warehouse floor. The wolf transformed partway into a man but then froze before completion. A pool of blood spread out beneath him. "Gray!" cried Colt. "I didn't see him there!"

"He's gone," said Adrian. "I'm sorry."

"No time for that now," said Flashpoint. "Get after the uranium. Don't wait for me." Adrian realized that the colored man had been shot and was holding a bloody rag against his leg.

Adrian wanted to say something, but had no idea what. At first, he thought it was his ears ringing from the explosion, but then he was certain that he heard the sound of an engine from the dock. He ran out of the burning warehouse and saw a motorboat pulling away from the dock with six men on board. He ran to the edge of the dock and released his arrow. A man on the boat tumbled into the water and didn't surface again.

Adrian drew back, fired, and sent another Nazi off to sleep with the fishes. Then he lowered his bow before firing any more arrows. "Out of range," he said to Colt as she ran up beside him. Tears ran down her cheeks.

"Only temporarily," said Colt. She pointed to where a small motor launch was moored. In a blur of motion she had the boat untied. Adrian slid into the seat behind the wheel. He thumbed the starter as Colt jumped into the other seat. The engine coughed twice, then rumbled to life. Adrian thrust the throttle all the way forward and locked it into place. The powerful motor roared and the boat's prow lifted out of the water as it accelerated away from the dock.

Even though it was late at night, there were still enough lights along the docks reflecting in the water that Adrian could see the path carved by the other boat. "Where do you think they're going?" He shouted over the din of the boat's engine.

"They've got to have a bigger ship out there somewhere. Something that will get them back to Brazil."

An idea occurred to Adrian. "Take the wheel a moment." Colt slipped in front of him, allowing him to pick up his bow. He reached into his quiver for one of his experimental arrows. He always carried three or four of them, different projects he was developing.

The arrow he drew forth had a pair of strange bulging packages wrapped around the shaft. He dragged the tip of the arrow along the boat's gunwale, igniting the phosphorous powder that in turn touched off the fuse. Before the fuse burned down to the flare, he pulled the bowstring back to his cheek and shot the arrow high into the night sky.

The flare package lit as the arrow ascended, burning magnesium powder to make a bright, white light. So far so good, thought Adrian. As the arrow reached the zenith of its arc, the secondary fuse burned through and the fireproof chute deployed itself. The flare arrow wafted down in the sea breeze, dropping like a star falling in slow motion.

"Nice," said Colt. "What else have you got stashed in that quiver?"

"I wasn't entirely sure that would work," Adrian said. Ahead, he could see the other speedboat heading for a tall, dark pillar.

Colt took one of her hands off the boat's wheel and pushed her pilot's goggles up onto her forehead. She squinted into the distance at the other boat's destination. "What is that?"

"Buoy?"

Colt shook her head. "No light on it."

The other boat slowed and pulled alongside the pillar. The water around it began to bubble and foam as it rose. A narrow, dark hull popped onto the surface, water draining away through dark openings.

A U-boat.

As the men on the other boat began to climb aboard the U-boat's deck, hauling the uranium-filled strongboxes with them, other men flowed out of what Adrian now realized was the conning tower. Some of them assisted the unloading of the boat, while the others unlocked the deck gun and swung it around toward them.

Colt spun the wheel hard and the boat heaved around a tight corner, nearly swamping itself as the gunners opened up. Adrian nearly fell overboard from the maneuver, only just managing to catch a tie bar. Heavy shells blasted fountains of water into the air, barely missing their boat.

"I'm not really equipped to take on a submarine." Adrian struggled back to the front of the boat. "What's the plan?"

"Plan?" Colt flashed him a brilliant smile. "You're the Eagle Scout. I'm just the cabbie." She whipped the boat around in another tight turn to avoid a trail of shell impacts.

"Okay, let me think for a second."

"No pressure, Doc. They're only shooting at us."

Adrian drew another explosive-tipped arrow from the quiver, which was now the lightest it had ever been in a single foray. "Well, I can do something about the shooting, at least. Can you get us to within fifty yards?"

"I better get one hell of a tip for this," said Colt. "Traffic is murder this time of night." She bounced the boat over a slow breaker and pointed the prow directly at the U-boat. The shells from the deck gun impacted closer and closer.

The shot would be impossible to aim using any type of conventional technique. The speed and rocking motion of the boat were too much. Fortunately, Adrian didn't aim so much as he fired instinctively. He always seemed to know exactly the right time, the right direction, and the right amount of pull for a given shot. He knew without conscious thought when to take the shot.

When the moment was right, he fired. The gelignite-filled arrow hit the U-boat's deck right where the deck gun was bolted down. The explosion blew the gun right off into the water, along with the gunners manning it. Nevertheless, in the short time it took for that shot, the other soldiers managed to get the strongboxes inside the vessel.

Adrian was about to say something to Colt but the words stuck in his throat. A Nazi officer was floating in midair, his body limned with a glow of pale energy that was visible even in the light of the flare. He glared at them with the contempt of someone confronting a nest of insects. The feeling of sheer power that came from the man was sobering. Adrian dropped an arrow from nerveless fingers; it splashed into the bilge.

The officer looked down at two wounded men on the deck, his face devoid of emotion. He raised his hands in an obscene parody of Christ. Raw energy flowed from his hands, incinerating the men and blasting seawater into steam. Satisfied that there was nobody left to be questioned by American authorities or superheroes, the officer landed upon the deck of the U-boat and stepped inside the conning tower.

The U-boat began to submerge. Colt throttled down. Adrian lowered his bow. The flare arrow finally hit the water and fizzled out into darkness in a few moments. He dropped into the seat next to her.

"They win this time. We'll have to find out what they're going to do with the uranium and get it back."

Colt nodded. "Jim said that his unit had investigated the creation of a Nazi parahuman back in the war."

"You think that was him?"

"God, I hope so. Otherwise it means there's more than one." Her hands were shaking.

"Are you all right?" Adrian took her hands in his.

She nodded. "Combat shakes. I get them every time." A weak smile crossed her face, now lit only by moonlight. "By the way, I'm Judy."

Adrian returned her smile. "Adrian."

Those Who Came Before:
Dust to Dust

Thou turnest man to destruction; again thou sayest, Come again, ye children of men.

-The Order for The Burial of the Dead,
The Book of Common Prayer, 1928

September, 1985
Kansas City, Kansas

"Ashes to ashes, dust to dust," said the preacher. "Go in peace, and God bless you all."

In turn, they each took a handful of dirt and dropped it on the grave containing Thomas Whitman, also known as Stormcloud, but Faith would only ever think of him as Tornado, the soft-spoken boy with the rockstar golden hair and serene smile. It wasn't until after the Blackout of '77 that he'd left behind his sky-blue and white costume for one that was hooded and dark, that matched the moodiness of his new identity and the swirling black clouds in his heart.

AIDS might have waited until 1985 to take his body, but his soul had died years earlier.

Faith Thompson was uncomfortable thanks to the unusually hot day for September. She was six months pregnant and nine months retired from Just Cause. Bobby, her husband, stood with her, gently stroking her back. He had retired from active superhero duties years earlier, but had taken on the job of Team Administrator, and divided his time between following Faith's pregnancy and keeping Just Cause operating smoothly.

All living Just Cause members and alumni had come to the funeral. From the original American Justice team of the late '40s came Adrian and Judy Crowley, Faith's parents, still fit even into their sixties. Lady Athena, who had grown even more elegant over time, stood with the Crowleys, her luscious black curls having long since gone gray underneath the burgundy of her hood. The only other living founder of Just Cause, known more by his heroic guise of Kid Crash than his birth name of Elliott Hines, was no longer the happy-go-lucky underage hero who'd charmed his way into America's hearts. He'd had double bypass surgery, and the whispers among the parahuman community was that his prognosis for long-term survival was, at best, poor. The White Knight had died in a car crash in '64, and Isaiah Mohammed, who'd never felt like he truly belonged among all the white parahumans of American Justice and Just Cause, had died just two years ago, angry at society all the way to the end when a stroke felled him in front of his typewriter.

All members from the Just Cause of the Sixties and Seventies had come as well. John Stone had forsworn his normal fedora for a pair of oversized dark glasses and a jacket bigger than anyone could buy from a Big and Tall men's clothing store. Lionheart, still looking heroic despite several years of retirement, filled out a dark suit and tie. He was starting to develop a paunch but his mane was as full as ever, framing his face like a tawny halo. He wouldn't meet Faith's gaze; there was too much history between the two of them. Beside her, Bobby glared at the lionish man and said nothing. Likewise, too much history.

The active members of Just Cause wore their costumes out of respect for the dead. They had known Tornado the longest, and his death had hit them the hardest of anyone. The Steel Soldier stood along with Imp, Javelin, and Sundancer, looking as somber as possible for a robot.

Three generations of the Devereaux family had crossed the Atlantic to be there. Although Georges, the man with whom it had all began, had died thirty years ago, his son Lane, granddaughter Grace, and great-grandson Jean-Michel had all arrived only that morning. Lane had taken his father's fortune, amassed an even greater fortune, and used it to become the benefactor to the team. Grace was one of the world's foremost experts on parahuman physiology, and her Institute of Parahuman Medicine in Paris was at the forefront of all research. Jean-Michel was ten, and looked like he'd rather be anywhere but at a funeral.

The current Just Cause team stood together across the grave. Sundancer's younger sister, Estella, was a tactical genius and the leader of the team. Ten years younger than her sister, she'd taken the name Sunstorm as a tribute. Beside her were Foxfire, the Timekeeper, Danger, and Fast Break. The newest, youngest members of the team were Juice and Crackerjack. They were still in college, and were strictly part-timers.

It was the largest collection of parahumans the world had ever seen, all there to pay their final respects to the quiet, friendly man they had all known as Tornado. He had died from advanced pneumonia, although they all knew that it was the compromising of his immune system that had allowed him to contract the deadly illness in the first place. AIDS was the watchword of the day, and despite Thomas Whitman's sexual proclivities, it was still a terrible shock to all who knew him when he was forced to retire as diseases began wearing him down.

Nobody knew how long he'd had AIDS, or even from whom he'd contracted it. In his final weeks, he'd worked to try and track down those men with whom he'd had relations, to warn them lest they might continue to spread the infection. In the end, not one of them had come forward to see him, or even contacted him. Thomas had died surrounded by only his teammates, who certainly loved him far more than any of his lovers had.

The group began to break up, somber and quiet, each hero lost in his or her own thoughts at the graveside.

Lady Athena hugged Faith carefully as Adrian and Judy looked on with a mixture of sadness and pride. "It's wonderful to see you again, Faith. You too, Bobby."

Faith wiped her eyes. "I just wish it could have been under better circumstances."

Lady Athena's own eyes were bright under her hood. "Your daughter will be a beautiful baby, and will be a great hero in her lifetime. This I know."

"Thank you," Faith whispered.

"Take care of yourself, Bobby." Lady Athena's gaze strayed to Bobby and seemed to grow troubled.

He nodded and put his arm around his wife. "I will. Can you join us for dinner tonight?"

"Of course."

Faith's parents walked away with Athena, quiet and introspective. It was an unwritten rule that superheroes died doing their duty, like Flicker and Strongman. Dying young was a privilege of the parahuman condition, and they had somehow avoided feeling death's sting. It was like living on borrowed time, her mother had told her, so they cherished every minute knowing it might be their last.

"Would you bring the car around please, love?" Faith asked Bobby. "I need to sit down for a minute." He walked away and she found a bench and eased herself down onto it, wishing she had a pillow to sit upon.

"How are you feeling?" Estella Echevarria walked up with her older sister a pace behind. Her costume sparkled with warm colors in the bright sunshine of the early afternoon.

"Like a blimp with legs," said Faith, absently stroking her belly and feeling her daughter kick. Her superspeed powers had vanished literally the moment she conceived. She had been in a panic, for they had never forsaken her before. She flew to Paris on the first available flight to visit Grace at her clinic, sick the entire way. Grace had come to the clinic at three in the morning and run a battery of tests. She hadn't been able to explain why Faith's powers had suddenly stopped working, but when Faith described the symptoms of her *illness*, Grace ran one more test. The discovery that she was pregnant was so startling to Faith that she'd fainted and spent three days in bed under Grace's watchful eyes. She asked Grace if her powers would come back. Grace couldn't say. Perhaps it was her body's way of protecting the unborn baby. All they could do is wait and see. Grace prescribed a strict diet and exercise regimen which Faith had given up her fifth day home and replaced with walks in Central Park and lots of tin roof sundae ice cream.

"I envy you so much," said Sundancer. "Bringing a new life into the world."

"You could have a baby if you wanted one, stupid," said Estella.

"Shut up already, pest."

Faith sighed, wishing she could take a really deep breath. "I've missed you guys. I miss Headquarters. I even miss your staff meetings," she said to Estella.

"Hey, they aren't that bad. Are they?"

"Oh yeah, they suck," said Sundancer.

"How are the new guys working out?"

"Well, James is pure business. No fun in that boy at all. Jack's his complete opposite. And, oh, is he a fox!" Sundancer shivered. "Too bad I'm old enough to be his, uh, stepmother."

"It beats me why they're such good friends. It's like the *Odd Couple* or something," Estella laughed.

Bobby pulled up in the Skylark and put it into Park, letting it idle while he got out and opened Faith's door for her. "Ooo, how gallant," Sundancer said. Bobby's brow furrowed suddenly in an expression that Faith recognized meant he'd heard something.

"Bobby?" She asked, worried. He swung his head slightly from side to side, zeroing in on the source of whatever he was hearing. He turned around suddenly and looked up. Faith followed his gaze, as did Sundancer and Estella.

A plane was falling on them.

It was some kind of private jet. Its engines were off and the only sound was the air whipping past its hull as it fell in a corkscrewing tumble. Faith would later replay the scene over and over in her mind, torturing herself and wondering if she could have done anything. It seemed like everything was happening in slow motion, but even her advanced perception abilities had vanished with the pregnancy. Several people were running in their direction, but they, too, seemed to be hardly moving at all.

Faith's instincts were to run to Bobby, but she struggled to even get up off the bench. Estella wrapped her arms around Faith and pulled, flying as hard as she could to get clear. Sundancer and Fast Break both lunged for Bobby as the plane came down, hitting the ground hard only a few feet from the Buick.

A puff of warm air blew past Faith. Estella's powers protected her from heat and she was able to extend the envelope to cover Faith as well. Pieces of the jet and the demolished car whirled outward in every direction, jagged razors of scorched metal. Faith saw a chunk of wing neatly decapitate Danger as he ran. His body took several more staggering steps before falling to the ground. Something long and sharp hit Lionheart in his abdomen and knocked him flying back into a gravestone, which shattered.

Estella set Faith down about thirty yards away from the crash site. "I can't carry you any further," she said, panting with the exertion, "but you should be safe enough here. Are you all right?"

Faith nodded. She felt a sharp twinge in her abdomen that might have been a contraction. *Where was Bobby?*

Estella's body became consumed in flames as she activated all her powers and truly became Sunstorm. She flew off like a phoenix, heading for the burning wreckage with a vengeance. She drew the flames away from the plane, pulling them through the air into her own fire.

Faith gasped as another contraction rocked her. *No, it's too soon!* In a few seconds it was over, and then Grace Devereaux was kneeling down next to her, holding her hand and calming her. Faith could see Lane towering above, standing protectively over them. Unwilling to leave his daughter, he dug in his pocket, considering, then handed his keys to Jean-Michel.

"*Apportez l'auto,*" he said.

"*Mais, Grand-père . . .*" the boy began nervously.

Lane smiled at the boy, sadness in his eyes from the events that had transpired. "*Je vous fais confiance.*" *I trust you.* Jean-Michel gulped and ran toward the distant car, keys held in front of him like a holy talisman.

The other heroes tore apart the plane with frantic intensity as they searched for the missing. Danger was in two pieces, obviously dead. "I can't find a pulse!" Crackerjack shouted. He was hunched over Lionheart. Imp was shrinking pieces of the plane while Juice tossed them aside.

Faith suffered through another contraction, squeezing Grace's hand, seeking strength. She tried to remember her breathing techniques, but she and Bobby weren't due to go to Lamaze classes until next month. *Where was Bobby?*

Sunstorm gave a roar of dismay, the sound of a plasma jet slicing through sheet metal, as she found her sister amid the wreckage. She gathered up the body in arms aflame and lifted her as easily as if she were a child. Sundancer's arms and legs dangled in a way that would be impossible if she were still living.

"*There!*" Imp cried, and pointed at a piece of wreckage, shrinking it to the size of a postage stamp. Juice pushed another piece aside and came upon the remains of poor Fast Break, who had tried to knock Bobby clear of the plane only to be crushed by one of the engines. Somehow, though, he was still alive. He gasped in agony through the shattered remains of his crash helmet.

Juice shouted, "Timekeeper, get him into stasis!"

The Timekeeper stepped up and created a bubble of frozen time around Fast Break.

Where was Bobby?

They found him underneath the tail. Fast Break had nearly succeeded in saving Faith's husband. He was alive, but only barely with a critical head wound.

"Bag him up, Timekeeper," said Juice.

"Already on it." Another bubble of frozen time formed around Bobby. There was still hope.

Faith heard sirens faintly, and her next contraction wasn't so severe. "Help's on its way," said Grace, as the Timekeeper put another stasis bubble around Bobby.

"Where the hell is the pilot?" Juice shouted. He'd torn open the remains of the canopy. "There's nobody in here!"

A high-pitched whistling sound rose over the confusion. Foxfire was the first to get it. "It's a trap! *Incoming!*" An object was diving from on high, and it was moving fast, a pair of contrails streaking in its wake.

Steel Soldier's eye lenses whirred as it focused on the intruder. "*BATTLESUIT. UNKNOWN CONFIGURATION. HOSTILE INTENT ASSUMED. INTERCEPTING.*" The Soldier snapped on its wings and blue alcohol flames shot out, incinerating a hedge. The robotic hero blasted into the sky like a missile. Half a second later, Sunstorm and Javelin followed suit.

Imp shrank Bobby and Fast Break down to doll size within their stasis bubbles, then she and the Timekeeper hurried to get them to safety inside a nearby mausoleum.

Foxfire had no obvious powers. Like the original Dr. Danger, she depended largely on athletic prowess and technological assistance to battle for Just Cause. Instead of arrows, her specialty was explosives and demolition. She followed the others into the mausoleum, pulling her first aid kit out.

Another contraction hit Faith, and she winced with the pain. *Not yet*, she told her unborn daughter. *You're not finished.* She faintly heard the sound of an engine and a car braked uncertainly behind her. She craned her head around to see Jean-Michel peeking over the rim of the steering wheel of a Cadillac. Lane ordered him to help Grace with Faith, then slid behind the wheel.

Between the wiry ten-year-old and his mother, they managed to get the ungainly Faith into the passenger seat of the Caddy. Grace and her son climbed into the back and Lane put the car in gear.

"No," said Faith, choking on her own tears. "We can't leave. The others might need us."

"We've got to get you to a hospital," said Grace. "I don't have anything with me to get your contractions stopped, and it's too soon for the baby to be born."

"Absolutely not!" Faith clenched her teeth, willing her body to obey her. "I won't leave without Bobby."

"All right," Grace said. "But I'm timing your contractions. If they get any closer together, I don't care what you want, we're leaving."

The armored figure dropping from the sky fired braking rockets and slowed. Sunstorm, Javelin, and the

Steel Soldier surrounded it. The angular armor was a uniform dark blue and looked like something out of an imported Japanese cartoon show. The head turned slightly, examining the Just Cause heroes surrounding it.

"*DO NOT MOVE*," the Steel Soldier said. "*WE HAVE YOU SURROUNDED. STATE YOUR BUSINESS*." The fifteen-foot-high battlesuit raised a hand and spat a bright globule of energy at the Soldier. The Soldier attempted to dodge but the globule expanded and enveloped the robot in a nimbus of sparks. "*SKZZRRT . . .*" The Steel Soldier's voice failed as the halo of energy condensed into an actinic point in its torso.

Then the Soldier exploded. Pieces of arms and legs flew in all directions. Irreplaceable components burned and shattered.

"*Stupid machine,*" said a digitized voice from the battlesuit. "*I never should have fixed it in the first place.*"

It was Harlan Washington, the Destroyer.

"Oh, no!" Faith groaned.

Javelin shouted, "Cook him!" He and Sunstorm cut loose with full power. A curved shield unfolded from each of Destroyer's arms. Sunstorm's flame splashed across one, harmlessly deflected into the sky. The other shield blocked Javelin's energy bolts, simply trapping them in whatever material from which it was made.

There was a flash of smoke and flame from a unit mounted on Destroyer's shoulder. Twelve miniature missiles, each no longer than a foot, arced out, zeroing in on Javelin. He yelped in surprise and dove for the ground as the missiles turned to follow like a horde of angry bees. He bounced off a heavy gravestone, sparks flying from his burnished armor. The missiles struck the gravestone and exploded, sending granite splinters flying in all directions.

Destroyer trained his hand-cannon on Sunstorm. "*I've got nothing against you. This is personal between me and them. Leave now.*"

Sunstorm growled and sent a bright stream of plasma hotter than the sun at Destroyer's weapon hand. "Personal? I'll show you personal!" Metal bubbled and ran like melting butter. "You killed my sister, you son of a bitch!"

"*Your problem, hero. Here's another.*" Something sharp and shining lanced out from Destroyer's damaged arm, struck Sunstorm in her chest, and poked out of her back. It was a wickedly barbed spear.

Sunstorm looked down at it in surprise. She raised her head slowly, red flames flashing in her eyes. "You stupid asshole. You might as well try to spear a campfire." To illustrate her point, she simply moved aside, letting the spear slide out of her flaming side.

It gave Destroyer pause, and he dropped out of the sky like a stone before she could light him up with another plasma stream. Powerful shock absorbers took the impact of the heavy battlesuit striking the ground. The suit's feet sank a few inches into the dirt.

Juice crouched down by one of the lampposts along the path, tore open the electrical access plate, and grabbed hold of the wiring. The lights flashed and then burned out in a tinkling of broken glass as he drained electricity from the surrounding grid to fuel his own abilities.

Javelin picked himself up from amid a pile of granite pieces. He stood gingerly, bleeding from several deep gouges. His left arm hung useless and broken.

Imp flew in front of Destroyer, scolding him like an angry hummingbird. "Harlan, just what do you think you're doing?"

Destroyer batted a hand at her that would have turned her into paste if it had connected. "Just a little payback, dear sister. I spent five years in hell because of you people."

"Juvie hall," called Javelin. "And you earned it, you little bastard. They shoulda locked you up for good."

A multi-barreled gun lifted out of Destroyer's undamaged arm and fired, barrels spinning in a blur. Jack leaped in front of Javelin, who was caught unawares. The stream of bullets drove him back and both men went tumbling over the rubble. Javelin hollered as his broken arm twisted.

Juice came crashing in, wrenching the gun loose in a shriek of overstressed metal. "I'm going to tear your ass right out of there," he shouted. "And when I'm done with you, you'll wish you were back in juvie!" He sank his fingers into the armor plating and tore a piece free.

"Watch it, Juice, he's clever," Imp warned, but not in time. A puff of white gas shot out of a hidden nozzle into Juice's face. The dark-skinned man coughed once, then his eyes rolled up and he dropped heavily to the ground.

"Get clear, Irlene!" Sunstorm opened up, raining flames down on Destroyer as if she had opened the very gates of Hell.

Destroyer staggered under the onslaught, trying to hold the shield up. With his other hand, he yanked a gravestone out of the ground and hurled it at Sunstorm. The heavy missile splashed right through her and melted into slag. Her body reformed once again. "I'm coming after you next time, you bitch!"

"There won't be any next time. You'll burn before I'm done with you." Sunstorm's flame was so bright it was actually painful to look at, casting new shadows in the daylight. Jack dragged Juice clear, clothes smoking from the nearness to the inferno Sunstorm had unleashed.

Something exploded in the battlesuit, causing everyone to look away. Faith saw something rising very fast out of the torso, riding a pillar of flame that paled in comparison to Sunstorm's. As she watched, stubby wings snapped out of it and it accelerated at an unbelievable pace. Sunstorm made a half-hearted attempt to pursue, but it was much faster than her and she was exhausted from the amount of energy she'd expended. She sank to the grass, shaking and spent.

In the distance, Faith heard all the sirens in the world approaching. She felt faint and realized she'd been holding her breath. Unable to take a deep breath because of her daughter pressing against her diaphragm, she panted a little and spots appeared in her vision. It occurred to her faintly that she hadn't had any more contractions. Grace was massaging her wrists.

Bobby.

"It'll be all right," Grace kept saying, like a soothing litany. "Bobby's in stasis."

"Eight years," Faith murmured, watching numbly as emergency vehicles began pouring into the cemetery.

Grace asked, "What did you say?"

"Eight years," said Faith. "He's been nursing that grudge against us for eight years. We can't fight that kind of hatred. We can only hope to survive it."

Roll Call
The Teams of the *Just Cause Universe*

Project Circus

Project Circus, known colloquially as *The Freakshow*, was formed in the summer of 1940 by the U.S. Army in conjunction with a French researcher, Dr. Georges Devereaux. It was a team of special operatives designed to exploit the first documented American parahumans. In 1941, the four *exceptional talents*—Strongman, Flicker, Meteor, and Sounder—were sent to operate in the European theater and were instrumental in helping the French Resistance.

Meteor and Sounder were killed in action in 1942 with the destruction of Aufstein Castle, and Strongman and Flicker were seriously injured. Project Circus was officially disbanded later that same year.

Project Shetland

Project Shetland, also known as *The Dog and Pony Show*, was formed in late 1941 by Georges Devereaux after he discovered additional American parahumans: Colt, Gray, and Flashpoint. If Project Circus was a low-profile operation, Project Shetland was practically invisible. With a membership that included a woman, a black man, and an American Indian, the team was very unpopular and was given missions of little consequence in the Pacific Theater. Despite the lack of support, Project Shetland functioned very well and succeeded brilliantly in every assigned mission.

Project Shetland was officially disbanded in 1943.

American Justice

American Justice was founded in 1946 by the surviving members of Projects Circus and Shetland. Having served their country across two oceans, the heroes turned their attention to America's growing crime problems. In 1949, Flicker and Gray were killed battling Nazi agents and mobsters in New York. Later that year, Dr. Danger joined American Justice. Strongman was seriously injured in 1951 and later died from his injuries.

Between 1950 and 1953, three more heroes joined American Justice: Lady Athena, Kid Crash, and the White Knight. In 1953, Georges Devereaux was called before the House Committee on Unamerican Activities. When he refused to disclose the secret identities of the unknown members of American Justice, the team was blacklisted. In response to the actions of the committee, Devereaux moved to Paris; the White Knight returned to his home in the South, and Flashpoint retired from the team to study alongside of Malcolm X. Colt retired from active hero duties to marry Dr. Danger and have a baby.

American Justice officially disbanded in 1953 and reformed as Just Cause in 1954.

Just Cause

Just Cause formed as a covert team in 1954, consisting of Lady Athena, Dr. Danger, and Kid Crash. Dr. Danger led the group for ten years, retiring in 1964. New members joined during this period, including John Stone, Lionheart, Danger (Dr. Danger's handpicked successor), and Tornado. In 1964, Lady Athena assumed command of the team. During her tenure, Just Cause made the slow transformation from covert operations to gaining public approval and sanction.

Eventually the laws enacted in the Fifties were repealed, due largely to the actions of Georges Devereaux and Adrian Crowley (Dr. Danger) and metahumans were no longer considered a criminal class. Although Georges died in 1955, his son Lane took up the cause and continued to fight for metahuman rights. An equal rights bill for metahumans was passed in 1969.

Lady Athena retired in 1971, leaving Lionheart in command of the team. Danger left Just Cause to operate as a solo vigilante. Kid Crash retired in 1974. Tornado remained active. New members joined including Sundancer, the robotic Steel Soldier, Imp, Pony Girl, Audio, and the Javelin. In 1974, Just Cause relocated to a new headquarters in Two World Trade Center. By the mid-70s, Just Cause had become a true "supergroup" and were celebrated by the press and their fans alike. In 1977, Just Cause battled Destroyer for the first time.

By the 80s, Just Cause had become its own corporation. The new commander, Sunstorm, was Sundancer's younger sister. Danger returned to Just Cause after his solo stint in 1983. New members joined the group: Foxfire, the Timekeeper, Fast Break, Juice, and Crackerjack. John Stone and Lionheart retired in 1979. Tornado died of complications relating to AIDS in 1985. His funeral was attacked by Destroyer and several Just Cause heroes were killed including Sundancer, Danger, Lionheart, Audio, and Fast Break. The Steel Soldier was destroyed as well.

By the 90s, Just Cause expanded into two separate teams with large memberships. The organization had become the single most powerful collection of paraahumans ever assembled. They battled such groups as the Zodiac and the New Malice Group, but were essentially unchallenged in their success and authority.

In 2001, Just Cause headquarters were destroyed in the terrorist attack on the World Trade Center. Several members of Just Cause perished in the attack: Timekeeper, Javelin, Foxfire, and Imp were all killed.

The surviving members of Just Cause—Juice,

Doublecharge, Desert Eagle, Crackerjack, Glimmer, and Forcestar—relocated temporarily to the JCST headquarters before moving out to a new facility built in Denver, Colorado. A presidential order made Just Cause an official part of the newly-created Department of Homeland Security.

In 2002, Just Cause added its first graduate of the Hero Academy: Mastiff. In 2004, Mustang Sally, the daughter of Pony Girl and granddaughter of Colt, was added to the roster.

Forcestar and Glimmer were both killed in action in Guatemala in 2004.

Children of the Atom

The Children of the Atom was a team of young metahumans that formed in 1960, inspired by the growing popularity of Just Cause. The Children of the Atom were never as well-organized as the larger group, and had many stops and starts with varying memberships. Two heroes that remained in CotA through all its various incarnations were the Neutralizer and Photon.

The Children of the Atom disbanded in 1972.

Just Cause Second Team

Just Cause's Second Team was formed in 1995. The team roster consisted of MetalBlade, Icebreaker, Superconductor, Alloy, and Mosaic. Hero Academy graduate Orbital joined the team in 2002. The Second Team is based in Richmond, Virginia.

The Lucky Seven

The Lucky Seven is the oldest active independent team in the country, having been in existence with the same roster since 1990. They are led by Spark, who has no parahuman powers and uses his athletic prowess and electric gadgets to meet parahumans on even footing. The rest of the team consists of Bullet, Juliet, Tremor, Stratocaster, and Carousel. Trix was killed in Guatemala in 2004. They have not yet replaced him. The Seven are based in Chicago, Illinois.

The New Guard

The New Guard began operating in 1999. Based in Los Angeles, the young team has seen a lot of action in the short time since they came into existence. Their leader, Javelin, is the daughter of the first Javelin and his wife Imp. The rest of the team—Seahawk, Chrome, Ogre, and Blueshift—follow her in their exploits.

Divine Right

Divine Right consists of six heroes who believe their powers are gifts from God. They took their names from books of the Bible: Matthew, Mark, Luke, John, Esther, and Ruth. Interestingly enough, not one of them has tested positive for the gene linked to parahuman abilities. They are based in Atlanta, Georgia and have operated since 2000.

Young Guns

The Young Guns are a team formed by the 2003 class of Hero Academy graduates (except for Mustang Sally and Orb, who joined Just Cause, and Vapor, who left active superhero work after graduation). They operate in New York City. The roster consists of Bombshell, Surfboy, Johnny Go, and Toxic.

The Hero Academy

The Hero Academy was established in 2000 as a place for young parahumans to receive training in the use of their abilities as well as providing a moral and ethical foundation for them. It is a fully-accredited high school, and students can continue on to achieve an additional two years of post-high school education.

Since Just Cause became an official part of the government in 2002, graduates of the Hero Academy are now licensed as Federal law enforcement officers.

The principal and several faculty members are retired heroes, including Sunstorm, John Stone, and Photon.

Deep Six

Deep Six is the prison facility established by Just Cause in 1994. Located six kilometers under the ground in Montana, it is capable of holding up to two hundred parahumans in solitary or group confinement. The warden, Neutralizer, used to be part of the Children of the Atom. There were thirty-seven prisoners being held in various levels of security in 2004.

ABOUT THE AUTHOR

 Ian Thomas Healy dabbles in many different genres. He's a ten-time participant and winner of National Novel Writing Month and is also the creator of the *Writing Better Action Through Cinematic Techniques* workshop, which helps writers to improve their action scenes.

When not writing, which is rare, he enjoys watching hockey, reading comic books (and serious books, too), and living in the great state of Colorado, which he shares with his wife, children, house-pets, and approximately five million other people.

Ian is on Twitter as @ianthealy
Ian is on Facebook as Author Ian Thomas Healy
www.ianthealy.com

~~~

ABOUT THE COVER ARTIST

Jeff Hebert is the creator of the HeroMachine online character portrait creator. He splits time between Austin, Texas and Durango, Colorado pursuing his lifetime dream of drawing super-heroes all day while not wearing pants.

Made in the USA
Charleston, SC
03 June 2014